JANUARIES

TOR BOOKS BY OLIVIE BLAKE

THE ATLAS SERIES
The Atlas Six
The Atlas Paradox
The Atlas Complex

Alone with You in the Ether
One for My Enemy
Masters of Death

AS ALEXENE FAROL FOLLMUTH
Twelfth Knight

JANUARIES

OLIVIE BLAKE

TOR PUBLISHING GROUP

NEW YORK

JANUARIES

Copyright © 2024 by Alexene Farol Follmuth

Endpaper and interior illustrations by Paula Toriacio (polarts)

A Tordotcom Book
Published by Tom Doherty Associates / Tor Publishing Group
120 Broadway
New York, NY 10271

www.torpublishinggroup.com

Tor® is a registered trademark of Macmillan Publishing Group, LLC.

The Library of Congress Cataloging-in-Publication Data
is available upon request.

ISBN 978-1-250-33068-0 (hardcover)
ISBN 978-1-250-37237-6 (international, sold outside the U.S.,
subject to rights availability)
ISBN 978-1-250-33069-7 (ebook)

Our books may be purchased in bulk for promotional,
educational, or business use. Please contact your local bookseller or
the Macmillan Corporate and Premium Sales Department
at 1-800-221-7945, extension 5442, or by email at
MacmillanSpecialMarkets@macmillan.com.

First Edition: 2024

Printed in the United States of America

0 9 8 7 6 5 4 3 2 1

this is my mixtape for you

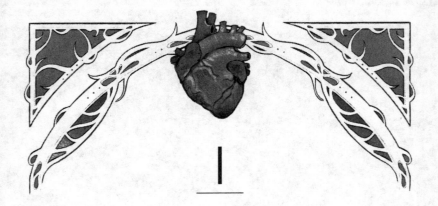

I

Spring

At the best of times, spring hurts depressives.

Angela Carter, *Shadow Dance*

To my love, whom I have no plans to murder. (For now.)

The Wish Bridge

There is a bridge that appears with every full moon. It isn't an ordinary bridge, clearly, and it is both more and less helpful than others of its kind. It doesn't lead anywhere (not really, anyway—it's not a portal to another world or anything), and it has some restrictions.

To cross it, for example, one must face the guardian who stands at its gate.

The guardian is a woman, or something that looks very much like a woman, though she is inhumanly beautiful and unnaturally still. There is something in her that resembles a river itself, in that she seems both placid and restless; eternally in place, and yet constantly in motion. She doesn't have a name, though most people don't bother to ask. To most people, her identity is inextricable from her purpose.

"I can grant you a wish or tell you a truth," she says when you meet her, "but not both.

"I can forgive you a sin or permit you a wrong," she adds, "but not both.

"And lastly," she murmurs, "I can give something back that you've lost, or I can remove something you wish to have excised, but not both.

"Once you choose," she says, "you have chosen. Once I speak," she promises, "I have spoken. There are only three choices. Choose carefully, for no matter what you choose, you will almost certainly pay more than you know."

If it sounds as though she's said this before, it's because she has. Many times, in fact, and to many supplicants, most of whom have heard of this bridge via stories and legends, and who've spent much of their lives trying to find it. She repeats the offer to anyone who comes her way for an entire night, but when the sun rises, she and the bridge disappear, and the promise she offers is gone with the stars that fade from the sky.

How do I know this, you ask?

It's sort of a long story.

Well, it's *my* story, actually, because the guardian of the bridge is my mother, and today, the first blue moon of the year, she passes her vocation on to me.

"What if I don't want to?" I ask, and she flashes me a look of impatience. When she is not in service to the bridge she doesn't have any particular face to maintain, and when it comes to me, this is the one she often chooses.

"Do you think I wanted to?" she prompts knowingly, and I sigh. "We're made for this, daughter. This is our purpose, our calling. It is a summons like any other, and we have no choice."

"But where will you go?" I implore her. "Why must you leave?"

"Because I'm done," she says, closing her eyes. I think she feels it in her bones. She seems to feel most things in her bones. I'm young still, so I don't feel much of anything. I feel sadness, I think. My world has always been very small, and my mother (aside from the bridge, which is enormous—the length of several trees, at least) has been the largest thing in it.

I was born with a vastness inside me, and sometimes I feel it will swallow me up.

"Are you ready now?" she asks me, sparing me a bit of gentleness. I think she understands in some abstract way that I resent our ties to the bridge, but she seems convinced I will grow to accept it. Not love it, of course, but accept it, as she has. I suspect, though, that she and I are more different than she thinks.

"I'm ready," I say, because it's what she wants to hear, and because this is only the first wish I will grant. Considering it's for someone so close to me, I try very hard to make it a truth.

My mother sends a kiss of luck my way, like a breeze that settles my hair around my shoulders.

And then, as she has done for so many others, she disappears, and the bridge and I are alone.

*   *   *

The first traveler who finds me has come a long way. His nose is very dirty, and his clothes are a bit torn. Part of me hopes he will ask for a new set of clothes, though I know perfectly well that would be a wasted wish.

I recite my part as my mother has always done, but the man is so eager to ask for whatever he's come here to ask that I scarcely get to any theatrics.

"Once you choose, you have chosen," I say, "and once I speak, I have spok—"

"Okay, here's the thing," he interrupts me, and while I think that this is very rude, I allow him to continue. After all, there might be many supplicants this night; then again, there might not. This is a very remote river. "I know what I want."

"Well, that's promising," I tell him, which is something that would make my mother's eyes cut to mine with dismay, but she isn't here anymore. "What is it, then?"

"I killed someone," he says.

"Oi," I reply. "Yikes."

"I know," he ruefully agrees. "So, here's the deal: I need to be certain I get away with it. It was the man with whom I had previously quarreled over a woman's heart. My sweet Katya," he explains, giving me a piteous look. "The death of my rival, Ivan, was an accident. We were only fighting," he concedes with a grimace, "but now, sadly, he is dead."

"Is that your wish?" I ask him. "That you want the people of your village not to know it was you?"

"Yes," he says.

I cast off the truth he might have received (like whether Katya actually loves *him*, which seems like an important truth to know, but he didn't ask for my opinion) and grant the wish. Nothing will tie him to the crime.

"What else?" I prompt expectantly.

"I need the sin forgiven," he says to me.

This, too, is easy enough. "Done," I say.

He hesitates before the final part.

"Ivan," he begins, and then his grimace deepens. "He's my brother."

"OI!" I reproach him firmly. "You didn't tell me that!"

I wish, now, that I hadn't forgiven him. Service to an eldritch bridge can be so restricting.

"I know," he says sheepishly. "I didn't mean for it to happen, but we have both loved Katya for some time, and now . . ."

He trails off.

"I can give you something back that you've lost," I remind him for his final wish, "or I can remove something you wish to have excised. But not both," I add hastily, in case he's forgotten, though that seems unlikely. He seems clear on the rules, which means that someone in his village must have spoken to my mother before.

"Excise my memories of my brother, please," he begs me. "The pain."

"The memories," I clarify, "or the pain? Because they are not the same."

He thinks about it.

"Or is it the guilt?" I prompt. I shouldn't interfere, I know, but he strikes me as a man prone to doing stupid things. "Perhaps it's your guilt you wish to have excised?"

He nods, relieved.

"Yes," he says. "It's very burdensome, and I wish to be rid of it."

I nod.

"Okay, then," I say. "It's gone."

"Thank you," he exhales, having been holding his breath. "Thank you, thank you, thank y—"

"You can go now," I inform him, gesturing behind me to the length of the bridge. My mother always suggested I not stand idle too long. Queuing for this type of thing can be a disaster. "You have to cross the bridge to finish the transaction."

"Oh," he says. "Well—" He shuffles uncomfortably. "Thanks."

I step aside, permitting him to pass.

Then I turn back toward the night, waiting for the next petitioner.

*　*　*

I grant a few more wishes. An old woman with a sick granddaughter who wishes for the ability to turn straw into gold. Not very creative, but she's relatively well-meaning, so I send her on her way. There's a younger woman, too, who wishes for the affection of someone she's long admired. I want to tell her that perhaps he won't be worth the wishing, but she seems so happy when I grant her his love that I can't bear to tell her my suspicions.

All in all, I find the entire process a bit overwhelming. I find myself not at all as serene as my mother would be.

This next petitioner is a very skinny boy-man. I think he's probably a man-man, but he has elements of boyishness; his legs are too long for the rest of his body. Perhaps his torso is long, too. He seems entirely too long, in my opinion. I wonder if that's what he's here about.

He also has very messy black hair. I wonder if he'll wish for a comb.

"Oh," he says, stopping as he sees me. "Who are you?"

I blink.

There's a speech for this, but for whatever reason, I've sort of momentarily forgotten it.

"This is my bridge," I say, gesturing to it, and then I grimace. "I mean, I'm this bridge's guardian."

The boy-man looks over his shoulder, and then back at me. "The villagers nearby didn't tell me there was a bridge here."

I gape at him. I think possibly he might be stupid.

"There isn't normally a bridge here," I explain slowly, as if I'm talking to a child. "It only appears once every full moon."

"Oh," he says. "And where does it go?"

"I—" He's definitely stupid. Where does any bridge go? "Across the river."

"Oh," he says again. "And who are you?"

"I told you," I begin to say, but he cuts me off.

"I meant what's your name," he amends quickly, and then adds, "I'm Nile."

I want to still be irritated, but unhelpfully, it fades. "I've been there," I say excitedly, because the Nile is a river, and one that I've seen several times.

He nods happily. "And what can I call you?"

"I don't have a name," I tell him, "so I guess you can't call me anything."

"Well, that just seems wrong," Nile remarks, and frowns. "How can you not have a name?"

"I don't need a name," I remind him. "I'm not really a person."

"What? Where did you come from?"

"My mother. I think."

"You think?"

"Well, I assume."

"What about your father?"

"I don't have one."

"How can you—"

"I just don't." I pause, glancing upward. "I like to think the moon is my father."

"Well, I've heard stranger things," Nile says kindly. "But if you don't have a father, how were you born?"

"I wasn't, I don't think."

"What?"

"Well, I think I manifested."

"I—What? So you weren't ever, like, a baby?"

I pause to consider it. "I've always been this way," I tell him, gesturing to myself.

"You were born fully grown?"

I shrug. "Maybe."

"Huh," Nile says, frowning.

Nobody has ever asked me this many questions. Not even my mother.

I can't actually tell if I like it.

"So, do you want to hear my monologue now?" I ask him, but he frowns.

"What language are we speaking?"

"I don't know," I tell him. "I speak whatever you speak."

"What about your hair?"

I blink. "What?"

"Your hair," he repeats, stepping forward. "I don't think I've ever seen anyone else with hair this color."

"Oh," I say, surprised. I've never actually given much thought to my own appearance. "What color should it be?"

"Well, it doesn't have to be anything," he tells me, and then, abruptly, he steps much, much too close, staring at something on my face. "Oh, your eyes are purple, too," he says softly, as I carefully nudge myself back a step. "Interesting."

"Interesting?" I echo. It doesn't sound like that's the word he meant, but then again, I don't even know what language we're speaking.

"Interesting," he says firmly. "I'm going to call you Mauve."

I make a face. "I don't like it."

"Fine. Lavender?"

"That's a plant," I say.

"True," he agrees. "What about—Lilac. Lila," he amends, blinking, and I give a slow nod.

"Okay," I permit warily. "Okay. You can call me Lila."

"Right, then." He exhales, grinning his boy-man grin at me. "Lila, I'm Nile."

He offers his hand.

"What am I supposed to do with this?" I ask, because there's nothing in it.

"Shake it," he says.

I grab his smallest finger and give it a jiggle.

"Well, close enough," he says spiritedly. "Anyway, you said you had a monologue?"

"Oh, yes," I say, and a good thing we've both remembered, too, because the sky is starting to get that hazy sensation of light—as if somewhere behind a swath of curtains, something is illuminating. "Right. I can grant you a wish or tell you a truth, but not both—"

"Why not both?" he interrupts me. I sigh.

"*Because*," I say. "Can I finish?"

"Right, sorry," Nile agrees. "Continue."

"Right." I stop. "Where was I? No, don't tell me—Yes, okay. I can grant you a wish or tell you a truth, but not both," I recite. "I can forgive you a sin or permit you a wrong, but not both."

"Wait," Nile interrupts.

I glare at him and he withers for a moment, but persists. Evidently his curiosity on the matter cannot be assuaged.

"Is the distinction then that you can forgive me a *prior* sin or permit me a *future* wrong? Is this a time-reliant question?"

I give him the sort of look that would make my mother's mouth tighten with frustration.

"Right, sorry," he says hastily. "Keep going."

"LASTLY," I say, with perhaps too much emphasis, "I can give something back that you've lost, or I can remove something you wish to have excised, but not both."

"Ooh, that's a good one," Nile says. "I like that one, that's a fun one."

It's my favorite too, but that doesn't seem worth mentioning.

"So?" I ask him, and he stares at me.

"So what?"

"So, make a damn wish," I remind him. "Or, you know. Ask for a truth. Something!" It's been a long night, and obviously my limited patience is even more limited than usual. I find he doesn't react much; he appears to be mostly lost in thought.

"This seems like a very big decision," he says. "People really make this decision on the spot?"

"Well, most of them have been looking for this bridge for a long time," I grumpily inform him. "Very rarely do people stumble on it by accident."

He considers this.

"Well, I'm going to have to think about it," Nile says. "Obviously I can't possibly decide this right now. That would be crazy."

At this juncture I feel quite sure that he's stupid, and now I suspect he might be crazy, too.

"You will likely never find this bridge again," I tell him sternly. I've never gotten to admonish someone before, but I see now why my mother enjoyed doing it so often to me. It's very invigorating! "It isn't very common to find it, and now you'll lose your only chance."

Infuriatingly, he smiles.

"I think I can manage," he says, and gives me something of a bow. "Until next time, Lila," he tells me, and then he turns and heads back through the forest, whistling something as he goes.

*   *   *

The next full moon takes me to an extremely remote river near a series of marshy fields. I hear something like waves, so I must be close to an ocean. I can't see it from where I am, though.

Only three people find me this evening. One of them is a village healer (?) who appears to be a fraud. He tells me he'd like for the powers he claims he has to be real, which strikes me as somewhat backward.

"I never intended to fool them for this long," he says sheepishly, "but now I've grown comfortable, and I've taken a wife, and—"

This doesn't interest me. I grant him his wish and dutifully attend to his other insecurities before sending him on his way.

Next is a teenage girl, a runaway. Surprisingly, she doesn't ask for a wish. Instead, she asks me what her purpose is. Of course, in order to answer the question, I have to sift through her consciousness a bit, which leads me to a startling discovery.

"Oh," I say, surprised.

"What is it?" she asks nervously, and I tell her not to be nervous.

"Your friend Rose," I say. "You're in love with her, aren't you?"

She doesn't say anything. I think I see now why she's run away.

"You're meant to love her," I say, and normally I would think of that as such a very, very small calling, but in this case, it seems monumentally important. "You have to go back for her," I add. "You must go back for her, and soon, because you need to save her, and love her. And . . . live." I clear my throat, which is unexpectedly tight. "That's your purpose."

Once the girl leaves, I feel a sense of accomplishment. It's soon undone, of course, as I grant a selfish man riches and watch him go, knowing his greed will one day corrupt everyone else in his life, and that he did not think to ask me to prepare him for that.

Then I wait.

The sun starts to come up, slowly showing its golden face, and I sigh.

The bridge and I disappear.

*   *   *

The next few moons pass without anything interesting. It's quite tedious, actually, glimpsing only a fragment of other people's lives. Only little flashes of what they want, and while those flashes can be intensely revelatory, they can also be somewhat off-putting. Sometimes I wonder whether the supplicants really deserve the things I offer them, but then I am reminded that it doesn't matter. I have no choice but to give it if they ask.

I sigh, wistful, and my breath escapes into the night air in the same moment that a young woman finds me.

"I'd like a wish," she says, and she's very beautiful. It's difficult not to notice, though naturally I say nothing. "I'd like someone brought back from the dead," she explains.

This is a questionable wish, but there are no rules against it. "Who is it?"

"The man I loved," she says. "His name is Ivan. His brother Oleksandr wishes to marry me, but I cannot let go of Ivan. In my village they say if I find this bridge, I'll be granted a wish, so—"

"Oi," I mutter under my breath, hoping I'm wrong about my suspicions. "What's your name?"

"Katya," she says sweetly.

"*Oi*," I grumble, rubbing my temple as I recall Ivan's brother's visit some months ago. "You're sure this is what you want?"

"Very sure," she says, and unfortunately, her singsong voice doesn't tremble.

This is a terrible idea, obviously, given what I know about the circumstances of Ivan's death. But if it's what she wants, there's nothing I can do.

"Ivan will be waiting for you on the other side of the bridge," I tell her. "As for the other elements of our deal?"

Forgiveness of a sin or permission of a wrong. "Forgive me for having been torn for so long between two brothers," she says. "I did not know then which one I wanted, and I'm sorry for the pain I caused them both."

Well, it's a nice effort. "Forgiven, then."

"And please," she beseeches me, "can you return my virginity?"

"Oh no," I say. "Oleksandr?"

Her cheeks flush pink. "Yes. And I wish for Ivan to have it."

Inwardly, I groan. Outwardly, though, her request is obediently granted.

"Cross the bridge," I say again, "and Ivan will be on the other side."

She throws her arms around me. She smells like flowers and not at all like the disaster that will almost surely come her way.

"Best of luck," I say, awkwardly disentangling myself from her.

* * *

The next full moon is closer to a town. It has a more urban feel to it, though of course, I can't fully explain why. Only that there seem to be fewer trees and a bit more cobbled stone, and something else I hadn't expected to see.

"Oh," says a voice when I appear, and I blink.

"Nile?" I ask, and he clambers to his feet with a broad grin.

"Lila!" he exclaims, yanking me into something that I suppose is an embrace, but feels a bit more like a very pointy ambush. His limbs are somewhat sturdier than they were before, and his skin a bit darker in a way that I'm given to understand means sun exposure, but he is still helplessly lengthy. "Where have you been?"

"Oh, you know." I offer a droll flap of one hand. "Eternally in service to a magic bridge."

"Can't you leave it?" Nile asks. He pulls something out of his bag—the remains of a loaf of bread. "Want some?" he offers, and I shake my head. "Come on, Lila. Li. It's really good." He takes a bite. "Baked fresh this morning."

"I'm sure it is," I tell him, "but I don't really eat."

"Well, have you ever tried?" Nile counters. "And you didn't answer the question."

"What question?"

"When it's not a full moon," he says, gesturing up. "Where do you go?"

"Oh," I say. "Nowhere, really. I think I just stop existing for a while."

This halts his oppressive chewing. "Really?" he asks, his mouth full.

"Yes, really," I say, exasperated. I have no idea why I would lie. "Where do you go?"

"Oh, I wander," he says, swallowing, and smiles at me. "I'm a wanderer. My mother laments it as often and as loudly as she can."

"And where do you wander?" I ask.

He shrugs. "Nowhere. Everywhere." He holds the bread out to me. "Seriously," he says firmly. "Have a bite."

"Have you decided on your choices?" I ask, gesturing behind me to the bridge.

He tilts his head. "Have you ever left it?"

"What?"

"The bridge," he says emphatically. "Have you ever tried leaving it?"

"No." I'm necessary, or so my mother always told me. I'm surprised to find that I agree with her far more vehemently than I ever thought I would, because for about one of every ten selfish wishes, there's someone I genuinely want to help.

It isn't the worst thing to serve a purpose.

"Well, give it a try," Nile tells me, and gestures over his shoulder. "There's a very good tavern over there," he adds, jutting his chin out toward it, "but I don't think they allow bridges."

"What would I do in a tavern?" I ask brusquely. "I have a job. A vocation."

"Oh, right," he says, snapping his fingers with sudden clarity. "Right, this. This is a job. But still, you haven't even tried?"

I think about it.

My mother never tried.

At least, not that I know of.

"No," I admit.

"Well, try," Nile suggests. "Just for fun. You don't have to go to a tavern or eat bread if it works," he adds wryly, "but think of it as an experiment."

I sort of don't want to, mostly because he's making such a spectacle of it, but also, I think I might have to. After all, now my own interest is piqued, and I've never been very good at denying my own curiosity.

"Stand over there," I say, gesturing to a spot a few feet away, and Nile immediately shifts over, giving me an eager nod.

I take a step, glancing around.

Everything's fine.

Emboldened, I take another step.

"THIS IS SO EXCITING," says Nile, at the top of his lungs.

"Hush," I tell him, and take a third step.

For a second, this, too, is fine, but the moment I try to take a fourth step, I find myself back where I started, as if I never took any steps at all.

"Oh," I say, hoping I don't sound as discouraged as I feel. Then I look up at Nile, who seems impossibly far away now, and he looks sad enough for the both of us. "Stop it," I say as he opens his mouth. "It's fine."

"Lila," he groans, coming over to me. "Li. It's not fine. It's very much not fine. Have some bread," he says, tearing off a piece and putting it in my palm. "It'll make you feel better."

"I feel fine."

"Lila, no offense, but you're not a very good liar," Nile says very seriously. "Have the bread."

I give an audible sigh. "Will it really make me feel better?"

"Well, it's not magic bread," Nile provides as a caveat. "But it certainly has convincing qualities. Go on," he urges again, and I do feel something sort of vacant and empty in something that's either my stomach or my heart, so I give in, placing it in my mouth.

I look at him. "Well?" I say, my mouth fitting uncomfortably around the bread.

"You have to chew," Nile says, looking as though he's fighting a laugh. "You know—" He mimics the motion of his jaws gnashing together. "Chew. Eat. Like a normal person."

"I *know* that," I say around the effort of chewing. After all, at this point I've certainly watched him do it enough.

"Then swallow," he adds loudly, and I glare at him, permitting the bread to go down my throat.

"Well?" Nile prompts eagerly, and for whatever reason, I can't bear to disappoint him.

That, and the bread was delicious. Or something I assume is delicious, though I have nothing to compare the sensation to.

"Good," I say, and Nile throws his hands up in triumph.

"Excellent," he says, pumping one fist in the air. "I feel vindicated, even if we do know you can't leave the bridge."

"Well, it's fine," I tell him. "I'd never actually considered leaving the bridge until you told me I should try it, so I really didn't lose much."

Only about ten seconds of hope, which were, of course, insur-mountably crushing. Not that he needs to know about that.

Nile sighs. "If you say so," he says, finishing the last of the bread before glancing over his shoulder. "I'm supposed to meet someone," he tells me. "At that tavern. Well, I'm supposed to go to work," he corrects himself, and gives me a sheepish look. "I need a little money before I can keep going."

"Go to work, then. I'm working myself," I remind him, gesturing to the bridge. "Though, since you're already here, you could always wish for money if you wanted."

He frowns. "I can't take money from you."

"It's not from *me*." I groan. "It's the bridge. You can make a wish, remember?"

He tilts his head, thinking about it.

"I can make money," he informs me after a moment or two, "so that's not a very good wish. And besides, what if I want a truth?"

I'm a little pleased he remembers the options, but I'm also rather displeased he still hasn't made up his mind.

"My goodness," I lament. "You're very indecisive."

"Yes," he agrees. "My mother says I'm eternally adrift."

"Well, better get to work. You found the bridge twice in one life-time," I add, which to my knowledge has never happened before, "so maybe you'll get lucky a third time."

Nile spares me a smile. "I think I'll manage to find you just fine, Lila," he tells me, and then, in a moment so fleeting I barely register its existence, his lips brush my cheek, leaving only some crumbs and the feel of his breath before he lopes out into the night, whistling.

*　*　*

Impractically, I start to catalogue my life less by the number of moons I witness and more by the moons that pass until I see Nile. There are sixteen of them before I see him again.

"Lila," he says, stopping dead in his tracks and mumbling it to himself. I think I'm near a city this time, by the looks of it. "Lila!" Nile exclaims again, and bursts toward me and the bridge, wrapping his arms around me the moment he is able (which, given his absurdly long reach, is far sooner than I can prepare myself for). "What brings you to the Thames?"

"Certainly not eternal servitude to a magic bridge," I say coolly, but he smiles anyway. His hair is longer now, tied back into something of a small, lawless ponytail, and he looks a bit grimier than usual, but a bit more muscular, too.

His limbs are still too long. His smile is still too broad. But even so, I think the moonlight looks well on him tonight.

"What's new?" he asks me, which is a crazy thing to say. He's terrifically stupid.

"Nothing. And you?"

"I'm a farmhand at the moment," Nile says, and his grin broadens. "I'm terrible at it."

"I can imagine." And I do. "Do you like it?"

"I like the people I work for," he says, and I start to wonder if there's anything he doesn't like. I would find it an annoying quality, I think, except he wears it better and more comfortably than he wears his mile-long legs. "What about you?" he asks.

"What about me?"

"Oh, I don't know." He shrugs. "I just wanted to know something about you."

"You already do," I remind him, but he shakes his head.

"Tell me something else," he says. "What's your favorite place?"

I don't know. I never stray far from the bridge, obviously. I've never really thought to consider it.

"I don't have one," I say. "I always wanted to see more," I add slowly, "but—"

I gesture to the bridge. I meant it to be more mocking—*see here, you silly fool, you know perfectly well I can't go anywhere*—but I catch a reflection of my own sadness in his face, so clearly it's much more helpless than that.

Nile grimaces. "Sorry," he says hurriedly, but I shake my head.

"Tell me about the people you work for," I suggest, and he does. He flails his long limbs while he talks, rising and sitting and gesticulating wildly as he sees fit, alternately eating blueberries and offering them to me as he narrates. He goes on for so long that I almost don't notice when someone appears, glancing hesitantly at the bridge with the sort of intention that belies a lifelong search.

"Oh," I say, smacking a hand into Nile's gut to get him to stop eating, or at least stop talking. "Are you here about the bridge?" I ask the petitioner.

"Oh, do you have a wish?" Nile asks, scrambling to his feet. "Interesting. How did you decide what to wish for?"

The petitioner frowns at Nile, and so do I.

"Ignore him," I assure the petitioner, giving Nile a warning glare. "I'm so sorry. Do you need to hear the monologue?" I ask the petitioner, and he glances uncomfortably at Nile, who's still eating blueberries with that stupid grin on his face.

"Are you just going to stand there?" the petitioner asks him.

"I mean, I could leave," Nile offers genially.

The petitioner and I both give Nile a withering look.

"Okay, okay, I'm leaving," Nile sighs, shaking his head and shoving some blueberries back into his pocket. "Bye, Lila," he says, and steps forward, almost as if he's going to kiss me again—it would more than likely leave a purple stain against my cheek, and strangely, my hand rises to where he might have left it, preemptively coveting it in my palm—but he turns instead, waving, and disappears.

"So," I say to the petitioner. "I can grant you a wish or tell you a truth, but not both."

Inwardly, I consider what it might be. If it isn't truth, then it's almost always money, power, or love.

"I want revenge on my father's killer," he says.

Well, that's new, I suppose.

"Okay," I sigh. "Then I suppose we should get started."

*   *   *

The rivers that run through forests are always the ones more petitioners frequent. Maybe living in cities dulls a person's ability to believe in things like magic bridges and tutelary spirits. Here, though, amid trees older than most of the villages, people seek me with vigor, with desperation. With the particular insistence of longing.

"I need a wish," says a man who looks vaguely familiar, after he lets me make my way through the entirety of my opening song and dance. I'd call it politeness, only he mostly looks tired. "Can you grant it?"

"I can, yes," I say. "Though you have to tell me what it is first."

The man shifts uncomfortably. "I don't know exactly what to wish for," he explains, "I just know I want a wish. I know that I *need*," he clarifies on an exhale, "a wish."

"Try me," I suggest.

"Well," the man says. "I have a wife. Named Katya."

"Oi," I say, recalling now why he looks familiar.

"I also have a brother," he says, "named Ol—"

"Oleksandr," I grumble, pinching the bridge of my nose. "Yes. I'm familiar."

"I'm Ivan," says Ivan.

"I know," I say. "So, what do you want?"

Ivan hesitates.

"Did I used to be dead?" he asks, which is, under the circumstances, a mildly hilarious question, but I think it would be uncivilized of me to laugh.

"You can't ask me questions," I tell him, "unless you wish for me to tell you a truth rather than grant you a wish."

"Shit," he says unhappily, and for a moment I consider telling him that I know someone else with a similar inclination for indecision, but it doesn't seem the time to bring it up. "Okay, well, I really feel like I used to be dead."

"Interesting," I say, in a different tone of voice than the one Nile used when he said it to me. I never really used to think about different tones of voices, but sometimes words are painfully unhelpful. "And what do you want, then?"

"I think I want to die again," Ivan says. "Or at least recover the feeling of being alive."

"Oh, well, you could wish to feel alive again," I say, because that's a new and interesting angle. Most people I deal with are already alive, so this hasn't been a problem before. "You could wish for, oh— invigoration, possibly."

His face brightens slightly, but not much. I suppose I'd have to grant the wish before he could really work up to it.

"Yes," he says, "do that. And permit me a wrong," he adds, "rather than forgive me a sin."

"What wrong are you planning to commit?" I prompt.

"I'm going to leave my wife, I think," Ivan replies.

"Oi." I sigh. "Really?"

"Yes," Ivan confirms, frowning. "I don't think I love her as much as my brother Oleksandr does, and I wish for him to be with her."

"I can't grant that wish," I remind him. "You already made one."

"Right," Ivan says quickly. "Well, for the last thing, I'd like to recover the relationship I once had with my brother Oleksandr."

This is so exhausting I suddenly feel an immense desire to sit down. I feel as if my very bones are aching from fatigue over how little some people can be helped.

"Fine," I say, waving a hand. "Cross the bridge and the transaction is complete."

"Thank you," Ivan says gratefully.

"Don't thank me," I tell him, grimacing. "Seriously," I add, folding my arms over my chest and wishing pointlessly that even one of them had thought to ask any of the others for a truth. "Don't."

*   *   *

There are twenty-one moons before I see Nile again, and this time, like the first time, he doesn't find me until the night is almost over, which is a shame as I'm already tired and a bit cold. Though, when I catch a glimpse of his messy black hair magically appearing well before he makes his way through the mountainous pass, I find myself . . . not entirely disappointed.

No, not disappointed at all.

"Lila!" he pants, nearly stumbling over himself to get to me. "Do you know I had to climb part of this mountain?"

He holds up an ax.

"Impressive," I say. "I hope you've come to a decision, then."

"What?" he asks, frowning. "Oh, right. The wish."

"Yes," I reply dryly, "that."

He sets his climbing accoutrements on the ground and then proceeds to lay out a rough, uncomfortable-looking blanket before

beginning to unload things from his rucksack. Food, mostly. Unsurprising. I'm not sure how a person can eat so much and still be so
defiantly skinny.

But then I remember I only see him every once in a while, and
perhaps he does other things when I'm not there.

"So," Nile says absently. "I've been thinking about your predicament."

"What predicament?" I ask. "Your constant reappearances?"

He waves a hand. "No, no," he assures me. "Your whole trapped-
by-the-bridge thing. I was thinking, there's a village nearby with a
shaman, and—"

"What?" I ask.

"Well, I bet there's ways to sever it," Nile says. "You know, yourself from the bridge. If it only appears during full moons, then you
should be able to do other things in the interim, right? Also, if you
have a mother, does that mean you're going to have a daughter?" he
asks tangentially, leveling a strip of cured meat at me while he talks.

This startles me. "I have absolutely no idea," I tell him, because I
don't.

"Well, how long before you can pass this on?" he asks.

I never asked my mother how long she did this. "I don't know."

"And when you're not here," Nile continues, "is it like you're sleeping, or—"

"Why?" I blurt out, unable to prevent it, and he looks up, startled.
"Why," I ask again, with a slightly more dignified tone, "do you care
if I can be severed from the bridge?"

He blinks.

In that moment I realize, strangely, that he's neatly parceled out
two sets of everything he's unpacked so far.

One of them is in front of him, and the other is in front of me.

"What are you doing?" I ask him.

"I'm trying to solve a mystery!" he shamelessly trumpets. "Who
are you, Lila? You're a girl in service to a bridge, and you don't even
have a favorite place. It just seems fundamentally wrong, somehow."

"What about you?" I demand. "You're a wanderer who's been all
over the world. What are you looking for?"

He stares at me.

"Myself, for a while," he says slowly, and then, even slower, "But I think since I met you, I've been looking for you."

For reasons I cannot explain, I am furious.

"Well, you took too long," I snap at him, gesturing to the lightness behind the mountain peaks. "The night's over, and now I'll be gone again!"

"I'm sorry," Nile rushes out instantly, hurrying to his feet. "Lila, I'm sorry. But if there's something I can do," he insists, with an earnestness that confusingly makes me want to deposit him at the bottom of the river even as I long to clutch him to my chest, "—if there's a way to, I don't know, allow you to leave—"

"I can't leave," I say, my voice less certain than I would like it to be. "I can't leave, because this is important, and because it's all I am. The bridge doesn't exist without me, and I don't exist without it. I'm not even Lila," I add painfully. "I don't have a name, Nile, and I don't have a place, and I don't have anything but this *bridge*—"

"Lila," Nile says, taking my face in his hands and leaning down to press his forehead to mine, his long arms folded into his sides like a pair of wings. "I'll find you again," he tells me, and I can feel his lips move near mine. I can feel the words as they melt into the cold air between us. "I promise," he says, "no matter what happens, I'll just keep on finding you."

I want to tell him that he can't promise that, but he's always been too stupid for his own good. I don't think he'd believe me.

"Nile," I start to say sternly, but he pulls my lips to his, and I know in my head that this is a kiss, but my lips only register it as something strange and terrifying and exhilarating, and I hold tightly to his stupid, too-long arms, trying not to fall.

"Lila," he says, but when his eyes open, he frowns. His voice changes. "Lila?"

The sun's coming up. I look down and realize I'm not where I should be, which is in his arms, being pressed against his chest.

The day breaks. The bridge is gone.

And by the look on Nile's face, I can see that so am I.

* * *

Four moons after I last see Nile, I find myself in another forested river, waiting again for what the petitioners will ask. The first this evening is a man who looks surprisingly clean and well-dressed, holding a jug of water to his lips as if to say he intends to remain well-hydrated, thanks very much.

I recite my usual monologue without much interest, and though he listens intently, he seems to know what he wants.

"I want a wish," he says.

"Groundbreaking," I reply.

He blinks. "What?"

"Nothing," I say. "Go on."

"I wish for the resurrection of my friend Ivan," he says, "who was killed by his brother Oleksandr."

Inwardly, a heavy sigh. Outwardly: "Which time?"

"What?" says the man.

"Sorry, nothing," I mutter, raising my voice to add, "So you wish Ivan resurrected? Why?"

"Ivan returned from his travels newly, um—invigorated," the man explains, "and he chose to leave Katya, his wife. But Katya was so distraught that she came to Oleksandr in her grief, and in a fit of vengeful feeling, Oleksandr killed Ivan."

This is unfortunately very unsurprising.

"Yes, fine," I ambivalently allow. "But why do *you* want Ivan back?"

"I love him," the man declares.

"Oh no," I say.

"And I require permission for a wrong, as I plan to kill Oleksandr," he adds fiercely.

"Oh *no*," I say.

"And lastly, I'd like my previous feelings for Oleksandr fully excised, stricken from my constitution—"

"What?"

"Oleksandr destroyed my heart when he chose Katya," the man says gruffly, "and I will no longer stand for the grief that he has caused me."

"Oi," I grumble under my breath, furious. "This is what you wish, then? This is what you prize above all else? Love excised to permit murder, and yet death reversed in order to further love?"

"Yes," he says stubbornly.

"And what if Ivan doesn't love you?" I demand. "What will you do then?"

"I—" The man looks taken aback. "What?"

I don't actually realize I'm angry until the anger itself boils over.

"You only want what you want!" I shout at him. "Not *one* of you has asked how the others of you feel, and none of you deserve the gifts that you get! But go on," I snap. "Cross the bridge. He'll be waiting for you, and best of luck. *Such* luck to you," I seethe, "because you will sorely need it."

The man looks dumbly at me.

"Okay," he says, stepping onto the bridge after a moment's hesitation.

I consider kicking him in the shins, but I don't. It's beneath me.

"Go," I say, and fold my arms over my chest, turning moodily to wait in the dark for the next supplicant.

I find, though, that I don't have long to wait at all.

"Nile," I say when I see the shape of him manifesting from the darkness, but he isn't grinning like he usually is.

"Lila," he replies, his brow slightly furrowed. "Did he upset you?"

"Who?" I ask, and then realize he must have been watching the whole time I spoke to Ivan's would-be lover. "Oh," I say, and shift from foot to foot. "Yes, sort of." I grimace. "Not just him."

"Just people in general?" Nile asks.

"Yes," I say. "Yes, precisely that."

Nile steps in closer. "You didn't seem happy with his wish," he tells me, with a little more of his usual buoyancy. "Was it not a very good one?"

"No." I force a swallow. Not any worse than the others, I think, but still. "No, it wasn't a very good one."

"Not many of them are," he notes.

"No," I bitterly agree. "But it's my job." And worse, it's all that I was given.

As if he hears my thoughts, Nile exhales.

He's very close now, all his long limbs tucked between us.

"What would you wish for, if it weren't your job?" he asks me.

I don't answer.

I don't *want* to answer.

I can't answer.

If I do, it will be like the time I tried to leave. It will hurt too much to think about, and only leave me feeling trapped in the end.

"Ah," Nile says, sensing my reticence. "I suppose that's an insensitive question."

I clear my throat. "It is."

"Well," he says. "I suppose I am sort of insensitive. Kind of foolish."

I roll my eyes. "'Kind of' is an understatement," I mutter, eyeing my toes.

"But I know what I wish for now," Nile tells me, at which point I look up so sharply I almost knock into his chin. Or I would, anyway, if his legs weren't so upsettingly long. Either way, the effect of crashing glances is somewhat jarring.

"Give me the speech again," he says. "Only do it slowly, okay?"

My heart thunders, and I nod.

"I can grant you a wish or tell you a truth," I say, "but not both."

He nods solemnly.

"I can forgive you a sin or permit you a wrong," I add, "but not both."

He tilts his head, thinking, and then nods again.

"And lastly," I murmur, "I can give something back that you've lost, or I can remove something you wish to have excised, but not both."

Nile swallows, clearing his throat, and nods again.

"Once you choose, you have chosen. Once I speak, I have spoken. There are only three choices. Choose carefully," I implore him, "for no matter what you choose, you will almost certainly pay more than you know."

He pauses, taking a sharp breath, and nods a final time.

"I wish to take your place," he says, and my entire body freezes. "I wish to trade places with you, so that you can see the world and I—" He swallows again. "I can take your place."

"Nile, *no*, don't—"

"I'd like you to forgive me," he continues. "I don't think it's a sin, really, but I think it counts. I think I'll need to believe I've been forgiven, anyway, or it might be a very difficult thing to endure."

"Nile!" I shout desperately. "Stop talking, *you can't take it back*—"

"I have this need to search, and keep searching," Nile says, glancing down at his hands. "I think it won't suit me for bridge-servitude, so I'd like you to take it from me. The wandering." He looks up, his smile slightly worn. "I'd say to keep some of it, actually, for yourself, but I think you have plenty. So will you do that, please?"

I can feel a wetness in my eyes, dripping slowly down my cheeks. I wonder if it will wash into the river, or if perhaps I'll float away myself, so that I will never have to grant another wish.

"Okay." Nile exhales, satisfied, and then frowns. "Wait, I don't feel any different. Should I?"

"You have to cross the bridge for the transaction to be complete," I tell him, even while something in my chest breaks off and buries itself in my stomach. "Once you cross the bridge, then you'll have it. Your wish. But Nile—"

"Oh," he says, looking disappointed. "I'd hoped to stay longer with you. But if those are the rules, then—"

"Nile, *please*—"

"Goodbye, Lila," he whispers, and ducks his head to kiss me again, the taste of my tears leaking terribly into my mouth and turning the taste of him to rot, to sourness and sorrow. I hold him close, my fingers burying themselves in his ratty clothes and tightening around his interminable limbs, but then he pulls firmly away from me, and he sets one foot on the bridge.

He turns like he might say something, some new impossible thing that lingers on his tongue, but then he gives me a broad, unforgivably happy grin.

And then I watch him lope away, finding his fate on the opposite side of the bridge, farther away from me than ever.

* * *

At first, I don't notice that anything's different. I'm still standing where Nile left me, only I'm trapped in place by something else this time—by terror or excitement or sadness, or perhaps all those things equally—and while I wait, my feet seem to grow roots, holding me in place. I stand there and stare until I see lightness start to appear above my head; a flood of color that rises up from the trees, dissipating into wide-open sky.

I stare at the sun until it's risen enough to blind me, striking me square in the eyes, and then I turn around to look at the bridge.

It's gone, of course.

The bridge is gone, but I remain.

I have never seen a sunrise before. I have only ever known darkness, actually, though I learn very quickly over the course of several different types of moons that there are some darknesses that are even darker than others. Sometimes the moon is only a sliver in the sky; sometimes only a slice. Sometimes the moon is scarcely present at all, though it makes the stars seem brighter. It's a curious thing, darkness. The looming swell of the horribly unknown.

Strangely, though, I find it relatable. After all, I was born with a vastness inside me, and now, at last, the world is at my feet.

It's a very freeing thing, really, to be granted a wish.

Even if it isn't technically mine.

*　*　*

For a while, I no longer live my life by the moon. I live it by the steps of my feet, by the beat of my heart, by the places that make my blood rush to my head or plummet to the tips of my toes. For once in my life, I'm permitted to be a wanderer, as Nile once was, and unlike the terrible supplicants I encountered before, I make certain to use every moment of the gift he gave to me. I climb to every summit I can find and dive into every depth. I wander endlessly until my (significantly more limited) limbs are sore and my back is aching, and while I never have more than a bit of money in my pockets, I have treasures of knowledge, and riches of stories, and for me they are more than enough.

Sometimes, too, I find ways to be close to Nile. After all, he was a wanderer himself, and for as vast as freedom is, the world itself is only so large.

"Ah yes, I knew a young man like you once," an older woman tells me when I'm wiping down the tavern bar, telling her about my latest trip to Turkey. "He was always chasing a river, I think. Always keeping close to a river's edge."

By now I have told her all about the spice markets in Istanbul, the churches in Budapest, the ruins in Athens, the spectacular warmth of the sun in Capri.

"What was his favorite place?" I ask her, absentmindedly polishing a glass, and she tilts her head, considering it.

"You know, I don't know," she recalls thoughtfully. "He only ever said anything about a bridge—a bridge," she repeats, "and a girl with eyes of lilac. Like yours," she adds curiously, her gaze softening on mine.

I keep my secrets to myself. When I have the money to leave, I do, and I make certain my travels take me somewhere new, and always somewhere far.

For a long time, I find that everything satisfies me, but by the same token, nothing truly does. I think I had seen the world as a pail to be filled, a collection to completed, but I find that the more I see, the more I wish to see.

The more, in fact, I feel as if I've seen nothing at all.

Over time, my feet and my wandering heart take me far, as far as I can get while walking along the edges of coasts and maps, until I find myself on an island that drops abruptly into the ocean. I turn and face the waves, and there, on an early morning when I have reached a place of inexpressible quietude, I discover something that makes my entire body sing.

That's when I begin looking for rivers.

* * *

I think I underestimated how much effort Nile put into finding me. No, I don't think I underestimated it. After only a handful of full moons, I know I did.

There are *countless* rivers, each of them incredibly long and far apart. Even if I were to guess the correct river and get there in time to arrive for the full moon, I'd have to walk along the curves of it for hours, and I do.

I do, because I have something to tell him.

I do, because I have seen and been and wandered, and now, at last, I have something to say.

It takes me thirty-one full moons to find him, but eventually I manage it.

"Nile," I call, stepping out into a clearing, and he looks up. I may have cost him his signature need to wander, but his grin is still exactly the same, and he is as gangly and sprawling as ever.

"Lila!" he says, and takes a step as if to throw his arms around me, but his service to the bridge renders him still. Even so, he isn't one to bow to disappointment, so he launches into a tirade instead, flailing his too-long limbs. "Lila, you won't believe how much has happened. Do you know how many people have truly awful wishes? Insane wishes, Li! I know I probably shouldn't say anything but, you know, from time to time I can't really help it, I mean some people should really learn to take more time with this decis—"

He breaks off when I wrap my arms around his neck—again, no easy task, but I manage it—and drag his lips to mine, parting his messy black hair (much longer now, and still terribly managed) with my fingers and sliding my hand up the back of his neck.

"Skye," I tell him breathlessly when we part.

"What?" he asks me.

"Skye. The island," I say. "In Scotland."

His eyes light up. "The Old Man of Storr?"

"The embankment above it, when you climb up the pass—"

"The waves?"

"The waves!" I exclaim. "The cliffs!"

"The *cliffs*," he crows in agreement. "Aren't they so—"

"Austere? Breathtaking?"

"They make you feel impossibly small," he agrees, and I nod vigorously, my arms still tight around his neck.

Nile clears his throat, glancing down at me with a flush that creeps slowly over his cheeks.

"So," he says. "Does this mean you have a favorite place, then?"

"Yes," I say, and he looks something slightly softer than smug. Proud, I think.

"Well, where else did you go?" he asks eagerly. "What else did you see? Tell me everything, tell me all about th—"

I should have known he would still be helplessly given to babbling.

"Nile," I interrupt him firmly, taking his face in my hands. "Don't you have a job to do?"

At that, he smiles his brilliant, foolish smile, and I am made stupidly happy by the sight of it.

"Do you want the full monologue," he asks me, "or will memory suffice?"

I kiss him again, luxuriating in it this time.

"Grant me a wish," I tell him, "and I'll tell you the entire story."

The Audit

DAY ONE

7:15 A.M.: I'm trying something where I wake up early. It's not going well.

9:45 A.M.: Okay, this time I'm definitely up. I have an interview at eleven and according to my roommate—let's call her Frances—I am, quote, unbearable when my blood sugar is low. She says I need time to digest and a person can't live on black coffee. I point out I'm currently fully alive and she says fully is a stretch. Frances is the kind of person who makes me want to go back to bed. I love her and assume she will leave me someday.

10:15 A.M.: I've drunk all the coffee and picked irritably at a bagel. Frances looks over my shoulder and asks who I'm talking to. I say the internet. She makes a face and says am I journaling and I say kind of, not really, it's just something I have to do for the audit. She says I had better explain what the audit is. I tell her the only people reading this will already know what the audit is. She glares at me so I guess I'll explain.

10:35 A.M.: The Life Audit pilot program uses the latest AI technology to determine a person's capacity for accumulated lifetime wealth. The idea is that youth is wasted on the young, who have no money. Frances looks over and says I am being too facetious and to really explain myself. Fine. By the time a person enters their fifties or whatever age involves sufficient discretionary funds to go places and do things, they're mostly too tired, which is the root of most middle-age crises, or seems to be, as far as I have understood the impetus for any of this. It's frankly astonishing that this pilot program even passed. I think the older generations dying off left some room for social experimentation. Frances says don't say that but it's too late, I said it. Anyway,

I'm not sure how this works exactly, but I wanted to travel and I didn't want to work, so I signed up as soon as I graduated. Basically, they're going to determine how much money I'm likely to make, and then they'll give it to me up front as a loan, and I'll have ten to fifteen years to get my kicks before I have to start working. The small print says that if you die before the loans are repaid the plan is to take it out on your family, but my parents are already dead and they had no living relatives either. So mostly this is robbing the bank. Frances agrees although she has chosen not to participate in the pilot program. She says it feels too much like astrology, which she is far too practical for, being profoundly a Virgo.

10:39 A.M.: The agoraphobe downstairs shoves a broom into the ceiling because apparently we're being uproarious. For the millionth time, I tell Frances that we're moving as soon as the audit check clears. She says not to count my chickens because I might still be considered worthless. She means it, too. The agoraphobe slams the broom again, beseechingly. I begin to two-step from a place of vengeance.

10:55 A.M.: Well, I'm going to be late.

11:17 A.M.: I'm late, but so are the auditors—when I check in, the receptionist tells me they're running thirty minutes behind schedule. I settle into a sterile-looking office chair with my forms and a granola bar that Frances shoved into my hand after I stomped around the kitchen and someone immediately calls my name.

11:34 A.M.: An auditor dressed more like an HR rep than a lab technician shows me into a room with a surprisingly banal touch screen tablet. When I make a joke about playing a game or getting my biometric data sold he grimaces and says the technology is more important than the hardware, which feels a bit like a comment on penis size. I can tell I've gotten off on the wrong foot so I ask how his day is going and he says well, we're behind schedule, so, you know. Then we stare at each other for a second before he points to the tablet. Just press start, he says.

12:37 P.M.: I stumble out of the auditing room with the sense that I just came from a really intense therapy session. I've only been once or twice because I couldn't afford real therapy, just whatever was offered at the student counseling center, which was honestly not very illuminating. Most of the audit involved me answering questions that got more and more ephemeral as I went. At first it was simple demographics and then it was questions about what I thought would happen to my soul after death or had I ever really known a love without obligation. I have at least three headaches. I ask the receptionist when I'll find out the results, and she says they'll be emailed to me as soon as they've been reviewed by an auditor, likely twenty minutes or so. I say I've seen pizza delivery take longer and she says haha in a polite way. So I leave.

12:55 P.M.: I'm on the train when my results arrive in my inbox. The results are so destabilizing I immediately send a screenshot to Frances. She says she's leaving the office and will meet me at the apartment, please don't have a meltdown. I say no promises.

1:23 P.M.: I throw my keys on the dish we keep on the bookcase and pick up one of Frances's daily affirmation cards. I forgot to pick one up on my way out. It says, "Embrace the unknown." Fuck you! I shout. Then the agoraphobe picks the wrong day to slam a broom.

4:56 P.M.: Well, here is what happened when I went downstairs to pick a bone with the agoraphobe. First, I noticed he was not an eighty-year-old Italian woman like I had assumed. Second, I realized he was a hoarder. His apartment was a strange labyrinth of bookcases that led to a tiny bistro table with those blue rattan chairs you see in Paris in the one spot of light in the entire place, next to which was the broom, propped against the window. The shelves were packed with books facing every which way. I forgot to be angry, sort of. I explained about the audit and the agoraphobe said he'd done the audit as well. How much did he get? I asked. He opened his mouth to tell me but then I heard an incredibly unbelievable din, such that I was completely distracted. What the fuck is that, I said. Well, it can't be you, so it's probably your roommate, he replied. So then I remembered about Frances and came up to tell her I was fine and she could go back to work because I wasn't going to have a meltdown, it could wait until dinner. She pursed her lips and said fine. Then I went back downstairs to the agoraphobe, who explained to me that he had a special exception to do the audit from home, it wasn't necessary to go down to the office. I said, glumly, did you get forty million dollars too? He looked hard at me for a second and I realized he was young, maybe even younger than me. No, he said, I got a very reasonable seven hundred thousand, which is about as much as the average American woman makes over her lifetime. I said but you're not a woman, in a questioning tone, in case I was wrong. He said no, that was exactly why it seemed fair. Then he poured me some tea and asked me what I planned to do with forty million dollars. I said I had no idea, that was part of the problem. He said part of the problem? And I said yeah, the other part of the problem is that when I turn thirty, I have to start working, and I have to do the kind of horrifyingly dull, capitalist work that produces forty million dollars, and I have to do it until I die, because that's the deal with the audit. Oh, bummer, said the agoraphobe.

5:15 P.M.: Frances is reading over my shoulder again. That's it, you went over and drank tea? Yeah, that's it. Then she's quiet for a second and asks if I want to order pizza. For some reason I can't stand the thought of it so I suggest Thai instead.

9:18 P.M.: We eat companionably and watch some baking competition shows and Frances doesn't ask me what I'm going to do with forty million dollars. She does ask me when I get it, and I say actually, it's in my account right now. She says do you have to pay taxes on it? And I say no, the pilot program has an exemption, because the taxes come into play later, when I'm actually earning the money. She says hm interesting and asks me if the audit told me what career I'm going to have. I confirm yes, part of the reason my deadline is thirty instead of thirty-five or later is because I have to go to grad school, first for chemistry and then for law. I'm going to be a very particular kind of executive officer that I currently lack the technical background for. Woof, says Frances. And she's a paralegal.

10:38 P.M.: Frances goes to bed. The agoraphobe texts me (I gave him my number because I am really tired of the broom, to which he said in a slightly not-joking tone that I can pay him cold hard cash to stop). In the text he says: Did your audit ask you if robots dream? No, I reply, and then ask him if his audit asked him what heaven looks like. No, he says. We keep going like that back and forth for a while wondering why my answers were worth forty million and his were worth a literal fraction of that until I feel myself drifting off. So I tap lightly on the floor. No need to shout, he texts me.

11:58 P.M.: I expect to fall soundly asleep but instead I lie there thinking about grad school, which I was trying to avoid, because I really thought that only aimless people who didn't know what to do with their lives went to grad school. And ironically, I was so sure about my life for a second there.

DAY TWO

9:43 A.M.: Frances asks me how long I have to do this journaling thing for and I tell her just a week. She gives me a look, like, hm. I say what. She says nothing. I say seriously what and she says you're already behind, I heard you moving around at six this morning and you're only now starting to type. I ask: Are you implying something? She says: No, I am stating it directly. The agoraphobe texts me to keep our voices down. I text back no offense but something is seriously wrong with your apartment. Come down and listen, he suggests. I roll my eyes and tell Frances not to move at all for twenty minutes, to prove a point.

10:16 A.M.: The agoraphobe and I ended up having a consultation over coffee. He asked me does this taste sour or bitter to you? And it took me a while to decide. He explained sour means the beans were ground too fine, bitter means they're too coarse. I said I think it might, possibly, be sour. He said okay I'll brew some more. By the time I remembered I'd meant to go back upstairs, there was an incredibly ominous din from overhead. "You see? You're animals," said the agoraphobe. Then he asked me if I wanted more coffee and I said yes. It wasn't really that sour.

11:25 A.M.: I realized he was having to journal as well and asked him how that was going. He said oh it's fine, it's no different from what I normally do, and then he asked me what I normally do, which is when I realized I was two and a half hours late for work.

12:15 P.M.: My boss isn't happy with me. More later.

8:46 P.M.: I ended up having to close and do inventory with Quintina, who is mostly fine but lately has been talking a lot about a mole she needs to have looked at. She keeps forgetting I am not a doctor.

9:27 P.M.: Frances tells me I'm supposed to explain where I work and why I didn't quit my job today despite having forty million dollars in my checking account. I work at a used bookstore that is also a café. I am sometimes a bookseller, sometimes a barista depending on whether people are feeling a more pressing need for literature or caffeine. It's a very covetable job in that the owner is very rich and makes most of his profits selling rare books to private collectors, so it doesn't really matter whether I am any good at my specific job (I'm not). Frances points out that I, too, am rich. So rich that it doesn't really make sense for me to keep the retail job that I specifically said I was going to quit the moment the audit money came through. But that was last week, I point out. She asks me what's different about this week. The answer was obviously everything, even though it was nothing. You're handling this very immaturely, said Frances. She was wearing a face mask to improve her healthy glow. The agoraphobe took issue and texted me to say he was trying to sleep.

10:11 P.M.: The agoraphobe opened the door even before I knocked. He wasn't wearing pajamas and had a book in his hand and was clearly not going to sleep. I realized I didn't even know where he slept. Is there a bed in this mess? I asked. No, he said, every night he shrinks down and sleeps in a little shoe that he keeps on the window ledge. It took me a few seconds to realize he was fucking with me because something about his apartment feels absent the usual rules of time and space. Sit down, he said, I'll put the kettle on.

12:57 A.M.: He does have a bed. There isn't much to say about it. It's a bed with a blanket and a pillow and next to the bed is a tower of books, on top of which sits a rotary phone he says could be used as a weapon if necessary. I said are your parents dead too? And he said interesting question, no, they're alive, they're just profoundly divorced. I thought this was an interesting choice of words. We seemed to bring out the interestingness in each other in a way that seemed mutually impressive. He explained that this apartment belonged to his maternal grandmother and most of the stuff in it was hers—he wasn't personally a hoarder, he just didn't have the energy to move it all to storage, and anyway he was making his way through the books (some of which were very bad, others just deeply anti-Semitic). I asked about the agoraphobia and he said well, I don't care for disease. The way he said it made it sound reasonable, like any wellness choice he had made and stuck to. He said not to be insensitive but what are you doing with your journaling week? And I said why would that be insensitive? And he said you just seem, you know, emotionally constipated. I thought about being insulted and chose not to be. Then, below an unbelievably chaotic noise that must have been Frances getting ready for bed, the agoraphobe asked if I could place an order for a book for him tomorrow, one of those coffee-table art books he already has hundreds of. I said wait a minute, I never asked, what did the audit say about your life that it was only worth the average American woman's lifetime earnings? Then I realized how horrific that sounded and felt embarrassed. Don't be embarrassed, said the agoraphobe, it's not your doing. Then he added that he was going to continue doing what he already does, which is essentially freelance journalism. Think pieces for very niche audiences. I said why did you do the audit? And he said well I mentioned the disease thing, right?

1:15 A.M.: Eventually I went home and tried to sleep, although it was difficult because I was thinking about how to spend the forty million dollars. I might as well spend it, because I owed it no matter what—it was contractual. Before the audit, I signed a really long agreement

(Frances read it for me) that said no matter what the audit said, I would have the money and owe it back. So now I have it, and I owe it back. But I don't like this thought exercise so instead I think about the agoraphobe. What is he journaling about? The bitterness of his coffee? In retrospect, I think the end result was fairly well ground.

DAY THREE

8:35 A.M.: Frances comes into my bedroom and suggests I really do something today, something expensive. She says she's been thinking about it and she thinks we should sign some sort of financial agreement. I ask what she means and she says well, she didn't really think I'd end up getting so much money, so she hadn't considered it before but what if I wanted to live somewhere really fancy and she wasn't contributing as much? And I say what if I wanted to live alone? And she says well, do you? And I say no and she says I really prefer you don't waste my time with stupid questions, and then she says don't write that down. But Frances isn't the boss of me even if in many ways she absolutely is.

9:00 A.M.: I make it to work on time. Many hearty congratulations to me.

12:15 P.M.: Break for lunch. Quintina asks me if the mole seems darker today. I ask if she means like a mood ring. Then she asks me about the audit and I tell her my results. She asks me if I'm worried that someone might kill me for the money, and I say they don't get it if that happens, it's not like normal money, it doesn't really belong to me in a way where it can be transferred to another person. It's not inheritable, because I owe it back. I can't transfer the loan to anyone else either, it has to be me. She looks at me hard for a minute and says wow that's lucky. Then she asks for a bite of my peanut butter sandwich and I say Quintina, please. But I give it to her because I don't even really like peanut butter. It's, you know, fine.

5:14 P.M.: I'm closing up at the front when my boss comes over to tell me he heard about the audit. If I'm going to quit I have to give him two weeks' notice. I say I don't know yet if I'm going to quit, I mean, I wanted to travel, so I was probably always going to quit, but I'm not sure yet of my exact timeline. Don't you have a limited amount of time to spend it? says my boss and I have a weird little panic inside of my chest. Oh god, I have to see the whole world before I turn thirty. I mean sure, maybe I could have traveled later in life like a normal person, but until I turn thirty I have *complete freedom* and then it ends. Wasn't this supposed to let me be young? I should be making mistakes right now. I was ready to be reckless—that was my whole plan. So why am I suddenly so terrified of making a mistake?

6:47 P.M.: The agoraphobe pats my free hand while I breathe into a paper bag. It's not so bad, he says. Maybe I should just spend some of the money, dive in cold. I ask him what he's doing with his money. Mostly grocery deliveries, he says. But what about your recklessness? I ask, and I'm grateful he doesn't ask me to explain. I did rent a movie last night that I might otherwise have tried to stream, he says, and asks me if I ordered him the book he wanted. I forgot. What's the deal with rococo? I ask. It feels reckless! he says enthusiastically—like, with so much enthusiasm I realize I've never seen him get excited before.

8:19 P.M.: I ask him about the profound divorce of his parents and what made it so profound. Oh, they hate each other so much and so specifically that it's obvious they used to have a thriving sex life, says the agoraphobe. I ask does it bother you, observing sexual tension between your parents? He asks me does it bother you, having dead parents? I have to think about it for a second. My mother died when I was really young of a disease she'd been struggling with for a while, and even though he always knew the end was near, her loss made my father very quiet. Or maybe he was always quiet? We didn't talk very much although he was extremely diligent about our nightly dinners. The food was usually simple, and lunch was always a neatly packed bento. He was much older than my mother and died after some struggle with heart failure. I used to take the train back every weekend to sit with him for an hour on Saturdays and then return to school. He told me not to visit at all and focus on my studies, so the weekly visit was, like most things between us, a very quiet compromise. He never wanted me to be anything in particular except for focused on my studies. He did get to see the telecast of my graduation, so there's that. And then he died on a weekday, between visits. Didn't you just graduate a few weeks ago? asks the agoraphobe. Yes, I say. He doesn't say anything else, just pats my hand again. Upstairs Frances has brought in a mariachi band, or she's just getting things together in the kitchen for her nightly salad. From down here it's not very clear.

DAY FOUR

7:04 A.M.: Frances points out that I've been spending a lot of time at the agoraphobe's and asks if I, too, am becoming agoraphobic. I say no but I don't really like heat. Or bugs. Or crowds. She lifts a brow and says nothing in a way that's very offensive. I say I'll go outside today, just to prove it. She asks what expensive thing I have planned, if I'm going to charter a jet to Paris or something and if so, could she come with me. It occurs to me that's totally plausible given that it's Friday and we can just go for the weekend, it wouldn't be a big deal, literally nothing is stopping me except that I have work tomorrow, which I could very easily quit. Two weeks' notice is honorable but, like, does it matter? I sit here thinking about it for so long that Frances leaves for work.

9:17 A.M.: "I know I don't leave my apartment but I do technically have a schedule," says the agoraphobe when I knock on the door. I say okay, can I check your coffee for you? And he sighs loudly but says fine.

10:23 A.M.: The coffee today is slightly acidic so he makes a fresh pot. I notice he has a small vegetable garden on the ledge outside his kitchen window, which I didn't pay attention to before. I ask him if he misses the outside world. He says no, he's kind of always been like this, it's just that now he's allowed to stay inside instead of being forced to go places or do things. I ask him what he's used his money for today and he says he bought himself good butter and pink salt. Why is it so easy for him? I was paralyzed in the bodega by two kinds of chips. I'm out of ibuprofen and can't decide whether to buy name brand or generic. I should see a therapist or something. The agoraphobe says I can talk to his therapist if I want. I say I didn't realize he had a therapist. He says of course, everyone does, plus he can be agoraphobic and mentally healthy at the same time. I ask if that's actually true and he thinks about it for a second. Yes, he says.

11:37 A.M.: I would miss the first weeks of spring. I would miss the fall, the leaves crunching underfoot. I would miss walking by to see the first Christmas lights twinkling on in shop windows. I would miss those hot summer days when the city feels alive again. I would miss, most of all, the feeling of walking around and knowing that nobody knows where I am, or what I'm doing. And anyway, sometimes bugs get inside the house. Even the agoraphobe has a flyswatter.

12:31 P.M.: I go to the park for a bit because the agoraphobe has to write. I decide I'm going to honor my first instinct and do whatever I want to do, whatever it is, whenever it occurs to me.

1:15 P.M.: "Why are you here?" says my boss.

3:45 P.M.: Quintina's mole does seem a little oddly shaped today. I knew it, she says in a melancholy voice. Then she tells me the book I ordered will be in on Sunday, which is another day I have off. I tell her I'll come in anyway, and then I do some inventory.

5:47 P.M.: I think about getting flowers for Frances, to put on the kitchen table. I think about buying a loaf of fresh bread. I think, Frances would want some chocolate, and then I stare at the chocolates in a fancy shop for almost forty minutes. In the end I buy nothing and go home. And then I stop and go back to the florist.

6:32 P.M.: The agoraphobe answers the door and looks confused. I don't understand, he says, you brought me flowers? I said yes, I don't know, I guess. He says those are definitely flowers, and they're definitely for me, so . . . He trails off. I realize he's making a point and

say you can say no if you want. He rolls his eyes. Come inside, you're
making a racket upstairs, I have a migraine.

7:01 P.M.: He fingers the petals so gently I have the strangest feeling,
like I want to sweep up his fingers and press them to my lips. Recklessness. He asks me what I'm smiling at and I say oh, I didn't realize
I was smiling. He asks if his book has come in. He asks if I remember what perfume my mother wore. I close my eyes and think
only of sun coming through the open window, a soft pink shade of
cotton they only seemed to make in the late eighties, the way the
house used to smell. The agoraphobe says his mother wears a vintage peach-scented perfume, something almost saccharine, he's been
trying to figure it out but he can't—he points to a package of three
different perfumes that aren't it. He closes his eyes and smiles. I want
to ask where his mother is now, and I think maybe it's too invasive,
and then I think no, it's fine, if he never wants to speak to me again
I'll just move. Where's your mother now? I ask. He laughs. Indoors,
he says, and I laugh too.

8:34 P.M.: I hear Frances clomping around and come upstairs. The
flowers are beautiful, she says. Then she says, there's some kind of
party this weekend at one of those fancy rooftop bars. I say do you
want to go? And she thinks about it for a second and says no, I want
to stay home and read, this antitrust case is so labor-intensive and I
spend all day trying to avoid this one senior associate who thinks I'm
prettier when I smile. I'm too tired to grind on some guy, she adds,
the weight of my youth is just too burdensome. She yawns widely
and asks if I'd be okay rewatching a show we've both seen four times
all the way through (it was canceled halfway through its second
season). I say sure, why not?

11:44 P.M.: Frances falls asleep on the couch. I pull the couch blanket
over her. The agoraphobe answers the door and says I just remembered that my audit asked me a math problem, did yours require any
math? I say no, did he know the answer? He says maybe, it involved
the Pythagorean theorem, which I know because there's a song that
goes with it, so maybe I solved it correctly, I don't know. I wonder

what makes me so valuable when I am unquestionably the most boring person in my life. Hey, thought, announces the agoraphobe, what if you put some of the money in a savings account, wouldn't the interest generate enough money for you to pay back some of your loan? An interesting loophole, I say. I didn't read my contract so I don't know, and Frances is asleep so I can't ask her. Let's find out, says the agoraphobe.

1:23 A.M.: Looks like nothing specifically prohibits it, says the agoraphobe. I've stopped reading because my eyes hurt. The ceiling twinkles with plastic glow-in-the-dark stars. Has my book come in? asks the agoraphobe. Are you dying? I ask. The agoraphobe turns to look at me. How did you know? he says.

1:35 A.M.: Oh man, I say, oh man. I can't do this again.

2:01 A.M.: The agoraphobe texts me. We're all technically dying, he says.

DAY FIVE

7:15 A.M.: Frances is on the couch reading a book I got her last month when I had no money and also no second thoughts about my lack of money. She laughs to herself and I think, I knew it was a funny book. I met Frances when we lived in the same hall in our freshmen dorms. She slept with my roommate, then they dated for a while, just a couple of weeks, long enough that Frances and I ended up walking in and out of the building together sometimes. Then she sat next to me in the dining hall and when we both ended up in the same French literature class I sat next to her and it kept going like that until I stopped knowing how to define myself without Frances as a benchmark. For example, I am funny at parties, but less funny than Frances. Let me pay your law school tuition, I say. She looks up from her book with a frown. No, she says. But I want to make things easier for you, I say. She sighs heavily and says things being easy isn't the point, but let me know when you charter that jet to Paris.

9:00 A.M.: "If you're going to quit, I need two weeks' notice," my boss tells me again. Quintina mocks him from where she's stacking the orders that have just arrived. When my boss leaves to take a phone call, I ask Quintina if she needs money to see a doctor about her mole. Oh, I'll get around to it someday, she says with a shrug.

12:00 P.M.: I ponder my lunch choices. Sushi? Pizza? Expensive patisserie? In the end I have a peanut butter sandwich and am reminded of everything that is wrong with me. I wind up so furious that I storm into the travel section and pull three books off the shelf at random. Sofia. Lagos. Seoul. There, job done. I pull up a browser page on my phone to book flights. Then Quintina tells me the book I ordered got here early, and that by the way, I could use it to incapacitate intruders. She mimes lifting a boulder as she drops it on the table in the back room where we all eat lunch and leave rings from our coffee mugs. The coffee back here is bitter. My brain is pressing in and I flip through the pages. Rococo. Characterized by elaborate, ornamental stylings. Maximalism. Wealth.

5:25 P.M.: The agoraphobe doesn't seem all that surprised to see me. It's not an imminent death, he says. I hand him the book and he says thank you. He closes the door and I go upstairs.

5:32 P.M.: Frances hasn't moved, although there are chocolate wrappers all around her and crumbs on her sweatshirt. She pats the spot next to her on the couch and I sit. There is a really good joke, one that makes me laugh-cry every time, and I do. The agoraphobe texts me to keep it down up there.

8:12 P.M.: What do I want? I have all the money in the world. What do I want? What do I want? Time feels like it's slipping away from me. It's already been five days. I can't breathe.

10:16 P.M.: You know, I know we don't know each other very well, but it seems to me you're handling this uncharacteristically poorly, says the agoraphobe, pouring me some herbal tea. He says he tried four different blends before he arrived at this one. I ask him what he writes about, and he thinks about it for a second. I have a tendency to intellectualize my emotions, he says, and also lately I've been writing about you. Can I see? I ask him. He shows me his recent entry, which is much longer than mine. He has basically recorded everything I said verbatim. I have a very good memory, he tells me. I say wow, this reads like a play or something, did I really say all of this? Sometimes I embellish, he says. Me too, I say.

11:01 P.M.: I owe you an apology, I say. Then we both sip our tea for several minutes in complete but companionable silence. It's pretty good, and I'm not really a tea person. I'm thinking I'll try bone broths next, the agoraphobe says. I lean over and kiss him on the lips. He seems surprised for a second, then slowly melts into it. His lips are soft. He smells a little too sweet, like an overripe peach. Was that the apology? he says. No, it was a different thing, I say. I kiss him again, then a third time. I trace the back of his neck with my fingers. I think about holding his hand in the snow. I think about the way the moonlight falls on his sheets. I think about bright white linen. I think about what matters to me and come up empty, except for Frances. I have so much time, I realize. So much time to fall in love. So much time to choose my future. So much time to call a therapist, any therapist, I can afford to have several therapists at once, which I really need to do. Why am I so weak for a ticking clock? The agoraphobe kisses me back and pulls away. That was nice, he says. Thank you.

12:46 A.M.: Later, when we're lying in his bed and looking up at the glow-in-the-dark stars, I think about high interest yields and whether the contract gets forfeited if I go to prison. What if I literally rob a bank? Take my youth away from me, I don't deserve it, I don't know how to use it. The agoraphobe looks over at me and says there must be a hell of a mess going on in that head. I can't remember who I used to be. I can't remember who I want to be. Maybe money *is* the root of all evil. Maybe they made a mistake! I sit up in bed, forgetting I'm naked. I'm going to tell the auditor he made a mistake, I say. The agoraphobe leans up to kiss my spine. I bet he'll love that, he says.

DAY SIX

4:43 A.M.: I wake up with a jolt and the agoraphobe is writing, one leg propped up on his chair, wearing only his boxers. He looks over at me and says nothing. I ask him if he ever sleeps—I'm realizing now that I've never seen him do it. He says he's on a dozing schedule. Part of me wonders if this is a complex psychological thriller, if he's meant to represent some part of my inner psyche, he's too weird to be real. Seems a highly congratulatory thing to think about yourself, he says, and goes back to writing.

6:15 A.M.: At some point I must catch his dozing schedule, because when I wake up he's nudging me with a fresh cup of coffee. He reminds me I was going to confront an auditor today. I say yes!! Thank you for reminding me!! I sip the coffee almost without noticing and then I say wow, this one is good. The agoraphobe looks smug. Yes, I really think I cracked it, he says.

7:02 A.M.: Frances doesn't think this is a good idea, but she says that at least I seem like my usual self. She says what are you hoping for, you know, from the new audit? I open my mouth as if I have a perfectly reasonable answer and then I realize the thing I'm about to say is nothing. I hope they say I'm worth absolutely nothing, the whole deal is off, I'll just have to figure it out on my own, the way real people do. But that is absolutely insane, and not even true, because I want to travel. I really like to travel. In theory, that is all I want to do. I quickly google what seems like an appropriate lifetime earning for mid-level management, which sounds boring but might not require too much additional education or extensive work hours. Something that would allow me to come home at five and take a few weeks off during the summers. I do the math and come up with about five million. Okay, thinking five-million-dollar thoughts for you, says Frances, toasting me with an iced latte that I really should have bought for her before I decided to give my fortune back.

9:17 A.M.: The auditor isn't happy to see me. You're already in the system, he says. Your audit has already been run through the program.

This is it. I ask him if he, by chance, wants thirty-five million dollars. Please leave, he says.

10:21 A.M.: The agoraphobe doesn't answer the door when I knock. For a moment I have a panicked thought: Could he have gone out? Is he dead? I knock again and he answers. I'm on with my therapist, he says, and asks if I want to join in.

11:05 A.M.: The agoraphobe's therapist says it's not appropriate for her to treat me but she does think it's worth asking myself why I'm so paralyzed by my unexpected windfall. She suggests that I try to turn it into art. I ask, turn what into art? She looks very tired.

12:34 P.M.: My theory is she's assigning you homework so that your overthinking becomes someone else's problem, the agoraphobe tells me after we make out a little on the bistro chairs. The sun is streaming in and I can only think of pastries. Come with me, I say. No, he says. But I just want to sit in a café with you. No. Come on, it's not that bad. No. The sun will feel so nice, the pastries will seem fresher, the air is—No. What if we went for a walk? No. Is being trapped in this apartment even good for your health? Irrelevant. I don't understand, you're young and free and the whole world is your oyster, what is so fucking wrong with you that you want to stay trapped in here? Wow, he says, and closes the door in my face. Goodbye.

4:12 P.M.: I take myself for a walk. I buy the pastries. I don't charter a jet but I book two tickets for Frances and me to Paris, first class. I google "capsule wardrobe" and buy everything the article recommends. I buy a new pair of shoes and an outrageous hat. I buy expensive champagne to celebrate the trip that Frances and I are taking to France. I buy Frances a new capsule wardrobe in multiple sizes, in case I get some of it wrong. I email the funeral home and request a more lavish headstone for my father. I put a quarter of the money in the highest-yielding account I can find. I hire two accountants, without telling them I've done so, to check each other. I book appointments with fifteen different therapists. I buy the fancy weed.

9:56 P.M.: I mean, I'm excited about Paris, says Frances, but I don't know if I can get the time off. Just quit your job! I say in exasperation. She looks at me with a grimace. I'll figure it out, she says, but don't do it again. Next time you spontaneously book a vacation, consult my calendar. I realize I need to quit my own job.

10:11 P.M.: I begin drafting my two weeks' notice to my boss. I get distracted by my phone, which has no messages. Then I change my mind and ask for a week off. Personally I find Paris overrated and you'll need to ask Quintina to cover your shifts, my boss replies. I look over at my phone. No messages. I stand up and start to stomp around in a figure-eight pattern. Nothing. After several minutes of this I email my boss back. Thanks, I say. I think about asking him what he does with his money, but I guess I pretty much already know. He buys peanut butter for the break room, for the store he owns that doesn't really make money in its day-to-day business, that he opens himself every morning and chooses not to leave, just because he can.

DAY SEVEN

7:01 A.M.: I check my phone. Nothing. Frances knocks on my door and reminds me to eat breakfast. I call back yeah okay. She leaves for work early, so she can get some stuff done before we leave for Paris, even though I tell her again that she can just quit her job. She says you are really testing my patience. I feel a moment of crushing fondness.

7:16 A.M.: The agoraphobe doesn't answer the door when I knock.

7:32 A.M.: I'm sorry, I text him from outside his door.

7:45 A.M.: I text him: I shouldn't have said or done any of that. I just want you to feel how I feel, that's all.

7:56 A.M.: I almost go back up the stairs when I see that he's typing a response. I see the shadows of his feet on the other side of the door. I like it in here, he says. I rush to type back. I know (Delete.)

I was just (Delete.) I shouldn't have (Delete.) I like being with you I just (Delete.) Can you forgive (Delete.) I know we don't really know each oth (Delete.) I just have all this money and (Delete.) I guess I'm kind of freaking out because I (Delete.) I just want (Delete.) Do you think you can (Delete.) What if I stayed h (Delete.) Do we have a fut (Delete.)

8:07 A.M.: The message I send says: If I make sure there's no disease, can I bring you something?

8:09 A.M.: I see his feet pace slightly on the other side of the door. Okay, he says.

12:43 P.M.: Frances texts me: Eat lunch.

2:32 P.M.: Frances texts me again: Make sure you have comfortable shoes for Paris.

2:56 P.M.: Frances texts me again: I should really just quit my job.

3:41 P.M.: Frances texts me again: Do you think you could pay for an accident to befall that senior associate. Burn after reading. Lol

3:44 P.M.: Frances texts me again: Don't literally burn but yeah delete just in case we do go through with it.

4:41 P.M.: Frances texts me again: What are you doing, anyway?

9:54 P.M.: It took me most of the day to finish my errand, but eventually I send Frances a picture. It's an arrangement of paintings on loan for twenty-four hours from a bunch of private collectors. Most are rococo but I did choose a few others, like van Gogh's sunflowers and *Wind from the Sea* by Andrew Wyeth. It's of an open window with translucent lace curtains, blowing in a way where you can almost taste the salt.

9:56 P.M.: Frances texts back: Holy shit, that's what his apartment looks like?

10:04 P.M.: The agoraphobe stands in front of each painting for a long time. He looks at all of the textures and colors and pieces. He explains to me things I didn't know about composition, about the values of the paint, about where the subject matter came from and what it means, the profoundness of the ordinary. My fingers flutter beside his and I feel like I'm floating. I feel like money finally has a point. I feel like the clock is ticking. I feel my future weighing down on me. I feel the grains of my youth being wasted. I reach for another pastry, my hand still holding his. It flakes tenderly apart.

11:11 P.M.: We move the mattress to the floor and fuck with an extravagant view of all the paintings. Briefly, the agoraphobe dozes. Thusly, my week of journaling ends. I don't know what I'm doing, only that if I'm lucky it will hurt. Recklessness is mine at last.

Sucker for Pain

Her name was Sophronia d'Este, though neither of them called her that. Nora called her Madam or Mistress or Ma'am, depending on the situation. Edmund exclusively called her Mother. This distinction in nomenclature was very important, Sophronia repeatedly told them, as it was the basest of the many implied distinctions between them. Nora was nothing. Edmund, however, was everything.

And for much of her life, Nora heartily agreed.

Nora Denshaw was nine years old when she first met Edmund and Sophronia d'Este. Edmund was eleven. Sophronia was always ageless, waffling unidentifiably between forty and eighty for as long as Nora had known her. In retrospect, Sophronia might have been well over a hundred, but there was simply no telling at the time.

At some point (approximately twelve years before Nora met her), Sophronia had fallen in love with a mortal man. It was heavily implied, in Nora's mind, that Sophronia had used a potion of some kind, or maybe some sort of spell. Perhaps it was because Nora lacked any kind of magic of her own that she assumed magic to be inextricable from anything Sophronia did, but even after learning that love was always convoluted whether magic was involved or not, it still seemed a likely event. It wasn't that Sophronia wasn't her own kind of beautiful—she was, if anything, a handsome woman—but she had a certain inability to bend. She wasn't an easy woman to love; even for Edmund, who was Sophronia's beloved son, and for whom Sophronia spared no ounce of adoration. Nora felt she understood why Sophronia might have loved that mortal man so much, because Edmund looked nothing like his mother, and therefore must have looked like his father.

And if that were the case, then Edmund's father must have looked like heaven itself.

Nora had seen Edmund first on the day she met Sophronia—or maybe Edmund was the one who had first seen Nora. Hard to tell, the way the carriage was covered. He was peeking through the drapes, looking out onto the street, and Nora had been somewhere in the shadows. Maybe it was because he was a witch that he found her. Maybe it was simply extraordinary eyesight, or youth. Either way, Nora had looked up and seen him, and Edmund had looked down and seen her, and they'd looked at each other, quietly, and then his face had disappeared.

Then the carriage stopped.

And then Sophronia d'Este stepped out of it.

Nora still remembered that Sophronia had been wearing a dress like a cake; the fancy kinds she had seen in shop windows but never tasted. It was black, though, but ruffled, layered—*tiered*, even—just like an elaborate pastry, with fabric Nora had never touched and could certainly never dream of affording (at the time). She later learned this was the only sort of dress Sophronia ever wore.

"Where are your parents?" Sophronia had asked Nora. No greeting, no hello, no *don't be afraid, I won't hurt you*. Nora supposed Sophronia never made promises like that, especially not to dirty orphans in the street.

"Dead," Nora said.

"Ma'am," Sophronia replied.

"What?"

"They're dead, *ma'am*," Sophronia corrected her firmly. "You'll have to address me as 'ma'am' if you're going to be part of my household."

"I don't know what you mean," Nora said.

"Ma'am," Sophronia corrected, and Nora sighed.

"I don't know what you mean, *ma'am*," she conceded. Then Edmund's face appeared again in the window of the carriage, and Nora looked up, distracted.

Sophronia cleared her throat, jarring Nora back to the conversation.

"My son," Sophronia said, "wishes to speak to you."

"Oh," Nora said, and then quickly added, "Ma'am."

Sophronia's mouth twitched with amusement in a way that Nora found rather discomfiting, even then. As if Sophronia were a wolf who had just spotted dinner on the horizon. "Do you find my Edmund handsome?"

"I—" In truth, Nora had never seen anyone with a face like Edmund's, though he was too young yet to really be handsome. He still had a boy's prettiness then, or even one more like a girl's, with delicate features and long lashes and full, supple lips that curved with uncertainty at the sight of her, as if he were taking stock of something that had not existed in the world before. Nora wouldn't go so far as to say it was interest, but it wasn't nearly not, either. It was a very palpable curiosity, as if it might have soothed him to press his fingers to her cheeks, or underneath her eyes, or perhaps into her skull, digging them in with surgical precision to ascertain that he and she were made of similar materials.

"Yes, ma'am" was the answer Nora gave, though, because it was quite clear there were many wrong answers, and only one right one.

"Well," Sophronia determined with finality, ostensibly pleased. "Then gather your things, child," she instructed, gesturing, and waited.

She remained there, fixed and expectant, for a very long time, because Nora had no things. To possess a *thing* was in fact so far out of Nora's reach that she'd merely stood dumbstruck, which in retrospect had been both her earliest mistake and her greatest stroke of fortune. Later, she would come to realize that Sophronia believed her to be stupid. That misconception served Nora poorly, at first, and then extraordinarily well.

Though that is, of course, a later story.

Nora remembered little of the carriage ride to the d'Este estate. She'd been staring furiously at her lap, at the dinginess of her clothing and the unnerving stare belonging to Edmund, and so committed almost nothing else to memory. She remembered the gate, though. The black iron gate, which had wrenched open as if waking from an impossible slumber, and then a ride through at least an acre of ancient, weedy grass, the stalks grown high and obtrusive. As they passed, Nora had looked back, wanting to examine it closer, only to find that in the rear view the lawn looked perfectly manicured.

Nora hadn't seen magic until she arrived at the d'Este estate that day, nor had she understood it. She was still of an age to believe what she saw, though, so she didn't think to question it much at the time. It simply was what it was. What was illusion and what was fact were things that now seemed obvious, but as a child, she merely believed what her senses informed her, which was that things became more beautiful the closer she came to the heart of Edmund's life.

Nora didn't have to remember the house as she'd first seen it because it didn't change at all during the entirety of the time she lived there. It was probably a typical manor house, minus the grisly artistic choices that appealed to Sophronia's taste for violence (all rich shades of crimson, all Baroque, all twisted and gruesome and in motion and therefore bringing to mind the word "excruciating"), but Nora had never seen anything like it before; thus, her conception of wealth would forever be tainted a little bit with blood. To be wealthy, to be powerful, was to bleed. She would later find this observation to be both very mistaken and hugely correct.

It was clear to Nora from the start that she would live there now and belong to Sophronia in some way or another, mostly in that she could not refuse her. Nora was given a plain black dress, stiff textured cotton that wasn't much softer than it looked, and a small room with a narrow bed tucked away at the back of the house, with a little tinkling bell just beside the doorframe. For two or three days Nora learned to respond to the sound of the bell, her quiet footsteps echoing throughout the house as she wandered the empty corridors. It took about a day for her to realize that although she never knew where she was going, she somehow always arrived. Even when Sophronia hadn't called for her, Nora didn't move independently throughout the house. That would have been more autonomy for her than Sophronia would have permitted. Instead, the house shifted around her, determining for her where she would go.

A week passed. Nora learned to make tea to Sophronia's expectations. She learned to clean things, to fetch things, and where to find the things that needed to be cleaned or fetched. She came and went, day and night. She learned not to distinguish between day and night, instead merely between sleeping and waking. Another week, and Nora learned not to ask questions. She learned not to ask why the fire was always lit when nobody seemed to be there to light it, or who made the picked-over food that always sat partially consumed on ostentatious platters around the house. Most important, she learned not to ask where Edmund was or what he was doing, because then Sophronia's face would light up, overjoyed with unspoken triumph, and she would refuse to tell Nora anything.

Sophronia was the only person Nora had ever met who was worse when she was happy. It usually meant that someone else was being hurt.

Two more weeks passed before Nora found Edmund. He was sitting in the library, an expansive room that Nora avoided because the doors were too heavy for her to open. She froze, startled to have come upon the open doorframe, and the motion caught Edmund's eye.

"Well?" he said, looking up when he spotted her in the corridor. "You're not just going to stand there like an idiot, are you?"

(His first words to her.)

"I might," she managed to reply.

(Her first to him.)

He sighed. "Come in," he said, and added, "Come tell me what you think of this."

She obeyed, walking tentatively into the room and pausing just before where he sat in a large, clawed armchair, a candelabra flickering beside him to cast an invigorated shadow over his face.

"This book talks of magical properties as if they are things that cannot bend," Edmund said, "but that can't be true. Why would magic be subject to rules? Isn't the whole point of magic that it *defies* the rules of nature? Things that are solid are solid except for with magic, after all, so I can't think why it should have any rules to begin with, unless it's witches themselves who make the rules for some reason—to control each other, I presume, which seems an abominable waste—and, in fact, magic itself is boundless. What's even the point of something that has rules?"

Nora blinked, opening her mouth to reply, but discovered nothing.

Edmund sighed. "Never mind. Just read this to me," he said, handing her the book and flopping back in the chair. "My eyes are tired."

She glanced down at the book.

Then up at him.

Then down at the book.

Then up at him.

He cracked one eye. "What?" he prompted impatiently.

"I don't want to," Nora said.

Even then, this did not seem to change anything.

"You mean you can't," Edmund determined tartly.

"I—" Nora hesitated. "I can't. But also, I don't want to," she insisted.

Edmund reached forward with a long-suffering sigh, yanking the book back from her.

"Come on, then," he said, and rose to his feet, heading into the corridor. He didn't check to see if she was following him; for a moment, Nora thought she wouldn't, just to see how he liked it, but in the end, she was compelled by curiosity, and by a pull of opposition from somewhere in her chest at the thought of watching him walk away. She hurried after him, sighing to herself, and struggled to keep up, his eleven-year-old legs already much longer than hers.

"Mother," Edmund said, walking into a room where Nora had not yet been. It was a workspace of sorts, which smelled of something vaguely herbal, and Sophronia turned to look at them, her eyes narrowing as they fell on Nora.

"What is it, darling?" Sophronia asked her son, pointedly turning away from Nora.

Edmund, meanwhile, gestured with his chin to where Nora was standing. "I want her to come to my lessons," he said. Nora blinked, surprised, but said nothing.

"Why?" Sophronia asked.

"Because she does me no good at all if she can't read or do anything or think," Edmund replied impatiently.

I can think, Nora wanted to argue, but she figured it wouldn't help. Besides, she was too curious to argue. She wondered what Edmund was talking about.

"She's a mortal," Sophronia warned. She said it in the same voice she might have said "refuse" or "castoff" or "useless bit of filth." Later Nora would learn there were many classes of paranormal species deserving of disdain (vampires, for example, whom Sophronia held in particularly low esteem), but none so prodigious as mortals. "Edmund, sweetheart, it's very generous of you to think of it, but—"

"It's not generous," Edmund interrupted. "As she is, she's positively useless, Mother."

Nora thought that was a bit harsh.

"Mother," Edmund said again, lifting his chin, "you *promised* me—"

"I know what I promised you," Sophronia purred, mulling it over as she glanced at Nora again. "Still, she can never be a witch, Edmund. She isn't like you."

Nora glanced at Edmund, wondering what he would say. He set his jaw, stubborn.

"You promised," he repeated, and to Nora's amazement, after another moment, Sophronia grudgingly relented.

Nora didn't know what the promise in question was, but she did know that once Edmund had insisted on her joining him for lessons, she suddenly had much less time on her hands. Each week, Edmund was assigned a series of tasks by his mother, along with a pile of books. Sometimes Sophronia was physically present; sometimes not. Sometimes Edmund spoke to the books and they spoke back. Sometimes he spoke to the lamps or the tables or the chairs. Sometimes he abruptly stood up, went outside, and summoned an animal, a fox or a bird, and asked them questions. He was constantly reading, or talking, or asking to be read to, or posing discussion topics about which Nora was supposed to be informed. She couldn't do any of the summoning, but she was expected to know the principles involved. She was expected to know all of the enchantments Edmund knew, even if she couldn't perform them. She was expected to read everything he read, too, so that when he was finished, he could recite a line and demand her thoughts on it.

The first time he asked for her opinion, she told him she had none. He scowled, snapped his book shut, and walked away. The next day, when she came to find him, he was nowhere. It was as if he'd simply disappeared; as if the house had folded in on itself like a book and he was somewhere hidden within the spine. The next day, the same. And then another day. And another. Suddenly Nora was filled with the very specific fear that Edmund would never forgive her, never return, and she scribbled in half-decent (only recently learned) handwriting that she was sorry, that she wouldn't do it again, that of course she had thoughts and wouldn't he listen, please, because actually she found it very interesting, and perhaps troubling, and also, what did he think about it?

The next day he was waiting for her in the library, and she never made the mistake of not having an answer again.

By the time Edmund was sixteen, he was officially handsome. *So* handsome, in fact, that girls were starting to come to the house in droves, finding their way to him like flies to honey. Society witches, Sophronia called them disdainfully, though she regularly checked to see that Nora was sufficiently upset by the presence of the many beautiful girls. One of them would marry Edmund, Sophronia informed Nora gleefully, when the time was right. When he'd learned everything he needed to know. When they found the *right one*. The right one would be beautiful, Sophronia pointed out. Much more beautiful than Nora, and more powerful, too. A powerful witch, Sophronia would say as if she were casting a spell, who was worthy of Edmund.

Privately, Nora doubted Sophronia would ever find a witch worthy of Edmund. Even if there was one (which Nora personally didn't believe), Sophronia would never approve of her. As for Edmund, he didn't seem to care either way—or in *any* way, really. He didn't care that Sophronia forced Nora to serve the other witch-girls their claret, watching them bat their lashes at him as she struggled not to flush with envy and heartache and shame, but he also didn't care that the girls were batting their lashes. He wasn't entirely without skill when it came to flirtation, but this, too, he approached like his studies.

"So, what do you think about Della Ailey?" he would say to Nora about some new and terrible society witch.

"She's very pretty," Nora would say, which was true, but Edmund would wave it away.

"But what did you *think*," he would insist. "Is she authentic? Or is her authenticity contrived? Is it an act, and if it's an act, is it a good one? How many faces do you suppose a single witch can have?"

Nora sighed. He expected honesty, always, even—or perhaps especially—if it was unwillingly given. "She isn't quite clever enough to keep up with you," she reluctantly admitted, loath to part with her practiced ambivalence, "but she's a good study. She has a very good idea of what to say to obscure how little she actually knows."

"So she's not totally stupid, then," Edmund mused.

"No, not stupid," Nora permitted hatefully. "But hardly worthy, either."

Edmund's mouth twitched, amused. "Are you jealous?"

"Of what?" Nora asked, indignant.

"Of *Della*," he would say, rising to his feet. "Perhaps you wish me to see you as a palatable option, instead?" he might ask, standing much too close to her. He was doing this quite a lot by the time he was eighteen; he was masterly at it by nineteen; an infuriating expert by twenty. "Nora Denshaw, do you perhaps wish me to love *you*?" he would ask her, and it would always sound so tempting, as if he were daring her to tell him, to confess so that he could finally take her in his arms—only, she had studied him as much as she studied anything. Edmund always looked most like his mother when he was daring Nora to admit that she loved him.

"You can stop," she told him, sighing. "It must be very exhausting."

"What is?" he asked.

"This," she said, pursing her lips. "You're practicing on me, but surely by now you must have practiced enough."

And then he would laugh, taking a step back from her.

"Good girl, Nora," he'd say, and then he'd launch back into something else; whatever he was studying that week.

Sometimes Nora would catch a glimpse of black slipping past the doorframe at these moments and realize that not only was Sophronia listening, but furthermore, she was pleased. Nora knew Sophronia well enough to know her true colors by then; after all, Nora had spent ten years observing not only Edmund, but Sophronia as well. Sophronia d'Este, who was only pleased when someone else was suffering. Sophronia, who had loved a mortal man and had her heart broken, resulting in a lifetime of mourning. Sophronia, whose life's purpose seemed to be to make certain her son's heart was harder even than hers.

It shouldn't have taken ten years to sort it out, but that was when Nora learned what she was. She wasn't just a servant; nor was she even a companion, even in the most patronizing sense. She was merely a pet, a lamb raised for slaughter, and now that Edmund was twenty-one years old—an age of significance in witchery, as Sophronia often said—Nora had a feeling her purpose in his life was about to take a drastic turn for the strange.

* * *

"This looks stupid," Nora said, "and I can't breathe."

"You're being dramatic," Edmund replied, not looking up from his book.

"I'm being *strangled* is what I am," Nora countered, shifting to look at herself from the side view. "Can't I wear my usual clothes? This corset is utter nonsense."

"You absolutely cannot wear your usual clothes," Edmund said impatiently, his gaze flicking up briefly from the page. "If you're going to accompany me on this trip, Nora, you certainly won't be doing it dressed like a street urchin."

"I *am* a street urchin," she reminded him.

"Not when you're with me, you're not. I have a reputation to uphold."

She rounded on him, glaring. "Why must I come with you at all?"

He arched a brow. "Would you rather stay with Mother?"

She grimaced.

"Thought so," he said smugly. "And anyway, all witches have familiars. You're mine."

She sighed. "I'm a mortal, Edmund. Not a cat. I keep telling you this."

"Well, true, you shed less." Edmund rose to his feet, setting the book on the table and walking toward her. "You look nice, kitty," he commented, catching her gaze as she turned back to her reflection. "I don't see why you're complaining."

She watched his attention wander over her back, pausing idly on the shape of her waist.

"Looks aren't everything," she informed him stiffly. "Funnily enough, Edmund, I find it rather beneficial to move."

He chuckled, and then reached out, hooking a finger in the fabric at the back of her dress. There was a bit of pressure at her back, like a balloon expanding, and then, with what felt like a rush of air, she felt the boning of the corset easing slightly against her aching ribs, permitting her to take a breath.

"There," he murmured, his breath warm across her shoulders. "Better now?"

"Yes," Nora sniffed, but Edmund didn't move. Instead he leaned closer, bending his head, and toyed with one of the softened waves of her hair, gently coiling it around his finger. His lips were perilously close to her neck now; troublingly present, really. Nora took advantage of having been gifted a charmed corset by letting her lungs expand, indulging in the necessary amount of oxygen to stabilize her other, more recalcitrant parts.

"I thought you'd appreciate an opportunity to get out of the house, Nora," Edmund murmured, his thumb brushing the bone of her clavicle. "But if you'd rather not join me, all you have to do is say so."

Was it *more* miserable that he would say such a thing, or less?

"You know I would never leave your side even if you asked it of me, Edmund," she said, half closing her eyes.

His lips were near her ear now, buried in her hair. "Yes. You're mine, aren't you, Nora?"

She stiffened as his hand crept around her waist.

"Stop it," she said, and looked into the mirror to find him with his lips curled up in a knowing smile, having been caught in his usual game. "Edmund," she growled, smacking his hand, and he released her with a laugh, dancing out of reach.

"You make it so easy, kitty," he told her, as she spun around to glare at him. "I can't help it."

"I hate you," she informed him.

"You don't," he corrected her, in the same tone of voice he might use to address a loyal cocker spaniel, and she hated that he wasn't wrong. He glanced at the clock. "It's nearly time to leave. Are you ready, kitty, or do you need to complain some more?"

"I'm ready," Nora said, clenching a fist.

Edmund's gaze flicked down to her whitened knuckles and he smiled, but let out a sigh.

"You know I'd sooner die than be without you, Nora," he said.

This, too, was meant to hurt her; to give her some softness of his to float on for a few days, until he inevitably broke her again. He did this, always, and he did it so well, and because Nora was a fool, she let him. Because she couldn't think to do anything other than love him, having been out of practice at anything else for nearly her entire life.

Still, she wouldn't dignify his arrogance with a response. "What are we even looking for?" she demanded instead. "What do you expect to find out there that you couldn't summon for yourself right here?"

At that, Edmund's easy smile wavered, and then tightened.

"A mark," he said.

Nora swallowed.

"Oh," she replied quietly.

* * *

Edmund was half mortal and half witch the same way a coin is half a face at any given time. While he was objectively both, he could still only really *be* one side or the other. Usually he was a witch, and as the son of Sophronia d'Este, he was of the finest magical stock; a prince among men. Sometimes, though, he was a mortal, and during those times he was something of a lower-tiered noble, descended from a bastard line of aristocracy. He wasn't invited to social events very often, but when he was, he and his mother usually took advantage. Sophronia was a proud woman—shamelessly so. She dolled Edmund up and boasted him about like a trophy: *See here, my fine handsome son, more beautiful than any of your weak-chinned excuses for boys.*

Sophronia and Edmund typically left for a weekend, and while they were gone, Nora slept. For good reason, too. The one time she had not been sleeping, she had seen Edmund and his mother return with a body.

"You know why," Edmund had said impatiently when she'd asked. "You've read the books too, Nora. You know precisely where power comes from. Do you think they just sell mortal organs at the market?"

He was sometimes crueler when he was guilty, so she didn't push the point.

This trip, and this particular society party, was to be Edmund's first one without his mother. He was of age now, Sophronia had said, and therefore she no longer had to waste her time communing with a lower species.

"Then Nora is coming with me," Edmund had said, which had made Sophronia's mouth tighten with impatience just as it made Nora's heart leap in her chest.

"No," Sophronia said.

"Yes," Edmund replied. "Nora goes, or I don't."

"Nora is *my* ward," Sophronia said, "and I say she stays."

"Nora is of mortal age as much as I am of witching age," Edmund said, "and she is no longer anyone's ward. And if anything," he added brusquely, "if she belongs to anyone, it's me."

Nora was very familiar with this sort of treatment as property. Sophronia, however, was clearly not enjoying the idea that her property could transfer ownership.

"What am I supposed to do without her?" Sophronia demanded.

"I think you can make your own tea, Mother," Edmund said.

"She's a commoner," Sophronia tossed out, switching tactics. "They won't like it."

"I'll dress her up," Edmund said. "And besides, she isn't *accompanying* me, Mother. She's just coming along."

"Like a servant?" asked Nora, and abruptly, Edmund remembered she was there.

"No," he said, giving her his usual ruffled look. "Like . . . like an associate."

"I don't think that's how it works," Nora began to say.

He glared at her, and she quieted.

"Absolutely not," Sophronia said, her final word on the subject. "Nora isn't going, and that's that."

"She is," Edmund said. *His* final word.

As usual, Edmund won out in the end, though it wasn't until Nora was alone with him in the carriage that she realized why she'd really been brought along.

"You're scared," she noted, and to that, he looked furious. "What? You are."

"I'm not scared," he snapped. "I just don't relish the thought of carrying a corpse by myself. They're very heavy."

Nora figured they probably were, and Edmund was artfully

slender, all long limbs and elegant fingers and decadent, opulent features. Certainly not a suitable vehicle for death.

"What if I don't want to kill someone?" she posed as a theoretical exercise.

He gave her a sour look that meant *too bad*.

"You'll do as you're told," he reminded her. "And anyway, I thought you'd be glad."

"Why?" she asked, but of course she already knew why. This was to be the only weekend in Nora's life since she'd first seen Edmund that Sophronia d'Este would not be somewhere nearby, observing Nora's movements from the shadows of their morbid house. In fact, Nora could reach out right now, could caress Edmund's hand (he would let her, of course, and then abruptly pull away and laugh, but still, for a moment it might be worth it), and Sophronia would not suddenly descend from the ceiling, swooping down to tell Nora to get her urchin tentacles off Sophronia's beloved son.

To her silence, Edmund merely lifted a brow, saying nothing.

The weekend was to be spent at Claxton Manor, a few hours from the d'Este estate. Nora, who hadn't been any farther than the edge of the d'Este gardens in ten years, was amazed to see that the world had carried on in her absence. It was late spring, and quite warm (Sophronia preferred the house to be at a temperature just above arctic), and Nora delighted in the sun that streamed in through the carriage until they arrived at Claxton House.

Others had arrived before them, wandering about the halls. "That's Sterling Wakefield," Edmund muttered in her ear, in reference to a rosily plump man who seemed to be constantly laughing. "Bit of a silly idiot, but fine enough."

"Looks wealthy," Nora noted.

Edmund nodded. "Too wealthy to go missing without much fuss," he said.

Nora caught sight of a woman peering out a window. "Who's that?"

"Adelaide Attlay. Notoriously paranoid." He grimaced. "Too much work."

"Ah." Nora looked around, about to ask after a very short man in a very large hat when she accidentally locked eyes with someone across the room. It was quite a young man, though perhaps a little older than Edmund, who was looking directly at her. "Edmund," she said, nudging him with an elbow. "Who's that?"

He, whoever he was, was extremely attractive. Not like Edmund, because Edmund was untouchable, but certainly very handsome of his own accord. This man was broad-shouldered and charismatic-looking, his head topped with coppery-brown curls that caught in the light, and Nora could see from her vantage point across the room that his eyes were an earthy, mossy green, like the rolling hills they'd passed before they'd arrived.

It was very clear that Edmund didn't like him, whoever he was. "That's Ives Cavendish," he said distastefully. "Bit of an overstuffed pheasant."

"Pheasant?" Nora echoed doubtfully, and Edmund shrugged.

"Plumage, you know." He glanced at her. "You know what I mean."

She didn't.

"He's looking at you," Nora noted, and he was. Ives was *staring*, in fact, with something of a half smile on his face, as if he were pointedly taking stock of Edmund's refusal to glance in his direction.

"He's a menace," Edmund muttered. "Barely aristocracy, and yet he never misses a party."

"Aren't you barely aristocracy?" Nora asked him.

Edmund glowered at her, and she bit back a laugh.

"It's just interesting," she remarked. "I never thought to wonder whether you had any enemies."

"I don't have enemies," Edmund snapped, and looked up, inadvertently catching Ives's glance.

Edmund's mouth tightened. Ives, on the other hand, smiled widely.

"I'm a witch," Edmund said to Nora under his breath. "Were I to make an enemy, he would surely find himself dead soon after."

Then he turned sharply back to her, his face a collection of grim lines.

"Come on, kitty," he said. "Let's dress for dinner."

* * *

"So," said a voice behind her. "You're Edmund d'Este's pet, I take it."

Nora turned to find herself face-to-face with Ives Cavendish, the pheasant himself.

"Is that all a woman can be?" she asked him.

"No," he replied, inclining his coppery head. "But it's what you are, aren't you?"

He was aiming for a reaction, she knew. She was familiar with the technique, so she opted not to give him one.

"How do you know Lord and Lady Claxton?" she asked.

"Ah, distant cousins, you know how it goes," Ives replied, shrugging. "I'm Ives Cavendish, by the way, though I assume Mund's mentioned it to you already."

Mund. Sophronia would have slit his throat just for that.

"Nora Denshaw," she replied. "Do you know Edmund well?"

"About as well as any man can know a shadow, I'd wager," Ives replied, in a way that made Nora bristle. "I know more *of* him than I know from any interaction *with* him." His gaze cut slyly to hers. "But it isn't him I came over here to talk about, if you catch my meaning."

"Subtle," Nora remarked dryly, sipping her wine. It hadn't begun to make her feel dizzy yet (Edmund usually made her have a drink with him after dinner when he was particularly enthused about a text, so she wasn't entirely unpracticed) but it would soon, and certainly sooner if Ives continued encroaching upon her breathable space. "I think you might be able to find a much more advantageous game elsewhere."

His grin broadened. "I never like to win too easily."

"I hope you like to lose, then," Nora said coolly, and looked up, gambling on whether a stare would unnerve him.

It didn't. In fact, it unnerved *her* when he didn't look away.

"I don't lose often," Ives murmured. "Never, in fact."

She exhaled. "Well, there's a first time for everything."

"Don't I know it," he remarked with a chuckle. "I'm guessing being kept by the d'Estes made you a predator, didn't it? Or at least prey with considerable teeth."

"She isn't prey," came a clipped voice behind them, and Nora turned with relief to find Edmund standing there, holding a spare glass in his hand. "Here," he said, handing it to her with no particular warmth. She hadn't finished her wine, but she knew better than to refuse. She accepted it and said nothing, and Edmund turned to Ives. "Cavendish."

"Evening, Mund," Ives said cheerfully. "I was just having a chat with your pet."

"I'm not his pet," Nora said, knowing full well that was precisely what she was, as Edmund said, "She isn't chatting."

"Mund, really, you must learn to share your toys," Ives remarked. "You come to what, one party every season? And you're only now bringing Miss Denshaw out from her cage? A criminal offense, in my view."

Nora hazarded a glance at Edmund, who had gone stiff with temper.

"Careful," Edmund warned through his teeth, and Ives laughed.

"Always so tense, Edmund. A relentless pleasure." He drained his glass, placing it on the table, and paused before leaning toward Nora. "If you find your cage restricting, pet," he murmured, "do come and find me. Mund here spends far too much time playing with his cauldron," he added, as Nora fought to keep her eyes from widening. "Couldn't please you if he tried, and we both know he wouldn't."

He leaned away, winking at Edmund, and then strode to the other side of the room, moving to chat with someone else while Nora slipped closer to Edmund.

"He knows," she said, at the same time Edmund said, "I'm going to kill him."

"What?" Nora asked. "But I thought—"

"It could look like an accident. Like he slipped out in the night and got himself killed in a tavern or something. He's not exactly subtle, or viceless." He paused, glass halfway to his lips. "Wait. What do you mean he knows?"

"He *knows*," Nora said, and dropped her voice. "He knows you're a witch. He said something about your cauldron, and—"

"Well." Edmund scowled. "Then consider that decision made."

* * *

Nora nervously paced the floor of Edmund's guest room. "So, what do I have to do?"

"Nothing," Edmund sighed, pulling at the collar of his shirt. "I'll kill him. You just have to make sure I'm not interrupted."

"And how would I do that?" she demanded. "I may know the charms to keep people out, Edmund, but you know perfectly well I can't cast them."

"You have a brain, kitty," Edmund reminded her. "Two working arms. Two legs. Surely it can't be this difficult to wrap your little mind around a simple task, Nor."

"You *say* that," Nora retorted, frustrated, "and yet you forget, *I* am mortal, and perhaps I am worried about the consequences this will have on my *fragile constitution*—"

"Nora." He sighed, and then his voice changed, softening. "Come here."

His instructions were always laced with commands. She shuffled over to him, furiously averting her gaze, and he reached up, offering her a hand.

"I can soothe you," he said. "If you want."

She knew the spell for it. She could speak it aloud right now (*Mitigo, Mulceo, Consolor*), could mimic the motions of his hands, precisely as he would do, only it wouldn't accomplish anything. It would only work if *he* said it, and yet for her, he could very well say nothing, and she would still feel everything. Funny how magic worked.

"I don't need to be soothed," she grumbled. "I just think it's wrong, that's all."

"He can't know about me," Edmund warned. "It's trouble."

"You wanted to kill him before that," she reminded him.

"Yes. Of course I did." He paused, and then said, "I didn't like the way he was looking at you."

"That's not a reason to kill a man, Edmund," Nora scoffed.

"Well, maybe I hate that he calls me Mund. Maybe I think he's entitled and insufferable. Or maybe I watched him with you and suddenly thought I could stand to see him gone, to wipe him out."

It was already too much. Nora shut her eyes, flinching. "Don't play with me, Edmund, please. Not now."

"You always think I'm playing. You always think it's a game."

"Because it is."

"What if it wasn't?" Edmund asked her.

"What if you meant it, you mean?" Nora echoed with a scoff. "That would make you a different man, Edmund. A more sincere one, which we both know you aren't."

He rose to his feet, pausing for a moment, and then stepped closer, brushing the backs of his knuckles along her cheek.

"What if nothing in my life is real?" he began, and she shivered. "What if it's all an illusion, Nora—what then? What would I have left, after you stripped everything else away? My magic or my money or my birth? Without all of that, do you think I'd have a society witch for a wife, or any invitations to mortal parties then? I wouldn't."

She sighed, miserable. "You know you'd have me, Edmund."

"I do know that." The corridors outside their rooms were silent, and Nora swore she could hear her own pounding heart. "And is *that* a game?"

It was too much. Much, much too much.

"Edmund." She half gasped it, burying her forehead in his shoulder, and suddenly wished that Sophronia would appear, to force them apart before Nora let herself go too far. "Please don't."

He paused for a moment, his hand hovering over her shoulder, and then he brushed the tips of his fingers down her spine, capitulating with a nod.

"Why did you bring me here, Edmund?" Nora whispered to him.

He stroked her hair, letting his fingers curl around the back of her neck.

"Because I hardly know what I am without you," he replied. "If there was ever a time I existed without you, it is long gone now. In a different world, or a different life. As if the universe itself rearranged to fill the gaps, and before you, there was no me at all."

Nora swallowed hard.

Mitigo, Mulceo, Consolor.

"This," she said, "is not what I want to hear before I kill a man, Edmund."

"You aren't killing him, kitty," Edmund reminded her. "I am."

"Still." She exhaled shakily, pulling away. "We should probably go."

That was enough. He nodded carefully, drew his shoulders back, and flipped the coin of what he was. He was Edmund d'Este again, son of Sophronia d'Este, and a witch beyond Nora's comprehension. She, meanwhile, had no place in his life as anything other than what she was.

A pet, as Ives had called her, and as she'd already known for so long.

"Yes," Edmund agreed. "Let's go."

* * *

Ives Cavendish was clearly a favorite of the Claxtons, having been given one of the more privileged rooms on the second floor. He had a balcony that faced the gardens and slept brashly, with his windows open, daring everyone outside to see just how splendid his accommodations were.

"Ridiculous," Edmund said, tutting.

Nora didn't find it surprising that Edmund thought so, but she found herself unmoved. She could see well enough from her one conversation with Ives that he was exceedingly charming, in a way that surely persuaded everyone he met to give him precisely what he wanted. Social generosity was probably all compelled by benevolent selfishness; a transactional exchange for simply being in Ives's warmth.

"It should be fairly simple," Edmund continued under his breath. "I'll levitate us both onto his balcony, unlock the door, and then bind his wrists while he sleeps. Once I've stabbed him—"

"Stabbed him?" Nora echoed, sickened.

"Stabbed him," Edmund confirmed, "I'll need you to help me drain the blood. It's very important," he added, "as—"

"—the blood from a fresh corpse is especially good for solstice rituals," Nora grunted, which she would have known having heard Sophronia say it even if she had not read countless books on the subject herself.

Edmund smiled. "Very good, kitty."

"Don't," Nora warned, and he shrugged, waving a hand once to draw them both up onto the balcony.

"You're right," Edmund said, and reached forward to tap the lock, listening for the telling shift of the latch and holding one finger to his lips. "I'll praise you later," he murmured, and she rolled her eyes, cautiously following him inside.

It wasn't like she was afraid. She was never afraid when she was with Edmund. Even if he were any less talented a witch, Nora was always far too occupied with other things about him to feel fear, like the breathlessness of watching him work. He had a light footfall, a light touch. Ives had been right to call him a shadow. Edmund was a slip of nothingness in the room, and if anyone had asked Nora if she'd thought Ives Cavendish was about to die, she would have said yes, no question. There wasn't a world that existed for her in which Edmund did not get precisely what he wanted.

But, as is bound to happen once or twice in any given lifetime, Nora's entire world changed that night.

"He's not here," Edmund said, frowning.

"Are you sure?" Nora whispered back, glancing around. Ives certainly wasn't visible, though at that time of night his absence seemed highly unlikely. "Do you think he just left temporarily? I could try to find him, and then—"

"My, my, you *are* a good pet, aren't you?" she heard behind her, and let out a gasp that was rapidly smothered, a hand sliding roughly over her mouth. "An accessory, even, and to murder, at that."

"Let go of her," Edmund commanded, stepping forward with his fingertips outstretched, but Ives shook his head, one arm snaking out to trap Nora's waist.

"Don't try any of your magic on me, Edmund d'Este," Ives warned, and for some reason, Edmund only blinked, as if the words had washed over him and pinned his arms at his sides, cast around him like a net. "Stay where you are. You know I could do far worse to her much faster than you could even lift a finger against me."

"Don't" was all Edmund said.

Nora, meanwhile, struggled with confusion, twisting around to glare at her captor. "Don't touch h—"

She broke off, startled, as she noticed Ives's teeth, and more important, that they were not teeth at all, but *fangs*. His eyes, which had been so green the entirety of the evening she'd been watching him, had grown bloodshot and red, his skin an incandescent glow amid the darkness of his room.

By then, Nora had read enough books on the subject to know

what she was looking at. His inhuman speed, those teeth, and Edmund's unwilling paralysis all confirmed it.

Ives Cavendish was a vampire.

"Edmund, *run*," she cast wildly over her shoulder, as the corners of Ives's mouth slid back to a grin that was wider than ever, accommodating his unearthly set of fangs. "Edmund," she shouted, writhing around to look at him, "just *go!*"

"Nora," Edmund croaked, trying again to reach for her, but Ives tutted his disapproval, shaking his head.

"Listen to your pet, Edmund d'Este," Ives purred. "I would have great need of a witch like you, Mund, but circumstances being what they are"—he tilted Nora's chin up toward his—"I'll make do with her."

"Edmund," Nora said again, desperate now. Sophronia abhorred vampires, and even Nora knew well enough what a vampire could do with a witch's blood. It would explain why Ives was able to wander around in daylight, and why he'd been able to conceal his identity, even from a witch. "Edmund, please!"

She wished, then, that she had just let Edmund kiss her when they'd been alone together in his room. So what if it had only been a game to him? It still would have been a kiss, and even if it would have haunted her for a lifetime, that meant very little now that she was clearly about to die.

"Are you a witch, too, sweetheart?" Ives asked her, stroking a curved finger along her cheek, and Nora shuddered as Edmund made a low noise of pain.

"Yes," Nora lied. "Yes, I am. I'll give you what you want, just let Edmund go."

Ives laughed and turned her around again, his arm still around her waist.

"Tell him to give you up," Ives whispered in her ear, and Nora shut her eyes, fighting tears. "Tell him it would be a waste of his time to pick a fight with me. He's only ever known mortals and witches, hasn't he? He isn't prepared to fight me. If you want him to live, pet, then you'd be wise to tell him to go. Tell him to go, and not to come back."

Nora stared at Edmund, forcing herself to speak.

"Go, Edmund," she choked out, unable to say anything more, and for a moment, Edmund simply stared at her.

Then he disappeared, vanishing into thin air, and Ives whipped her back around, smiling down at her.

"Now," he said. "About that lie you told me—" He leaned forward, brushing her hair back to speak directly in her ear. "—*mortal*."

Nora shuddered. This was the end.

This was the end, and Edmund was gone.

Then Ives Cavendish leaned forward, brushing his lips against her neck with a terrible, monstrous softness, and sank his teeth into her with a sigh.

* * *

Nora woke slowly, her head pounding, as something soft and smooth was being pressed against her mouth.

"Drink," came a voice. "You'll feel better."

Somewhere in her mind she knew it was skin that was brushing her lips, and that "drink" was not a command typically associated with skin, not without a puncture, and of course she couldn't puncture anything, seeing as she had very nice and normal-sized teeth. Somewhere, her mind knew that only a vampire would say such a thing, and that only a vampire would drink, and thus if "drink" meant "drink *blood*," then of course she must *also* be a vampire, only that would be thoroughly implausible. That would be *impossible*, actually, because she was nothing very special at all, and she certainly wasn't dead, and if she wasn't dead then she obviously couldn't be *un*dead, so naturally, none of this was happening.

Her mind said all these things, of course, but instinct told her *drink,* and so she suckled at Ives Cavendish's wrist like a calf to its mother, lapping it up with a shaky sigh until she felt almost drunk, a sleepy contentedness settling low in her belly. Then she licked at the wound at his wrist, closing it up.

"There," Ives said, stroking her hair. "How's that, pet?"

Nora nodded, curling up in his arms, and then jolted upright.

"WHAT," she shrieked, and Ives chuckled, sitting up to look at her.

"You didn't think I would really kill you, did you?" he asked. "No, pet, I like you. I like you quite a lot. Couldn't you tell?"

"But—" Nora was gasping for breath. "But—but now I'm—"

"Well, it's not good for me to have a mortal around. I've wanted to bite you," he murmured, stroking a finger along her neck, "since the moment I first saw you. But I had to contain myself, of course. Might have killed you if I hadn't. Luckily restraint is only one of my innumerable skills."

"But—" Nora stared at him. He was handsome again, hardly frightening at all, only she was more terrified than ever. "I have to get back to Edmund," she said, scrambling out of what she realized now was Ives's bed, and Ives sighed, moving quicker than light to catch her as she stumbled to the doorway.

"Careful," he warned. "You've only just turned. Unless you want to get staked through the heart by Sophronia d'Este, I'd advise you to take a bit more care who you go storming after, pet."

"It's Nora," she grumbled, though even then, she was struck by a very interesting but unhelpful thought. Edmund's nickname for her was essentially the same thing, only when Edmund said it, it was as if to remind her: *You belong to me.* Ives's use of "pet" was somehow . . . affectionate. Playful.

Interesting. But, again, unhelpful.

"Nora, then," Ives said. "Do me a favor and sit down, Nora."

She sat. She wasn't sure if he'd manipulated her into it with magic (was it still considered magic when it came from death?) or if she'd simply become numb to instruction, letting it wash over her like a wave. Ives knelt down in front of her, gently, and took her hands in his.

"It's quite a lot, I know," he offered sympathetically. "But surely you could see the d'Estes were only using you."

Yes, she certainly knew as much, but how did he?

"Because," Ives said patiently, "they are rather famous, Nora. Infamous, you might say. Sophronia is an abuser of mortals and creatures both. Countless have died at her hands. Did you really not know?"

Nora blinked.

"It's a wonder they let you live." Ives sighed. "My guess is that Sophronia was using you for something more long-term. Sometimes we give the young ones animals, you know, to teach them about responsibility. About what it means to care for something. Then they have to kill them, of course, to learn the hardest lesson of all, that to truly care for something else is to sacrifice a bit of yourself. Did you ever wonder if Edmund was going to kill you, pet? Did he ever look at you as if one day you might be gone?"

Edmund didn't, Nora thought.

But Sophronia nearly always did.

"Maybe one day you'll realize I saved you," Ives continued. "It doesn't upset me if it isn't today. I have eternity to wait, you know. But I can't permit you to go back, Nora. I cannot save your life merely to un-save it."

Nora stared down at her hands, unwilling to believe him, but also unable to look past one unassailable fact.

"What is it?" Ives asked, tilting her chin up, and because she couldn't think to do anything else, she let her eyes meet his.

"I'm hungry," she said quietly.

Slowly, Ives smiled. "Yes," he said. "You must be starved."

* * *

"How is it?" Ives asked, as Nora wiped the smear of blood from her mouth.

"Good," she answered, stepping back from the glassy-eyed butler's body. "Is it sweeter when they're older?"

"Yes. Ages like wine," Ives confirmed approvingly.

Nora nodded, then faltered. "Edmund would know how to clean this up," she remarked ruefully, glancing down at the mess she'd made. She'd never been so strong; she'd wrestled a grown man into Ives's room with almost no trouble at all, despite never having done much of anything aside from making tea and carrying books. The windows were sealed shut, though, as even a sliver of light gave her a headache, so it wasn't all victories.

"So do I, and so will you. More importantly for the time being, though, what you need is a witch," Ives informed her. "Witch's blood will permit you to do certain things from time to time, like attend stuffy noble parties. I'd give you some," he added, "only we'll have to go home for that. I don't keep anything that valuable just sitting around."

"I'm not going home with you," Nora said.

"Yes, actually, you are," Ives told her. "You can't go back to the d'Estes now. Sophronia will kill you. She probably would have either way."

"Edmund wouldn't let her," Nora said.

Ives arched a brow. "Are you sure?"

No. No, she wasn't sure.

"Then I want one witch in particular," Nora said abruptly.

To that, Ives looked delighted. "Edmund?"

"No," Nora said, thinking instead of Edmund's favorite of the society witches. "Della. Della Ailey."

"Interesting," Ives said, which sounded more like "oh, you poor thing," or "sad, sweetheart, *sad*," but Nora didn't care. She was a vampire now, wasn't she? And Ives seemed to want to please her. So if witch's blood was what she needed, she knew just the witch she wanted.

"Well," Ives said. "We'll need to stop off for supplies, but then we can go and find her, I suppose."

"Don't you have the rest of this party to attend?" Nora asked him.

"Hm? No," Ives said. "Funnily enough, whenever I stay the whole weekend, somebody usually dies."

Nora glanced down at the butler, who stared blankly into nothing.

Ives smiled. "Come on, pet. Off we go."

*　*　*

The Cavendish house, much like the d'Este estate, was an elaborate manor house filled with spectacularities, featuring intricate statues that lined the halls and fountains that leapt up like stardust before crashing into pools of wonder. It was filled with both wealth and magic, and as they walked, Ives murmured in her ear about the origins of things: This, his mother's. This, his great-grandfather's. This, he stole.

"I am proudest, of course, of the things I've taken," he said to her, his hand hovering above the small of her back but very pointedly not touching it. "They are more carefully selected than anything else in this house."

She shivered, and said nothing.

Ives was not the only person who lived in his house, nor was he the only vampire.

"This is Cassius," he said, introducing her to what she would have guessed was another young nobleman had he not openly flashed her his teeth, letting his incisors scrape opals of white into his lips as he bowed his raven-black head. "When I was turned, Cassius turned with me. He's a rather close friend."

"Who turned you?" Nora asked Ives.

"That would be me," said another, older gentleman, this one named Otto. He had the sort of look Nora associated with material wealth, and though he didn't bare his teeth, he *was* wearing an alarming number of blinding jewels.

"Otto had grand aspirations for a life of leisure," Ives affirmed in Nora's ear. "I suppose that made me and my fortune rather impossible to resist."

"That, and your marvelous flesh," Otto assured him, which Nora supposed was meant to be a compliment, though it sounded more salacious than anything.

"It can be both," Ives informed her, which was when she realized (quite late, of course) that he could read her mind.

"Can all vampires do that?" she asked him.

He shook his head. "I can with you, and I suppose Otto could with me, if he cared to," he told her as Otto made a face of profound disinterest. "There's a special relationship after siring. You'll be able to read mortal minds, but not another vampire's. It's considered poor form," Ives added, half smiling, "but as it's so novel, I suppose I can't resist."

"How many others have you turned?" Nora asked, and he turned his head, glancing plaintively down at her.

"Only the one," he said. "I was a virgin before you."

She felt her thoughts jolt, and he smiled.

"I read that, too," he said, "but as I'm such a gentleman, I'll keep it to myself."

His house was as grand as Sophronia's, but with substantially less witchery. It didn't shift around Nora as she walked. There was also no bell summoning her. Ives led her to a bedroom that was easily four times the size of the one she'd had at the d'Estes', and once he left her, she was alone. *Truly* alone. For someone who couldn't recall having any space or movement of her own, it was difficult not to immediately fall in love with solitude. Nora fell back against the bed, relishing the knowledge that nobody was expecting her to be anywhere or do anything, and fell into a long, delighted doze.

When she woke, it was to a quiet knock on her door. Nobody barged in. Whoever it was, they waited for her answer. She crept quietly to the door and cracked it just slightly, determining the amount of space she wanted to give.

"Evening," Ives said.

"Is it that late?" asked Nora.

"Early," he corrected. "And we'd better go, if you still want to hunt yourself a witch before the sun comes up again."

Nora hesitated.

"What am I supposed to do here?" she asked him. "Just . . . live forever? With you?"

"If you want to," Ives said. "You're certainly safer here than anywhere else."

"But—" She paused, trying to determine how to phrase it. "But, seeing as you're doing something for me, would I then have to—?"

"Oh, heavens, no," Ives said, looking repulsed. "Do you really think I need to force you to love me? Or fuck me? No, pet, that's up to you," he said, as her cheeks flushed, or would have flushed, had they not been considerably immune to blood-rushing. "If you don't want my company, Nora, you're free to refuse it."

She frowned. "But then why—"

"Why did I turn you? Oh, I don't know. Boredom, I suppose. You were going to die anyway, and isn't it better this way? But as I was saying—this *Della*," he said, abruptly changing the subject. "Is she a very good witch?"

Nora didn't want to sound rude, but by then she was accustomed to the expectation of candor. "No."

"Well, excellent," Ives said. He was rather irrepressibly cheerful, Nora thought, for something so dead. "Good instincts, pet. Shall we be off, then?"

Was it really only a couple of days ago that she was complaining about a corset? One relief, she supposed, was that it no longer felt quite so restricting. For whatever reason, once the life in her lungs had suspended, she finally felt she could breathe.

"Yes," she said. "Yes, let's go."

*   *   *

Della Ailey looked up groggily, her head lolling to the side.

"Oh," she said, upon sight of Nora. Her eyes were nearly as glazed as the dead butler's, though it looked more like intoxication than death. "It's you. The servant girl."

"My name is Nora," Nora informed her, and gestured to Ives. "This is Ives."

"Hello, handsome," Della said, catching her head just before it jerked back. "Where's Edmund?"

Nora's stomach tightened. "Not here."

To her surprise, Della scoffed. "Good," she muttered, as her head fell forward. "He's a real piece of work, you know."

"What?" Nora asked.

"He's—unfeeling. Cold." Della lifted her head with difficulty. "And far too attached to his mother."

"I like this witch," Ives remarked. "I'm glad you didn't kill her."

Nora glanced at him.

"Don't worry," he said. "I like you more."

"Stop," she told him.

He shrugged, playing unconvincingly at innocence.

"What do you mean Edmund is cold?" Nora asked, turning back to Della. "Maybe he just didn't like you."

"Maybe," Della permitted, voice slurred. "Or maybe he only loves murder."

"What?" Nora demanded. "Edmund doesn't—he doesn't murder anyone. He's—that's why he—he wouldn't—?"

Ives reached out, stilling her.

She exhaled.

"What do you mean?" she asked Della, trying again.

"Edmund's a witch-killer," Della replied. "I caught him once. Told me he'd kill me, too, if I said anything, so I didn't. Until now." She smiled vacantly. "He and his mother, they buy and sell witch blood. It's how they have all that money." She blinked. "You're not going to sell mine, are you?"

"No," Nora said, frowning. "I was just going to drink it."

"Maybe save some for a rainy-day snack," Ives contributed.

"Oh," Della said, glancing at where her dress had been shifted from her shoulder. "Did you already bite me?"

"A little," Nora remorsefully confessed.

Della's blood had been delicious. Not too acidic, not too tart. A burst of sweetness, like a perfectly ripe strawberry.

"That's why you feel like that," Ives added to Della.

"Like what?" Della asked. "High?"

"Oh good, so you're familiar with the sensation," Ives said, and glanced at Nora, explaining, "To a witch, a vampire bite can be somewhat intoxicating. Almost tantric."

"Better if the vampire's good," Della said, which Nora assumed was meant to be a compliment. "Virgins don't normally take to the bite so naturally."

To that, Ives arched a doubting brow.

"I'm rich and beautiful," Della replied in answer. "I've experimented."

Nora blinked, very much taken aback by all these turns of events.

"Can I come back?" Della asked them. "You can have as much as you want, as long as you don't kill me. *And* as long as I don't have to go back right away," she added with a grimace. "My mother will be positively unbearable if she catches me like this." Nora frowned, and Della shrugged. "Still have to find a proper husband. You know how it is."

"I don't, actually," Nora said.

"No, of course you don't," Della agreed, gesturing idly to Ives. "You already have one, don't you?"

"He's not my husband," Nora said.

"Well, then you're an idiot," said Della. "Can you bite me somewhere that won't show in polite company? Like here, for example," she said, and tugged down her décolletage to display the swell of one ample, creamy breast.

Ives and Nora exchanged a glance.

"I suppose I could do that," Nora said eventually.

"Wonderful," said Della, closing her eyes.

* * *

When the sun no longer bothered Nora (thanks to Della's blood, in which she admittedly overindulged at first) she took herself on walks outside in Ives's gardens. She'd never been able to spend much time outdoors at the d'Este estate unless Edmund had wanted to. In fact, Nora was so used to living on Edmund's clock that it was a somewhat startling luxury to realize she could sleep and wake when she wanted, eat whenever she liked, go wherever she pleased. She would tense up, at first, whenever she heard Ives's voice, or ran into Cassius or Otto. But rather than expect anything from her, they would merely tip their hats, or tip imaginary ones, and then disappear.

Gradually, Nora gave in to the indulgences of freedom. She read books for pleasure. She went into town sometimes, though never when she was hungry; that was asking for trouble, and Ives had warned her about leaving bodies lying around. ("It's unsanitary," he said, "and we are gentlemen.") Della came around about once a week, chatting with Nora about what was going on in the outside world.

"They say Edmund's killing vampires now," Della remarked, warming herself by the fire, which was lit despite its lack of impact on the undead things that lived in the house.

"I wonder why he never killed me," Nora murmured.

"Maybe he was going to," Della said.

"I suppose," said Nora, charitably. Ives had certainly thought so.

"Or maybe he was in love with you," Della said.

"I doubt it," Nora replied. "If he was, he wasn't any good at it."

"How could he be, with a mother like that?" Della asked.

Nora felt suddenly flustered. "I don't know," she said, and she didn't.

Della shrugged, lifting her skirt to prop one leg on the arm of Nora's chair. "How about here this time?" she suggested, gesturing to the curve of one ambrosial thigh. "I've already got bruises on my stomach."

Nora blinked.

"Okay," she managed, and leaned forward, sinking her teeth in as Della let out a contented sigh.

* * *

Ives, like all vampires, was unnaturally quiet, though he was kind enough not to sneak up on Nora when she wasn't prepared.

"Knock, knock," he said, tapping at the doorframe.

"You don't have to say it *and* do the thing," Nora told him.

"Well, pet, it's too late to change me," he said. "I'm really quite set in my ways."

She rolled her eyes, but gestured for him to sit beside her. "Would you like to know what I'm reading?" she asked.

"If you'd like to tell me," Ives replied.

She opened her mouth to answer, then immediately clamped it shut. It felt too much like something she used to do with Edmund.

"Nora," Ives sighed. "This isn't—"

"Don't read my mind," she said.

He fidgeted. "I don't mean to, you know. It's difficult to turn on and off, and really, I'm just as inexperienced with it as you a—"

"Don't read my mind," Nora pressed on, "because I'd like to tell you what I'm thinking. In words. Out loud."

Ives froze, falling unnaturally still. Had Nora not already been certain she wouldn't find one, she would have checked him for a pulse.

"What would happen," she began carefully, "if we . . . ?"

He waited.

"You know," she said.

"Pet," Ives told her slowly, "those aren't words."

"It's—" She toyed with her fingers in her lap. "It's undignified to say aloud."

He considered her a moment.

"I see," he said eventually. "Well, I'm not sure. I do know one thing, though," he determined, rising to his feet, "and it's that if I hear the name Edmund in your mind while I'm—*you know*," he said pointedly, lifting a brow, "I will have something of a problem with it."

Fair enough, she thought.

"I knew nothing but Edmund for years," Nora reminded him. "Sometimes I can't help it."

Ives was tender when he touched her shoulder. "I have all the time in the world to wait," he advised, leaving the room with hardly another sound.

* * *

"The witches have themselves a serial killer," Cassius said. His feet were propped up on the living room table and he said it very casually, as if he were sharing nothing more than a little bit of gossip. "They say even Sophronia d'Este has gone into hiding."

"How do you know that?" Nora asked, looking up at him from Della's arm.

"*Everyone* knows that," Della informed her drowsily. "And keep going, please. I have to be back in twenty minutes."

"You know, for someone being drained of her blood, you're awfully entitled," Cassius noted.

"Thank you," Della replied. "Anyway, like I said, everyone knows. My mother heard from Alma Radford's mother that Sophronia was hiding out in some sort of cave. Shameful, honestly."

"Sophronia?" Nora asked, wiping her mouth. "Hiding from her own son?"

Cassius shrugged. "I suppose that's what happens when you raise your son to be a murderer of witches," he said. "She probably never suspected he'd wake up one morning and realize she was a witch, too."

"None of this sounds like Edmund," Nora said, frowning. "Sure, maybe he killed some people—"

Della rolled her eyes, mockingly mouthing the word "maybe."

"—but he hated doing it. I saw it," Nora insisted. "I saw it in his eyes."

"Well, something's clearly changed him. He's no longer the witch you knew," Cassius said, rising to his feet. "You should probably stay away from him. And if you're quite finished," he added, gesturing to Della, "the lady does expect to be numb with pleasure, and you're much too distracted to finish your drink."

Della smiled brilliantly at him, but Nora felt dazed.

"What cave?" she asked.

Cassius bent before Della as she placed her foot in his hand, letting him lift her leg onto his shoulders.

"Ask Ives," he suggested, ducking his head under Della's skirt.

*   *   *

"Sophronia," Nora called, catching sight of her from a distance. One thing to be said for vampirism was her excellent night vision; despite the blackness of the cave, she could see the old witch's form where it was shrouded in darkness, tucked deep among the shadows. "Funny seeing you here."

Sophronia squinted at her, eyes narrowing. "Nora."

"And Ives," Nora genially acknowledged, gesturing over her shoulder to where he stood. "He insisted on coming along to see you."

"I wasn't letting you go see Sophronia d'Este alone," he reminded her, in a voice that meant *if we're going to fight, we're going to do it in private*, which Nora chose not to acknowledge, shifting closer to Sophronia instead.

"Well. The great Sophronia d'Este doesn't look like much anymore," Nora remarked, kneeling to lock eyes with Sophronia in the dark. "I wonder why, hm?"

Sophronia kicked at her. "Get away," she growled. "I have no interest in seeing you."

"Why not?" Nora asked. "I thought I was your property. Until that whole rumor that you wanted me dead, that is."

"Of course I did," Sophronia spat. "You were supposed to die the moment you returned. I was going to make him kill you, in fact. So that he would learn. So that he would *learn*." She fidgeted, beginning to rock herself back and forth. "I made you his heart so that I could destroy it, and all that was left would be power. Now he is power and nothing else, and oh, how I've suffered for my mistake."

Sophronia put on a look of theatrical misery, which Nora ignored. "You made me his heart?" she asked instead, bemused, and Sophronia glared at her.

"Edmund's father made a fool of me," she snapped. "I loved him, and when he tried to leave, I killed him, though it broke my heart to do it. It broke me, but it made me stronger. It increased my power tenfold." She quieted, staring at her lap. "I thought giving you to Edmund, ensuring that he would bury his softness in you, would do the same. I thought he would love you, kill you, and then be stronger for it."

"But Edmund never loved me," said Nora.

"Of course he did, you stupid girl," Sophronia said impatiently, and Nora remembered that Sophronia had always considered her a fool. "He *only* loved you. I thought you being gone would be a blessing, and for a time, it was. He was ruthless." Sophronia spoke of it, of Edmund, as if he were one of her beautiful, gruesome paintings. "But when you were gone for too long, he was different. Then he turned against me."

"Well, what a surprise," Nora said. "You made him a monster. Did you really think that was what he deserved?"

Even in the dark, she could see the loathing in Sophronia's eyes.

"You are nothing," Sophronia snarled. "It was a mistake to bring you into Edmund's life. You were born nothing, Nora, and you will die nothing."

"I'm already dead," Nora told her. "You might have heard?" She let her incisors flash briefly, knowing the tips of them would glitter in the dark. "Maybe I did die nothing. But I'm certainly something now. Something you probably shouldn't mess with, *ma'am.*"

It was a cheap shot, but an effective one, in that it was met with further rage.

"You'll never have Edmund," Sophronia taunted. "He doesn't know what love is. He'd kill you just as soon as love you. He'd kill you, you stupid fool, and not even know it was love until after you were already dead."

"If that's what he is, then it's your doing," Nora reminded her. "You brought this on yourself. He was already powerful. You're the one who made him heartless."

"Better that than see my son with someone as low as you," Sophronia spat.

To that, Nora blinked.

"I'm not nothing," she told Sophronia d'Este, saying it aloud for the first time in her life. "I was never nothing. Perhaps it would have done you some good to see that, Sophronia."

Then she stood up to leave, turning to Ives. "Let's go. I'm done with this."

Ives nodded, offering her his arm.

"I hope Edmund kills you!" Sophronia screeched at her back.

In response, Nora froze.

"You don't have to," Ives murmured in her ear.

But she did.

She really, really did.

"I'm hungry," Nora whispered to him, and turned her head, brushing her lips softly against Ives's cheek.

Then Nora took a step toward Sophronia d'Este, burying her smile in the dark.

* * *

"How did she taste?" Ives asked when they arrived home. The sun was only just beginning to rise, so Nora had pulled him toward the garden, suggesting they take a walk.

"Not very good," Nora said. "Sort of . . . overripe."

"Ah," Ives said sagely. "Well, that can happen. If we'd had more time, I would have advised the use of a decanter. Sometimes, with the older ones, you really have to let it breathe."

Nora paused him beneath an old oak tree.

"Read my mind," she suggested.

He looked down at her, green eyes bright with bemusement.

"What do you see?" Nora asked, tilting her head.

He swallowed.

"Me," he said.

"And?" she asked.

He blinked. "Me."

She stepped closer. "And?"

"Me." His voice grew ragged. "I only see me."

"And what do you suppose that means?" Nora asked him, taking another step.

He closed his eyes. "Pet," he said hoarsely, clearing his throat.

"Nora," she corrected him.

"Nora," he agreed. "Nora." She took his chin in her hand, guiding him toward her. "Nora," he murmured, and she slid her arms around his neck, drawing him closer and closer and *closer* until they, and every spare inch of them, found a counterpart in the other. "Nora," he said, and she kissed him, with all the softness of fresh grass and warm spring nights and other, living sensations. "Nora," he said while he kissed her back, enveloping her tongue with the taste of him until they were both gleaming, beautiful things.

"Nora," he whispered, and while the other times had been a proclamation, a jubilant series of rewards, this one was a question.

"Ives," she said in answer, and let him lay her gently down among the moss.

* * *

"We have to kill Edmund," Nora said, lying with her head on Ives's chest.

She'd had a dream, which was normally something she associated with being alive. Only living things had dreams, she thought. To be dead was to lose a certain amount of internal spark, which meant that it was probably unnatural. Rarely did a vampire see a witch's face in her head, and even more rarely (Nora suspected) did said witch whisper, *Come to me, kitty, I'm waiting, I know you're alive and I'm waiting,* which meant that Edmund d'Este must have used his unbounded witchery to break into her mind.

"He must know his mother is dead," Nora continued. "I suppose he'll come for me now."

"Of course he'll come for you," Ives said. "He loves you."

"He doesn't know what love is," said Nora.

Ives tilted her chin up. "Do you?"

She hesitated.

"I know what it isn't," she replied.

Ives kissed her forehead, his lips cool and grave against her skin.

"Then I suppose let's kill Edmund," he remarked, curving his palm around her cheek.

* * *

"There's another one of those mortal parties," Della said. "You know, one of the weekend ones. At the Crawleys' this time."

"I hate those," said Nora.

"You liked the last one," Ives told her, a smile twitching at his lips.

"It worked out," Nora permitted, "but that doesn't mean I liked it."

Ives glanced down, pretending to read his book. "You liked it," he murmured, as Nora returned her attention to the porcelain of Della's bare waist.

"Edmund's going," Della said, hissing slightly as Nora sank her teeth in. "Has to make appearances, you know. It's been almost five years since the last one, and people are beginning to wonder."

"How do you know so much mortal gossip?" Ives asked her.

"I'm a countess, when I want to be," Della replied, smoothing a hand over Nora's hair.

"That explains a lot," Ives remarked. "So you're sure Edmund will be there, then?"

"Very sure," Della said, her voice airy and intoxicated again. "He loves a good party."

"I thought he loved murder," Ives said.

"Yes," Della said, her eyes falling shut. "But who doesn't also love a party?"

She shuddered and gave a small moan. Then Nora pulled away, licking blood from her lips.

"I could do a party," she said.

*　*　*

The Crawley house was so eerily similar to the Claxton house that it was as if Nora had fallen back in time, collapsing into the same room, surrounded by the same people, with the same sensation that perhaps everyone could see through her, straight through to what she was. She recognized some of the faces Edmund had once pointed out to her, identifying them from the recesses of her mind; but still, one face stood out among the others, as it always had.

"Edmund d'Este," he said, holding out a hand for hers. "You must be Nora Denshaw."

"Nora Cavendish, actually," she told him, and watched him blink, momentarily off-kilter.

"Quite a rise," he murmured, regaining control of himself and sipping from his glass of champagne.

"From pet to noble," she asked, "or from witch to vampire?"

He spared her a cautioning glance. "Kitty," he said.

"I'm not your familiar anymore, Edmund," Nora said. "I'm not a cat. I never was."

"Maybe not," he said. "But you were mine once, weren't you?"

She paused, glancing around, and caught Ives's eye across the room before turning back to Edmund.

"I still am," she said.

His eyes narrowed. "You're lying."

"No, actually, I'm not." *And that's the saddest part,* she thought. "I may not like it, Edmund, but I've always loved you. I've always been yours, even when I didn't want to be. *Especially* when I didn't want to be. Always." She looked up at him. "Before you, Edmund, there was no me at all."

He stared at her.

And stared.

And stared.

"Nora," he whispered, his gaze curling around her cheek as if he might have touched it, and perhaps once he might have. Perhaps he might have, and she would have let him, and in a moment just like this, had it happened five years ago, then she would have been alive, and so would he.

"Come find me tonight, Edmund," she murmured softly.

Then she turned away, rejoining Ives where he stood across the room.

*   *   *

He came to her. She'd had her doubts that he would, insisting he would surely smell a trap, but it was Ives who'd convinced her Edmund would do it. *He won't be able to resist,* Ives had said. *How do you know?* Nora had asked. *Because I wouldn't,* Ives had replied, and then he'd kissed her long and hard, as if that were explanation enough.

But doubts aside, Edmund did come to her, and Nora was sitting at the foot of her bed when she heard the latch creak of its own accord, and saw him enter from the balcony.

"Hi, kitty," he said.

"Hello, Edmund," she replied.

He stepped forward. She rose to her feet. It was all very halted and mechanized, as they were out of practice. Eventually, though, muscle memory took over, and it seemed that Edmund's feet still remembered how to carry him to her. Nora's chin remembered how to tilt up toward his; Edmund's fingers remembered how to fit themselves to her waist; Nora's lungs remembered how to fill and burst at the sight of him.

"We could run away together," he said. "My mother is gone now."

"I know," Nora said, and added, "You've been very bad, though, Edmund. Very bad."

He dodged her glance. "I'm powerful now."

"You always were. What's different now?"

"Everything." He sucked in a breath. "With you, Nora, it could all be different."

Something lived in the unspoken: *If it hadn't been for Sophronia . . .*

But then, if it hadn't been for Sophronia d'Este and her insistence on breaking her own son's heart, perhaps Nora would never have known Edmund at all. Because there *had* been Sophronia, and thus all Edmund and Nora could ever be together was sorrow, just as it was all they could ever be apart.

"Why didn't you look for me?" Nora asked him instead.

"I thought you were dead," he said, flinching. "I thought . . . until my mother was killed. Until I found her. Then I knew."

"And while you thought I was dead?" Nora asked him. "What did you do then, Edmund?"

"I—" Edmund faltered. The Edmund she remembered didn't falter. "It doesn't matter. None of that matters."

"Oh, but it does, Edmund." Nora sighed, resting her hands gently on his chest. "It does matter. You hurt a lot of people."

He didn't deny it, and she was glad of it, albeit a little (immensely) anguished. Part of her—the stupid part that had once stumbled upon a boy in a library—still clung to the hope that Della was wrong.

"I can change," Edmund insisted instead. "I—With you, Nora, it's different. When you're here, I feel—I *feel* things, things that don't exist when you're gone. It's why I brought you with me the first time, kitty, because I can't stand to be without you—because when you're not there, I can't—everything just goes dark, and I—"

"Edmund," Nora said. "You're a murderer. You know I can't simply forget what you've done."

"You can't?" Edmund asked, pained.

She swallowed. "I can't," she confirmed, and nodded over his shoulder.

Edmund's eyes widened the moment Ives's knife buried itself between his ribs, stabbing into his lungs. He lurched forward, collapsing to his knees, but Nora continued to hold him, arms wrapped steadily around him as he fell to the ground, trying and failing to speak.

"Edmund," Nora whispered to him, stroking his hair back from his face and cradling him, rocking with him as he bled. "Oh, Edmund, my love," she said again, and let her fingertips trail down the back of his neck, guiding his head to fall heavily against her shoulder. "Isn't it just awful what we are to each other?"

He didn't answer.

By then, his entire body was still.

*   *   *

Her name was Nora Denshaw. I called her Nora or Kitty or Nor, depending on the situation, but she only ever called me Edmund. She never made me a diminutive of what I was; never broke me into pieces. Not until the end, that is, which turned out to be my beginning.

When I woke up, it was to the taste of something coppery and sweet; a mix of both, like sugar and salt. I lapped at it, unabashedly, and felt her fingers in my hair and thought it was a dream. Perhaps I should have known what I was doing. Perhaps I should have refused. But it was such a relief to be in her arms that I didn't mind it, and when I was done gorging myself on the taste of her, I curled into her arms, and she whispered in my ear that everything would be different now.

"You'll feel better soon," she said to me, brushing her lips against my forehead and soothing me with a touch, like magic. "We'll get you some witch's blood, pet."

And this is what I am to her now: a pet. Rather than feel shame over it, though, I'm glad for it. I owe her, after all. I've spent my whole life owing to her what she had always offered to me, freely, without ever being asked. With Ives she has love and companionship;

with me she has the devotion she has always deserved. He doesn't begrudge her any time spent with me; I don't begrudge her any time spent with him. He's not so bad, Ives Cavendish. I, on the other hand, am a monster, but I am *her* monster, and so I wait patiently for her to choose me, whenever she does. However she does it.

I have always belonged to Nora Denshaw, in whatever form she or I take, and I wait for her, as I have always done. Maybe tonight I'll be alone, as I am from time to time, and I'll take solace in my memories. Or maybe tonight she'll be with me, and I'll be with her, and it will hurt us both. It will be a bit of softness to float on for a couple of days, until we both inevitably break each other again. It will be what it is, and what it always has been, and what it will always be.

Just then, she knocks at my open door, and I turn to look at her. She's spent her day wandering in the garden or gossiping with Della or making love to Ives or maybe doing something else entirely; something I don't know about, and won't ask. I think she enjoys her little secrets. I also think she's earned them well enough.

"Hi, kitty," I say, feigning surprise, and her lovely smile broadens.

"Hello, pet," she replies, and slips inside.

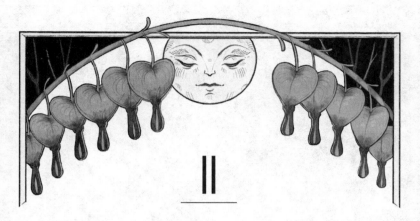

II

Summer

Summer bachelors, like summer breezes,
are never as cool as they pretend to be.

Nora Ephron

I never properly loved summer until I loved you.

The Animation Games

Part I: Once upon a Time

Once upon a time there was a small, unassuming village called Camlann's Strife. It wasn't a particularly well-manicured village, or even an especially interesting one—two villages over there was at least a chicken who could predict rainfall to a near-reliable degree, thus leaving *something* for people to discuss as they passed through—but one thing of significance did happen there.

(Specifically, it happened at the well.*)

The story opens, as many stories do, with a boy and a girl; a boy who, like many you have been told of before, was handsome and bold and dauntless, and a girl, similarly, who was headstrong, clever, and lovely. With a boy like Bran Barza and a girl like Rhosyn Viteri, sparks were no doubt going to fly—but this is no tale of ordinary love, nor of magic that constitutes a blessing. In fact, the trouble strikes on the very eve preceding Bran and Rhosyn's would-be wedding, on which they were visited by a rather unfortunate mishap: a ghastly, untimely death that tore the young would-be lovers apart.

Specifically, Rhosyn's death.

A tragic occurrence, of course, as with any great loss, and Rhosyn herself being such a rare beauty, too—but don't worry; this isn't a tragedy. In fact, this story is hardly even sad. Rather, there is a pearl of wisdom to be gained, for when one has lived a life such as Bran Barza and Rhosyn Viteri have lived, one is given to learn a very important lesson indeed.

That sometimes, the end is just the beginning.

---

* Wells, of course, have a long history of magical phenomena. Whether this has more to do with some coincidental, anthropological reliance on the healing powers of water or with various mythology suggesting that such potable sources had been placed there by deities, blessed by saints, or granted by some other supernatural explanation altogether, there's no way of knowing. All there is to know is that in this particular case, there was a well, and in the next case, there was a resulting series of highly unnatural occurrences.

Part II: Endings

The first time that Bran Barza met Rhosyn Viteri, they were children scarcely over the age of ten. Bran, the eldest of four boys and the heir to his father's successful forge, had been healthy and strong, even then quite tall for his age, and his disposition plainly showed a knowledge of his own good fortune. He carried himself with pride and was known for his agreeable nature, his sense of humor, his charming laugh, and the makings he possessed of both successful heir and irredeemable scoundrel. Rhosyn, on the other hand, had been a tiny, pinched slip of a thing, her dark curls wild and unruly, with a perpetual scowl that had been particularly uncharitable when her father shoved her toward her fate.

"It will be a good thing for both of us," Lord Viteri promised in pleading undertones to Bran's father. "I don't have much for her dowry, but her stature can only aid your son's future. Please," he added, supplication that made Bran's chest swell with pride.* "I have great need of your services, and I'm afraid my daughter is all I can offer in return."

Unprofitable or not, the trade was accepted by Bran's father, the betrothal was made, and Rhosyn, who slid her hands uncomfortably down the front of her worn gown—by then it had been let out more than once, and many times refitted and restyled and resewn—stared unwaveringly at her feet, scarcely batting an eye as her father sold her off to the local blacksmith's son.

"You're lucky, you know," Bran told her proudly; a boy still, as he was. "I will be a good husband to you, and you will live a good life here."

Yet again, she scowled; he'd meant to comfort her, but it was obvious she'd taken offense.

"I'm a lord's daughter, and you are a blacksmith's son," she pronounced simply, "so it is you, I should think, who are lucky."

Bran arched a brow, his gaze traveling slowly over the worn material of her dress and back up to the sour expression on her face. He fixed his attention on her too-pert nose—the little stub of it sitting

---

* That such a fine nobleman would humble himself so plainly to beseech the Barza family was as profound an intoxicant to Bran as it was a humiliation to Rhosyn.

beneath unfashionably dark eyes that were too close together to be truly beautiful—and sighed. She was no sunny farmer's daughter and had no laughing gaze of cornflower blue, and would therefore likely mean a lifetime saddled with gloominess and drudgery. With a rush of displeasure, Bran newly doubted that he would enjoy the fruits of their union.

"We'll see," he said tartly, and Rhosyn left with a parting glare over her shoulder, trudging after her father as he went.

*   *   *

The second time Bran Barza met Rhosyn Viteri, it was to finalize the details of their marriage, when both had reached the age of seventeen. It was shortly after Bran's birthday and he'd had something of an unprincipled celebration the evening prior, having passed the time with a lovely girl called Bessie and (*perhaps*) overindulging in vice. He doubted he had much to worry about, however, anticipating Rhosyn's tepid scowl and considering her still the luckier of the two; after all, she was more a payment for services rendered than any sort of prize to be earned. And so Bran staggered carelessly from his bed, sparing little effort beyond a scrape of one hand through his fair hair and a moment's pause to slap the reprobate look of sleeplessness from his cheeks, scarcely even bothering to rid himself of the lingering tavern smell.

The moment he saw her, though, he regretted not having done more.

"You remember, of course, my daughter, Lady Rhosyn," Lord Viteri had said, gesturing to where her fingertips rested gingerly on his arm.

After some delay* Bran forced out "My lady" in a blustered exhalation, catching a twitch of satisfaction that stretched briefly across the face of a girl he might have dreamt into being, but certainly did not remember having met.

For Rhosyn Viteri's face now suited her name, the little rose of her father's failing kingdom. Whereas everything about her expression

---

* Bran's father had been forced to smack Bran hard in the gut, prompting him to shut his gaping mouth and bow.

before had once been too close and too cramped and too small, she had now grown elegantly into her features. Her dark hair had been tamed into a long braid, slicked serpentine down the path of her slender back. Her eyes remained dark and discerning, but her nose, her cheeks, her lips were as if they'd been brought to life by angels, blooming across a painterly smile that was no less stunning than it was completely false.

"Mister Barza," she acknowledged warmly to Bran's father, offering a small curtsy before turning to Bran. "And you, Master Barza, are quite well, I hope?"

He choked on something that might have been an answer as she swept her gaze up through coquettishly batted lashes.

"I hope you have not been too lonely while we have been apart," she commented, and Bran knew with a burning in his chest that she could see quite clearly what he had been up to over the course of the preceding night. "What a shame that would be, indeed, given that I am not so terribly far away."

"I regret not having known more of you these past seven years" was Bran's ungainly bleat in reply.

Wordlessly, his father glared at him. Rhosyn, however, gave a brilliant, elusive smile and reached magnanimously toward him, civilly proffering one hand to be kissed.

Pulse inconveniently thundering, Bran came as close as protocol allowed. It was near enough for Rhosyn to speak in his ear, her fingers tense and clawlike in his.

"You don't yet regret anything," she whispered, the words audible only to Bran as he brushed his lips against her knuckles, "but you will soon, won't you, beloved?"

He stiffened, pulling away with a feigned smile that became a poorly concealed grimace. So, the dream was slightly less ethereal in certain lights. He forced himself to shove aside the yearning in his chest he'd first suffered at the sight of her, finding it confusingly misplaced. Yes, through some miracle or cataclysm she'd become a painfully beautiful woman, but such things were only skin deep. The impulse to fling himself at her feet vanished the moment he realized his bride's disagreeable nature had only been cleverly masked.

Satisfied with his horror, Rhosyn seemed newly subdued, even sweet. Placated, like a wild animal, licking satisfaction from the tips of her canines and promising him with a glance that whatever cost she had paid for her pride, his would be markedly worse for his pleasure.

"Oh, how I long for our marriage," Bran muttered, watching her long braid bob along the line of her spine as she laughed, reveling in his dread.

*   *   *

The third time Bran Barza met Rhosyn Viteri, nearly two years had passed. He was no less handsome and restless and she was no less beautiful and oppositional, but this time, the years that had passed in isolation had molded them both to something far more somber. Rhosyn had lost her mother, the Lady Viteri, and her father had been quick to take another young wife. As a result, the proposed marriage between Bran and Rhosyn was nearly dissolved; the promise of more Viteri heirs and the injection of the dowry belonging to Lord Viteri's new wife renewed the family's prior wealth, and so the always unflattering (at the very least, highly unequal) betrothal had nearly been cast aside.

Surprisingly, it had been Bran who hadn't wanted to let it go* and he urged his father not to let Lord Viteri upend the deal they had made nearly a decade prior.

"I hear that you fought for me," Rhosyn remarked without preamble, startling Bran by appearing outside his father's forge one day.

"Lady Rhosyn," he said, glancing around in alarm. "You shouldn't be here alone."

"Why?" she remarked drolly. "Are there any terrible rogues I might encounter?"

"I'm serious," he told her sternly, though he felt his mouth twitch into a laugh, and felt something else twitch, too, at the sight of her hips swaying toward him. "You're a lady. You should have an escort."

---

* Perhaps he fancied himself deserving of a lady now, or possibly it had something to do with Rhosyn herself, although given their previous altercations that seemed both unlikely and profoundly ill-advised.

"Oh, don't bore me, Barza," she retorted.* "I simply want to know what your reasoning was. My father may yet keep to his promise, you know, if I say I want the betrothal," she clarified neutrally. "But if I do not . . ."

She trailed off pointedly, and Bran arched a brow.

"I take it you want me to convince you," he guessed, and she tilted her head.

"Say that I do," she agreed. "Are you so opposed to actually courting me?"

"I—" He hesitated. He was beginning to understand that everything with her was a game, though he didn't yet grasp how to play it. "I want a wife who keeps her promises," he replied instead, seeing a window of something clever, "and if you are willing to be that sort of wife, then I would be happy to see to it that you are courted as you wish."

"Smooth." Her look in reply was sardonic, but not unamused. "Get a little bit cleverer and perhaps I will marry you after all."

Ah, so the game wasn't so unfamiliar, then! Bran took a daring step closer, waiting to see if Rhosyn would retreat.

She didn't, though she arched a judgmental brow.

"I'm not some kitchen maid you get to lie to sweetly," she told him, her gaze slipping sideways to the townspeople that passed. "Don't try to conquer me, Barza," she muttered, "because I promise you, it won't work."

He smiled. He liked a challenge, and Rhosyn Viteri was officially the most challenging woman he'd ever met.

"Meet me, then," he decided. "Tomorrow night. Let's be alone," he suggested, and she tilted her head warningly,† but he held up a hand for pause. "Not for that," he assured her with a wink, a brief lift of his chin. "But convince your father to uphold his agreement, and I swear, I will give you the romance you want." He stepped closer, as close as he was sure any man had ever been to her, and watched her swallow.

* For a moment, Bran recognized a flash of the sulky girl Rhosyn had been and did not necessarily hate it.
† It did, after all, imply an air of indecency as far as propositions went.

"I will sweep you off your feet," he promised.*

After taking a moment for her dignity, Rhosyn spared him a slow nod.

"Tomorrow night, then," she said carefully. "At the well?"

He smiled.

"Tomorrow night at the well," he promised her.

*　*　*

The final time Bran Barza met Rhosyn Viteri, it was just after sundown on a clear, cloudless night, after he'd slipped away from his father's forge and made his brother swear not to tell where he was going. It was foolish, of course, to partake so deliciously in secrecy when he was only going to meet the woman who would soon be his wife, but still, anticipation thrilled through his bones. Bran crept by the light of the overbright moon[†] to the well on the edge of Camlann's Strife, just outside her father's lands.

He caught the outline of her in her cloak and swallowed hard as she turned.

"Hello, Master Barza," Rhosyn called to him, her voice unwavering as ever in its tone of conceit. For whatever reason it was beginning to affect him bodily, and Bran felt his fear dissipate from his shoulders.

"Lady Rhosyn," he offered, sweeping her a low bow, and she laughed, shaking her head as she approached him.

"You bow too low," she informed him, tapping her fingers lightly against his back to adjust his posture.[‡] "I'm not a queen, after all, and then what will you do when you meet one?"

"But you're *my* queen," he teased, or meant to tease. It came out more like the overwrought declaration of a boy who couldn't hold his tongue, and Rhosyn smiled radiantly, her beauty effervescing in

---

* It is perhaps worth noting at this point that Bran Barza was standing very close to Rhosyn Viteri, close enough that prior promises delivered by Bran at this proximity were often—how to put this delicately?—lies. To his credit, Bran did mean this particular promise in some abstract, rose-tinted way, and at the moment he spoke those words to Rhosyn, he could not yet know the lengths to which he would go to fulfill this particular oath.

† It was full, which was . . . probably coincidental.

‡ A surprisingly sensual gesture.

the moonlight that broke through the crown of trees, rendering the landscape that much more ethereal.

"Would my queen like a dance?" Bran asked, playfully grabbing at her fingertips, and Rhosyn shook her head with a regal look of feigned indifference.

"A pavane?" she guessed. "Gavotte?"

"Put your fancy words away and let me show you," suggested Bran, sweeping an arm around her waist and spinning her wildly, delivering them both to feverish laughter until they collapsed, breathless, in the grass.

They turned to look at each other, their breaths gradually quieting, and for several moments she simply stared at him and he at her, feeling something shift and change between them.

"I wanted to marry for love," she confessed, looking down at her hands. "Which is a foolish conception for a girl like me."

"Why?" Bran disagreed. "Hardly seems worth being born a nobleman's daughter if you can't do anything you choose."

Hope drove her gaze upward, meeting his. There was something behind it, something calculating but not cruel. Measuring, perhaps.

"Will you be fair to me?" she asked him. "Will you let me be your partner in life?"

He frowned at her, bemused. "My equal, you mean?"

"Yes, that."

"But you are above me," he reminded her, mimicking the insouciant tone of her youth. "You are a *proper lady* and I am at best a craftsman, as you've reminded me many times—"

She gave him a shove. "Yes, but once I am your wife, I will only be that." She seemed lost for a moment. "Only your wife, and nothing of my own—"

"That's not true." Bran lurched upright to take Rhosyn's hands in his, ignoring her startled jump at his unprompted boldness. "That's not true. My life is not very grand, fine," he conceded, "but I have money, and a household to run, and I want . . . I want a wife who can think for herself." He paused, and carefully—so carefully he could hear both their hearts pounding—he brushed her hair from her eyes, tucking a loose, midnight-colored curl behind her ear.

"I promise you," he said quietly, taking the curve of her cheek in one hand, "that marrying me will not lessen you, Rhosyn. I will share this life with you. Equally," he added with a hint of avowal.*

"Let's get married, then," she said, and Bran blinked in surprise. "Tomorrow, even," she urged, rising hurriedly to her feet. "The sooner the better, before my father tries to marry me off to some doddering, ancient nobleman who wants nothing more than to keep me in a cage—"†

"Tomorrow?" Bran repeated vacantly, uncertain. "But—but a wedding requires—"

"What do we need?" Rhosyn protested, cutting him off with a sudden reach. Bran glanced down, his breath trapped within his lungs by the featherlight brush of her fingers on his chest. "A priest, a witness, that's it. And then we'll be wed, and my father can say nothing against it. Will you do it?" she whispered, gazing up at him. "Please," she added. "You said you wanted to marry me, didn't you?"

Bran swallowed hard, staring down at her in disbelief.‡

"See, I was right, then," he commented eventually.

Her dark brow furrowed. "About what?"

"That I would be a good husband to you," he said seriously, fighting a laugh, "and that you would be lucky to have me."

It took a moment, but once she saw that he was teasing her, she let out something that was half laughter, half mesmerizing groan.

"Let go of me, you ingrate—"

"Never," he swore, and pulled her closer to press his lips to hers, capturing the sound of her gasp and the pliant willingness of her oath on a breath shared communally between them.

The moment he kissed her, he wanted more; wanted her in his bed, or better yet right there, beneath the too-bright moonlight on the mossy ground beside the well, where no one but the two of them would know what they had promised each other. But she was a

---

* He felt wildly goonish making such a claim, but he could see that it had been the right thing to say when she smiled up at him, gratitude spreading across her lips.

† The truth? Rhosyn lied about being able to sway her father's decision as to the matter of her betrothal. Her father had his own agenda and she belonged, as a matter of possession or real estate, to him. But it had seemed to her like it would be fun to toy with Bran, and up until this particular moment it had been. Now it seemed far less recreational.

‡ It seemed . . . stupid. And simultaneously too sweet to be true.

maid still, and as yet uncertain, and so Bran released her with a sigh, stroking his thumb along the lower line of her mouth.

She stared up at him, likely the first man she'd ever kissed,* and turned furiously, resolutely pink, the flush in her cheeks visible even beneath the cover of night.

"Are you thirsty?" she asked, turning to the well with her hand self-consciously over her mouth, and Bran cleared his throat, managing a nod.

"Yes," he said, "it's quite a warm evening."

"Unseasonably," she agreed. "And the moon quite so unusually bright."

"I wonder if there's magic in it," Bran joked, stepping toward her as she lifted the wooden pail from the well and rested it atop the stone ledge. "Do you think we'll be blessed?"

"Silly stories." Rhosyn dismissed him with a shake of her head and cupped her hands together for a sip, closing her eyes as she drank. "It is refreshing, though. Would you like to—?"

She trailed off, her proffered hands waiting, and Bran leaned gently forward, his lips brushing the inside of her thumb as he took a sip from her hands. He let the water coat his lips, seeping coolly onto his tongue, before it slithered gradually down his throat and settled conclusively in his stomach.

He glanced at her face, his fingers lingering around her wrists, and again fought to suppress the urgency he felt to hold her, instead opting to clear his throat and offer her another silly bow.

"Another dance, Lady Rhosyn?" he suggested. "Might as well, as I doubt we'll conjure up much festivity tomorrow if we'll have only a priest and a witness."

She set the pail on the ground to grant him a coquettish curtsy of her own, looking up at him through her lashes.

"Better make it a good one, Master Barza, or how will I possibly be bonny and blithe at bedtime?" she offered serenely, and he yanked her into his arms with a growl of poorly tempered longing, spinning her about until she had thrown her head back with laughter, holding tightly to him as they danced.

---

* He was, and would be the last.

It all happened so quickly from there.

It might have been his fault; he'd spun her so wildly he hadn't seen where he was going, and neither could she, having taken his lead.

It might have been her fault; she'd set the pail down in such an inconvenient place, and they'd both forgotten it had been there, having been caught up in closeness.

It might have been no one's fault; perhaps eldritch spirits conspired against them, having grown envious of the young couple's blossoming love.

It might have been anyone's fault, but however it happened, it happened too quickly to prevent; Rhosyn spun free from his arms, stumbling backward as she collided with the pail, and then there was a moment; a *breath*, even—disastrously brief and yet so tormentingly long—wherein her eyes widened enormously, and Bran understood two things: that she could not prevent herself from falling, and that he could not move quickly enough to catch her himself.

She stopped breathing the moment her head hit the stone wall surrounding the well, her chin knocking forward and then, disastrously, off to the side as she collapsed on the ground. Bran dropped down beside her, crying out in dismay, but even before he fell to his knees, he already knew it was much too late.

In an instant—a breath—Rhosyn Viteri had died, and his future, his promises, fled with her.

At first he felt nothing but sorrow; a gripping, terrible loss.

Gradually, though, the chill of grief gave way to fear, and then, as Bran held his sweetheart in his arms, he felt his veins run cold with recognition.

Lady Rhosyn Viteri, an unchaperoned noblewoman who'd come to him in secret, had died, *and he would almost certainly be held responsible.*

Bran choked on a breath of panic, his grip tightening on her corpse.

He could not return to his village, nor could he return her body to her father.

He would be punished for certain, possibly killed, and then—

He swallowed, glancing down at her motionless face, and pressed his forehead to hers.

"I'm so sorry, beloved," he whispered in her ear, just before he tossed her lifeless body into the well.

* * *

He'd gambled that Rhosyn wouldn't have told a soul where she'd been going, and he found he'd been correct. News soon spread from her father's house to the village of Camlann's Strife that Lady Rhosyn Viteri had fled without warning, and for the entire day following, no one could speak of anything but the intrigue regarding her disappearance.*

All looked to Bran, expecting devastation, and they certainly found it in spades. He walked as mournfully as a ghost, dumbstruck by the loss of his betrothed.

"Didn't you see her that night?" his brother asked, and Bran forced out a lie. After all, what was yet another, when there were so many worse things he'd have to live with?

"She didn't come," he replied, as steadily as he could manage, though out of his brother's sight, his hands shook from the weight of his falsehood.

He waited for someone to find her body, to notice something amiss in the well; after five days, his sense of discomfort peaked. Determining that he could no longer wait to find out, he snuck out as soon as he was able to evade questioning by his father, and was immediately struck by a most disconcerting observation:

Rhosyn Viteri's body was no longer in the well.

He supposed he should have been relieved. Perhaps someone else had found her and been equally unwilling to take the blame for her death. That would be a reasonable enough explanation, and Bran clung to it, hoping to put his conscience to bed. Her death had been a terrible accident, a cruel twist of fate, and was it not better for both of them that he not suffer further in the wake of her devastating loss? It pained him to lose the promise of her, to grieve the life they might

---

* Some guessed she'd taken a lover, had run off with him in the night; others speculated that Lord Viteri's new wife, Lady Rhosyn's stepmother who was only two years her senior, might have done away with her herself, so that only her future progeny would inherit. (Speaking candidly, it had crossed Lady Viteri's mind.)

have had together, but at least there were not two lives wasted in the process.*

At first, Bran honored her memory by keeping his distance from his usual vices, from excessive drink and rowdiness with his brothers and friends, from pursuing women who still passed him teasing, sidelong glances, perhaps even more frequently now that tragedy had struck. After all, he could not put Rhosyn's kiss from his mind; could not rid himself of the way she'd curled into the circle of his arms, the warmth of her pressed inescapably against the length of him as he'd drawn her into his chest. She had always been the woman he'd wanted most, and now would want, perhaps for as long as he lived. For a time, he considered that no other woman would do, and that he'd take no lover at all outside the paramour of his memories, forever bound to the ghost of the woman he'd lost.

For a time, he really believed it.

Eventually, though, he became restless. Why not live, after all; why survive Rhosyn's death if he did not truly make use of his survival? He would need to take a wife, to bear sons, to live a life as he might have done otherwise, Rhosyn or no Rhosyn. Once several weeks had passed, he realized he'd hardly known Rhosyn at all, and so perhaps such a period of mourning was in fact an insult to her memory. And besides, was *he* not to have anything in life?

He returned to his old ways before long, and his memories of Rhosyn eventually faded, drifting from his thoughts as though he'd only dreamt her into being once or twice. Every time she flitted through his mind, he became less and less convinced that the night he'd spent with her at the well had even happened; hadn't the moon been overly bright, the air unseasonably warm, her face inhumanly lovely? How was he to know whether any of it had been real?

Perhaps none of it had ever even happened.

"You must be terribly alone," Flora lamented, a silly girl who was in his arms with hardly any effort after coaxing him into her father's barn and letting him settle her on his lap. "You poor, poor man, abandoned by such a selfish woman, and to call herself a lady, too—"

"Hush, don't speak of it," Bran replied, his fingers moving hastily

* Or so Bran told himself.

down the front of her bodice. "Please, I am so distraught by her loss—"

"Oh, Bran," Flora wailed, tugging at his trousers, and Bran hid a smile in her shoulders, burying his lips in the line of her neck when he suddenly paused, a flash of something drawing his eye.

He looked up, his breath catching in his throat, and blinked.

For a moment, he wasn't sure what he was seeing. At first he processed only the sound of water—a slow, torturous drip upon the floor, growing oppressively louder and more percussive the longer Bran stared. After a few moments, even with Flora skillfully wriggling away on his lap, the vision before him became clearer, until Bran realized that what he saw was in fact the silhouette of someone painfully familiar.

"Rhosyn?" he croaked, trying unsuccessfully to clear his vision, and the image of her—or whatever it was—took a step closer, crooking a finger toward him from afar.

"No, sweetheart, you poor darling," Flora said, gripping the back of his neck. "Oh Bran, you poor, poor dear—"

But he wasn't listening, nor was he fully aware of her touch. He was lost instead to a vision he could have sworn was a ghost, blinking at it in wonderment with his breath trapped somewhere in his throat.

As the figment of Rhosyn approached, Bran realized that it was she who was the source of the dripping sound; that in fact she was soaked to the bone, her teeth chattering from a constant, unwavering chill. Droplets of water fell like tears from the gown that now clung to her every curve, leaving her hauntingly exposed and terribly, terribly beautiful.

He swallowed hard.

"Rhosyn." Her name fell from his lips as he fumbled to free himself from Flora's hold. "Rhosyn, please—"

"What is it?" Flora pressed, taking his arm to coax him back as he stumbled forward, into the emptiness where just moments ago Rhosyn had been.

"Did you see anything?" he demanded, eyeing the dry beams of the wooden floor. "Was there someone here, just a moment ago?"

"Of course not." Flora stared at him, and not in a teasing way. "Are you unwell, Bran?"

He knelt down, running his fingers over the beams of the floor.
Nothing.

No sign of moisture, even.

"I don't know," he said honestly, aghast.

But it was only in his mind, of course.

Of course. The stress of her loss, of his secrets.

That was all.

Unless—

Hadn't he been the one to wonder whether there was something
unusually magical about the well? *Silly stories,* Rhosyn had said, but
suddenly, Bran wasn't so sure.

"There's no one here," Flora said uncertainly, her voice a long distance now from where he knelt, and Bran closed his eyes, unable to
fight a chill up his spine.

"Go," he told her hoarsely.

"But—"

"Just *go,*" Bran repeated, and waited until the sound of Flora's
footsteps disappeared before giving in to a shudder of fear.

He heard a droplet of water fall behind him and turned; nothing.

Then, on his left, another.

Another.

Another.

Another, more, faster, falling and falling until they matched the
sound of his pulse, the erratic beat of his heart.

The echo of falling droplets ricocheted around his head, scattered
and frantic and violently arrhythmic. Bran dropped to his elbows in
rising panic, crying out in horror.

"Rhosyn!"

Like magic, the sound abruptly ceased.

Bran sat up slowly, glancing around.

The floor was wet.

The room was empty.

"Master Barza," he heard in his ear. An insouciant little taunt as
he choked on a gasp. "Tell me, beloved, are you sorry?"

"Yes," he rasped. "I'm so sorry. I'm so sorry. I'm sor—"

"No, you're not." Rhosyn's voice was hard, crueler than it had ever
been in life. "But don't worry, Barza."

He swore he felt the moisture of her lips as they hovered, frozen, over the back of his neck.

"Bran, my beloved," Rhosyn Viteri whispered in her sweetheart's ear. "You're not sorry yet, but you will be."

Part III: Vengeance

The last thing that I remember is spinning and falling, peaks to valleys, high to low. The last thing I feel is a joy so incomprehensibly sharp I almost don't notice when it convulses into fear. There is part of me that knows I am ending even as I am so filled with beginnings, and I don't suffer any pain; I only feel numbness, and then an abject chill.

When I wake, the chill has not subsided, and I'm freezing; I'm incomprehensibly cold. I'm not where I was before, either. I rise to my feet awash on the shore of a river, the clothes I'm wearing clinging to my arms and legs as droplets of water trickle down from my limbs. I stand in the sun but feel no warmth, nor do I manage to dry.

There is only one thing on my mind when I open my eyes, and it is Bran Barza's face, even as I look up to familiar moonlight. I imagine him telling me again that the well is filled with magic, and this time, I don't laugh. Perhaps now I am one of those silly stories. I even think, childishly, that perhaps this is a love so strong that death itself bears no authority over our lives. That thought is the only thing that warms me as I make my way back through a half-familiar wood.

I keep myself hidden at first, because even I can see I am not as I was while I lived. I am eternally, wretchedly cold, and water seems to follow me wherever I go—in fact, it now seems part of me, and in time I find that I can control it almost as equally as it controls me.

Part of me knows I have died. Part of me understands that I remain dead, though I breathe and see and hear and feel just as I did before. I learn, however, that my whereabouts are as yet a mystery to the village; Bran has not told them what happened to me. They do not believe I am dead. In fact, most of the townspeople believe I have shamed my family, run off with someone in defiance of my promises, in an affront to my position and my name.

In death, my reputation is tarnished.

Bran Barza has let them tarnish me.

In this version of my body, anger feels cool, like raindrops on rooftops, like waves that crash upon sand, but whether my fury is ice or fire, I feel it passionately, deep in my bones. I know I must find him; I know, somehow, that there is a debt I must yet collect, though I don't know yet how it will be paid.

Then I find Bran with his arms around another woman, and the moment I lay eyes on him, I know precisely what he owes me, and I know exactly what I will take.

"You're not sorry yet, but you will be," I whisper to him. He may not realize yet that I am here, that it is really me, but what he knows or doesn't know no longer matters. I have done enough reckoning for the both of us.

I know exactly what I will take, Bran Barza.

I will take your life, as you have taken mine.

*   *   *

The moment that Rhosyn Viteri realized she had Bran Barza at her mercy, her lips pressed lightly against the back of his neck, she knew that whatever she gained from a quick death could not possibly be enough.

No, Bran would have to give her much more than that.

He would have to suffer equally as she had suffered.

Rhosyn Viteri had not lived much of a life, after all; how could she? She was a nobleman's daughter, but for most of her life Lord Viteri had been a poor nobleman with little to his name, and whatever dearth he'd possessed as a lord, he'd come up even shorter as a father. He had been quick to discard Rhosyn as payment when he'd needed weapons and plows, then equally quick to cast off his word when he no longer had need of the arrangement. Rhosyn had gained little from her tepid aristocracy save for persistently damaged pride. She had been treated as nothing but an object, cast aside even in death, and having never had a hobby pursued purely for her own pleasure, she saw at last—at *last*—an opportunity to take something selfishly.

So she started by letting Bran go, even as she held him in her grasp.

"Rhosyn," he begged. "Rhosyn, please, if it's you, I have to see you—just tell me if this is real—"

Ah, and wouldn't certainty be a gift! Instead she withdrew into the shadows, finding satisfaction in his confusion as his eyes went wild with fear.

For the next few days she followed him, keeping to the shadows in his home, lurking quietly around his forge. She could slide in and out of sight as easily as water itself now, and not only that, she seemed to control whatever water was in her sight; she was magic, just as Bran had said.*

As for her patient study of him, the whole thing was incredibly rewarding. For days, every time a drop of water hit the floor, Bran jumped half a foot in the air, staring around the room and pressing a hand to his chest to settle his frantic heart. Every time she knocked over a glass of his water or caused a pitcher of it to burst, the contents splattering over his face, he let out a whimper of "Rhosyn," and she was forced to fight a laugh.

Much to her pleasure, he called for her, and often.

"Rhosyn," he said one night, lurching upright in his bed with a shudder, and she sighed.

"Yes, Barza?" she asked, waiting for him to find her and turn toward her in the shadows, his eyes bloodshot and dim.

"Are you haunting me?" he asked her.

"Yes, Barza," she replied, "obviously."

He lay back down, still looking as though he didn't quite believe it.

"Are you going to kill me?" he whispered.

She sighed again.

"Yes, unfortunately for you, beloved, I plan to," she told him. "But I wouldn't worry about that yet."

She watched him breathe, the motion of his chest quiet and anguished. "I made you angry, didn't I?"

"Yes," she replied shortly. "I find I'm rather displeased with you."

"I would have loved you," he told her. A whimsical thought.

She shook her head, rising to her feet to watch him cower beneath his sheets.

"No, beloved, you wouldn't have," she said. "For a while, perhaps,

---

* She'd have given him more credit for being right if he hadn't dragged her reputation through the mud after flinging her corpse into the well.

but you'd have tired of me and moved on. If this is your faithfulness, Barza, then better to suffer it dead than alive," she murmured,
watching him squeeze his eyes shut as droplets fell heavily from the
tips of her fingers to crash against the floor beside his bed. Drip.
Drip. Drip.

"That's not true," Bran managed, and Rhosyn made a face. "I
wouldn't have tired of you."

"You know, you might as well be honest, since you'll be dead
soon," she advised.

He was silent for a long moment.

"What about you?" he asked eventually.

Rhosyn balked.* "What about me?"

"What will you do once you've killed me?"

She paused, considering it.

"I hadn't thought about it," she admitted.

He closed his eyes.

"I don't recommend it," he said. "Being alone, I mean."

Rhosyn eyed him warily.†

"You're just trying to save your own life," she scoffed after a moment, unimpressed.

His eyes fluttered open.

"Maybe," he allowed, and turned his head, looking at her long
and hard as if to drink her in. "You're so beautiful," he sighed regret-
fully, one hand rising as if to stroke her cheek. "We might have had
a beautiful life together."

Rhosyn made a face. "Don't ruin this for me."

He smiled.

"Are you going to kill me tonight?" he asked.

"No," she told him. "Not tonight."

"Good," he said. "Then sweet dreams, Rhosyn."

"I don't dream," she informed him.

"Right," he agreed, "because you're a ghost."

"I'm not a ghost," she corrected. "I'm just haunting you."

---

* Needless to say, Rhosyn was unaccustomed to others reflecting on her well-being, or
her presence, or her existence, or anything generally relating to the fact that she drew
breath. In death things were not so different from before.
† Has it been mentioned yet how handsome Bran Barza is? Perhaps not by Rhosyn.

"Right," he repeated. "Sweet dreams, beloved."

She rolled her eyes.

"Go to sleep, Barza," she replied.

* * *

"So how are you going to do it?" he asked, aiming the question over his shoulder as he worked. "Have you thought about it?"

She'd meant to stay hidden, but under the circumstances, silence seemed somehow less fun.

"Blunt force trauma," she replied.

"That's nice," he said. "Romantic, really, to pattern it off our first night together."

"Is that how I died? I can't quite remember."

"Yes," he confirmed. "You hit your head."

"Stupid," she lamented. "What a terrible way to die, frankly."

"I agree," he said. "And it left me in quite a predicament, too."

"You?" She glared at him. "Who cares about you? You're alive. *I'm* dead."

"Well, to hear you tell it, I will be soon," he reminded her. "And frankly, being haunted isn't much of a life."

"Well, good," she muttered stiffly. "I hardly think you should be permitted to go about things as normal. Or was throwing me in the well not betrayal enough?"

"I sort of assumed you were the regular kind of dead," he said, and paused before adding, "I also didn't realize you'd be so upset."

"Of course I'm upset," Rhosyn snapped. Elsewhere, a pot of boiling water exploded. "You shamed me. You dishonored me. You *forgot* me—"

Bran paused then, looking up with a curious expression of recognition.

"Are you . . . jealous?" he asked with a note of something unforgivable,* to which Rhosyn scowled.

"No. I'm angry."

"Sure you are." Bran chuckled then, and Rhosyn was furious.

She'd had enough, she decided.

---

* Patronizingly like fondness.

He'd grown too comfortable, and haunting him wasn't fun any-more.

Now he'd have to die.

* * *

She decided to do it in his forge.

That had a nice bit of irony to it, she thought, considering how he seemed to feel so safe there, and it would be easy enough to pull off. Plenty of heavy things around. Plenty of ways to be rid of him afterward.* Flames, she figured, would be a nice, poetic alternative to being thrown in a well, if she decided she felt up for the task by the time she got around to it.

Mainly, she was in it for the death bit. What happened after that was purely whatever struck her fancy.

She practiced quite a bit with his hammers and things, making certain she could lift them. Even the hot ones, the tools that had been recently put to work against various metals, were still slick and chilled in her hands, so she decided it would be simple enough. She pictured the impact; imagined it to be satisfying.

After all, she'd waited long enough.

She bided her time until he was nearly done for the day, watching him wipe sweat from his brow as he went about setting things in order.

The fire lit warmth into his cheeks, and he looked remarkably, indescribably handsome.

She couldn't wait to see the light go out.

"Rhosyn," Bran called, as he usually did. It was a habit he'd de-veloped over the past few weeks. "Beloved, am I going to die today?"

"Yes," she replied. "Shortly, in fact."

She watched his mouth quirk up in a smile.

"You're going to hit me, are you?" he remarked to empty air. "I doubt you can lift these things, Rhosyn. Even I had to train with them for years. Maybe you should choose another method."

---

* She knew how Bran had disposed of her body because she had asked him, and he, somewhat inanely, had told her the truth. In retrospect, knowing the details made every-thing much worse, except when it came to her own preparations.

"I don't need help murdering you, Barza," she snapped, carefully picking up one of his hammers. "In fact," she added, taking a careful step closer, "I think I'll manage it just fine."

She paused, reconsidering, and he tilted his head.

"Didn't want those to be your last words to me?" he guessed.

"Shut up," said Rhosyn.

"Go ahead," he urged. "Try again."

She sighed crossly.

"What did you say to me?" she asked.

"Nothing," he reminded her. "Your death was an accident."

Fair. "Then what did you say before you threw me in the well?"

He swallowed, his chin dropping slightly as she maneuvered herself closer, ever closer. Not long now.

"I said 'I'm so sorry, beloved,'" he answered.

Rhosyn smiled, grimly satisfied, just as she stepped within arm's reach.

"Say it to my face, then, Barza," she invited in his ear.

Instantly, he pivoted to face her, ducking out of reach just before she swung the hammer at his head.

"Oh, *hell*," he swore, dropping to his hands and knees. "Seriously?"

"You're not allowed to duck!" Rhosyn growled, swinging again at his back and nailing him right between his shoulder blades.

Bran let out a yell of displeasure, stumbling upright. "I'm not just going to *let you*," he snapped, scrabbling forward and promptly slipping in the puddle of water that had pooled at her feet, swearing his opposition as he went. "This is hardly fair—"

"Fair?" Rhosyn demanded. "You think you deserve *fair*?"

She swung again, hitting him hard in the torso this time just before he ducked behind a rack of cooling swords.

"How's this for fair?" she snarled, tossing the hammer aside and picking up a still-hot dagger and throwing it, javelin style, at Bran's retreating back.

Instantly, he fell to a rigid halt. Then an incoherent yowl of pain tore from his lips as he staggered forward, collapsing against the forge with one arm. With the other, he reached around for his back, yanking the blade free with a squelching sound of ruptured viscera, the blade degloving from carnage as if from a sheath. Then he tried to take a step toward Rhosyn and failed, collapsing with a groan at her feet.

"Rhosyn," he gasped, tugging himself upright by the wet material of her skirts. "Was this really necessary?"

She waited until he slid flat against the floor, his eyelids fluttering in pain.

"Yes, this was fine," she informed him, hefting one of his newly finished broadswords aloft in her right hand and eyeing the blade experimentally. "But this, I believe," she murmured, "will be a bit gratuitous."

"Don't do it," said Bran, or maybe he said something else.*

Rhosyn knelt down to speak close to his ear, just to be sure that he could hear her.

"So sorry, beloved," she told him softly, "but I'm afraid that I must."

And with a motion so fast that it hummed through the air, Rhosyn Viteri plunged the sword into Bran Barza's chest, finishing him off in one stroke.

*　*　*

Rhosyn could move as easily as water, and so after she'd murdered her would-be lover, she seeped down through the floors, resurfacing outside his forge at the moment his brothers and father discovered his body. There was much wailing and shrieking, she noted, counting the many women who appeared a little too distraught for comfort over Bran Barza's death, and for a second she lamented she hadn't done more. After all, it wasn't quite fair, was it? He was painted as an innocent victim, remembered for his looks and his easy charm, while she'd been horrifically slandered.†

As soon as he was gone, though, she found that Bran had been right—it was a curse of its own being the one left over. She had nowhere to go, and no one she could speak to. For a time she tried heading back to her father's house, following him around, but he was far less interesting than Bran. He didn't seem to miss Rhosyn in

---

* He was somewhat less intelligible than usual.

† Men. Even in death, they had it easier.

the slightest, and though Lady Viteri was very much traumatized by Rhosyn surfacing in her quarters,* Rhosyn found the entire thing prodigiously underwhelming. After hardly any time at all, people had forgotten entirely about her, and there was no one left who cared.

Eventually she wandered over to the graveyard, moistening the still-fresh mound of earth that had been layered over Bran's body. She bent down, staring morosely at Bran Barza's name, and before she quite realized what she was doing, she'd begun clawing dazedly at the loose dirt, not stopping until she'd hit the shroud he'd been buried in.

She stopped suddenly, her breath suspended, and flattened her palm against it, closing her eyes.

The shroud was empty. She was sure of it—where his head should have been there was nothing but more earth.

She swallowed hard, processing this thought slowly.

Bran Barza, whatever he was now, was almost certainly not dead.

She let out the breath she'd been holding.

It carried on the wind, chilling her once again to the bone.

And then, on a whim, Rhosyn smiled.

*   *   *

The last thing I remember is looking up at her face—my lost betrothed, my terrible darling, my most cruel and my dearest beloved—and in that moment, she is strange and beautiful and cold. I know that she is the only woman who has ever delivered me to such primal fear, to such unmatched awe and wonder. I wish, as I have wished for so long, that she had never died. That I had gotten the chance to hold her, to touch her, to be with her and to consume her, devour her as my own. To own all the parts of her I was never able to possess.

And then, just as the thought occurs to me, I realize something.

I realize that part of what I desire so much about Rhosyn Viteri is my own strange, sharpened need to destroy her, if only so that she loosens her unyielding control over me.

So, the moment I open my eyes, I resolve to find her.

I know right away that I am not quite as dead as I should be, and when

---

* She, at least, had the decency to faint on sight.

I come to life again I have the strength of a thousand men, breaking my way through the earth of my burial and climbing up through jagged stone. Part of me wonders if perhaps the only thing keeping Rhosyn in any state of living was her need to exact vengeance on me—it's possible that now she is at rest, or something like it—but somehow, I feel sure that she will be waiting for me. Somehow, I think she knows that I'm the one deserving of revenge this time. After all, my death was far more gruesome than hers.

I think we both know that some degree of pain is owed.

I find her near the water, which is apt. And though I am strong, stronger than I have ever been, my footfall is soft, so that she doesn't hear me coming until it's too late. Until I am so close I could do away with her in an instant, with one hand wrapped tightly around her slender neck.

Her eyes flutter open, and I realize now why she couldn't kill me right away.

I'd be lost without the sight of her, as she must have been without me.

"Is that you, beloved?" she whispers, and again, I struggle not to think of how it might feel to take her in my arms. For a moment, it tempts me.

For a moment.

"Hello, sweetheart," I say.

She smiles.

"How will you kill me?" she asks.

"Slowly," I promise.

Her beautiful smile broadens.

"Perfect," she declares.

Part IV: The Animation Games

Round 1: Bran

"What if I don't come back?" Rhosyn asked, wiggling her fingers as Bran tied her wrists to the branches of a forest tree. "You'd miss me, Barza."

"Of course I would," he agreed, testing the restraints around her wrists. "But I suppose it's worth it, isn't it? The attempt?"

"It was very satisfying," she permitted curtly. "Killing you, I mean."

"I know," he confirmed. "You made that very clear."

"Well, say that I *do* come back, then," she prompted. "What then?"

"You'll have to find me," he said. "I, unlike you, look quite normal. I think I'll just . . . carry on living my life."*

"You wouldn't dare." Her fingers curled into a fist; behind them, the river's current crashed atop the shore, drawn asunder by her fury.

"I would," he purred, stepping back to survey his handiwork. "Why be alive, after all?" he posed to her, stroking his thumb gently along her frozen cheek. "Have to enjoy it, or it's just a waste, don't you think?"

He reveled in her look of fury; delighted quietly in her rage.

"I don't understand why I miss you when you're gone," Rhosyn seethed. "You always cast me aside so easily, Barza."

He fought a scoff, glancing up at her, and shook his head.

"I'll never be rid of you, beloved," he reminded her, knowing she'd be a fool to think otherwise. "I simply don't care to be dead in your absence."

She scowled, reminding him again of who she'd been as a child, and he leaned forward with a laugh, resting his hands on the sodden hips of her still-wet gown.

"I knew you couldn't love me," she told him bitterly, and he leaned forward, wondering if she'd ever realize the truth.

"I hope I see you again, Rhosyn Viteri," he whispered in answer, and pressed his warm lips softly to her frozen ones, letting moisture bleed from her mouth to his. "Don't take too long to come back to me, sweetheart."

"Is this it?" she muttered into his mouth. "You're just going to leave me here? You know I won't die of starvation or thirst," she reminded him dully. "I don't need those things anymore."

"No, beloved," he corrected her gravely. "I'm afraid you'll die of blood loss."

And then he dug the dagger between her ribs, leaving it there, and stepped back to watch the crimson of her blood mix with the water that poured forth from every pore of her skin, dripping beatifically from her solemn, sorrowful eyes.

"You've never been more beautiful," he said, touching her cheek.

* It was the worst possible thing Bran Barza could do to Rhosyn Viteri, although who is to say whether he knew it to be or not? (He did.)

She dragged her gaze up to his.

"You are going to die a very painful death when I return," she choked out.

Bran nodded, heading back to the forest path. "I don't doubt it," he murmured to himself.

* * *

He came back to check on her a week later.

There was no sign of Rhosyn, and Bran smiled.

"See you soon, beloved," he said, turning over his shoulder and heading back into town.

Round 2: Rhosyn

It took months, but eventually she found him.

Naturally he couldn't go back to Camlann's Strife, having died there and been buried, but she wasn't certain at first where he would go. Luckily, this time upon her return she wasn't nearly so out of place in a crowd. This version of her reanimated self was dressed quite normally, and wasn't subjected to terrible temperatures, though the chattering in her head was perhaps not entirely ideal.*

It was weeks before she learned to toy with the levels of things, tuning some voices louder and softer. She listened intently for Bran, but it took a while; luckily she was well acquainted with his weaknesses, and after scoping out a tavern some villages away, she finally heard something familiar. A young woman's voice pined unrelentingly for a certain brawny blond that Rhosyn would have recognized from any description, whatever he foolishly called himself, and so she decided to make an introduction.

"River, really?" she asked dryly, sliding into the seat beside him in the tavern booth and watching every hair on his arm stand on end.†

"Creative, darling, but not very covert."

---

* It took her several days to get used to the sound of it before she realized what she was hearing; that no, the world had not gotten louder, but in fact, she was now exposed to the volume of *others'* thoughts.

† His grimy white shirt had been pushed up to reveal the muscle of his forearm. It was certainly no fault of Rhosyn's that that was where her eyes had gone.

"Hello, sweetheart," he said without looking at her, bringing his cup of ale to his lips. "I see you managed to find me."

"Don't be too impressed." She gave him a scathing look that he resolutely ignored. "You barely made it difficult."

"Well, I wasn't totally sure you'd be back," he reminded her, winking at the barmaid who'd had him so perennially on the mind. "And it's been some months, in case you haven't noticed."

"How long did you wait?" she asked, feigning levity. "An hour?"

"Oh, don't sell yourself short, beloved." He finally looked at her, eyes alight with something too bright for mirth. "For you? I managed a full day of mourning."

She fought a sullen retort, knowing it would only amuse him.

"It took longer this time," she noted, drumming her fingers against the table. "I wonder if it's because the method of death was gorier."

"An interesting theory," he judged. "Will you kill me quickly this time, then?"

She considered it, watching the barmaid smile at him from across the room.

"I haven't decided," she pronounced unhappily, and he turned to face her in the booth, fixing her with his bright, breath-arresting gaze.

"What did you come back with?" he asked. "Abilities, I mean. I find I'm curious."

She paused, toying with the levels in her mind.*

"What, tell you and give away the game?" she asked neutrally, reaching for a sip of his ale before sliding it back to him with a shrug. "That hardly sounds fun at all."

"Oh, so it's a game, is it?" he prompted with a hearty laugh, raising the tankard to his lips. "Then I presume the first round went to me."

"Well, presume all you like," she told him stiffly. "I doubt the first round matters much in the scheme of things, does it? We're just getting started."

"True," he agreed, taking a long swallow and setting the tankard down with a smile. "So," he continued with a wink, "shall we celebrate

---

* *Rhosyn*, she heard his voice say in her head. *My Rhosyn, my love, you've finally returned.*

our respective animations, at least for a night? Surely you're not *so* eager to be rid of me as to—"

He stopped, his eyes widening, and drew a hand to his throat.

"Oh dear," Rhosyn said falsely. "Beloved, are you unwell?"

He coughed loudly and retched, struggling for breath. Rhosyn slid her hand along his thigh, the small, now-empty vial pressed firmly into his leg.

"Would you like me to hold you while you die, sweetheart?" she asked him, as his eyes rolled back in his head, his tongue lolling out from between his lips. He careened sideways into her lap, foaming at the mouth. "Oh *no*," Rhosyn called in feigned distress, gesturing for the whoring barmaid. "I think he's been poisoned!"

"No, not River!" the girl cried in dismay, sprinting for help as Rhosyn fought not to roll her eyes.

"No," she agreed sourly, "not River."

She looked down in time to see Bran Barza gargle up something incoherent, leaving her to sigh as he vomited blood in her lap.

"Terrible last words, Barza," she told him. "I presume this round goes to me?"

His convulsing body fell still.

"Alas, beloved," she whispered to him. "See you soon, my love."

Round 5: Bran

The next few deaths were unremarkable, being the forays into academic study that they were.* Bran, returning from his poisoning with powers of telekinesis, used it to strap Rhosyn down and brandish a wide variety of kitchen implements, leaving her in a rather messy state of parts. Her return, however, nearly two years later, was one so thoroughly infused with rage that the slitting of Bran's throat meant a very brief period of reanimation. He was back within a matter of weeks, this time with the highly unhelpful ability to slow time to a syrupy crawl, which only bought him worthless spare minutes plotting his next moves against a very difficult opponent.

That round, Rhosyn was near invincible, her skin impenetrable to

---

* There had been some merit to the idea that animation took time; the more brutal the murder, the longer it took to reanimate after death.

either impact or laceration; Bran figured it would be easier to simply take the loss.

"Fine. Just do it," he grunted, watching her sketch lines into his skin and lamenting again how unhelpful his gift had been this round. "What's with all the extra body art, anyway?"

"Oh, I'm thinking I'm going to distribute the pieces of you this time, scatter them around," she said absently, drawing a line across his mid-thigh. "See how long that takes, you know?"

"That's very clever, sweetheart," he said. "You're not going to do it while I'm alive, are you?"

"No," she said, making a face. "Seems excessively bloody."

"You do love to do things in excess," he reminded her.

"True," she agreed. "But I think I'll enjoy winning two rounds in a row, and the extra time to savor it sounds rewarding enough on its own."

"May I ask what you have in mind?" he prompted, and she tilted her head, thinking.

"Sure," she permitted. "It's not very complex, really. I'm just going to shoot several arrows into your head," she explained, gesturing to the bow and quiver she'd procured, "and then I'm going to get the knife and—"

"Never mind," he cut her off, feeling queasy. "I think I grasp the concept."

"It's a win for sure, though, isn't it?" she prompted, and though he hadn't wanted to admit it, he conceded the point.

"It's a win," he admitted with a sigh, and she'd smiled.

Rumor had it, though, once he'd returned, that a woman had been put to death shortly after being found dismembering a man.

"Witchcraft," the innkeeper had told him, shuddering to speak of it. "Some sort of unholy ritual, clearly. They burned her at the stake."

"Oh really?" Bran asked, amused. "Did she say anything?"

"Oh, who can remember the details," the innkeeper sighed. "Must have been what, five years ago? They say she said something funny before she died, though," he recalled. "Sounded like 'it still counts, beloved,' or something—"

"Ah," Bran said with helpless pride, chuckling to himself. "She never did like to lose."

"What?" the innkeeper asked, his brow furrowed.

"Nothing," Bran said quickly.

But mentally, he adjusted the tally.

That round no doubt went to him.

Round 11: Rhosyn

Bran was never very good at hiding himself; he regularly left a trail of people who adored him in his wake. Even the strangers he encountered would always regale her with tales of having come across a cheerful blond man of considerable height, and though Bran was at times more effort to trick, he was always exceedingly easy to find.

That particular round, though, both the finding and the tricking were so easy as to be very nearly unfair.

"Fancy a dance, handsome?" Rhosyn asked Bran, having taken on the appearance of a young farmer's daughter.* "You look like a man who knows his way around a place like this."

He glanced at her, a wolfish hunger instantly filling his face, and Rhosyn fought not to gift him her signature scowl—he was always so foolishly predictable. Only a single dance was enough to lure him out to the barn, where she lay stretched out beneath him on the hay as his lips floated over her neck.

She hadn't expected to like it.

She hadn't expected, either, to want more—*much* more. She'd possessed the ability to kill him within seconds after arrival, having hidden a knife beneath one of the bales, but to her severe disappointment, Rhosyn realized that she now understood what was so very appealing about Bran Barza to the many, many women he'd encountered over the years.

"Tell me," he murmured to her, his lips traveling over her—*not mine,* she reminded herself, *some silly farm girl's*—ample breasts. "What's your name?"

"I'd prefer we didn't talk," Rhosyn managed roughly, and he paused, glancing up at her.

"Really?" he asked, mildly suspicious.†

* Whom she'd tied up temporarily amid the towering grains.

† Time had certainly passed, but it was not yet the era for this kind of sexually radical ennui.

She squirmed in his arms.

"Continue," she instructed, shifting his hand under her skirt, and he frowned, watching her a bit too closely.

"Why me?" he asked, and Rhosyn realized the question sounded empty without his usual terms of endearment for her. Without "sweetheart" or "beloved" the words merely felt cold, and she wondered if this empty charade was the reality of him for others.

"Perhaps I thought I'd be lucky to have you," she said, and though she froze for a moment, wondering if she'd unintentionally shown her hand, he seemed to have lost interest in conversation. Instead, his lips found hers as his hand traveled slowly up her thigh.

He was gentler with her than she thought he would be.

The whole thing was sweeter, really, than she'd expected; he seemed to hold her penitently, achingly, and with a coveting touch that part of her hated, wanted to rail against, because she wanted those parts of him to only be for her. As things progressed, she felt her heart grow heavier even as desire sharpened.

She was furious, and weak.

She was saddened, and ignited.

"Bran," she whimpered, her fingers tightening in his hair, and he sighed.

"Rhosyn," he said softly, "I know it's you."

She bristled, stiffening in his arms.

"I'd rather have you as you, sweetheart," he told her, so tenderly she flinched. "Perhaps you might find it in you to kill me later?"

She paused, considering it.

"But then who would win?" she countered, and tiredly, he sighed.

"Must there always be a winner and a loser?" he asked, but she knew better.

"You only say that," she reminded him, "because you're winning, six to five."

He grinned.

"I know," he agreed, and she closed her eyes.

"Kiss me again," she told him, and he greedily complied, his lips finding hers as intently as if they'd journeyed there for pilgrimage.

He didn't notice when she gripped the knife in her left hand.

He did, however, cry out when she dug it into his kidney.

"Rhosyn," he sputtered, glaring. "Was that really necessary?"

"It was, rather," she replied. "And I'd like to see you find me, Barza, when you don't know what face I'll wear."

He groaned, fading fast.

"I'll always find you," he promised her. "I always do, beloved."

She sighed.

"Would you have held me like this?" she asked. "If I'd come to you as myself?"

"Longer," he said, his eyelids falling steadily. "Closer."

"Hm," she murmured. "That sounds nice."

His lashes fluttered once, then stilled.

She slid out from under him, eyeing the bloodstains on her gown.

Part of her wished he hadn't confessed knowledge of her identity until later, until after her curiosities about his performance had been assuaged. Though, wouldn't she have rather had him in her own body?

"Well, but I'd rather not have him at all," Rhosyn protested aloud.*

Round 23: Bran

Proving even more difficult than the time that Rhosyn could change bodies—a task that had taken him nearly three years until he'd finally caught a woman sneaking out to the well at Camlann's Strife, half asking to be caught—was the time she could become invisible. He would catch up to her and promptly lose her, watching her vanish entirely and leave him with absolutely no hints as to how to continue. His own gift, control over metals, was almost no use; until, that is, he determined that his manipulation of light sources made her easier to spot, and then he discovered after a few days of trial and error that *she* had actually been following *him*.

"I know you're here, beloved," he called into the air. "This is just like the first time, isn't it? You do have such a tendency to follow me around."

"I do not," her voice returned.

He glanced around but didn't see her. "Are you bored, Rhosyn?" he asked. "You must be. It's been quite a long time."

"Bored?" she scoffed. "*Bored*, watching you chase your tail, Barza?

---

* By then, nobody was there to tell her she was lying.

Peering into shadows, staring desperately into space? Hardly a trace of boredom to be had."

"Well, *I'm* bored," he ruefully informed her. "This, of course, is a useful talent for smithing," he said, manipulating the sword in his hand and bending it, just so she could see. "I wish I had been able to make use of it when we still might have had a life together."

He heard her swallow.

She was always so sensitive to nostalgia.*

"You wouldn't have stayed true to me," she said again, her usual argument. "Even now, you don't."

"Actually, I do," he corrected her. "Lately I find that other women have a frustrating tendency to be . . . how shall I put this?" he considered, cocking his head. "So very *not* you."

He heard a satisfying waver of doubt in her voice. "You're lying."

"I'm not," he said with a shake of his head. "Why bother with a woman who doesn't know me as intimately as you do? You are the woman who has caused me the most pain, and the most horrific suffering," he reminded her. "Therefore you are the only woman who has ever truly known my strengths, and who has given me the greatest of adventures."

He listened to her hesitate; placed her by the sound of her breath in the room. She was close enough to touch.

"Do you love me yet, Barza?" she whispered sadly.

"I have only ever loved you," he said sincerely, even as he aimed the carving knife in his palm in her direction.

He felt the impact of it, the sound of her gasp, and watched the blood that dripped onto the floor; he watched her hover in and out of sight and then carefully took her in his arms, catching her as she fell against him.

"This won't kill me," she said, gesturing to the wound in her shoulder.

He wrenched the knife free from her shoulder, waiting for her to hiss in pain, and then replaced it, driving it into the steady beat of her heart.

---

* He knew it, because so was he.

"Come back to me however you like," he told her, "just come back to me, beloved."

He watched a smile flit across her face, gone as quickly as it came.

"Bran," she whispered with her final breath.

Round 30: Rhosyn

"This is crazy," Bran told her. "Rhosyn, sweetheart, you do realize this is *mad*, don't you?"

She tilted her head, considering it.

"Rhosyn," he pleaded, "if you do this, you only hurt yourself. Is that even part of the game?"

"I don't know," she said, frowning. "I hadn't considered this before."

They'd already tested it several times, unfortunately.

This time, the gift (curse, more like) was a connection; when he hurt, she hurt tenfold. When he was enveloped in warmth, she burned like the sun. When he felt joy, she melted into it; when he felt sorrow, or anger, she was helpless but to drown. When he keened at her touch, she felt herself delivered to euphoria, and whatever it was that had dragged them apart and forced them back together, she knew this was the worst of it.

This, to feel as he felt, she simply couldn't abide.

"I have to do this," she said numbly. "Otherwise, why are we even here?"

He pressed his forehead to hers, his thumb rising to stroke the lines of her cheeks.

"Who would win?" she whispered, because by now, she felt she knew nothing else.

"I would surely lose," he said plainly, and shuddered. "I could only lose, Rhosyn."

She wondered how to respond.

Wondered, sighing, for perhaps too long a time.*

"How do you want to die, Barza?" she asked, not unkindly.

"In your arms," he replied.

"That can be arranged," she assured him, and stabbed the

---

* Long enough to have answered a question neither she nor Bran had thought to ask.

poison-tipped arrow into his back, feeling the matching, blinding pain in her own.

"Do I win?" she murmured, her vision blurring as they stumbled to the floor.

He didn't answer.

She closed her eyes.

Part V: Resolutions

They met again outside of Camlann's Strife, at the well between the village and the land that had once belonged to Lord Viteri, who had long since passed away.

"Hello, Master Barza," she said, greeting him as she arrived. "Have you been waiting long?"

"Not long at all, Lady Rhosyn," he replied. "Though, even an hour without you seems long enough."

"I find I've lost count," she said. "Of the game, I mean."

"It is difficult," Bran agreed. "This one took quite a long time."

"Years?" she guessed, and he nodded.

"The village is so different now," he commented. "I can't quite believe how much time has passed."

"No one would recognize us," she remarked, scrutinizing him with a glance. "And I see you didn't bother to hide."

"I didn't," he agreed, and then added, tepidly, "I couldn't."

She waited, not quite ready to lean toward hope.

"What can you do now?" he asked tangentially, meaning her talents—her gifts that sprung forth from the well.

She'd tried it extensively; done as much as she could.

"Nothing," she confessed, and by the look in his eye, she could tell his answer was the same.

"Do you ever worry that we won't come back?" he asked.

"Always," she said, and paused.

"Do you ever think," she posed carefully, "that we should have just had a life together?"

She waited for him to blame her; to fall back on methods tried and true.

Instead, he surprised her.

"Don't we have one?" he asked simply.

"Do we?" she countered, bemused.

He gave her a solemn nod.

"I think," he murmured, taking a step toward her, "that we have had so many lives together, Rhosyn, we may very well be soulmates."*

She gave a sigh of exhaustion, feeling the weight of those lives (and deaths) settling firmly in her bones.

"Could this, perhaps, be the gift, then?" she asked.

"What?" he echoed. "You and me?"

"A life together," she corrected, "certain, at last, that there is no one else for us."

Bran Barza's lips cracked a knowing smile, as they always did.

"I have always been certain," he told her.

She considered the value of her truth.†

"There has never been another," she reminded him, confessing it plainly this time.

It seemed an easy ending; once again, beside the well, it seemed a promise that was far too sweet to be true. But by then, they had both witnessed magic aplenty, and no longer had trouble believing in anything at all.

Instead, they glanced aside, at the well that had started everything, and contemplated how very far they'd come.

"Thirsty?" she asked him.

His lips quirked up.

The game was to finish in a draw, it seemed, and they both recognized the offering.

To her surprise, though, he shook his head, and offered her his arm.

"I think my thirst is sated," he replied, and together they set out, venturing back into life.

---

* Soulmates: a term used here to mean two tired halves of a battered whole, though also those traveling along the same cosmic path, which in this case is both circuitous and eternal.

† Found, ultimately, that the alternative was wanting.

Part VI: Happily Ever After

In a small, unassuming village of no particular interest, something extraordinary happened; many things, in fact, but one in particular. A love story, one that all started with a well, and that ended with one, too.

Wells have always been places of strange phenomena, and this one is no exception—though, as with the others of its kind, there are no scientific conclusions to draw from the circumstances of events that have passed. There is no explaining the curious events befalling Bran Barza and Rhosyn Viteri, and with such uncanny happenstance, perhaps there never will be. What, then, is the truth? Perhaps magic bests our mortal minds yet again—or perhaps the only truth worth remembering is the one that Bran and Rhosyn shared in the end.

For the story *does* end, as most stories do, with a familiar tale of a boy and a girl, and a happily ever after. But this tale concludes with a lesson, too: that the end is never the end.

For the gift, the magic of it all, is in the sharing of a life together.

The House

Charlene and Danielle, let me begin by ruminating wildly about marriage. After today, people will continuously ask you the same questions, which at this stage of life and love will be "Does it feel different being married?" (Later these questions will be more pertinent to one or more uteruses, so good luck.) I had a friend who was particularly exhausted by this question—which, in fairness, does seem to demand a specific but unguessable answer—and her pet answer was no, of course it doesn't feel different being married. In her words, she chose to get married in the first place because she didn't want anything to change. She liked her life exactly as it was and thought, *Cool, let's do this forever, then.* A totally reasonable answer that I will now invalidate brutally behind her back.

Because actually, things will be very different after today. Maybe not right away, but soon you will begin to notice something that I like to describe in terms of architecture. To me, marriage feels like you have taken up residency in an unfinished house with a very, very long hallway, such that you cannot see the end from where you stand, and you are only allowed to progress through one room at a time. Which means that today, you're standing in a beautiful room full of exquisite, exhilarating beginnings, but right outside this room is another endless stretch of as-yet-unmaterialized rooms, each one containing an unpredictable number of things you know absolutely nothing about. So what can you build next if you don't yet know what rooms will be required? What can you create at this moment, with the tools you currently have, that can account for one of the rooms you haven't yet seen? Conversely, can you afford to take any room for granted knowing you may not be allowed to stay there long? You can merely accept the room as it is and continuously make the choice to keep going. To say yes to every room that follows, regardless of what might ultimately live inside.

Which is to say that in marriage, there are consequences. The decisions you make today will impact an argument you have ten years from now; ten years from now, learning something new about the person you already know by heart will sweeten the promises you make today. Because you, as you are now, will not exist in this form forever. Your spouse in the future is technically someone you have yet to meet. Your marriage is, likewise, a shape-shifting entity, one that demands evolution, and while all relationships are alive in this way, marriage is particularly architectural. By choosing marriage, you are entangling lives and thoughts and beliefs and dreams that can never be fully extricated. You're making vows to each other that will be significant self-fulfillingly, because you made them at all. You are looking each other in the eyes and saying the word "forever," and while the act of making a promise of such magnitude is already a blind leap of faith, the act of choosing to accept it is terror itself, and therefore this, today, is an act of incredible dauntlessness. You, as you stand here today, are a miracle of happenstance and faith.

Because to allow yourself to be known is to allow yourself to be wounded. If intimacy is handing someone knives and saying please don't stab me with those, then marriage is shedding your armor, too. It's saying to the person you've chosen that you accept their love and plan to honor it. That your vulnerability comes at a high price, but a worthy one. That you will willingly suffer when they suffer because your solitary peace is unmatched by the peace you share with them. That you understand you are building a house of many mysterious rooms together, even when your co-architect in this matter can never be wholly understood.

And in the end, what a dazzling decision! No one will ever know this house as you have known it. No one can ever knock it down without your consent. No one but you and the person you build it with can ever do the work to fix it. And no one but the two of you will ever know how truly breathtaking the many beautiful rooms can be.

You could build this house on your own, but I think we all know it wouldn't be as interesting. It wouldn't be as weird, and I mean that in the truest sense—that real, awe-inspiring greatness only comes from divergence, from the weirdness that invention brings. It comes from the place where your passion and theirs intersect. So, to answer this incredibly annoying question for you: Will it feel different being married? Yes, and what a luxury it is to be this in love, and to build this life from nothing! After today, everything will be different—you will each be braver, steadier, and capable of dreaming bigger dreams, because you both know you have a place to call home.

To Make a Man

Day 250

"Well," she exhaled, turning her head to look at him. "Clearly I'm a very good teacher."

She looked best this way, stripped down in the low light of his bedroom. He'd never met a woman so comfortable naked, though that was true of how she looked in any situation: comfortable. She didn't seem to care what he thought, or what anyone thought. She seemed thoroughly uninterested in the opinions of others, which was probably half her appeal. Maybe more than half.

He rolled onto his side, facing her, and slid his hand over her torso, from her ribs down to her hips. He traced over her bones with the edge of his thumb, watching her breath catch. He contemplated something nameless as he looked at the various pieces of her; breaking her down to clues, maybe.

She closed her eyes, letting him. It had taken months for her to let him, but now she always did.

"A siren," he said after a moment, and she permitted a slow smile.

"You guessed that already."

"I know." He leaned forward, pressing his lips to the line of her sternum. "It's something like that, though."

"Want me to tell you?"

"No, I told you. I want to guess."

"Mm." She let her eyes float open, dark lashes sweeping up from cheek to brow. She was every shade of golden, warm olive skin with mahogany eyes. "You're running out of time, you know."

"Am I?"

"Yes."

He rested his cheek against her stomach, letting her nails trace the shape of his spine.

"Are you going to eat me?" he asked her. "Consume me? Devour me whole, spit out my limbs, build a nest with my bones?"

He'd nearly made her laugh. "I've already told you what your death will be, and it's not at my hands."

"What if I don't like the one you told me?"

A shrug. "Change it."

"That easy?"

"That easy."

"You should stay," he said, looking up to rest his chin in the dip below her rib cage.

She fixed him with a doubtful glance.

"What," he asked, "that's not as easy as me changing my own death?"

"No."

"Why not?"

"You're exhausting."

"Am I? You seem to like me."

"You're perfectly suitable."

"Then why not just . . . stay?"

But he'd already lost her. He could tell. Her mind was elsewhere, distant, even if the rest of her hadn't moved.

He stretched his palms over her ribs, spreading his fingers out like frost. "Why can't I resist you?" he asked her. "Something about you calls to me. It . . . summons me."

She glanced down at him.

"Whatever you are," he told her, "it's not normal."

She closed her eyes again, scraping her nails along the nape of his neck.

"No," she agreed, and didn't speak again.

Day 1

Marcelo spat some blood onto the side of the ring, beckoning to his opponent. "Again," he said, with a laugh that hurt his probably-broken ribs. Still, laughter was key in situations like this. People always hated to watch someone enjoy themselves; joy sparked rage faster than anything else he'd ever tried, and like always, it worked.

Angel wound up and hit him hard, sending him stumbling into the barrier.

"That all you've got?"

A misplaced blow to the kidney. Would have been a knockout if Angel had ever learned to aim correctly, but no. This was a nightmare. "Shut up, Marcé."

"No, I'm serious," he said, straightening. "I thought you promised me a fight. Is that starting anytime soon?"

Angel threw a hook, then a cross, then another hook. Marcelo took them all, collecting them like raindrops, then threw two jabs, three. Angel was tired, clearly, already stumbling over his feet, and the audience was restless, bored.

"Pity your mother kept me up so late," Marcelo said. Uncreative, but it would have to do. Too many shots to the head tonight already. He smiled, then winked. "Think she'll nurse my wounds tonight, Angel?"

"My mother wouldn't touch you with a fucking pole, Marcé."

Probably false, but good sons were so easily deluded. Marcelo threw a couple of jabs to Angel's body, deliberately leaving his face open, and someone in the front row *yawned*. Throwing a fight usually ended faster than this.

Over Angel's shoulder, Marcelo caught a glimpse of something possibly useful.

"Is that what Mickie told you?" he asked, and Angel's brow furrowed.

She was easy to spot, like always, and Marcelo let his eyes slide to three places in particular. One, the scar on her shoulder. Fifteen stitches from the shard of a broken window. Two, the tattoo on her hip, where two sparrows circled each other in flight. Three, her eyes, which were on him.

It only took a couple of seconds for Angel, who was never the brightest even if he did run with the thuggest crew, to do the math.

"You fucking bastard, Marcelo," Angel gritted through his teeth, and that time, the blow to his ribs was wholly unexpected, as was the uppercut that sent him colliding skull-first with the wooden barrier.

He gave it a moment, cataloguing the places he felt pain, which wasn't something he felt often. Typically his reflexes were better than

that, but then again, he'd been letting Angel beat him up for three
rounds already. Even he couldn't take that many shots to the head
before things started to go south. From what he could tell? One or
two broken ribs, maybe some internal bleeding. Figured. Some shit
was wrong with his knee, too. Might've bashed it during one of his
earlier falls. He did them both a favor and stayed down.

"MICKIE, YOU SKANK BITCH," Angel roared, spinning on
his heel and heading for his girlfriend, who was probably soon to be
his ex-girlfriend. At least until they got back together again, anyway.

The fight was over, finally. Marcelo hadn't wanted to bring anyone
down with him, but if that was what it took, so be it. Unfortunately,
standing was going to be an issue, and he doubted anyone was going
to help him up. Consequences of fucking the wrong girl or taking
too hard a fall, whatever. Welcome to fucking Wednesday night.

"Marcelo Guerra," came a voice, and he looked up, half squinting
as someone came into view. It was a woman, with golden skin and
eyes. Not the usual over-tanned girl of the neighborhood, though she
wore its costumery of platform heels and a shirt that hovered above
her navel. She was either an angel or a delusion, he figured, though
more likely the latter. It would take a lot more than one fight to kill
him, and he would know.

She sank down to look at him, tiny skirt and all, and he stared
groggily back. The adrenaline of the fight was starting to leave him,
which meant pain would start soon. Very soon.

Marcelo struggled to sit upright, but she stopped him, the tips of
her fingers pressed to his chest.

"Why didn't you win that fight?"

If it wouldn't have hurt like a bitch, he'd have shrugged. "Didn't
have it in me tonight, I guess. Happens."

"Don't be ridiculous. You have it in you every night," she said.

She was pretty, sort of. A little older than he was, if he had to
guess. Maybe about as old as he was pretending to be, though she had
a bony sort of look to her. None of Mickie's hips and ass or Raquel's
tits as far as he could tell. Just golden eyes and a look of bored disappointment, and a skirt that made promises he wasn't opposed to
finding out if the rest of her would keep.

"Could have it in you if you wanted," he replied.

She gave him a slow, hateful smile.

"Marcelo," she said, "if things keep going how they're going, you're going to die one year from today." She glanced over her shoulder, pointing just outside the makeshift ring. "You'll be standing right there," she said, gesturing to where Mickie had been, "and you'll bleed out from a gunshot to your ribs while nobody says a word."

"Nobody makes me bleed," he said, which, considering the circumstances, wasn't strictly true. But it was, kind of.

Nobody made him bleed unless he let them, anyway.

"Someone will," she told him. "Eventually. Everyone's got a weakness."

"Not me."

"Then why'd you lose tonight?"

"Money." He decided to tell her the truth, just for fun. "Can't win every fight. Is what it is."

"The house is paying you to lose?" she asked, unfazed. Unsurprised.

He glanced around. Nobody was listening and it wouldn't do her any good even if she was some sort of cop, so he said, "On occasion."

"Thought you were your own man."

"I am."

She gave him another arched look of skepticism.

"Who was the girl?" she asked.

"What girl?"

"The one you got punched over."

"Oh." Micaela Riviera, called Mickie. "Friend. Ish."

"Ish?"

"Most of the time." Minus the times she wasn't, which she had been quite a lot recently. Something about boredom, or maybe wanting things he couldn't have.

The woman seemed unperturbed. She shrugged, saying, "She'll be there."

"What?"

"When you die, she'll be there," the woman said. "She won't do anything to help you."

He sat up slowly. Tried to, and partially succeeded. "Yeah?"

"Yeah."

"That supposed to be some kind of mystical bullshit or what?"

"Might be mystical," she said, "but it's not bullshit."

She was silent for a moment, and then she reached out, touching the swollen part of his cheek. He sat still, letting her run her thumb along the bone for a moment or so before he caught her hand, holding it steady.

"You an angel or something?" he asked her.

"Nah," she said, and then rose to her feet. "See you around, Marcelo."

She turned to leave. He caught her ankle, smoothing a hand around the shape of it, and glanced up at her.

"Come home with me," he said.

"No thanks," she replied, and stepped out of the ring, leaving him behind.

Day 23

"You're back," he said, spotting her. Today, she was wearing a black dress and high heels, big gold hoops. Standard outfit for a girl who went to places like this—only he had the impression, like he had before, that she was somehow in costume. "Gonna tell me what you are this time, or am I just going to have to keep guessing?"

He'd asked her last time if she was a selkie. The time before that, a succubus.

"Keep guessing," she invited curtly, turning to make her way across the room. He shot out a hand, catching her arm, and she gave him another look of boredom, or expectancy. "What?"

"What do you want me to do?" he asked her, though he wasn't totally sure he was serious. Maybe, maybe not. It depended what her answer was. "Just tell me."

"Be better than this," she said.

"Wow," he said. "Really had that loaded in the chamber, huh?"

She gave him a long look of consideration.

"You dropped out of high school," she said. "Never went to college."

He leaned forward, resting his forearms on the barrier. "Been asking about me?"

She shrugged. "Nah. Just more mystical bullshit."

"School's not everything, fresa. I had as much as I needed by the

time I was sixteen. Already knew all my state capitals and everything," he said, making a point of running his tongue slowly over
his teeth.

"School's easy for you?" she asked him, glancing down at where he
leaned against the barrier.

"Sure. Didn't your Ouija board tell you that?"

"Then why not go back?"

*Marcé, you're wasting your potential. You're so smart, mijo, why do you
keep getting in fights? Just keep your head down, be good. Get out of this
neighborhood and make something of yourself before it's too late.*

He leaned back, repulsed by the wave of memory, and the girl
gave him a long, unapologetic stare. It occurred to him that maybe
he didn't actually want to sleep with her this badly.

Except, fuck. He did.

"Tell me what you want," he said. Scratch the itch, be done with it.

"Be better than this," she repeated.

"How, exactly?"

"That's on you, Marcelo."

"You know my name. What's yours?"

"Doesn't matter."

"Sure it does."

"Why?"

"Because I need something to call you."

"When?"

"When do you think?" he asked, and when she didn't answer, he
laughed. "Fine, when I make you breakfast in the morning, then.
How's that?"

She gave him a look of contempt, moving away again, but he
matched her steps.

"Give me something I can do tonight," he said. "I can't just be
better in the next hour."

She scanned his face for something.

"Win this fight," she said.

"Can't," he told her. She gave him a tart look of disinterest.

"Rigged again?"

"They'll kill me." They would, too. He was treading on thin ice as
it was. The rules were simple, really. Do what you're told, get paid, do

it again when you're told to. Do anything else and get broken. Maybe your arms, maybe your legs. Probably not both, but why chance it?

"No, they won't kill you. You'll die in a year."

"A year?"

"Minus a few weeks, yes."

"You sound sure about that."

"I'm always sure."

"Sure enough to gamble my life on it?"

She shrugged. "It's up to you. You're the one who wants me. I never said I wanted you."

As if hard-to-get wasn't the oldest play in the book.

"You do, though," he said, leaning toward her. "I can tell."

She glanced up. "Mystical bullshit?"

"Eh, I'm lucky," he said, tipping her chin up. When she didn't move, he assured her, "Preternaturally so."

"Pretty big word, Marcelo." Might've been cliché, but her lipstick smelled like cherries.

"I told you, I don't need school."

"You do," she said, and he brushed his lips across hers, promisingly. Just enough to taste the softness of her mouth, to let her feel the warmth of his breath. He'd put his mouth anywhere she asked him to.

She pulled away. "Win, lose, up to you," she said, turning to leave. "Your choice."

He gritted his teeth. "It's gonna cost me, you know. Wouldn't you rather I take you somewhere nice?"

"I want a man," she said without turning around, "not a wallet."

"At least tell me your name," he called after her, and she paused.

He raked a hand through his hair. She was the frustrating kind. The lose-sleep kind. He couldn't quite figure it out, whatever quality she had that made him want to find a way to make her world stop when she looked at him. Whatever it was, it was foreign, unfamiliar. He'd been with better-looking women before, so it wasn't her looks. He'd been with plenty of bitchy women, too, so it definitely wasn't that.

It was something about the defiance in her eyes when she turned and told him, "Lina."

"Lina?" he echoed. It sounded like a lie. "That's what you want me to call you?"

She had turned away again, walking elsewhere. "Yes," she said.

She aimed herself at an empty spot in the room, near the back corner. He realized that, once again, she had come alone. She hadn't been there with anyone the first time, and she wasn't tonight, either.

So what was she here for, then?

"Don't make plans for tonight, Lina," he shouted after her.

She kept walking without turning back.

Day 34

"Lina," he said, and she turned. "You sure you're gonna be okay walking home alone?"

"Not like you can walk me," she reminded him. "I don't think you could do much about my safety."

"Could," he said defensively, and then glanced down at the cast. Legs, always legs. Though, he'd been right. Not both. "You know, you might have mentioned this was going to happen. Since you were doing all the other mystic shit already," he pointed out.

"Well, I told you you weren't going to die," she reminded him. "Wasn't my job to tell you how close you were going to come to death."

She probably didn't know, either. Outsiders never did. It looked bad, but it started so simple, really. Started with some high school kid from the neighborhood finding him on the playground, asking him if he wanted a few bucks. (Everyone here wants a few bucks, and when your mom works all day your prepubescent ass doesn't exactly have someone to point out you're signing a deal with the devil's less-literate associates.) All you have to do is carry this, be there for that. If something goes wrong, throw a punch, take a dozen of them. Oh shit, kid doesn't cry, good for him. Run when we say run. Here, hold this gun, stand there and be quiet. Don't lose this money, keep this out of sight, give it back when we tell you. After his mom gets sick a few fights prove him better than the other dumb shitheads who took the same deal, and you know what? He enjoys it. Not just the money—that, but the pain, too. Nothing hurts like an empty stomach.

Morality doesn't pay bills. He rises in rank, high enough that retaliation only comes when he does something stupid; *really* stupid. Like beating the shit out of the one person the crew said don't touch just because a girl swung her hips and tasted like cherries.

"Just stay the night," he said. "Please."

She shook her head. "Can't."

"But I said please?"

"Yes, I know. My hearing is fine."

Marcelo wondered when he'd become the sort of guy who begged. Over a week since the fight he'd lost and he'd gotten nothing out of her except her name and about five minutes of her time, most of which had been spent wandering silently around his living room.

"I could make you coffee? Pour you a fresh cup of blood," he amended, "if that's what you vampires prefer."

"Good night, Marcelo," she called, pulling the door open.

All right, he was officially a masochist.

"I won that fight for you, you know," he called after her, hobbling to the door in her wake. "Least you could do is stay."

She rolled her eyes.

"Next time, try winning one for you," she said, and shut the door behind her as she went.

Day 47

The funny thing about her was how well she fit into his world, optically speaking. He knew she wasn't from the neighborhood by the obvious: he'd never seen her before, and this wasn't exactly a prime spot for migration. But if she stood out in some or any way, it wasn't because of something he could fully put a finger on, like the way she dressed or the way she looked. Sure, she was beautiful, but she only became that way the longer he looked, and he might not have looked so long if not for . . . something. Something else. Like the air was different around her. It was something one of his other senses could determine—some foregone, vestigial instinct from when men were primates or hunting in caves or some shit—but his eyes always failed to register it in time to make it obvious.

He always found her. Maybe because he was looking.

"Hey," he said, darting into her aisle of the grocery store. "What's it going to take, hm?"

She looked up from where she'd been eyeing jars of olives, attention fixing on him from somewhere mentally far away.

"Do you know," she said, as if she'd been having part of a conversation in her head and was transitioning to having it aloud, "in my experience, if there's one way to be sure a man wants you, it's to refuse him. Why do you think that is?"

Her dark eyes slid to his, and he found himself prickly again, unsettled.

"You're something weird," he said. "Like a fairy or something."

She seemed disappointed, or irritated. "No," she said, and replaced the olives on the shelf, turning to leave.

She paused, though, brow knitting together as she angled her chin over her shoulder, glancing somewhere near his feet.

"No crutches," she noted, and he glanced down.

"Oh," he said. "Yeah." He looked up, shrugging. "I heal fast. Wasn't too bad."

She arched a brow, then continued down the aisle as he grimaced.

A whole thirty seconds. That had to be some sort of record, and not in a good way.

"Wait," he called, half chasing her, and she came to an unwilling halt. "I wanted you before you said no," he pointed out, and she pivoted to face him, ponytail whipping his face.

"Why doesn't it matter that I don't want you?" she asked, and he blinked.

"What?"

"I said no," she said. "What makes you think you deserve a yes?"

He usually had an answer for this.

He usually had an answer for everything, actually.

The way she looked at him was blinding with something. Not hatred, but certainly closer to that than anything else. Possibly revulsion, or just some disappointing lack of surprise.

"Okay," he said eventually.

Her mouth twitched. "Okay?"

"Okay," he said, and nodded, clearing his throat. "Okay, well. Bye, Lina," he said.

Her eyes narrowed, nearly to slits, and then she turned, walking away.

She didn't look back, either.

Day 56

He flipped to the back pages of the book, scanning the index.

Certainly not a harpy. Even if shape-shifting was part of the deal, there was nothing about them seeing the future.

Could she have been one of the Fates? A possibility.

She said she wasn't a siren. Probably not a nereid, seeing as she wasn't especially helpful. Mostly, she just seemed to get under his skin. Could she be some sort of . . . psychic nymph? That wasn't unheard of, though she hadn't really struck him as anything deified. She seemed more suspicious of him than anything.

He flipped the page, thumbing the worn corner.

Spartae were violent. Was she?

He shut the book and drummed his fingers on its cover, closing his eyes.

It was becoming upsettingly obvious that he didn't know enough about her.

Day 61

The next time he saw her was at a neighborhood barbecue. Mickie and Angel had made up (surprise, surprise) and Marcelo was gruffly clapped on the back upon entry, so maybe Lina wasn't mystical after all. He wasn't going to die in three hundred days; how was that even possible? Still, he kept his distance from Mickie, who was giving him the *eyes*.

She'd had bedroom eyes since she was a teenager, a gift and a curse. An ordinary magic, deeply feminine.

Lina was wearing a flimsy cotton dress, tied up around her neck with a little moisture at her back, like everyone else. This kind of heat was miserable, unbearable. They didn't have the luxury of a coastal lifestyle, left to the devices of inner-city asphalt. The blaze of propane didn't help, but at least it meant everyone's kitchens might have a rest for the evening.

She turned slowly, a beer dripping condensation from her hand as she raised it to her lips, pausing when she caught his eye. He hesitated, unsure if he was about to do something very stupid or if he should soothe it with a spare few minutes with Mickie upstairs, make it go away. She had hips like reggaeton, rhythmic and deafening. Time with her would be a blur of mindlessness, casting the unimportant away for just long enough.

In the end, though, he sighed and pushed through the crowd, watching Lina revolve slowly toward him.

"You've got to be some kind of demon," he said.

"Thanks," she replied, "but no."

She raised the bottle to her lips, tongue slipping out over them as she sipped.

"Let me ask you one more time," he said, and she stopped, the lip of the bottle resting against her bottom teeth. "I promise, if you say no I won't ask again," he told her quickly, "but I will ask you, one more time."

Her reply was reflexive. "Why?"

So was his. "Fuck if I know," he said.

And then, regrettably, "I just get the feeling I haven't done it right."

She seemed to warily accept the situation. Possibly because she was drinking, or because it was hot, or because she wasn't talking to anyone else, anyway.

"Please," he said, figuring that was a good place to start, "just spend an hour with me. We can do whatever you want to," he added. "Dinner, if you want. Coffee. A drink, up to you."

Her eyes narrowed again, and she took another sip.

"I like you," he said.

Again, her reply was lightning-quick. "Why?"

"I don't know yet," he said. "Maybe because you predicted my death?"

She said nothing.

"Look," he sighed, "I get the feeling I'll know why if you give me an hour, okay? Just one hour, and if you want nothing to do with me after that, I'm gone."

Risky offer. He loved a gamble, but hated to lose. *Don't say no,* he thought, and she glanced down at the beer in her hand, sliding a nail under the peeling corner of the label.

"Yeah?" she said.

"Yeah." She looked up sharply.

"Fine," she said, setting the beer on the table. "Let's go."

Day 63

"Night, Lina."

"Night, Marcelo."

She turned, about to pass through the doorway when he caught her hand, pulling her back to the threshold and pressing her against the frame. She let him line her spine against it, breath catching—yes, he felt it, the way her breath hitched, the way he was getting through to her somehow, the way he could tell she didn't feel nothing, how it proved *this wasn't nothing*—and he stretched out against her, their feet patterned like puzzle pieces, one fitting on either side of the other.

He smoothed her hair back from her face, fingers catching in the pitch-dark strands that fell against her tan lines, the shape of summer burned into her skin. He traced his fingers over the curve of her shoulder, rounding over it with the line of his thumb, smelling her shampoo and the sticky heat of desert air outside.

Her chest rose and fell against his, but she didn't move.

"Marcelo," she said, "whatever you think this is, it isn't. You can't have me."

Jasmine. That was the smell of summer, wafting like heat waves on holy ground to leave the barest hint of refreshment, a little chill for the benefit of searing skin.

He shifted, cheek brushing hers, to speak in her ear. "What can I have, then?"

Whatever she was, she wasn't immune to the proximity of his mouth, breath floating over her neck. He could feel her alternately tensing and relaxing with each motion from him, his lips touching the high bones of her cheek. He leaned purposefully against her, hips-stomach-chest, pressing her deeper into the wood until they could both be camouflaged against it, as much a part of the house's structure as the hinges on the door.

"You can have a little bit of time," she said, and he felt her lashes flutter, eyes falling shut.

"How much time?"

The sound of her breath in his ear was hypnotic.

He slid a hand down, resting it where her thigh stretched out from her torn jean shorts, and she slid from his reach, leaving him to catch himself with his elbow against the doorframe.

"Ask me tomorrow," she said, and descended the steps from his porch, slipping through the gate and disappearing down his street.

Day 116

"Like that?"

"No," she said.

They were sticky with sweat, the two rotating fans in her bedroom little help against the heat. The sheets were saturated and twisted around them, deposited on the floor, crickets from the street wailing up to the windows of her apartment.

"If you're going to touch me," she said, "do it like it matters."

As if it could possibly not. As if he hadn't been watching her, suffering every bit of closeness, for weeks, months, proverbial lifetimes. It had never been this difficult, or this long a wait. It had been years since he'd dreamed of real girls, no longer the horny teenager he used to be, but then there she was in his mind at all hours, in his bed even when she wasn't. Lina, Lina, Lina, like a pulse, the way her waist flared into her hips, the way she leaned against his counter, the way her brow furrowed when he spoke. How her mouth looked when she smiled, like an unfamiliar shape, a broken arch. The shape of her ribs, the way they curled around a heart he both could and couldn't feel. He could sense it pulsing—could prove its existence, medically speaking—but still, it was out of reach. Was she an angel, a demon?

Neither, she said, but he didn't believe her. She was so obviously both.

He sat up momentarily, disentangling them.

She slid back toward the headboard, propping herself upright.

"What are you?" he asked her.

She gave him one of her unwilling smiles. A sad one.

"You tell me," she said.

Day 130

Lina, Lina, Lina. You are the softness of your skin, the sharpness of your mind. You are the knife edge of your humor, which doesn't look like humor at first because, on you, joy looks like suspicion. You are the distance you so meticulously keep between us. You are the door, the latch, the key. I understand now that I am an invasion; even with my best intentions, you can only trust me the way you'd trust a flood. There's no choosing which parts of me you accept or which parts of you I want. We seep in through each other's cracks, all or nothing.

"Like that?"

She had a habit of smiling like she didn't plan on doing it.

"Yes," she said, and shivered. "Like that."

Day 140

"Already read it," he said, tapping the shelf and resting his hands on her hips.

"Which one, the *Aeneid* or the *Iliad*?"

"Both. And the *Odyssey, Antigone, Lysistrata, Metamorphoses*—"

"For school?"

"The first two, yes. The others for fun."

"What else?"

He scanned the shelf. "Most of it," he said, tapping the spine of *Trojan Women.* "I guess it spoke to me or something."

"Yeah?"

"I mean, I've read the Bible, too."

She glanced over her shoulder. "For fun?"

He leaned down, brushing his lips across her nose. "I've had more

fun doing other things," he said, losing interest in lesser arts of conversation and slipping his hands under the hem of her tank top.

"You know," Lina said, "there's more I could teach you. If you
want."

He glanced around before leaning in to brush his lips across the
side of her neck. "Thought you were teaching me plenty?"

"Yes, and you're a quick study. But I meant more along the lines of
this," Lina said, gesturing to the shelves. "Unless you already think
you know everything there is to know."

He had always thought he knew everything he needed to about
the world until he'd had her in his bed. By that point, the dearth
of knowledge—what she liked, how best to touch her, what sounds
she'd make if he did it right—overwhelmed him, and he put himself
in her hands to be molded, sanctified, blessed.

He'd given up school because it felt like a cage. *Do this, Marcé, be
this, make something of yourself. You're wasting your potential if you don't.*

Potential. As if he had ever asked for potential. Yes, please, give
me the means to disappoint everyone, hold me responsible for all the
achievements I can never unlock. Just because he could do something didn't mean he *should* do it, or so he'd thought.

But with her the world was suddenly vast, mysterious. It wasn't a
matter of his potential, just some irreconcilable matter of how much
of himself he should be, but how much of the world he could fill;
how much of it he could lay at her feet.

Her. He wanted to capitalize Her in his mind, making Her a
beacon.

"Goddess," he said in her ear.

She laughed, shoving him away.

"What, you don't believe in them?" he asked, teasing her.

"Oh, I know they exist," she replied, turning away. "It's just that
believing in them is another matter altogether."

Day 180

"How did you know I was going to die?"

"Because I saw your death," she replied.

"What, like a movie?" She shrugged a yes. "Is it always like that?"

"Sometimes. Sometimes not." She was washing the dishes, looking up at him as he put things away. "Is it bothering you that I told you?"

He shrugged. "Nah. Not really."

She arched a brow. "Hubris," she observed.

"No," he replied, "I just don't really believe fate is . . . static like that." He stepped closer to her, resting his hands on her hips and pulling the curtain of her hair aside, burying his lips in the side of her neck. "Besides, you said it was a matter of 'if,' didn't you?"

He felt her stiffen. "What?"

"You said *if* I kept going as I was, then I would die. But I didn't just keep going, did I?"

He thought it was a good point, but she hardly moved. If she was breathing, he couldn't feel it.

Her voice, when she spoke, was smaller and thinner.

"You believed me?"

"Well," he said with a laugh, "I suppose it depends. How was I going to die?"

"I told you. A bullet wound." She turned in his arms, resting her hands on his chest and then sliding them down, curving her palms over him. "Here," she said, drawing a thin line between his ribs with the nail of her thumb. "This is where the entry wound would be. There would be no exit wound."

She stared at his shirt for a moment, watching the placement of her thumbnail as he inhaled, exhaled.

"It's an argument," she continued. "You and your friend, you're fighting, you double-crossed him. He double-crossed you first but it doesn't matter, he has a gun and you don't. Your other friend, she could save you but she doesn't. You hear your mother's voice when you die."

Highs and lows, mijo. Everything turns, highs and lows.

It felt like a memory, even if he had never lived it. Like something he'd known in a dream. He fought a shudder, then tightened his arms around her.

"Lina," he said. "Tell me what I should do."

She shook her head. "I can't see that. Shoulds, ifs, those aren't my job. I see things as they are."

"Well, just tell me what you think, then."

"Why?"

"Why not?"

"Why?" she repeated. "You won't listen to me."

"Haven't I listened to you so far?"

She was silent.

"You believe me?" she asked again.

"Should I not?"

"Answer the question." She sounded serious, even panicked.

"Yes," he said, bemused.

She stared at him for a long time, dark eyes narrowed.

Then she leaned up on her toes, wrapping her arms around his neck. She felt small, fragile. He slid his hands under her shorts, toying with the fraying of her denim.

"What will happen to us?" he asked her.

"Nothing," she said.

"But you keep telling me you can't stay. Do we fight or something?"

"No."

"Because if we do, I apologize in advance."

"No, there's no fight."

"Okay, so if we don't fight, then what?"

"I told you, nothing."

"But—"

"It will be over soon," she told him.

"Well, maybe I don't believe that."

She shook her head.

"Either you believe me or you don't," she said, leaning back to look at him. "Do you believe me?"

He hesitated.

"Yes," he said.

"Good." She tilted her chin up, filling his nose with dish soap and chiles and the honeyed jasmine of her hair. "Better you don't waste a moment."

Day 257

"What was your name again?"

    "Marcelo. Guerra. Sorry I'm late."

You know, I was wondering. Whatever happened to nursing school, Mick?

Marcé, don't be stupid. You know I got no time. Besides, I clean up enough shitty drunks running with Angel's crew, what I gotta be a nurse for?

Hey, you never know, Mick. I could get shot or something. Maybe I'll get in trouble, need you to save my life someday? Never know.

Ha, that sounds right. Okay fine, culo, you go back first, then maybe I'll think about it.

"You've missed two classes already, Mr. Guerra. Have you done the reading?"

"Yes."

"All right, sit down, you've taken up enough class time."

"Thank you, sir."

Marcé, you in this weekend or what?

Nah, I'm deep in it, man.

That same chick? Shit man, you whipped.

Yeah, yeah, she's a hell of a drug.

You some kinda kept boy now?

Sure, fine, whatever, laugh all you want—

Don't stay away too long. We got big things coming, amigo. Big things.

"Let's start with Cassandra, daughter of King Priam, who prophesied the fall of Troy. What is the significance of her visions?"

"Tragedy," someone said. "Deep insight combined with helplessness."

"Anything else?"

"Irony," said Marcelo.

The professor fixed him with a look. "Meaning?"

"Knowing a tragedy could have been prevented isn't just tragic, it's ironic. Hubris," he added. "She warned the Trojans what was coming and they laughed in her face."

The professor paused, then nodded.

"And how has Cassandra the character become an enduring archetype?"

Day 279

"If you could just tell me which goddess you are, I promise to worship you when you go back," he said in her ear, toying with her hair. "Build shrines to you. Carve statues. Write a series of tomes in your honor."

She rolled her eyes. "You're so dramatic."

"So you're really not a goddess?"

"No, and not a succubus either, but thank you for the vote of confidence."

He twined her hair around one finger.

"You're something different from me," he said softly. "You're made of something different." He released the lock of her hair, letting it fall against her shoulder. "I don't know what it is, but I can feel it, the way we aren't the same."

She turned her head, half smiling.

"For once, Marcelo," she said, "I think you might be right."

Day 301

He noticed her eye before he noticed her.

"Mickie," he registered, frowning, and she spooked.

She ducked into another aisle but he caught her arm before she disappeared.

"Mick, what the fuck?" he said, frowning at the bruising on her face.

"Mind your business, Marcé," she said in that bossy voice she'd had since they were six.

"Did Angel do this?"

"No."

"You're lying."

She wrenched from his grip. "It's fine. I'm handling it."

"Mickie, if he's hitting you, you need to get out—"

"Oh," she scoffed, "*do* I? Just *get out,* Marcelo, that's it? Silly me, didn't think of it, what with all my other options."

"I didn't mean—"

"What *do* you mean, then, Marcé?" she asked, cutting him off. "No wait, don't tell me. Tell me what it meant when you were fucking me, hm? You didn't seem too eager for me to leave Angel back then. Now it's not convenient for you, so you want me to go?"

"Mick, I wasn't—"

"What about when you told Angel about us, huh? What did you mean to happen then?"

The weight of his selfishness stung. "I didn't know" fell out of his mouth.

"Know what? Nothing to know," she said bitterly. "We got nothing between us anymore, probably never did."

"That's not true." He wanted it not to be true. "You think I don't care about you?"

"I think between the guy who stays and the guy who disappears it's not much of a choice."

"Mickie. Please."

"Please what?"

"Just—" He fumbled. "If things are bad, or—"

"You think this shit is new?" Her lips were a thin line of contempt. "You know how this goes. You know the ups and downs. This shit just fucking turns," she said with a darkened laugh. "Highs and lows. It's been bad before, it'll be bad again. It'll be good again, too. We all got our cards, Marcé, we just play what we're dealt. Highs and lows."

"I just want to help you," he said dully.

"Yeah, well, I don't want your help." She turned to leave, pivoting away and taking off until she was halfway down the aisle.

Then she stopped, falling to a rigid halt as he waited, silent.

"I thought you were gone, asshole." She angled her chin over her shoulder, addressing him without looking at him. "Haven't seen you in weeks."

"I've been . . . busy."

"Oh, yeah?"

"Yeah."

"That girl?" She sounded contemptuous.

"Her, yeah. And I went back to school," he said. "Just a few credits, just to see. Like you said."

She turned sharply, facing him with anger, or surprise. "Me?"

"Yeah, you. You told me to, didn't you?"

She looked, for a moment, as if he'd slapped her.

Then she stormed up to him, closing the distance so rapidly he nearly took a step back.

"Stay out, okay?" she warned, expression hard. "Don't come back. Don't take his calls, don't come when anyone asks. Disappear—no matter what they say, no matter what they tell you, no matter what they promise to give. You got that?"

Her voice was low, ominous. Familiar.

Mijo, I knew it when I held you in my arms, you were meant for so much more than this.

"How bad is it?"

"Bad. Bad enough," she muttered, impatient, "or I wouldn't say nothing."

When you die, Lina's voice reminded him softly, *she'll be there.*

He hesitated.

"Mick, if it's that bad—"

"I told you," she said, "I'm handling it."

"I know, but if you need help—"

"You already got a girl, Marcelo. Gonna throw this one away, too?"

"It's not like that. We're friends, Mickie. Always."

She gave him a doubtful look, suspicion shadowed by the green-purple-blue of her cheek. "Just promise me you'll stay away," she said gruffly. "Got it?"

"I—" He grimaced, then nodded. "Yeah, fine, I promise."

"You remember you promised me, Marcé. If they try to tell you you owe them anything," she said fiercely, "remember you owe me first. Got that, pendejo?"

She was always sweetest when she was mean. "I got it, Mickie."

"Good." The word, said with defiance, was as curt a dismissal as any. "Get far, as far as you can and stay there. You're different," she told him stiffly. "I don't know what you are anymore, but I know it don't belong here."

He was an expert in goodbyes. Enough to know one when he saw one.

"Mickie," he began, but only managed, "Please."

She softened for just a moment, reaching up to touch his cheek.

"Send me a postcard when you get where you're going," she said.

Then she released him, turning away and disappearing at the end of the aisle.

Day 315

It's easy to tire of beautiful things. Watch the sun rise from your bed each morning and it loses its majesty, becomes white noise. Reverence collapses, terror fades. Boredom is woefully accessible. There's an oppressive sameness to doing things that will never change, to living days that are carbon copies of each other. Repetition is the beast of captivity, habit the tyrant of awe.

He would have traded euphoria just to keep her, to make her the subject of his tedium. To live a colorless life in the shade of her bones, in the sound of her breath, knowing and eternally recounting the monotony of her details until he ground himself down to nothing, never learning or experiencing another beautiful thing.

Some creatures were more dangerous than others. Addiction was a venom.

"Don't go," he whispered in her ear.

Lina reached around for him, letting him curl around her.

"It won't be me who leaves," she said.

Day 364

When he woke up to an empty bed he crept outside, leaping over the creaky spot in the floors of his old house. It never rained much here, desert that it was, but it was raining that day, gloomy and gray amid that strange, off-colored blue of early morning. The clock on the microwave read just before six, and he found her in the garden that had not been a garden for many years; not since his mother had died.

She was standing with her feet bare in the dirt, eyes closed, chin turned up toward the sky. Her hair was slicked back from the rain, her clothes soaked through, and even from afar he could see she was shivering. He could see the pebbling of her skin, the shudder of her breath. The way she contained herself, arms folded, shrinking and bursting at the same time.

Then he saw it. How fragile, how small.

How woefully, irreversibly doomed.

"You're human," he realized aloud.

Her eyes opened.

She turned to look at him, contemplating him without expression, and then held a hand out for his, waiting. He took the steps to reach her, the pads of her fingers brushing the expanse of his extended palm before she pulled him close, her hands on either side of his face.

"I'm human," she said, and touched her lips to his forehead, to each of his eyes, her hands running over his back, his spine, his shoulders. They came around to his ribs, resting there.

This is where the entry wound would be.

There is no exit wound.

"I'm human. But you," she whispered, shivering a little in the cold. "You're something else."

Day 250

"Well," she exhaled, turning her head to look at him. "Clearly I'm a very good teacher."

He looked best this way, stripped down in the low light of his bedroom. There was something particularly glorified about his nudity; about having escaped the captivity of fabric. There was some victory to his exposure, some divinity to it. He was a man unthreatened, unburdened, and he pulsed with his own freedom, temporarily without the frailty of a shell.

He rolled onto his side, facing her, and slid his hand over her torso, from her ribs down to her hips. He traced over her with the edge of his thumb and she caught her breath, slowly, while watching him. He was contemplating something nameless as he looked at her; breaking her down to clues, maybe.

"A siren," he said after a moment.

He never tired of guessing. Chronic persistence, a remarkable disease.

"You guessed that already," she reminded him.

"I know." He leaned forward, slipping his tongue over the line of her sternum. "It's something like that, though."

"Want me to tell you?" She knew he wouldn't.

"No, I told you. I want to guess."

"Mm." She let her eyes float open, finding his dark gaze on hers. Unsettling, the way he had his father's eyes. They sparked like lightning, but his mouth must have belonged to his mother. It was soft, vulnerable.

He had more of her than she'd expected.

"You're running out of time, you know," she told him.

"Am I?"

"Yes."

He rested his cheek against her stomach. She traced her nails down the shape of his spine.

"Are you going to eat me?" he asked her. "Consume me? Devour me whole, spit out my limbs, build a nest with my bones?"

"I've already told you what your death will be, and it's not at my hands."

"What if I don't like the one you told me?"

A shrug. "Change it."

"That easy?"

"That easy."

"You should stay," he said, looking up to rest his chin in the dip below her rib cage.

She imagined telling him, just for a moment. Just to see what it felt like.

Then she gave him a doubtful look.

"What," he guessed dryly, "that's not as easy as changing my own death?"

"No." Or maybe it was.

"Why not?"

She no longer knew. "You're exhausting."

"Am I? You seem to like me."

"You're perfectly suitable." Troublingly so.

"Then why not just . . . stay?"

It was difficult, knowing what he was. Knowing that by the time he understood it, it would be over.

"Why can't I resist you?" Misery struck such a perfect chord in his voice. Clear, low, aching. His confusion was rare, and perfectly tormented. "Something about you calls to me. It . . . summons me."

She glanced down at him.

"Whatever you are," he told her, "it's not normal."

She closed her eyes again, scraping her nails along the nape of his neck.

"No," she agreed.

We have a deal, remember?

I know, she thought.

I know.

Day 1

What would he look like?

Like power incarnate. Tragic, really, that he would take this form with all its power only to lay waste to it if permitted to go unchecked. This is the problem; this is why I asked you for help. Because he will be so much more than a man, and that will draw people to him. He will fail to understand that a lifetime of being what he is will only render him less.

Was she supposed to love him?

No. No, in fact better if you don't. We're only asking you to teach him. To make something of him.

What made them so sure she could?

We're not. But better you than nothing. What do you foresee for him?

"If things keep going how they're going, you're going to die one year from today," she told him. She glanced over her shoulder, pointing just outside the makeshift ring. "You'll be standing right there, and you'll bleed out from a gunshot to your ribs while nobody says a word."

So you see why you're so necessary, then.

"Nobody makes me bleed," he said.

He won't know why not, of course. Not yet.

"Someone will. Eventually. Everyone's got a weakness."

"Not me."

It's like this every time.

"Then why'd you lose tonight?"

"Money. Can't win every fight. Is what it is."

"The house paying you to lose?"

"On occasion."

Times have changed. Regrettable. People used to love a victor. Now they only love the spoils.

"Thought you were your own man," she said.

"I am."

Even injured, beaten to a pulp, he was magnificent in a way people were so often not. He had a blinding quality to him, and she was certain that others, possibly even he himself, had spent twenty years mistaking it for chemistry, or for magnetism.

Was it just his looks, then? His physicality?

No. He has weaknesses, like any of his kind. A pity that his true strengths, untapped, will be his downfall.

Unless she helped?

Unless you help.

But she was nothing, really. Just a girl who saw too much.

Yes. True.

But why should that not be enough?

"You an angel or something?" he asked her, staring through the cracks of swollen eyes.

His name is Marcelo Guerra. You have a year to make him something.

Make him what?

A man.

"Nah," she said, and then rose to her feet. "See you around, Marcelo."

Day 4

He was charmingly unbearable. Smug, persistent, immune to hostility, amused by artless candor and flattered by the intimacy of her criticism. He delighted in the mystery of what she was, and was never frustrated by it. His imagination was bold, his language colorful, his energy merciless and violent. He was charismatic and handsome. He rose up like the center of her world with only a glance; a twitch of his mouth; a slip of his errant tongue.

He was spectacularly, masterfully easy to hate.

"You're going to destroy yourself," she told him. She had seen it happen, could replay it at any given moment. He didn't die regally. None of them ever did. His kind was so difficult to kill it was almost always a humiliation, dying in the last way they had ever dreamed they could.

"What are you, some sort of succubus?" he said. He didn't listen, of course. Had no reason to listen. His kind never did.

"No," she said. "What makes you think I am?"

"The mystical shit," he said with a shrug. "That, and—"

He took an eyeful of her, snatched it. He had possession in his gaze.

Seduction had never been a requirement. Then again, men had not looked like Marcelo Guerra for some time, and she had not felt this in far longer. Let him chase her, let him want her, let him suffer for being unworthy. She would punish him for his cravings.

We have a deal, remember?

She'd been handed bad deals before. Why should this be any different? Let someone else suffer for once.

"You won't like your death," she told him.

"Oh yeah?"

"Yeah."

"Morbid," he said, smiling. It was a good word on him, especially with the way he curled his lips around it. The syllables were melodic from his tongue. "Anything else?"

She waited, watching him.

"Do you know the gods have children?" she asked him. "Millions of them throughout time. People stopped telling their stories after a while, deciding to put their faith in other things, but they still exist. Nothing changes. Their children are violent, destructive. They put their abilities to improper use without oversight, and the gods still take as they wish. They punish as they see fit."

She paused, and then: "In the end, nothing changes."

"Heavy subject for the produce aisle," he said.

His black eyes from the fight were already healed. She wondered if he had ever questioned why before, but figured he probably hadn't. His kind never asked themselves why they were the way they were. It was one of their worst faults, that they never asked themselves much of anything.

"Those won't ripen in time," she said, gesturing to the avocados in his basket.

He glanced down at them. "You think?"

"Yes." She could see him struggling with them in her mind. "You don't believe me?"

He picked up the avocado with one hand. "I'd be stupid not to, wouldn't I? But seeing as there's not a lot of shit to choose from, I guess I'll just have to try my luck."

"Guess so," she said, and turned away quickly, blinking.

She hadn't been listening, having found herself distracted.

The moment he had touched the fruit, her vision had shifted. No more problems. Now it was fine. Her mind, which lived in tomorrow while the rest of her lived in the now, told her his mother's recipe would yield a perfect guacamole, like always.

Had he done it? Changed its fate? None of her visions had ever been altered before.

"Hey," he called after her, "what did you say your name was?"

She didn't answer. She pulled her cardigan tighter around her, hurrying away.

Day 180

Everything was blurry with his hands on her, her breath too fast, her pulse thudding with the motion of his hips, her muscles aching, quaking, her sense of time wrung out and twisted, stretched and contorted, her nails in his skin, in the place where the bullet would enter, between his ribs that were pressed against hers. There—*right there*—his body would swallow it up and not let it go and neither would she with him; she wouldn't, let them take her, let them try, let their fates warp and wane and be lost because he was strange, he was different, he changed the things around him and now she, too, was changed. Faster and faster, building to something, just out of reach and so close, so close, his lips in her hair on her skin in her ear and this, this was not what she'd come for, this wasn't what she thought she'd find, she wanted to bury it without a map so that no one else would find it, it was hers. Filled to bursting, overflowing, wrenched open and gaping and—

Nails in his skin, digging in, indestructible until he wasn't. He only looked like muscle and bone, but he was something else, something invincible except for one spot. She slid her nail between his ribs and sliced, watching him choke out a shudder, sweat and carnage and—

She curved her hollow palm around the single inch of his imperfect fate and came.

Day 23

"What do you want me to do?" he said. "Just tell me."

She thought it was obvious. "Be better than this."

He was, above all else, a disappointment. She had known he would be, but still. He was a mediocre con artist, a walking scam. There was potential and then there was *potential*, and he buzzed with it. The ground beneath his feet shook with it, and he didn't even have the audacity to feel shame at what little he'd accomplished with what he'd been given.

"Wow, really had that loaded in the chamber, huh?"

"You dropped out of high school," she said. "Never went to college."

He leaned forward, resting his forearms on the barrier. "Been asking about me?"

As if there would be anything worth knowing even if she did.

"Nah. Just more mystical bullshit."

"School's not everything, fresa," he said. "I had as much as I needed by the time I was sixteen. Already knew all my state capitals and everything," he said, making a point of running his tongue slowly over his teeth.

"School's easy for you?"

"Sure. Didn't your Ouija board tell you that?"

"Then why not go back?"

That wasn't really the question she meant. What she meant was

Then why are you like this? but she figured that would be giving too much away. There was intriguing and then there was patronizing, and if she was either too easy or too difficult she would lose his attention. She would have to walk the fine line of neither, or both.

It didn't surprise her when he didn't give her much of an answer.

"Tell me what you want," he said.

Easy. "Be better than this."

"How, exactly?"

"That's on you, Marcelo."

"You know my name. What's yours?"

"Doesn't matter."

"Sure it does."

"Why?"

"Because I need something to call you."

"When?"

"When do you think?" he asked. He gave her that look again, with his father's eyes. For a moment there had been something else there, something she didn't know or want to know or trust, but just as quickly, he was back again, familiar. "Fine," he said to her silence, "when I make you breakfast in the morning, then. How's that?"

Let him want her. She turned away, but he caught her.

"Give me something I can do tonight," he said. "I can't just be better in the next hour."

We have a deal, remember?

Make him a man. But as far as she could tell, he already was one. A man, with all men's greed and ego.

"Win this fight," she said.

"Can't."

It was tiresome how minimally he accepted what he was, judging his fate to be sealed without even pushing it to see if it bent. It was the one thing that made him different from his predecessors, though she couldn't decide if that made him better or worse.

"Rigged again?"

"They'll kill me."

"No, they won't kill you. You'll die in a year."

"A year?"

"Minus a few weeks, yes."

"You sound sure about that."

"I'm always sure."

"Sure enough to gamble my life on it?"

"It's up to you. You're the one who wants me. I never said I wanted you."

"You do, though," he said, leaning toward her. "I can tell."

He wavered in and out between something she'd never seen and something she'd seen so many times it sickened her. "Mystical bullshit?"

He touched her cheek, her jaw. She felt something else mixing in with her revulsion.

"Eh, I'm lucky," he said, tipping her chin up. "Preternaturally so."

He probably was, too. His awareness of it annoyed her, irritated her somewhere she couldn't place, like an itch.

"Pretty big word, Marcelo."

"I told you, I don't need school."

"You do." And he did. He so clearly knew nothing.

He brushed his lips across hers, which was something she permitted because she had to. Because he was what he was, and he would want what he wanted. He touched her and she saw, behind closed eyes, something different. Like he had with the fruit, the avocado, he touched her, and something wavered and warped.

She pulled away. "Win, lose, up to you," she said, turning away and hiding her reaction. "Your choice."

"It's gonna cost me, you know. Wouldn't you rather I take you somewhere nice?"

What had he done? She couldn't tell yet. She wasn't sure. What had been clear before was obscured now, as if his lips touching hers had somehow fogged up the glass.

"I want a man," she said without turning around, "not a wallet."

Now her mind was buzzing, images darting. She tried to picture him bloody on the floor the way she had seen him before, the smoking barrel kicked aside, but couldn't see it. She could see parts of it, each person as she had seen them the first time, but something was gone. Where was the gun?

"At least tell me your name," he called after her, and at that, she paused.

She was nothing, really. Just a girl who saw too much.

Yes. True.

But why should that not be enough?

She couldn't be the same as she'd been. It couldn't be like it was then.

Who will you be this time?

She turned slowly and decided.

"Lina."

Day 248

"What's your real name?"

She glanced up from her cup of coffee, managing to pull a small half smile from some useless junk drawer in her mind. Within the same drawer were apathetic moans of pleasure, evasive murmurs of reassurance, the mechanical familiarity of prayer. Things she'd had to use until she met him.

"What makes you think I lied?"

He sat beside her, opening his mouth, and then apparently thought better of it, kicking her chair out just enough to place himself between her and the kitchen table, her face cupped between his hands.

"Tell me again about my death," he said, and she sighed.

"This," she said, "is called a fixation."

"Very mortal of me, I know," he said. "You probably don't have to think about yours much, do you?"

"I already know my death," she told him. "I've seen it."

"And?"

"And what?"

His nose brushed hers, his thumb passing over her bottom lip.

"Can you prevent yours?"

She shook her head.

"Then why can I change mine?"

"We're not the same, Marcelo."

"Because you're something else?"

"Because I'm something else."

She felt him smile.

"If I change my death," he said, "will you tell me your real name?"

"Whether you die or not changes nothing between us."

"Why not?"

"Why would it?"

He paused for a second, forehead pressed to hers.

Then he sighed, releasing her with a biting kiss, darting in and away.

"Okay, Lina," he said. "Let's play your game, then."

Day 34

"Lina," he sighed. "I could make you coffee? Pour you a fresh cup of blood," he amended, "if that's what you vampires prefer."

She shouldn't have come. He had taken a beating from his loss at the club and she, despite knowing better, felt guilty. The failures of her humanity nagged at her more when he taunted her, still so foolishly convinced there was anything she could be besides grotesquely, utterly what she was.

"Good night, Marcelo," she said, pulling the door open.

"I won that fight for you, you know," he called after her. "Least you could do is stay."

She wondered how to tell him that he was a deck consisting entirely of aces. Arrange his features any way you liked and he was still a winning hand.

"Next time, try winning one for you," she advised, and shut the door behind her as she went.

Day 116

The kiss had surprised her. Not the way it happened; they had already kissed in all ways but reality, breaths entangling like chains through the shared imaginings of what it would be. She knew it was mirrored behind the lids of their eyes, collecting in pools beside the space they slowly degraded between them, dissolving more each time they crashed against it.

The surprise was that it had happened at all. It wasn't as if restraint had held her back. She had simply thought *I won't kiss him* and then thought *Never mind, I will; in fact, I'll put my hands on him myself.*

She supposed it was curiosity that won out in the end. Curiosity, and not her own limbs that had pulled him closer, letting his hands travel under her dress in the terrible summer heat that felt so familiar, so looming, like a haunting from her past. She was slick with sweat, panting by the time things progressed, his body pressed to hers to anchor her against the dizzy spell of déjà vu, the contortion of past and present. He peeled the fabric from her body, running a hand along the lining of her thigh as curiosity met memory, trapping her there between boundaries of oblivion and fear.

"Like that?"

"No."

Let him think it a lesson, like something she was there to teach. Later he would put his mouth on her and charge her with something, running a current through her limbs that would make her muscles tense, and she would grit her sorry teeth and marvel. She would inflict tiny instances of damage, bites and scratches she would repair with little miracles, caresses and a mindless kiss. He would rearrange her pieces, shift her while she tore at fraying ends, and she would unravel him as he had done for her, clawing for a glimpse of his indecipherable core.

She saw a little glimmer of him darting into her mind, back out. A flicker of an imagining she'd seen before, only different. The gun was gone, the bullets. This time, Marcelo stood in front of her alone, hands empty and extended, and the closer she came, the more exquisite the torment, the more she shook with desperation while his Cheshire smile broadened, and when he didn't stop she dug her fingers in, tore at his skin, pried apart his ribs and—

What do you have that the gods don't?

She let out a gasp, shuddering.

Pain.

Exactly.

Day 47

He was stranger than she had expected him to be.

On the surface he was no different from the others, but there must have been something else, some other factor she couldn't see.

He called her Lina like it was a favor to her, a poem he read for her pleasure. Like he knew it wasn't her real name, but he wanted to indulge her anyway.

He seemed able to find her in a crowd without effort. She had found an apartment in his neighborhood on purpose, never far from where he still lived in his mother's house, but it had begun to feel like he was finding her, and not the other way around. It unnerved her, unsettled her.

He was also walking again within days of his beating.

"I heal fast," he said, like it was funny.

No. Not funny. Hadn't been funny for some time. He'd been beaten to a pulp and healed in days, months' worth of regeneration accomplished in hours. If she could tear his head apart and visit his brain, she doubted she would even find a memory of pain.

This was all becoming absurdly clear to her the more time she spent with him, which was increasing at the same rate as her misgivings. The first times their paths crossed had been about her finding him, but now he was starting to find her. She felt the rearrangement of pieces in her head each time he did it.

He had been so easy to hate, but something about him was untying knots, leaving her to fray, unraveled.

He was stranger than she'd expected him to be.

Day 364

The rain slid down his cheek, over his shoulders, down the crevices of him.

"What does this mean?" he asked her.

"If you don't die tomorrow, then I've done my job."

We have a deal, remember?

"What about you?"

She toyed with his hair, slicking it back from his face.

"What about me?"

"Can't your ending be changed too, if mine can?"

A lie would make it eminently sweeter, but she had always been cursed with truth.

"No," she said, tilting her chin to the sky.

Day 301

"Lina," he said. "Tell me what I should do."

"About what?"

"Everything. Life. Mickie. You." A pause. "Everything."

She shook her head. "I can't see that." She wasn't some sort of Fate, informed by some omniscient power she could tap. She only knew just enough to be a curse.

"Well, just tell me what you think, then."

"Why?"

"Why not?"

"Why?" she repeated. "You won't listen to me."

"Haven't I listened to you?"

She was silent for a moment.

"You believe me?" she asked.

"Yes," he said.

He seemed to say it without hesitation. She scoured him for a lie, still waiting for some other reaction. She was still thinking when she rose up on her toes, allowing his touch to wander over her skin, which was by then little more than a map of places he'd been before.

If it was a trick, it was a cruel one. She wondered if even that was enough to let her hate him again.

"What will happen to us?" he asked her.

"Nothing."

"Do we fight or something?"

"No."

"Because if we do, I apologize in advance."

"No, no fight."

"Okay, so if we don't fight, then what?"

"I told you, nothing."

"But—"

"It will be over soon," she told him.

"Well, maybe I don't believe that."

She thought of saying nobody ever did, but then stopped, shaking her head.

"Either you believe me or you don't," she said. "Do you believe me?"

Maybe it was a test. He hesitated, and she hoped he would fail.

She nearly dropped to her knees and prayed for it, for the safety of knowing he could not simply put his hands on something and change it, make it over into something unrecognizable and new. That was too much power, far too much, for anyone to have in their veins and not know it.

"Yes," he said.

There was such indelible cruelty in hope.

She smothered it quickly.

"Good. Better you don't waste a moment."

Day 0

"What will you call yourself this time?"

She stared out over the plains, considering it.

"This time," she said, "I get to be Helen."

"Is that really better?"

"No. But what's one curse compared to another? If I have to do it over, then better hers than mine."

"Curses are broken from time to time, you know."

She slid a doubting glance to her requester.

"No man cares for a prophetess," she said. "Better a prize."

"Oh? Perhaps he will be different."

"Or," she said, "perhaps if you continue to push me, I won't do it."

Her requester smiled thinly.

"You'd rather remain here?"

She glanced out over the fields again, considering it.

"Fine," she said, turning away and resolving not to look back. "One year. But that's it."

"Of course. As I promised."

"And you'll have to let me do it my way. One year, no interference."

A shrug. "I wouldn't. We have a deal, remember?"

Day 332

"I don't understand. Don't you love me?"

"Must I love you?" she asked him, sighing. "Can't it be enough that we're happy as we are?"

Over time she had learned Marcelo had the stubbornness of his mother. His resilience belonged to her, a small token of his finer inheritance.

"You always act like this has to end," he said. "But what if I want more? What if I want to be with you, to marry you? What if," he said, and stole forward half a step, snatching her hand up with his. "What if I want to change your fate like you changed mine?"

"You can't, Marcelo."

"Why not?"

"It's a losing battle. And besides, I can't, I have rules."

"I won once for you when it was my job to lose," he insisted. "Don't you remember?"

"Yes," she said. She remembered him broken and bloodied, the legs he limped on for days. "But my rules are different from yours."

He looked at her a long time without moving.

"Tell me your death, then," he said.

She shook her head. "It's not for you to know."

"Why not?"

"It's private."

"Please." He tightened his fingers around her hand. "Please, Lina, just tell me."

You wouldn't believe me stung the tip of her tongue. Old habits.

Still, he looked so desperate she slid a hand around his cheek, sighing.

"You won't like it," she warned. "You won't want to hear it."

"You've never once told me something I wanted to hear."

He was right about that.

"There is a curse on me," she admitted, letting him lean against her palm. "I refused someone once, and because of it, he cursed me. Because of him, I will live only long enough to see my world as I know it crumble down around me, and I will have no power to prevent it or to stop it, though I will be the only one to see how everything will end."

She paused, and then, "I end my life with a man who does not love me, who does not care for me at all, but I will be only one in a horde of many he doesn't love, and one of them will kill me. I will die far from home and alone, empty, with only my memories of violence to follow me eternally. Those and my curse are all I have.

"Except," she said, withdrawing her hands and becoming very small, shrinking within herself. "Except for the single year I spend with you."

When she managed to look up again, she found Marcelo with his eyes wet, sparkling with sadness, with pain. That, too, was a gift from his mother.

"I can't save you?" he asked her.

"No." It was half a lie.

"Then what can I do?"

She considered it.

We have a deal, remember?

"Save others," she said.

Day 365

Before he left, they lay facing each other on the bed, knees touching, curled up together like children.

"Do you want to hear your new death?" she asked him.

He shook his head.

"I'll meet it when it comes," he said.

Because he doesn't ask, she doesn't tell him he will be gray and old, fulfilled and wise, surrounded by generations of his progeny. She reaches out and touches the place he will not die; where he will simply grow tired of his mortal body, with all its inviable fibers and feeble organs and evidence of wear, and then, inevitably, his father will come to meet him, to favor him well enough to take him home.

Later, he will leave in the dead of night, closing the trunk of the car he rented while he looks up to her window, his friend Mickie in the front seat believing that if they're caught, they'll soon be dead. She envies Mickie her hope, that she can still find the risk worth taking, even without the certainty of knowing how it all turns out. The woman called Lina thinks if she had had Marcelo sooner or had even an ounce of Mickie's courage she might have lived a different life herself, which she does not say to him. Neither that, nor that

Micaela Riviera will not be the first or the last or the only woman he saves.

She doesn't tell him that he will not die; he will only retire from this form, transcending to another.

More important, though, he doesn't ask.

"Just tell me one thing," he whispered, catching her hand and holding it. "Was any of this real?"

She touched her fingers to his brow, to his cheek, to his mouth. He kissed the tips of her fingers lightly and spared her the indignity of having to confess, or to let the pieces of her heart fall from her tongue to land gracelessly in the chasm that will grow between them.

"Okay," he said, accepting her weakness for what it was, and kissed her. "Is this goodbye, then?"

She nodded, tired now, and blessed him with her silence. Someday, she thought, she would remember this for all that it was, and for all that it wasn't. She would resurrect this very moment into countless perpetuities and embrace the searing pain of it; suffer the boundless joy.

Because it had been real. Every moment of it. Every blessed thread.

As she closed her eyes, she heard him say it in her ear.

"Goodbye," he said, "Cassandra."

And it was hope, rather than the surety that had always been her curse, that whispered in her heart that maybe, maybe someday, they would see each other again.

Day 366

Returning to the Elysian Fields wasn't a particularly long journey. The divine arrangements were quick, relatively painless, the air changing the moment she left the city's arid winds. She removed the too-high heels and the low-slung jeans and tossed the costumery of Lina aside, digging her feet into cool, refreshing earth.

"So," came a voice, and she looked up. "How was it?"

"Fine," she said, and then, with a perfunctory bow, "Hera."

The Queen of the Gods, protector of women, smiled indulgently upon acknowledgment, taking a seat beside her in the Elysian grass. "Good. I thought he had potential."

"He does. Not all your husband's children have been so powerful."

"True, but that wasn't all of it, Cassandra." Hera paused, and then: "Or should I say Lina?"

"I said I would be Helen this time," she said, "didn't I?"

"You did." Hera turned, observing her closely. "And was it painful?"

"Mortality is always painful. Not that you would know." A bit petulant, but that was to be expected under the circumstances, she thought.

"Fine," Hera said neutrally. "Obviously you're not in the mood to be polite."

Dryly, she replied, "Should I have offered you refreshments?"

No answer. Aside from cleaning up her husband's messes, Hera wasn't easily provoked. Even when it came to Zeus, she had a remarkable way of reserving her energy.

Instead of replying, Hera leaned back, inhaling the sweet smell from the plains, and remarked, "Persephone's done wonders with this place."

Silence.

"Are you at peace, at least?"

You have only your lifetime of misery to follow you around the afterlife, Hera had told her a year and a day ago, when they first made their deal. *I have a husband who is irresponsible with his progeny on Earth. Perhaps, instead of both suffering the idiocy of careless men, we might do each other a favor?*

"Why did you choose him?"

Hera laughed. "I thought you'd look beautiful together," she said.

"And did we?"

"Yes."

"How charming." She was bitter, though that would fade. Bitterness, loss, injustice . . . in her experience, those sensations always faded.

What do you have that the gods don't?

Pain would fade.

Memories, on the other hand, would remain.

"Well?" Hera asked. "Are you?"

At rest, she meant. At peace.

I hope I gave you something, Lina, in exchange for what you gave me.

"Yes," said Cassandra.

Indulgently, the goddess smiled.

"Good," Hera said, and disappeared, leaving her to the solace of her afterlife.

Preexisting Condition

It's wash day. A lowly, humdrum day upon which I may recall things such as the progression of morning to noon and certain types of flora and how to properly purge a rug of bloodstains but not, for example, the day I was born or whether I have always had this particular set of hands. I have no specific cause for concern as to the nature of my hands—only that I have no recollection of them. Whether these have always been mine or whether they once belonged to, say, the butcher who died last winter remains a mystery to me. Mihaila is a vault.

The sky is gloomy again and soggy with humidity for the fortieth straight day, which speaks to the nature of my own personal malaise. I've made mention of my inner longings many times to Mihaila but she becomes lost in thought whenever I bring it up, as if the sound of my voice causes her to suddenly remember a task unfulfilled. I do remember Mihaila—she is the only person I remember with even the faintest bit of clarity—although from the rubble of my erstwhile mind she hovers as a distant specter, as if I am witnessing her hazily from a distance, behind a thick shroud. What she was to me in life I have no idea. I know only that I opened my eyes and she was there and it seemed right that she would be there, perhaps even good, and there were tears like jewels on her lashes at the sight of me drawing breath, and behind her, the plain stone walls shone like stars.

We do the wash in the river like always. Today, the clothes come out especially yellowed from the claylike mud lining the sodden banks. When everything is clean—by someone's measure—we return home to do the nightly simmering. The kitchen becomes ungodly hot as always and will stay this way for hours, like a preview of damnation. Mihaila wipes her forehead with the back of her wrist tiredly before scrutinizing me with a glance.

"You know, you do not look so well when you scowl at me like that," she says, breaking our usual companionable silence. "There is no earthly reason for you to seem so constantly displeased."

She motions for a bit of the ox blood and I hand it to her.

"I have been seeking a way to die more permanently," I admit.

She tilts her chin up to the sky as if beseeching the heavens for patience. She does this on occasion. I never know what to do while it happens, so I simply wait.

"For the last time," she begins, "I went through hell to revive you. I have cared for you, provided for you, comforted you, fed you, clothed you. Loved you, as I have always done, as no other creature has done for another. To the depths of my soul I have cherished you." She looks at me squarely. "Do you mean to tell me I have done all this in vain?"

"It does seem that way," I mutter. My reply is initially defiant, but almost instantly I feel the knees of my rage unlock. I shuffle my feet across the mud-stained floor and hang my head low, unwilling to look at her though I know it is owed.

Mihaila is very attractive and wise. Her eyes are the color of a beautiful steak. Her voice sounds like the hollows of eternity. She wants me to be alive and so I am alive. I do not understand what is so difficult about any of this except that it is nearly impossible to bear.

She seems sympathetic and rests a hand on my shoulder. Her fingers are tiny and frail, like the bones of a bird. I can identify birds still, somehow. That one is a sunbird. That one a nightjar. That one a cuckoo. And yet there is still so much I cannot name.

"Will you tell me whose hair this is?" I ask Mihaila, reaching up for a tendril resting jaggedly across my clavicle. I do not like it, this hair. It is an almost otherworldly burning. I don't know what it was before but I cannot imagine it looked like this.

Of course, just by my asking Mihaila knows I have moved on from my initial complaint, and so she tires of me immediately. "I cannot think there is any purpose to knowing," she says, straightening from the stews with a look of exhaustion.

Still, I feel a wicked need to press her. I do not imagine I was ever a saint. Were we lovers? Is Mihaila my mother? The significance of us lounges stagnant, eternal, bone-crushing.

Perhaps these questions are too heavy for a day of such gloom. I will try them again at breakfast.

"Was I always so tall?" I ask her instead. "I feel I used to see the world from a slightly different angle. I am certain I was not this tall."

"So I made you a bit taller," she says with a shrug. "Is that a crime?"

To my knowledge no, though there is no telling which parts of the criminal code I no longer grasp, or have ever known.

"My knees hurt," I whisper. I feel certain I used to be more compact. I fantasize sometimes about a version of myself encased in the richness of earth. Mihaila says I am iron-deficient.

"Growing pains," Mihaila replies.

*   *   *

The heat is a godless malevolence. It is, in a word, profane. Also, I fear I may soon succumb to my morbid urges. At night I dream of tomb-like silence and wake with liquid drying on my cheeks. The earth is calling to me.

"You're just depressed," Mihaila says briskly, reaching over me for the acacia and encouraging me to exercise.

As a measure of bonhomie I decide to give it a try, despite feeling more obstinate than usual. I did ask Mihaila this morning whether I had been someone important to her before, which I recognize now was somewhat improper wording. Of course the answer was yes. Had she not resurrected me with her own two hands, crafting me from a clay of raw materials, rotting carnage, and fresh tears? What did I propose we were, then, if not *important* to each other—mere acquaintances? Was I, where I stood at that very moment—alive, breathing, with a beating heart in my chest, with blood in my veins, with air in my lungs that she had put there by *sheer force of will*—was I not a miracle of love, born of such precious wonder that there could be no doubt we were once two souls living in perfect harmony? Did I *really dare* to ask such things when no matter what form she or I took, the core of that love would always remain?

To which even I in my obstinance could not disagree—the love between us seems to be the only thing that has not changed shape with resurrection. Besides, I sensed there should be no follow-up questions. She had already worked up a sweat.

And so I wade through the marsh with no particular thoughts in my head aside from the usual worms until I see him lying on the banks. A man, very handsome, though that's not what catches my eye. I am initially distracted by the sight of movement among the reeds, the motion of bare skin gleaming like the slither of a silver-backed fish. His breath as I approach is dynamic and occasionally withheld, punctuated by absence, a percussive staggering paired with a quiet slapping sound that grows increasingly aggressive. I realize he is pleasuring himself only moments before he finishes, long lashes fluttering lazily open only once he has reached his climax.

I remember sex, so presumably I've had it at some point. Truthfully, I'm left with the ringing sensation that I was quite good at it. In any case, something within me awakens by the time I recognize that the man lying on the banks wears the white council robes that Mihaila routinely sneers at. The fabric is parted boldly, insouciantly, and were there any sun piercing the goddamn gloom, it would glint off the muscular angles of his chest quite magnificently.

He catches my eye and I realize he is extremely beautiful, albeit not in a terrifying or awe-inducing way like Mihaila. More of a gentle beauty. His hair looks soft in disarray and his eyes are soulful, like a dog's. His brow furrows for a moment when he sees me, but I suppose he seems to realize I won't say anything. After all, who would I tell? Mihaila discourages me from socializing. I usually do not accompany her to do her weekly shopping in the village. But still, she's never told me explicitly to remain in the house. I'm not breaking any rules.

Though, in the moments before I return swiftly in the direction I came, I must silently acknowledge: he makes me feel as if I would like to.

* * *

"The council consists of three idiots, two motherfuckers, and two shit-licking cunts," Mihaila tells me later when she's molding the dense, chewy rolls we'll later stuff with sweetened yams. We have already finished the day's stewing. "Why do you ask?"

"No reason. Why the white robes?"

"To further cement their hypocrisy. You haven't spoken to any, have you?"

"No, I haven't."

"Good, don't. You'll cost a fortune once they realize you're something they can tax."

Interesting. "As a child? Or a spouse?" (Personally I lean paramour but am keen to test the outermost constraints for purposes of deduction.)

Mihaila gives me a quizzical look. "As a person," she says. As usual she sees right through me. Alas, but I do live with a vestigial admiration for her brilliance. An unfortunate palimpsest from the traces of who I was to what we are.

"More importantly," Mihaila adds, "as a collection of restricted rituals. You're at least four arcane rites, and that's only counting the ones they know of."

Hm, perhaps another route. "So, were I to encounter a council member," I pose in charitable deviation, "what specifically should I not say?"

Mihaila heaves a deep sigh and turns to me long enough to take my face between her hands. Mihaila is so tiny and fragile and yet so calm and wise and beautiful. For a moment I feel a pure, gushing love for her; a desire to consume her whole with the latent ardency of my fondness.

"My heart, there is nothing you need to worry about when it comes to the council. You are safe, and you are precious, and you are cherished."

In that moment my heart seems alight with affection, a softness I can almost call a memory, as if I lived this love before. And in that moment, perhaps it seems worth it to be alive again, to know that this love is not only possible but within my grasp. For what reason should I crave the whispers of a tomb when life can beam so shiningly, with such warmth?

"But if you so much as utter a word to that shit-licker Kamon," Mihaila says, "I will wait until you're asleep and then put roaches in your bed." She strokes my cheek with her thumbs. "The flying ones."

* * *

"I'm Kamon," says the handsome man from the marsh when I see him next. With all his clothes securely fastened, I realize the white robe does him no favors. It's not a bright white up close, more of a faded natural color, though the fact that I happen to know how bronzed his shoulders are beneath the fibers of the linen is perhaps the first time in this life that my memory has been a problem. "And you are?"

This is a very good question, so I act as if he did not ask it. Instead, I point out the more pressing indecency of what I stumbled upon him doing the other day. "Most people do that sort of thing in the house."

Mihaila does. I hear her at night sometimes, quick and business-like. Less like a secret she keeps from me and more like one she keeps from herself. I myself have done it several times, if only to familiarize myself with this body. It functions as well as can be expected. (Further clues! Mihaila must have wanted it to function, seeing as if she did not, it would not. Such is the nature of creation.)

"Yes, well, it was a nice day," says Kamon, as if that is answer enough. For a moment I think that's all the conversation we'll be having—which makes sense, as the threat of flying roaches does linger somewhere in the periphery of my thoughts, not unlike actual flying roaches—but then Kamon turns a bright smile on me and I am momentarily forced to squint.

"You remind me of someone," he says, and I feel myself react too strongly. I am dying to remind someone of something. To exist in a way of significance or meaning or even just sonically, like an echo from someone else's past. He sees it on my face, I think, because he smiles so broadly I know I have unforgivably transgressed. I already know there can be no forgiveness from Mihaila. And without Mihaila, who am I?

I feel a stab of rage so sharp it edges close to desire. On a whim I step closer to Kamon, who is near enough to my height; he has no choice but to let me see the startlement registering temporarily in his eyes. He is calm, though. I envy that. My fingertips brush the shape of his brow and he becomes even more placid, like a kitten being stroked.

"What do you do for the council?" I ask him.

"Oh, you know the council," he says evasively, closing his eyes. "What does anyone really do for it?"

His eyes open again and I notice that they are massive. The orb of his eye, it is like a lantern. Mihaila's eyes are lifted at the corners, making her look as if she is forever waiting for an ax to fall. I did not realize until this moment that perhaps I am, have always been, the terrible thing.

"I have to go," I say, but not before Kamon smiles widely.

"Same time next week?" he says.

I begin to lie, nodding yes even though I do not mean it, though I can't help but ask, "Who do I remind you of?"

He smiles again. "I'm not sure yet. Perhaps I'll tell you when I see you next."

Mihaila says the council members are all very wily, so it was probably my mistake to think I could ask a simple question and receive a simple answer. And what answer do I want? He is not very old, perhaps Mihaila's age. Would he have even known me?

I feel it is better, safer, not to know. I think perhaps I'll die tomorrow, anyway. I've been distracted these last few days and temporarily tired of my hobbies but I don't see that being a permanent condition.

"Goodbye," I say, and leave.

*   *   *

The following day is again wash day. It's my fault, I should have been paying more attention. Mihaila pries the knifelike branch from my fingers while I weep uncontrollably into the ashes of the fire. Eventually my sobs subside and become hiccups, then shuddering sighs. Then, gradually, I look up to find the expected look of disappointment on Mihaila's face, only this time it is sharpened by something. She finds me exhausting, I can tell. She does seem very tired lately. Only I seem to care for Mihaila, bringing back pretty rocks I find near the river or drawing pictures in the mudbanks for her to find. Plus, the stews. Nobody else comes to visit.

I understand then that my death would mean cursing Mihaila to a life of loneliness. It is no wonder she tried so hard to bring me back. The flip side of that is very disappointing. If I live on Mihaila's willpower alone, then of course I cannot die, no matter how skillfully I hide my weapons. Last month I tried eating cassava behind her back but she knew, somehow, and took me sharply with her hands and forced me to vomit with her own fingers. Her dress after that was streaked with blood that neither of us could remove, not even after several washes.

"Do something," she says in a toneless voice. "Find something. Music. Religion. An impossible problem." She thinks for a moment longer. "Food," she says, and then, "Are you hungry?"

"No," I say dully.

She gives me a look that means I am being very unkind. Once again, I think: Who is Mihaila? Perhaps without me she does not know the answer, just as I do not, and cannot, exist without her.

I am not a monster. The love I have for Mihaila is real, I know that much, and perhaps it does not matter what I call it or what form it once took. Besides, if I do not make some changes she'll just put me in the room again, the one where she first put me until she decided I was safe. Shudder.

Do something, she says. Find something. Where to start? I have very few choices. I only know one person who would possibly help.

And so, it appears I will have to risk the roaches.

*　*　*

Kamon is smiling cheerily at me when I join him at the riverbank. It is a bit late already, the sky another dull thud of gray, the sly suggestion of sun already slipping from grasp. I decide to do something drastic that is not likely to end in death, as a very honorable favor to Mihaila.

"That thing you were doing the other day," I say before Kamon says a word to me in greeting. "Do you prefer to do it alone?"

Surprise is indolent on him, an impotent spark. "Is that an offer?"

I feel suddenly shy. "I ask because I am looking for a reason to live."

"Ah," he says. "Well, that seems a great deal of pressure." His robe looks crisper today, though I can't tell if that's his doing or merely my imagining. "Though I can't say I know anyone who isn't doing the exact same thing."

He sits on the ground with no apparent concern for his robe, which tells me he doesn't do his own washing. (I hear this observation snidely, in Mihaila's voice, and push her temporarily aside.) I sit next to him carefully and we stay there in silence for several minutes, to the point where I begin to think I should go home. If I miss the stews, Mihaila will come looking for me.

As the sky grows darker and the air thicker with unseen bugs, I lurch forward as if to rise and then stop. "What do you do?" I ask him.

"Hm?" His eyes are distracted when they meet mine, as if they have traveled a long way to find me in that moment. He has been elsewhere, I can see that. Mihaila is often elsewhere but not nearly as distant. She is usually just to the left of wherever I am.

"You said you don't know anyone who isn't looking for a reason to live, which must include you. So what do you do?"

"Oh." He doesn't answer at first though he seems pleased that I asked, which Mihaila never is. She does not have an especially high regard for curiosity. I long for the struggle, resentfully, and resume my urgency to leave until Kamon says, "Well, usually when things are really shit I make something."

"Make something?" This intrigues me. It feels . . . familiar.

But Kamon merely nods and does not expound on the subject. The sun is nearly gone now, and Mihaila will not be happy if I'm not back before the stewing begins. I think perhaps it is a lonely time for her, although loneliness is one of the things I don't technically recall. I seem to know it as a concept but have no memory of it as a sensation. As if it were something I once read in a book.

"Well, goodbye," I tell him. He nods and closes his eyes and I do not think he is really a shit-licker. Masturbator, yes. Shit-licker, probably not.

*   *   *

I am not sure when exactly I begin looking for him. I would like to think I didn't technically start, since the first time I found him I was on one of my usual walks, of which there are three possible routes. Usually, I ask myself at the big stone partway from the cottage whether I would like to travel by mud, by grass, or by marsh. But lately I tell myself that mud is difficult to remove and grass has bugs in it, the kind that leap onto your ankles. So I always take the marsh.

Sometimes Kamon is there, sometimes not. When he is there he gives me answers, like "The council is made up of shamans" or "The robes are white because we couldn't agree on anything else" or "I don't really care for stew." I am careful not to bring up Mihaila because I sense that she would not like that, and I also do not think I will like the answer if I ask the question "Is Mihaila a good person," which anyway is fine because I already know that she is. She is really more like benevolence incarnate, which is different from goodness. But not in any relevant way.

I suppose I am falling in love with Kamon or something, even though I still dream about death like a postcard from a place I miss with my entire being. The insides of me clench sometimes with desire just at the thought of being back in the ether, or wherever it was I used to be (probably the marsh). But when I wake up in the morning, when I am not very excited to do the wash or make the stews or strain to hear Mihaila's silent ministrations from her bedroll, which as I may not have mentioned is not very far from mine—in those moments when I might have previously longed for death, then I do find myself looking forward to my walks, because sometimes I will see Kamon. And even if I don't see him, the feeling that I *might* see him is enough to keep me from seeking out poisons and barbs. So probably that's love.

I ask him how a person knows whether they are a shaman and he says it depends, shamans are all different and anyway a lot of them are freaks. Also, many of them are frauds. But surely some of them are real I point out and Kamon says I mean I guess so and then I say if they were all frauds then why would there be a council of them and he says I don't think you understand that government is largely an institution of frauds. I say but that would mean you are a fraud, are you a fraud?, and he barks a laugh and says he wishes he were a fraud because it would be easier probably! I ask him to explain that and it takes several meetings but eventually he expounds that there are three main kinds of shamans—herbalists, divinists, sorcerers—and they are basically contract negotiators with nature and the dead. There are rituals or whatever (those are his words). He is an "or whatever" of the sorcery branch, which means that occasionally, nature or whoever it is that is always poking and prodding

him when he's trying to do other things like eat or sleep (or masturbate, I think silently) will give him the ability to do something like
heal the sick or do the opposite. Sicken the healthy I guess is what he
means. Yeah, he says.

He continues that he didn't want to be on the council because the
council only allows him to practice his shamanism in certain ways.
He can't sicken anyone he wants to sicken or heal whoever he thinks
needs healing, someone has to petition the council for it and then
the council grants it and they set a price and then once they are paid
Kamon does it, basically like a glorified errand boy. Which he would
gladly be as an alternative, because he doesn't even want to be a
shaman, but nature is always poking at him. He said that already.
Anyway, he thinks things might have been a lot less interesting for
him in a good way if there were other sorcerer-shamans, but there
aren't. There used to be one but they left. Now the only other shamans are divinists who see the future (frauds who pretend to see the
future) or herbalists who can make healing draughts (frauds who can
make rancid soups and not blink too fast while referring to them as
miracles). I see! I say with some enthusiasm. Because it seems like
he is not normally allowed to talk for so long, and I sense that some
positive reinforcement is probably best. Mihaila is actually very good
about that.

But after a few weeks of this I start to think I might like Kamon's
company, and then I begin to think I like Kamon's company better
than some other things, and then I begin to think I like Kamon's
company better than most other things, and then like a line in the
marsh that I can't unsee, I realize that I like Kamon's company better
than Mihaila's.

Which feels . . . substantially problematic.

*   *   *

At night I close my eyes and the world fills with cool damp earth and
the eternal weight of nothingness and I am back in my old body. I
breathe in and try to see if my arms are shorter or if my hair is a different color, but I am pretty sure I am just dirt. Which is a deflating
thought, so I try to focus again on the nothingness. There. That's better.

Then I try something different and think of Kamon's weight on top of me. And that feels less good than nothingness. But only a little less.

*   *   *

"I think you should tell me something about who I was," I say to Mihaila like a dare, because I am once again feeling obstinate. The stews are especially hot today, and they are also—what word did Kamon use? Rancid. I knew that word felt familiar. It is also applicable to the stews. "Or at least tell me how I died?"

Her mind is slightly to the left of where I'm standing—I am always near her thoughts, if not actually in them, which causes me to feel a twinge of guilt over my ongoing betrayal—but she looks irritated at being made to glance back at me. "Why on earth would that be productive? You would only get nightmares."

"So my death was violent?" I ask hopefully.

"Isn't all death an act of violence upon life?" she replies.

At first I think this is poetic, but then I realize it is just Mihaila saying words meaninglessly in random order to try to distract me from the point. "Haven't you ever wanted more?" I press her. "Or, I don't know, less? Like, a lot less. Like to not think or move at all or breathe." I decide this would be best delivered with a smile but she doesn't even look up to see it, so that's a waste. "Okay, then what if I want to be with someone else?"

I worry a little that she will take this badly, or I don't know, emotionally, but she merely lets out a snort and fiddles with a row of small beetles. She arranges them until they align in the shape of a crescent, like a smile of unblinking eyes.

"Like who?" she asks with a small cackle. This is just her laugh. She thinks it is funny, this idea that I would go out and have a life separate from hers, which I guess makes sense as the last time I did that I died somehow. And it's true that I am still not able to imagine a version of my life without her.

"I don't know. Someone." I feel restless again. "I need to take a walk—"

"No, you need to sit here and wait." She plops me into a chair so worn that I feel sure I will fall through it. "You can go in a few minutes, when we're done."

I sigh. Beside me, the stew boils hotly.

"Did you bring me back because you were lonely?" I ask in a quiet voice, and that time, Mihaila's eyes snap to mine.

"I brought you back because life is a gift. *My* gift, specifically, to you," she points out.

"But I don't feel that way."

"Your feelings are irrelevant."

"But—"

"You are alive. That is a good thing. What does it matter if your elbow doesn't creak the way you want it to? Elbows never do. Life is short and hard. Tits sag. Bellies sag. Thighs stretch and then they, too, sag. The best parts are always fleeting. Love is never true. Men are mostly garbage fuckers. Women are deceitful and envious. Every day is hot as seven hells. Every waking morning is somehow worse and more despairing than the last." She is pounding the cassava roughly but then looks up for a moment, as if she forgot something.

"Life is a gift," Mihaila seems to recall, with a surliness this time. Then she points with her lips to the stew, calling for me to focus.

* * *

"If this person in your life really loved you," Kamon says, "she would want you to be happy. That's what love is. It's hoping that, if given the choice, all the worst things will happen to you instead of the person you love. So, if she loves you, then she will choose your happiness. It is just how love goes."

* * *

I can't help but think Kamon is very stupid, but in a way like a baby animal, helpless to the world. I lean forward and catch his smile with my lips. It feels almost as good as blinking out entirely—like being nothing more than a fleeting thought or a distant, dying star.

* * *

Things take a turn when Mihaila catches us. It is my fault, really, for staying back in the marsh with Kamon when I knew very well there was stewing to be done. She doesn't say much when she finds us, only looking at Kamon through slitted eyes before reminding me of our previous bargain. Then she stands there waiting for me, and while I do recall the threat of roaches, I realize I will go with her. There are no other persuasive alternatives and then my feet simply move.

"Goodbye," I say to Kamon. I am not sure yet whether I mean forever. He reaches for me, kind of. But not really.

"Mihaila," says Kamon, in a tone that is not really pleading, but not technically not. I hope there is something declarative coming, something decisive, but then he only says, "I didn't even realize you were still living around here."

She doesn't turn and neither do I, and I marvel for a moment how powerful our love must be, that the potency of my own betrayal is enough to drive me to my doom by choice. Because what exactly do I expect to receive now? Freedom? Answers?

*   *   *

I do not know how she caught this many roaches, much less managed to put them in my bed.

*   *   *

It becomes again very difficult to rise from my bed and the days bleed together like blood. Or stew. I am locked in that place again and there are nothing but carnal fantasies to sustain me. Even the roaches are now dead. I am only let out for the stews and Mihaila and I don't speak at first, because her anger takes up so much space, and because I know I have done something terrible even if I am not exactly sure what that terrible something was. But then my obstinance once again takes over, and after a few more days or possibly years of this half-alive misery, I finally decide to make myself feel something, even if it is rage.

"What is your problem with Kamon?" I ask her.

In answer, she puts a dead beetle in my hair.

"No, seriously," I press her. "Were you and I lovers first? Have I betrayed you?"

"I cannot believe," she says in a low voice, "that you had to choose Kamon, an imbecile. Of which there are a dozen other versions, each more stupid than the last."

"So we *were* lovers!" I say, my fury tinged with relief. "Then why do you stay over there in your own bed, pleasuring yourself alone as if I cannot hear you?"

She blanches. "Because you cannot be trusted. You never could."

But how can that be true? I have nothing from my past but her. "If I have always been yours, Mihaila, and no one else's, then why not simply *tell* me—"

She throws a yam so hard it bounces off the wall and back into my forehead. There is a little thunderclap of something and the impact is unnaturally explosive. I feel myself fading away, fading. Did she do this to me? All I can see is Mihaila standing over me now, her beautiful eyes rich with something that must be love, it must be. Or else everything she told me was not only wrong. It was cruel.

"Don't make me start over!" Mihaila shrieks at me.

I want to ask her what that means, but instead I melt heavily away.

* * *

From somewhere within my shroud of nothingness, I begin to wake in shards. The more pieces of consciousness I collect, the more I suddenly understand. Kamon may be an imbecile, but he's not wrong. Of course Mihaila doesn't love me! She *hates* me.

And then, as if an old elbow has suddenly sprung to motion, I understand something else. The heaviness, the significance of us, the constancy in which I'd put my faith, rightly but inaccurately. The truth I had so long chosen to misunderstand.

That I hate *her*.

* * *

There it is! At last, a spark of something familiar, a mechanism locked properly into place, just as a loud bang comes from somewhere outside my door. An intruder! I rush to slam on the stone as hard as I can, striking and striking as if someone on the other side might hear me.

They can. The wall parts and I fall forward into the waiting arms of Kamon. Sweet Kamon.

"I didn't realize," he says, pale as linen. I understand that it is meant to be an apology and decide not to ask questions such as what took you so long. More pressing matters await.

"Where is Mihaila?"

"She used to be on the council," he explains. "She was the only other sorcerer, and the best—well, second-best herbalist. We always thought she ran because she was sure to stand trial."

"For what?" I ask, even though I'm distinctly aware he didn't answer my question.

"Murder," he says.

"Oh." This makes sense to me in a way that nothing about my past or present lives has ever previously made sense. Finally, the answers! Though I realize with a profound disappointment in myself that in this life, I have always been the problem. I could have been so much worse so much sooner, and then I would have already known everything that I know now.

I return my attention to Kamon. "Where is she? Did you kill her?"

"What? No, she's passed out with the potions—"

Potions. Not stews. Potions. What an arbitrary thing to not remember, unless I simply didn't want to. Mihaila said to help her with the stews and I obliged. How insanely fatuous. No wonder she wanted nothing to do with me! I've given her nothing to properly hate, no loathing with which to be inspired. Invention, desire, a taste for destruction, I have given her none of these things since my death, only grudging obedience. How tiresome. A lackluster naivety in which to be routinely disappointed, not unlike Kamon's.

I recall Mihaila's issue with Kamon then, her half-hearted growl of ire. I understand now that to Mihaila, the betrayal was not the act of sex, love, or loyalty, but the choice of Kamon—someone common, a dozen like him. Which implies the same is not true for her or me, and again she is right.

"We have to go!" Kamon urges me, tugging my arm. "She could wake at any moment, Mirikit—"

She kept my name, I realize.

She changed my body, but she kept my name. And still Kamon does not recognize the truth of me, despite the fact that I am myself.

I push Kamon away and begin walking to the kitchen. Mihaila is on the floor in the shape of a sodden smile. She is wearing a dress that I washed for her just yesterday. I know how to remove blood. I know how to spill it. I know how to toxify it. I know a lot about poisons. I do not know how to cook. Mihaila had to teach me, but she did. She taught me.

I bend to the ground beside her as Kamon makes increasingly fluttering bleats of distress from behind me. "We have to go, Mirikit, we have to go *now*—"

I look up and find one of the previous stews. She never told me what it did, but I realize now that she didn't have to. I simply didn't ask why we were making it, but now I know.

Because occasionally, you need something on hand that will tranquilize unwanted hysteria.

* * *

After Kamon falls to the ground, I sit in the corner and wait for Mihaila to sit up. She is groggy due to the head wound. I wonder if she is seeing me through a veil the way I saw her. Probably not. Unlike me, she hasn't been dead yet.

She purses her lips, first at Kamon's unconscious body where I tied it to the stove. Then she looks at me. "What?" she snaps. Unbelievable.

"We aren't lovers," I tell her.

She scoffs. "No."

"We're enemies," I say.

"That's overly flattering."

"You're a shaman and so am I."

She grunts something in response.

"But I'm better," I remark, "aren't I?"

This time she openly snorts.

"Well, you needed me alive," I point out, gesturing around the kitchen full of potions.

Mihaila rolls her eyes, but she is alive now, too. Finally. "Your death was an accident, you self-involved cretin. But the council was going to have my head for it anyway, and since you're a suitable herbalist—"

"Suitable? You're completely dependent on me—"

"—since you're a *suitable herbalist*," she repeats, "but a shit shaman and an even worse human being. I swear you choked to death just to spite me, just so it'd look like I killed you—"

"Starting to think you deserved that," I mutter.

"—and anyway, I needed the practice. And an assistant. And an excuse to disappear." She looks at Kamon with that same expression on her face from before, like she smells something displeasing. "So, you're going to run off with him now and be disgustingly happy together, aren't you?"

"What's your problem with him?" I ask again, because there's nothing in my memory of relevance.

"I told you, he's a shit-licking cunt." She rubs her head, where he knocked her unconscious to rescue me. "He's the council's favorite little lapdog."

"You think he's pretty, don't you?"

She looks at me with such a familiar expression I nearly laugh aloud. To think I mistook that for fondness! Oh, she brought me back just to torture me, I understand that now. She resurrected me to punish me, to revel in my misery. To know with utter certainty that I hadn't gone to a better place, but a worse one. To match my loneliness with hers.

(And because she could not exist in the world without me, for better or worse. How devastating to know I share her feelings. The heaviness, the ugliness of us, like the tawny bloodstain splattered irreparably across her apron.)

I rise to my feet from the chair and hold a hand out for hers. She looks at me skeptically but takes it, letting me pull her upright.

"Will you kill me?" she asks in a tone so polished with false bravado it practically gleams in the dark.

As if I would let it end so easily. No, I will not kill you, Mihaila. Not yet. Not when the prospect of torturing you glitters so prominently as an alternative. My longing for death has fallen away, its contents as familiarly known as the shit-lickers outside these walls. What is the monotony of death compared to the thrill of reparation? Forget the void. Cast off the lure of nothingness. I choose pain and it is ecstasy. This life, it is a gift!

"I have one question."

She gives me her usual look of incomprehensible boredom. "What?"

"Why did you give me new body parts? Why not just go with the body I already had? It was you who was hiding from the council, not me."

"Internal organs were a mess," she mutters. "And you were ugly."

"No, I wasn't."

"Well, now you are." She smiles to herself, and I realize that I'm smiling too. This bitch is going to live forever. I am going to personally make sure of it. She is my choice and I am hers—in some way I have always known it.

"So," I say. "The stews?"

She contemplates me for a second. Does she know? I think she does. I think she welcomes it.

"Yes," she agrees. "The stews."

* * *

When New Kamon opens his eyes, I find it is a wonderful feeling. I do feel like a giver of gifts! I feel benevolent! Kamon was right, making things is very rewarding.

"I feel," he manages to croak, "as if something is . . . quite wrong."

Mihaila and I exchange a glance before sunning him with our twin smiles.

"Would we have wrestled the gates of death for something to be *wrong*?" I ask. "This life is a gift. *Our* gift."

"To the depths of our souls we have cherished you," adds Mihaila. "Do you mean to tell us that we have done all this in vain?"

New Kamon looks tormented for a moment. "No," he says.

Mihaila and I glance at each other in something I know to be rapture. Behold, nature speaks, and she delights in our inventiveness!

"Come," I say to New Kamon, beckoning. We have not yet decided on a name for him, but then again, why should he need one? It is not as if we will use it. He is here mostly for his looks and because I needed the practice. In case I ever need to drag Mihaila back from death myself, in which case I will shorten her tibias. Maybe enlarge her breasts. Just enough to strain her back by some tiny, marginal percentage—just enough so that she knows something is wrong, but cannot say what. The possibilities are beautifully endless. "It is time to do the stews."

III

Autumn

You have so many autumns; so many selves,
waiting to be shaken down.

Zhou Mengdie, "Nine Lives"

You are the weathered spine of every love story I will ever write.

Monsterlove

There was no real way to tell when it first started. She simply couldn't remember being another way. At some point she could grow teeth when she wanted, sprout them from her forearms like armor, use them to sink weightily into the ground until she could only peer out from her new home among the roots, so deep was she into the earth, so vast and impossibly shallow. Light as air, twinkling iridescence, like teardrops on the rustling blades of grass. No one will ever accept you this way, whispered her mind, and then she became stone, the kind ground to rubble by the tides. Coarse and flaky powder, diminished breeze by breeze the more solidly she stood. A whisper, flame-flicker, maybe it's a lie? Tender brush of knuckle-against-skin, they're not so different, sea and sky. She lets him see 92 percent of her selves, all of the good ones and some of the worst ones (he is polite enough to think the rotting scales a phase rather than a form) but still leaving one or two miscellaneous for herself. Alone, filled with echoes, a cave to hold her secrets, not her best her or her worst her, but still her, nonetheless.

*   *   *

A whistle of something. Longing. Suddenly the love has a shape, she can see it in the dark, she can feel it curling up against her skin. So much of it she overspills and, oops! Her branches reach skyward, joyful with presence, stretching up on a thrum-purr of instinct, something animal and alive. Her last form before she leaves this mold is primal-hot, no teeth for now. The roughness of a loving tongue, regurgitated nutrients, love is a wrenching and a retching. Gag. Love is construction, love is architecture. Love is ten naps a day to make a placenta. Love is perpetual sickness, the pulverizing sense that she is slowly being lost, her iridescent beauty flaked away for desert tundra. The tumor moves, it kicks. Suddenly, she has no other forms. She traded them for another self. A not-self. In this form, she is trapped.

*   *   *

In her dreams she screams and screams and no one hears her, no one wakes. The heartquake rages on unspoken. Something, anything! Give me back my claws, they're mine! Were she still capable of grotto she might whisper some secret truth: not anymore. But now she isn't emptiness. She is not her trillion individual drops of dew. They are collected in a captive pool, a marsh, motionless and painful. She thinks of her hips, those wordless bones, they shriek with such pain she can never forget them. They no longer flicker or swish or sing. They only lie.

*   *   *

Then!

*   *   *

The warmth on her chest is golden light swallowed whole, she didn't know this body could do that. (She has been a hot ball of gas before. But not like this. And not without serious risk of burning.) The newness glares raw in her head, a scream-pitch on the undulation of the ocean. She rocks along on the waves, delusory with the erotica of nurturing. The smell of the Head, the fragrant milkbreath, the lashflutter kiss. Who has the desire to take on other forms when there is such cream-love in this one, glistening with slather on the lips, slickly molten, fat and rich? Ravenous glutton, she gorges, gorgeously. Lovefucker. Monsterlove. Everything is too small a word for it, bite-sized, laughable crudite. She still looks boring skin-and-bone, but is she? The form you see reveals nothing of the odious. Ceci n'est pas une pipe. The partner tiptoes around the radius, not unwelcome but unable to join. You can't share ecstasy. It can't be cut down into slivers. It blazes. It's too bright not to see.

*   *   *

Long night. Long night. Long night. Long night. Long night. Don't sleep holding the child even if the child only wants to be held. Long night. Long night. Long night. Eyes open. Long night. Long night. Long night. One of your selves is now eternally out of your hands.

Long night. Long night. Long night. Long night. Long night. Isn't
it my duty—my privilege—to soothe? Long night. Long night. A
nightmare! Long night. Long night. Long night. How long can she
stay in this form? AS LONG AS IT FUCKING TAKES THAT'S
HOW LONG. THIS IS HER FORM NOW. THIS IS THE
FORM AND IT IS A GOOD ONE. IT IS A GOOD MOTHER-
FORM. IT IS THE PERFECT SHAPE TO PROPERLY
ADMINISTER THE MONSTERLOVE. DON'T LOOK AT
HER SHE'S FINE. Long night. Long night. Long night. Long
night. Long night. Long night—

*   *   *

She wakes up and now her feet are become pond. Her hair is 52
percent endangered swampland with bonus whooping crane. She
pulls it back together quickly, ahhhh! This is not THE SHAPE.
She remembers where her elbows go, she needs them. Reapply the
nipples. Reattach the battery. This is the only form. She will not
stray from it. The other forms are traitors, Bad For The Offspring,
safety hazards! A Good Mother is not fourteen thousand individual
teeth! The Motherform is not the hollow gutted sound of Void! Read
a goddamn book for once in your life. Everyone knows this. God.
Idiot. Everyone knows.

*   *   *

Please go to sleep. Please! She thinks it too hard and from the flicker
of the shadow on the wall (over the din of the noisemaker, the buzz-
god, the Almighty Sound Machine, pray for us sinners in the hour
of our need—) she watches herself change forms. She is a terrifying
mass of spines, at least seven unholy spines, stalagmite, stegosaurus-
like. A howl escapes and it is pain. The pain takes off its mask, aha
it has been anger this whole time! The anger hurts because—a dramatic reveal—it is actually guilt in disguise! Like a Russian doll it
keeps on going. Who killed the gentle parenting with the knife in
the nursery? She did! The shadow on the wall is proof, the wailing
cry is damning evidence! She has been four million forms of dooms-
day this whole time! NO. She retracts the mineral deposits because
she can do that. She can will herself into this one perfect shape.

Gentle. Patient. The monsterlove outlasts all things. The monsterlove outweighs all forms. It chooses the child, the Anti-Self. It glows
outward—no, it beams. Like an asteroid. It hurtles. She is falling.
She feels the danger. But she has looked danger in the eye before
without becoming it.

                         *   *   *

This will not always be the way of things. She would know. She is
not a hot ball of gas right now is she? So then nothing lasts forever,
not even torture. (Not even goodness, the dark matter in her left
lung taunts.)

                         *   *   *

She snaps again at night, in the pretend hours, where no one can
see. Still, she knows the Anti-Self can feel the benevolent monsterlove rotting into sticky hot lava tar. The Anti-Self begins to cry
from fear and immediately she shrinks back into herself. Underneath the anger is hate. But not hate for the Anti-Self. For the
Self, which despite her white-knuckle hold cannot retain this One
Good Form. IDIOT. DEMONTHING. If everyone could see
you now you'd make the tundra-form look nurturing. A lurking
thought becomes a forked tongue earworm. Hey you! Yes you! You
fucked up bigtime baby! B I G T I M E. (Nobody can hate her like
her other forms. At least forty-nine of them have Ph.D.s in sadism.
Four have active patents pending.) The Anti-Self cries out for its
motherform. Yes yes, I'm here. She weeps a soothing mist into its
wheatsoft hair. Everything is cool again, will remain this way, she
is resolved to be the Good One. She has the blueprint for the Good
One on hand, there's no reason she shouldn't rebuild it, over and
over and over, and over, and over, and over, and over, and over, and
over, and over, and over, and over, and over, and over, and over, and
over, and over, and over, and over, and over, and over, and over, and
over, and over, and over, and over, and over, and over, and over, and
over, and over, and over, and over, and over—

                         *   *   *

I mean, if you weren't willing to retain the metaphysical walls of this form permanently, why did you even have a child?

*   *   *

Count your blessings (you dumb bitch!). The Anti-Self grows and laughs and flourishes and wants her attention and smiles and coos and starts to play games and begins to grasp empathy and wants her attention. Like her, it loves to read books and has the partner's perfect eyes, the eyes she fell in love with, the eyes that seem totally fine with at least seventy-two of her forms. The Anti-Self babbles and sings and holds her hand and wants her attention and babbles and sings and wants her attention. It wants her attention and it does. Not. Want. To. Sleep. It wants to sleep but it can't, it just physically can't for some reason!! HAHAHAHAHA ISN'T THAT SO FUNNY. WATCH OUT. THE COSMIC IRONY WILL GET YOU EVERY TIME. The Anti-Self crawls and then walks and then runs. It hugs and sweetly kisses. It explodes her heart from the inside out. Folks, the monster-love is alive and well! The Anti-Self wants her time. It wants her eyes. It wants her body. It wants her attention. She gives it gladly. She gives it gladly. She gives it . . . less gladly. She gives it. She gives it. She gives.

*   *   *

The partner (another Anti-Self, whispers a rogue demonform—an Anti-Self insidious, in-disguise!) tells her, warmly kindly fondly, with a gush of healthy normal toothless love: You Are An Amazing Mother.

*   *   *

But the funny thing about this horror film is: the killer is already in the room. (The fifty-seven forms narrowly held at bay know the truth!)

*   *   *

She has the blueprint for the Good One on hand. So really, there's no reason she couldn't rebuild it, over and over and over, and over, and over, and over, and over, and over, and over, and over, and over, and

over, and over, and over, and over, and over, and over, and over, and
over, and over, and over, and over, and over, and over, and over, and
over, and over, and over, and over, and over, and over, and over, and
over, and over, and over, and over, and over, and over, and over, and
over, and over, and over, and over, and over, and over, and over, and
over, and over, and over, and over, and over, and over, and over, and
over, and over, and over, and over, and over, and over, and over, and
over, and over, and over, and over, and over, and over, and over, and
over, and over, and over, and over, and over, and over, and over, and
over, and over, and over, and over, and over, and over, and over, and
over, and over, and over, and over, and over, and over, and over, and
over, and over, and over, and over, and over, and over, and over, and
over, and over, and over, and over, and over, and over, and over, and
over, and over, and over, and over, and over, and over, and over, and
over, and over, and over, and over, and over, and over, and over, and
over, and over, and over, and over, and over, and over, and over, and
over, and over, and over, and over, and over, and over, and over, and
over, and over, and over, and over, and over, and over, and over, and
over, and over, and over, and over, and over, and over, and over, and
over, and over, and over—

*   *   *

Oh my god, she completely forgot that one of her forms is a literal
black hole. THAT WAS A CLOSE ONE.

*   *   *

Oh, I totally know what you mean, says another possessor of the monsterlove. Yeah right, she thinks. How many forms could you possibly
have? Maybe four on a good day. You think you understand this kind
of quantum material shape-shifting? Please. You really think we're
operating on the same level of cosmological phenomena? Please. You
wouldn't recognize my chimeric dynamism if it pierced your peanut
butter exoskeleton. YOUR Anti-Self sleeps through the night!

*   *   *

Nobody's Anti-Self is as delicious as her Anti-Self. Nobody, no form, no nothing can match the decadence of this cream-fat meal. She still gorges. She licks it from her fingers, she sucks it from the marrow. Oh, believe me, the monsterlove is *fed*.

* * *

It's just so fulfilling, the monsterlove. She's so fucking fulfilled she could cry!!!!!!!!!! The thing is it's not even a lie. It's just wearing a truthmask, and under the truthmask is exhaustion. Which doesn't untruthify the truthmask! Okay! So what she's saying is everything is fine.

* * *

The thing is, all of her forms know the world is shit and thus all of her forms know this was always an unethical exercise. There is so much out there lurking, waiting to destroy the Anti-Self, to tear it apart with its teeth. Like it or not we all RSVP yes to the live shooter at the combination hurricane-earthquake. And those are baby teeth compared to the wrecking balls of bigotry and unrequited love. Outside of the monsterlove there are things worse than all of her worst forms because at least all of her forms love the Anti-Self, even the ones that briefly fantasize about drop-kicking it across the room. (Only the worst forms think that. But they do think it. But they're the worst forms.) The point is, *she's* the creator-god of the Anti-Self. *She's* the ten thousand forms in a trench coat that dragged the Anti-Self into being. Why, because of some biological hormone-desire bullshit that only a handful of her forms even feel? (The rest could have been convinced to see logic if she'd only done the smart thing and held a symposium. God, and to think she used to be smart!) (She's forgotten about the loveformshape or whatever she said before because the One Good Form is so fucking tired.) So, like, basically what she's saying is it doesn't matter if *she's* happy. That's not what the monsterlove is about. The monsterlove is not about her at all. That's what makes it the monsterlove.

* * *

The older the Anti-Self gets, the harder it is to hold the forms at bay. Which is ironic. She's been the Good Form for so long, so dutifully, so unfailingly, and only now that the Anti-Self is beginning to form memories does the noxious bog start to slip through! She holds it back before she poisons the whole house but it's a close one. A close one.

*　　*　　*

A close one. A close one. A close one.

*　　*　　*

Until.

*　　*　　*

Maybe if she had just gotten that one more hour of sleep—if it wasn't three days before her period—if the partner had emptied the dishwasher—if she hadn't dropped the cereal box and watched it detonate across the floor—if the Anti-Self hadn't been tugging her sweatpants in the way she hated because it's just so humiliating somehow, the act of being unceremoniously pantsed by something she suffered so bodily just to make—if nobody had ever invented email—if everyone had just left her alone—if she could just—if she could just have one minute—if she could just—if she could just be allowed to have one—ONE—FUCKING—SECOND—TO—HERSELVES—

*　　*　　*

The form that breaks through is a ten-foot-tall cyclone and unfortunately it happens in the kitchen, where the knives live. Somewhere in the reserves of her brain or whatever operational system runs the forms she becomes aware of all the dangers. The Anti-Self will be Harmed. The Anti-Self will Cry. The Anti-Self will see that she is not and has never been the Good Form and she only invented the Good Form for the Anti-Self which means it has never been real. It is only the product of hoping so hard that she will not become, for the Anti-Self, Pain. That she will not make it feel what the world has made her feel. That the Anti-Self won't itself splinter into forms that are the doing of the World, the World that does not typically assign Social Security numbers to people who are part ecological disaster. The World has been so unwelcoming of her many variations, and she didn't bring the Anti-Self into this World just to give it her own Pain. But it is still there. In all the forms. Even the Good One. Actually she can see now that the Good One is always holding a knife, only it's shoved into her own chest, and the Anti-Self is guiding it in, and it is the monsterlove, and her other forms splinter upward from around its center, and it is the most alive she knows how to feel. From the cavernous opening of her monsterrage she screams, and then she becomes the scream, and then the scream is its own tornado, and then she is a tornado with ten tornado-hands. From inside the operational system—no, from the monsterlove— she sees with her monsterloving eyes—the Anti-Self is wide-eyed and frightened. The Anti-Self does not know her anymore. And the monsterlove twists. She has become the Worst Form. She knows she cannot become the Good Form again. The blueprint has been lost to the storm. Even if she shrinks back down again it will not be in the Good Form because now the Anti-Self knows the truth. The Anti-Self knows what is under the mask. The mask is not untruth but still, there is a bigger truth which is the rottenness. The collection of forms that are maladies, that are all, and have always been, her. She wants to beg the Anti-Self for forgiveness. She wants to wipe the Anti-Self's mind and reset. Even before she begins the descent back to bone-and-blood she already feels the heart-shatter of guilt, which is sadness wearing an untruth mask. Before she returns, she is the seagull cry of loss on an ocean breeze, a red sky of post-storm catharsis.

*   *   *

I'm sorry. I wanted to be the perfect form for you, the form you deserve, but I can't hold it. Even with the monsterlove, I am still only different forms of me.

*   *   *

The cabinets are off their hinges. The roof will need to be replaced. Somewhere she hears the slow trickle of water running over porcelain shards of broken dish-teeth. She remembers that she used to be the ether, that she likes to read for pleasure, that she is musical and prone to laughter, that she has a temper and desires, that love and truth share forms with horror, that shame and fear wear hope-filled hats.

*   *   *

The Anti-Self reaches up for her face and frames it with both hands. Mama, says the Anti-Self, as if to say, not a form but a collection. Not an entity, but a range. The Anti-Self begins to change, and through a morning fog of heady iridescence, she sees another set of forms is starting. Not an Anti-Self after all, but a world.

*   *   *

Together among the detritus of the kitchen they hold the monster-love. It is not too scary. It is not too heavy. She whistles a quiet breeze, a tide that gently beckons. And the youngling trickle of her ocean, the bone of her bone, says yes Mama, and sings.

How to Dispel Friends and Curse People

Letters from an Aspiring Poet to the Village Witch

You looked at me today
As I was gathering rhubarb
I hate rhubarb
It is practically a weed
What is it, a stalk?
That sounds fake

You said you'd curse me if I kept staring
So naturally I came closer
Not to stare
Just to look

You turned me into a rooster
I've only just turned back
And I have to tell you

I like that you are not a liar
You're clearly different
And I'll be back

I like you
Is that so hard to believe?
I like that you're so attentive
To your aesthetic
Which is great, by the way

My mother says you could ease up on the black if you wanted
I vehemently disagree
I admire your commitment
There's tenacity in that
Girls around here change like the weather
Sometimes they like blue, sometimes red
It's exhausting

I think you've got staying power
And coincidentally
So do I

Go away you flaming imbecile
You said
Which can't possibly be what you meant
Seeing as I brought you flowers
And combed my hair
And bathed thrice before my arrival

So I think what you meant to say was
Come in
But seeing as you are out of practice
I'll just wait here
Until you inevitably realize
You used the wrong words

Is it the way your eyes shine?
Is it the way your nose bends?
Is it the way your mind winds,
Your voice lofts, your hands tend?

Perhaps it's how you look at me
As if you wish that I were gone, or dead
Though, perhaps it's that you haven't killed me
That leads me to suspect you might like me instead

Well, I did not like being a goat
Please note that somewhere in the minutes
It's not that I don't enjoy being free
Or leaping
There was a lot of leaping, as I recall
But my stomach is a bit unsteady
This is going to sound crazy, but did I eat part of my house?

Though, while I'm at it
I have another crazy thing to say, and it is this
You look loveliest when you're cursing me
I really think you've found your calling
It really suits you

It's not easy, you know
Finding what you're meant for
Congratulations
And I'll see you tomorrow
So we can do it all again

I like that you don't ask me for things
You *tell* me to leave
You *warn* me that your patience is thin
You *ignore* me when I ask questions
You are very autonomous
Has anyone ever told you that?

Everyone else here is upsettingly polite
They never say what they think
They only whisper it when nobody's listening
You tell me you're turning me into a toad, and you mean it
And I admire you for that
Even if I do now have a sore throat

Do you ever get lonely in the woods?
Or scared?
I think I would get scared
Not all the time, obviously
But sometimes

I suppose the loneliness would be worse
Though you have things to talk to
Your plants and stuff
I heard you call them your pretties
I think you should be proud of them
And don't worry about talking to them
I think it's very normal

I think you're very normal
And also very extraordinary
And perhaps the most magical thing about you
Is how you are both those things at once

My best friend Roger wants to know where I've been
I said for the last twelve hours I was a parrot
He laughed so I think he thought it was a joke
Which is probably best

He also said my father is very angry
Apparently I've been slacking on my chores
This isn't your fault
I am generally not very good at my chores

Roger is very prone to conversation
You wouldn't like him very much
He told me Mary who lives next door is very pretty and I told
    him pretty is nothing
Pretty is a trick of the light
And he said what do I like then and I said power
And he laughed
I think actually Roger is the worst person I've ever met

We need more people in this village

I think today has been a breakthrough
You noticed I possess two arms and working legs
And said if I'm going to be here I might as well dig
I thought maybe bodies at first?
But to my relief you meant for plants

I would dig up bodies for you if you needed it
I think maybe that's a bad sign
I think maybe that might be love?
You might remember I mentioned that briefly
My affections et cetera et cetera
And you sighed
And turned me into a beetle

But that's okay
Not everyone is good at confessing their feelings
My mother says I am a prodigy at sharing whatever crosses my
    mind
She doesn't say it like a compliment
But I think that I've heard worse
Besides, a relationship is like a garden
It takes time
It has to grow
So take as long as you need
I've got all day

You told a joke today
I asked how you decided to become the village witch
And you said "my collection of eyeballs was getting out of hand"
And then you laughed a little bit

I like that you laugh at your own jokes
Too many people are afraid to and I don't know why
I think maybe you're outrageously brave
Or possibly you don't care what anyone thinks

You definitely don't care what I think
And you didn't ask
But if you were wondering
I think your jokes are pretty good
And also, if I can make you laugh
Half as well as you can
Then I think
I'll probably be happy enough with that

Bad news
My mother has sent for a priest
She thinks I'm possessed by demons
I tell her my love for you is not a demon
This is obvious to me
Sure, it feels a lot like hell
There's a burning sensation
And I sometimes have a tail
But still, a wise man knows the difference
Between possession and patience
Unfortunately
My mother disagrees

First of all, I have to apologize
I did not properly appreciate your line of work
I'm very sorry
You just make cursing look so easy
I thought maybe I could do it too

Turns out, no
I said it the way you said it
Flicked my wrist the way you do
Unfortunately the priest is not an orangutan
And I have been arrested

So moral of the story
Other people's vocations should not be lightly taken up
Lesson learned

My respect for you has tripled
Not that I didn't respect you before
Hopefully you know by now
Unless you don't
In which case
I'm not as good a poet as I thought

There's not much to do in here but wait
And think
And remember
I wonder if you're lonely too
Probably not
You have your plants
I suppose I have my poems

Huh, I think I just realized something
I was bothering you, wasn't I?
Disrupting your quiet
That must be why you cursed me so many times
Well, I'm sorry
Silence is kind of nice, isn't it?

Still
I miss your face

There have been a lot of words thrown around rather casually
Being that I am a harbinger of words
You would think this would be good news
But the more common ones seem to be "stoned" and "burnt at
    the stake"
So
I've heard better

Oh, "hung," that's new
I want to tell them it's actually "hanged" under these
    circumstances
Which is admittedly an odd quirk of language
And an easy mistake to make
But I'm afraid they'll think it's a suggestion
So I'm telling you instead

Do you think much about death?
I suppose you don't
Since I assume you don't have to
Die, that is

I really admire your agency
I think you must be very brave
I suspect I'm not very brave
Part of me is very upset about dying

Not the death part, though I assume that will hurt
But I think it will be sad not to be living
And to miss things
Like when your garden starts to bloom
And you threaten the insects that crawl on your tomatoes

I think your tomatoes are very lucky to have you
And I also think that you should have my bones
If it means that I can help them grow

Let me start by saying
That was very exciting
I didn't know you could break down walls
This is very strong brick!
I'm very impressed
But that's enough about me

You said you can't have him
And they said why not
And you said because he's my idiot
And they said what do you mean he's your idiot
And you said are you idiots too
And they said excuse me
And you said you heard me
And they said how dare you
And you said hey, poet, are you coming or what
And I said are you talking to me
And you said is there anyone else here who writes stupid poetry
And I didn't know actually because I don't know what other
    people's hobbies are
So I said did you just say I was yours?
And you blinked and said well, aren't you?
And I said

Well, actually I said nothing
I was speechless
So I suppose I am an idiot
But I am your idiot, so
That seems fine

Thank you for saving my life I eventually said
Then you told me you also turned my mother into a bird
I asked you not to because it isn't her fault she doesn't understand
    love

And you sighed
But said okay fine

And as it turns out you're a very good listener
I think I was right to love you
Communication is important
And listening is the hardest part

You said I'll have to write more absurdist poetry
If I intend to live in your house
Either that or plant more tomatoes

Absurd? I said
No, this is clearly the height of romance

Then you laughed
Which was not what I was going for
But I made you happy, so
I'll let you have this one
Since it means that we both win

Fates and Consequences

On Monday, June fourteenth, at approximately seven forty-five in the evening, Guy Carrington was hit by a bus.

"Ah, fuck," said Atropos. "Whoops."

"What do you mean 'whoops'?" echoed Lachesis, setting down her measuring rod to cast a chilling glare at her sister. "What've you done?"

Atropos opened with a promising "Look, don't freak out—"

"No promises," Clotho muttered, toying with a tangled thread.

"—but I accidentally cut the wrong thread." Atropos picked up the correct thread, for a Mr. Gene Cartman, and promptly gave it a snip with her finest shears of mortality. "See?" she said, letting the two pieces fall. "Done. No harm, no foul. What's one little mishap per millennia?"

"Give me that." Lachesis ripped Guy's threads from her sister's hands. "But this is *Guy Carrington*," Lachesis said emphatically, picking up the two halves and holding them aloft for her wretched siblings to see. "I had a whole thing planned for him!"

"Let me see that." Clotho, meanwhile, gave an affected sniff, plucking the nearest half of Guy's thread from Lachesis's grip to cast an omniscient gaze over his first two-ish decades. "Well, he's going to be rewarded, anyway, isn't he? Atropos is right, he'll be fine." She shrugged, tossing the apportioned thread back to her two sisters. "Who's going to blame you for a few extra years in paradise?"

"Uh," Lachesis corrected, glancing at the second half that remained in her hands. "Not exactly."

Atropos snatched the severed thread back from Lachesis, reconsidering with a glance.

"Ah, balls," she deduced with a sigh. "Hades is going to be *mad*."

* * *

Guy opened his eyes slowly, squinting around the cavernous room before letting his vacant round of scrutiny settle upward on the face of a man reclining above him—a blue-veined, heavily bearded stranger who sat comfortably on a charred-looking throne. The man, apparent judge of sorts, sipped casually from a pewter goblet, presiding over a court of thin, waiflike creatures who cackled quietly as Guy attempted to right himself, feeling his head throb. It was unreasonably warm—unseasonably so—and Guy's clothes were clinging to his skin; despite the humidity, however, Guy found himself shivering.

"What happened," he croaked.

"The short story," the man supplied, "is that you, Guy Carrington, were hit by something called a bus."

"What?" asked Guy.

"A bus," the man repeated. "It's like a car, only bigger."

"No," Guy offered apologetically. "I meant more along the lines of, you know—*how* I got hit by the bus."

"Ah," said the man. "Then you phrased the question poorly."

Guy rubbed the back of his head and looked down, noticing he was wearing the same suit he'd been in at the time. It was rather fuzzy, and fairly far away, but now that he was trying, he could just manage to recall the moment of impact. The bus had slammed into him and he'd felt nothing.

Well—excruciating pain, he amended thoughtfully.

And *then* nothing.

"So, where am I?" Guy asked, looking around the room. "Is this a hallucination?"

"Unfortunately, no. Bad news, kid," the man offered with an air of grim finality. "You're in the Underworld."

Guy laughed and laughed and laughed.

"No," he eventually managed. "That can't be right."

"Well, I guess it's time for the long story, then." The man took a gratuitous drag from his goblet, tossed it over his shoulder, then settled back in his throne.

"First of all, I'm Hades," explained the man who was apparently Hades. "Welcome to my home."

"It's . . . cozy," Guy managed.

"Yes, fine, lies are welcome here," Hades acknowledged, flapping a dismissive hand. "Here's the situation, Mr. Carrington—may I call you Guy?" he asked, and Guy nodded, unsure whether refusal was wise. "Look, Guy, here's the deal. Your string of fate was accidentally severed, and so you have died several years before your time. Now, the thing is," Hades continued, sounding very much like a doctor about to deliver a fatal prognosis, "at the moment you died, you were . . . a fundamentally good person. Sound morals, reliable ethics, generally pleasing temperament."

"Oh, I don't know about all that," said Guy, unable to prevent himself from preening slightly.

"*But*," Hades continued, "had you lived, you would have borne witness to an extremely tragic event—specifically, the death of your twin sister, Greta Carrington," he clarified, gesturing behind him to a picture of Greta that projected across the cavernous ceiling, "which would then have prompted, you know, a full psychological breakdown—"

"Is this a PowerPoint presentation?" Guy cut in.

"Hm?" Hades paused to glance over his shoulder. "Oh, that! Yes." He faced Guy again with a shrug. "I mean . . . this *is* hell."

"Right," said Guy. "Anyway, you were saying—mental breakdown?"

"Right," Hades confirmed. "So, it's a whole thing, but glossing over the complexities, you sort of form this vendetta and then you start hunting people down and killing them, and there's also a bit of a cult aspect involved . . ." He trailed off, frowning. "Candidly, Lachesis didn't really go into detail. Let's just say that this was clearly one of her more creative tyrannical murder plotlines."

"Plotlines?" Guy echoed faintly.

Hades shrugged. "Plotlines, lives—it's really all the same to us," he explained with a gesture to the figures around the room. "Anyway, your string of fate obviously ends with you here in the Underworld, so now that you're dead, your soul is mine."

"Wait," Guy interrupted, blinking slowly. "So you're saying that since I was *supposed* to turn into a—" He paused, glancing expectantly at Hades for confirmation. "A bad guy?"

"Sure," Hades agreed, yawning. "Let's go with that."

"So even though my fate's been changed, I'm still going to hell?" Guy said, suddenly feeling a slap of recognition as he noticed the pair of silvery translucent shackles that had wrapped around his wrists. "Are you saying that I'm—?"

"I'm saying you're in hell," Hades helpfully confirmed, toasting Guy from his seat on high. "Which is unfortunate, I suppose," Hades offered in apparent sympathy, "but rules are rules. I *had* thought Zeus might petition for your soul, which would have been very messy, you know, bureaucratically and logistically and such, but it turns out you're one of the lucky several that Zeus prefers to leave well-fucked." At Guy's tormented silence, his smile twitched slightly. "You do get the joke, right? It's a classic double entendre," Hades clarified, twirling an invisible mustache. When Guy failed to respond appreciatively, Hades looked to his minions around the room, shrugging. "Eh, you guys get it."

"But I'm not even Greek," Guy muttered in disbelief, staring at his hands.

"Yes, well, bummer about that," Hades agreed, not unkindly. "But, things being as they are—"

"So I'm stuck here," Guy summarized aptly, shaking his head. "I don't deserve to be here, but there's nothing you can do, so . . ." He faltered, drawing a hand to his mouth. "That's it? That's what you're telling me?"

"It is! Yes," Hades confirmed, sounding relieved. "You've got it perfectly, which I'm happy to say makes the whole situation far less complicated than I thought." Hades straightened and waved to someone behind Guy, gesturing them forward. "Take Guy down to Tartarus, would you?" he asked, and one of the waifs nodded. "You'll have to take the river, which is frankly murder this time of the day—no pun intended," he offered charitably to Guy. "Sorry. I suppose that's a bit on the nose."

"I didn't actually murder anyone," Guy reminded him, "so to be honest, this all seems a little bit . . . horrifying?"

Hades raised his hands in mock surrender.

"It's the Underworld, Guy," Hades said. "I'm just here to rule it."

* * *

The first day in hell was startlingly similar to one of Guy's worst days on Earth.

"Oh, well, it's not all fire and brimstone, dear," his mother remarked over her usual stuffy Easter brunch. "And sit up straight, would you?"

"I *am* sitting up straight, Mother," Guy remarked tightly, pulling at his constricting collar. "See? Straight."

"Speaking of straight," his mother ventured, violently pouring him another cup of tea. "You *are*, aren't you?" she asked, not for the first time. "So why haven't you found a nice girl to settle down with, Guy?"

"Because I'm twenty-five," Guy muttered, "and nice girls who want to settle down don't exactly come banging down my door. Oh," he added with a rough scoff of laughter, "and I'm *dead*, too."

"Drink that," his mother instructed, pointing to the tea and ignoring him. "Antioxidants. It's good for your digestion."

Finding no better option, Guy raised it to his lips with a roll of his eyes. "Fuck," he swore, the liquid promptly scalding his tongue. "Fucking *fuck*, that's hot—"

"Language!" his mother exclaimed, drawing her hand to her chest in theatrical horror before resuming her most brisk, businesslike tone. "Now hurry up and finish," she urged. "We have things to do, you know."

"Oh, good," said Guy. "Is fire and brimstone next on the list?"

She pursed her lips. "Do you *want* to be burnt to a crisp, Guy? Is that what you *want*? Because it seems to me you could show a little gratitude," his mother chided, leaning over to wipe something off his face. "Come here, you've got a little something—"

"Mother, *stop*," Guy growled, swatting at her hand. "How long is this brunch?"

"Thirty-six hours," she told him, scrubbing mercilessly at his cheek with her napkin. "Now," she continued, sitting back in the chair. "Explain to me again what you plan to do with your future, and after that—" She leaned down, pulling something from her purse. "I want you to teach me how to use something called Elon Musk's Twitter."

"You've got to be kidding me," Guy growled, throwing his hands in the air. "My mother isn't even dead!" he added, half shouting. "You're not actually her, are you?"

"No, I am not," not-his-mother confirmed, swiping through her phone and squinting at it. "Guy," she called to him loudly, "I'm trying to read this *Fifty Shades* book but the print is too small, so do you think you could read it out loud to m—"

"If you're not my mother," Guy interrupted, staring at her, "then who are you?"

His mother blinked, tilting her head slightly. "I'm Timothy Spade," she—*he*—said.

"Why are you here?" Guy demanded. "And more specifically, why are you my mother?"

"Oh, I invented a cure for nicotine addiction," Timothy Spade replied.

"That's amazing," remarked Guy, but his mother (Timothy Spade) held up a hand.

"I invented a cure for nicotine addiction, but I didn't *tell* anyone," Timothy Spade clarified. "I kept it a secret and then I sold it to a tobacco company for an unholy fortune."

"Yikes," Guy said. "Okay, then."

"And I'm here," Timothy Spade continued, "because I hate brunch. And people," he added, "and technology, and socializing, and memorizing lines."

"You have lines?" Guy asked, and Timothy Spade nodded.

"Apparently your mother has quite a speech for how disappointed she is that you've failed to live up to your potential," he said. "I was saving it for the halfway point, you know, for a bit of excitement in between looking at pictures of her cats and discussing the pitfalls of menopause—"

"Right." Guy sighed wearily, and then tilted his head. "Just out of curiosity, what do I look like to you?"

"Sort of a nice guy," Timothy Spade said. "Actually, you're not awful."

"I'm not?" Guy asked, pleased in spite of himself.

"No," Timothy Spade said. "You're really not so bad."

"Huh," Guy remarked, and then frowned. "But you still have to—?"

"Yeah, I have to carry out your punishment or I'll get electric shock therapy later," Timothy Spade said. "Which is another thing I personally dislike."

"Fair enough." Guy sighed again, leaning forward. "So, you said you wanted help with Twitter?"

"Yes," Timothy Spade said, giving him his mother's owlish blink. "And I'm also thinking of getting on the Tinder."

"Oh, Christ," Guy said. "Okay."

*   *   *

When brunch was over, Guy opened his eyes to find himself inside of a very small, very lemony white room.

"Hello," a man offered unenthusiastically. "I assume you know why you're here, Mr. Carrington?"

"No," Guy replied, frowning. He glanced down, realizing he sat at a table, and before him on the table was a box full of receipts alongside a poorly organized checkbook. "What's this?"

"I'm Edward Naughton," droned the man, "and today you're being audited, Mr. Carrington."

"Are you kidding me?" Guy asked, to which Edward Naughton shook his head.

"No," said Edward Naughton. "So, if you could just fill out forms 941, 1066, DE-6—"

"Oh, holy hell," said Guy, holding up a series of hastily scrawled association minutes. "These aren't even my financials!"

"Does that mean you've forgotten your identification, Mr. Carrington?" Edward Naughton asked him. "Because if so, then I'll need you to fill out a couple more forms. And if you'd like to run home and get it, I should warn you that this is actually one of the nightmare rooms, so you *will* feel as though you are jogging in place whilst something chases you—"

"So what's your deal here?" Guy cut in. "What did you do?"

"I claimed my son had cancer and asked my coworkers to donate to save his life," Edward Naughton explained.

Guy grimaced. "I take it your son didn't have cancer?"

"I don't have a son," said Edward Naughton.

"Okay then," Guy said. "And you're doing this because . . . ?"

"Because I was an auditor," supplied Edward Naughton, "and I deeply despise auditing."

"Fair enough," Guy agreed, sorting through the receipts. "Well,"

238   FATES AND CONSEQUENCES

he muttered, trying to make sense of them, "there's nothing that says we can't have a good time while you audit me, is there?"

Edward Naughton pointed to the sign behind him.

> **ABSOLUTELY NO GOOD TIMES.**
> **DO NOT ENJOY THIS AUDIT.**
> **SIGNED, MANAGEMENT**

"Right," Guy sighed. "Well, I'll at least try to—"

Edward Naughton wordlessly pointed to the slightly smaller placard below the first sign.

> **NO EXERTING OF EFFORT TO MAKE THINGS EASIER.**
> **SUFFERING ONLY!**
> **SIGNED, MANAGEMENT**

"Got it," Guy said. "Cool. Excellent. Marvelous."

"I hate that word," Edward Naughton muttered, glancing up.

"Which one?" Guy asked.

"All of them." Edward Naughton squinted at him. "But you're not so bad, I guess," he conceded.

"Thanks," Guy told him, and then held up a receipt. "Does this one count as a business expense?"

Edward Naughton tilted his head, lowering his glasses to glance at it. "Do you own a pornography-related business?"

"No," Guy said, startled, and pulled it back, staring at it. "I swear, a second ago this was a *gas* receipt—"

"Then no," Edward Naughton ruled sullenly, pursing his lips. "Moving on to form 542."

* * *

"How many more of these?" Guy whispered to Andrea Villanova, who he discovered had stolen regularly from an arthritic old man she'd nursed until the time of his death, at which point she'd escaped to Tahiti rather than face his disgruntled heirs. "These paper cuts are really starting to sting."

"You know, the whole making-endless-lemonade-with-paper-cuts is one of the more innocuous tasks," Andrea Villanova reminded him. "It's really more irritation than torture."

Guy hissed quietly in pain as he sliced open a new lemon, the juice of it seeping viciously into a crack in his cuticles. "Right," he said faintly, grimacing. "Sure. It's definitely better than—"

"Better not," Andrea Villanova cautioned, shaking her head warningly. "Hades'll hear you and get inspired."

"He doesn't actually hear *everything*, does he?" Guy asked, flinching again before tossing the lemon aside and forcing himself to pick up a new one.

"No," Andrea Villanova confirmed, "but there are a lot of shitty souls around here, so best to be careful who you say things to. Not me," she clarified, flashing him a somewhat unnerving grin. "I can keep a secret."

He looked up then, wiping at the sweat seeping from his hairline with the back of his wrist (it was, understandably, quite warm there, being what it was) before suddenly realizing they were not alone.

"Who's that?" Guy asked, gesturing to a woman who was stepping off one of the Styx riverboats. She appeared to be coaxing Cerberus, Hades' three-headed dog, which dragged along behind her on a leash.

Andrea Villanova glanced up briefly, looking unsurprised. "It's Persephone," she said. "Hades' wife. She must have just arrived for her six months."

"Six months?" Guy echoed, watching her. Persephone was a willowy kind of tall, slender and poised, her skin freshly tanned and glowing against the backdrop of the lightless cavern. Her dark curls were loosely knotted near the top of her head before spilling down in a messy array of decorative braids, all of it draped beneath a thinly woven crown of gold. Her gown, a green silk that was almost black, trailed down to her bare feet and hovered above the Underworld floor, almost as if she was floating.

"Yeah," Andrea Villanova confirmed, and then paused. "You don't know about Persephone? The whole kidnapped-by-Hades, ate-six-pomegranate-seeds, bound-to-the-Underworld thing?"

Guy supposed he knew the story, but it was just a story. At his vacant head shake, Andrea shrugged and continued, "She has six months on Earth to make things grow, and then spends six months as Queen of Hades."

Queen of Hades, Guy's mind echoed curiously, watching her toss a raw steak into each of Cerberus' drooling mouths.

At the feel of his eyes on her Persephone looked up, meeting his gaze across the river. Her eyes flashed like amber, like molten gold, and narrowed almost instantly upon meeting his.

Guy let out a captive breath. "Right," he murmured to nobody in particular, promptly looking down.

"Don't even think about it," Andrea Villanova warned, bringing her thumb to her lips and wincing as the lemon slipped in her hand. "Fuck, *ouch*—"

"Come on, Cerby," Guy heard Persephone coo, her voice low and musical as she spoke to the dog's three heads, tickling underneath one of his chins. "That's a good boy."

*   *   *

"Yes, yes, I'm naked," Guy muttered, trying awkwardly to cover himself. "I get it. It's hilarious."

"It's a nightmare room, bro," the young lacrosse player offered sympathetically. "We've all been there."

"Well, I don't know what *you're* all getting out of this," Guy snapped, bristling at the unexpected presence of a cool breeze that would otherwise not be unwelcome.

The athlete shrugged. "We're taking a midterm," he explained, holding up the sheet of paper he'd been writing on. It was nearly three feet long.

"Great," Guy muttered, shivering again as he looked around for the source of the unlikely break in ambient heat. "Why the fuck is it so—?"

"Well, isn't *this* interesting," he heard behind him; a low voice he faintly recognized. Guy caught sight of Persephone over his shoulder and promptly spun to face her, still trying unsuccessfully to cover himself. She, however, had her head tilted curiously to one side, a small smile playing across her lips as she tore her gaze from the curve of his backside.

"Not bad," she commented, offering up a quiet laugh as he felt his cheeks flush. "Who are you?"

He licked his lips, trying not to focus on the way her ivory gown clung so invitingly to her hips.

"I'm Guy," he said.

"I see that," she mused, making a small motion with her hands that brought his wrists flying above his head, leaving him exposed. She tilted her head again, smirking slightly as she dragged her gaze across his torso and then lower, salaciously resting between his legs. "I love a thing that's aptly named."

Despite the heat, Guy felt his skin break out in pebbled goose-flesh.

"Tell me, Guy," Persephone continued, taking a step toward him. "Are you the one my husband says isn't supposed to be here?"

Guy forced a swallow, watching her fingers as she brought them first to her lips, brushing one against the swell of them, and then out toward him, drawing one manicured nail down the path of his abdomen.

"Yes," he forced out, sucking in a breath at her touch.

"Hm," she hummed thoughtfully, her crown glinting as she took another step. She was nearly his height, he noted, only having to lift her chin slightly to meet his eye. "Interesting."

"Hey," the lacrosse player interrupted, "are you two going to—?"

"Go work at a soup kitchen," Persephone commanded, snapping her fingers.

In an instant, the entire class had disappeared, taking with them the academic scenery and leaving behind only the Queen of the Underworld—and, of course, Guy.

Who, as it turned out, felt more naked than ever.

"Put your arms down," Persephone instructed. "You look ridiculous."

"But you're the one who—" Guy sighed, lowering his hands at his side. "Fine."

"Better," she said, nodding at him. She made another hand movement and the room around them spun, changing in a breath; she daintily fell back against a bed that had materialized behind her, her honey skin a kiss of gold against a sea of emerald bedding. "Are you coming?"

Guy shook his head slightly, or tried to, feeling very conscious of his tongue as his bare feet settled against the beams of the cool wooden floor. "But you're married."

"Yes," she agreed, her expression unchanging. "But you have a strong jaw, and a queen needs a sturdy throne."

He gaped slightly at that but was unable to prevent himself from watching her long legs as she crossed left over right. She leaned back onto her elbows, glancing up at him expectantly.

"But," he said again, less convincingly this time. "You're . . . married?"

"Yes," she acknowledged. "But on the other hand," she reminded him, sitting up slightly, "you're dressed for the occasion."

At his tortured silence, she sighed in apparent long-suffering exhaustion, rising to her feet and letting her gown slip to the floor before stepping perfunctorily out of it. She was wearing nothing beneath the fabric and he marveled at the way her skin was so vibrantly lit from within; she was so gloriously *golden*, the edges of her curves seeming to glint and flicker, glowing like a candle flame.

"Guy," she said, taking a step toward him. "May I call you Guy?"

"Yes," he mumbled, the word sounding oddly slurred.

"Guy," she repeated approvingly, taking hold of his face and drawing it down to hers, her breath skating across his lips. "This is what it's like to kiss the Queen of the Underworld."

He opened his mouth to argue but hers was already there, colliding with his, a hungry, urgent wanting that tore the breath from his throat and then reached in and snatched it from his lungs as well, a kiss that was as much a blow to his constitution as it was a strikingly elegant promise—a deliberate taste, and nothing more.

Not enough, he thought with panic, realizing his hands had launched forward to grip her waist, his fingers digging into her skin of their own accursed volition.

"Now," Persephone whispered, her lips still touching his. "Would you like to see Elysium?"

*　*　*

"So," Hades said, materializing with a quiet pop beside him. "How goes it?"

Guy jumped, letting out a strangled yell as the doctor tightened his grip.

"Ah, prostate exam," Hades remarked knowingly, letting out an oddly delicate laugh. "Fun."

"It's going well," Guy said through gritted teeth. "Loving it."

"Not even remotely hellish?" Hades asked, frowning. "Pity. I suppose we could always—"

"No, no, it's fine, it's bad," Guy forced out, trying not to move as the doctor continued his exam. "I'm suffering, I promise."

"Well, that's a relief." Hades took a seat in one of the patient chairs and propped his feet up, offering Guy an absent-minded smile. "Hope you don't mind, but I thought I'd check in. I do that on occasion," he added. "At least, I do with the ones who aren't totally opposed."

"Are there a lot of those?" Guy asked, forcing his eyes shut.

"Honestly? No," Hades admitted. "I'm not very popular."

"You're kidding," Guy said dryly. "You sentence them to their eternal damnation and they don't even have the decency to adore you?"

"I know," Hades agreed. "I'm baffled, too. Hey," he added, as though a thought had just occurred to him. "You haven't seen my wife around, have you? Persephone?" he clarified, gesturing near his head. "About this tall? Brown hair? Wears a small golden crown?"

Guy bit back a breath of panic, forcing a smile. "I'm familiar with the Queen," he began unsteadily, "but no," he lied. "I haven't seen her."

"She normally doesn't do a lot of wandering," Hades murmured, half to himself. "Likes her gardens, mostly. But she seemed awfully interested in you." He fixed a long glance on Guy, who was still pointedly trying to look elsewhere as the doctor continued his exam. "I think she's quite taken with your backstory."

"My errant fate, you mean?" Guy asked, unable to prevent a stirring of bitterness. "Yes, I suppose it would be interesting."

"Not really sure why," Hades confessed with a shrug. "But, in any case, do let me know if you see her." He rose to his feet, offering Guy and the doctor respectively curt nods. "Until next time," he said, before disappearing with another quiet pop.

Guy let out a sigh of relief, suddenly feeling a cool breeze from somewhere near the door and fighting a smile when he recognized her presence.

"He's so nosy," Persephone sniffed, snapping her fingers to make the doctor disappear.

In an instant Guy was in her bedroom again, his elbows braced now against her emerald duvet rather than the exam table where he had been. "Now," she murmured, tracing a line down his spine with the tip of her finger. "You weren't having any prostate fun without me, were you?"

"Prostate *fun*?" Guy echoed, blanching.

Persephone laughed, reaching delicately between his thighs.

"We'll get there," she assured him, and from the reflection of her vanity he watched her flash his back a wicked smile.

*   *   *

"Tell me," he murmured to her, mapping patterns on her bare shoulder as he drew her loose curls away from her skin. "How does one come to live in the Underworld? I suppose it was an abduction," he recalled hazily, frowning, "but still, I don't see you as the 'abducted' type."

"It wasn't an abduction," she corrected him, suddenly irritable. "I chose it."

Guy paused his meandering fingers, tilting his head to meet her eye. "You chose it?"

She looked up at him, her heavy-lidded gaze narrowing slightly. "Do you know what it's like, being created for the sole purpose of nurturing things?" she asked, her expression darkening. "Vegetation, harvest, fertility—it was a life of being made to give with nothing in return." She closed her eyes, coiling her fingers in the soft silk of her sheets. "The world will drain you, Guy, if you let it."

He laid himself back against the pillows and drew her into him, settling her cheek against his chest. "The pomegranate seeds," he remarked slowly. "Is it true you were tricked into eating them?"

She scoffed. "Do you really think anyone doesn't know what they're doing when they eat food from the Underworld—much less *me*?"

Guy brushed his lips against her forehead. "Are you very brave," he asked slowly, "or just very desperate?"

She measured him with her amber gaze and opted not to answer the question.

"You're quite popular with the other souls," she commented tangentially.

He shrugged. "I try to be friendly. We're in the same boat," he explained. "Or river, as it were."

She nodded, her fingers tracing a line down his inner thigh.

"Pity there wasn't a man like you around when Hades offered me the pomegranate," she lamented, drawing herself up. She rested her knees on either side of his hips, dug her nails into his chest, and leaned forward to whisper in his ear, "I'd have swallowed the fucking thing whole."

*   *   *

"Hades is such a dick," Timothy Spade remarked on Monday as Guy played the role of his wife, the two of them shopping for an evening gown that both knew neither could afford. "It's not like there's anyone making him enforce these punishments. He just *likes* them."

"And considering there's only one of him and zillions of us," Edward Naughton said on Tuesday as he and Guy wheezed through a marathon, "it's a wonder nobody's tried to revolt."

"You'd think," Andrea Villanova mentioned offhandedly on Wednesday as she and Guy planned a deeply Pinterest-infused destination bachelorette for her older sister, "that having someone else in charge would really make a difference."

"Like who?" Guy asked innocently, and Persephone's voice laughed in his ear.

Like you, she murmured to him, as the image of him spending eternity in her bed (her legs wrapped around his waist, the shackles gone from his wrists, their need for secrecy abandoned) flashed before his eyes and then trickled down to his lips, curving them into a peaceful, beatific smile.

"What are you thinking about?" Persephone asked breathlessly, collapsing with him atop the sheets. "I know I'm good, but you look unusually euphoric."

He took her hand, brushing a kiss against her knuckles. "What do you think about a mutiny?" he asked her, biting lightly on one of her fingers.

She watched him for a long moment, seeming not to move or even breathe. "I think," she said slowly, "I'd be interested in seeing that happen."

He smiled again, rolling over to settle his hips against hers. "We could be free," he whispered as she traced her finger along his lips.

"Nobody's free, Guy," she told him. "But damn if I don't want to see you try."

He felt the corners of his mouth twitch, satisfaction nudging at his fingers.

"We could rule ourselves," he said to Timothy Spade the following Monday. (It came quickly, as Fridays and weekends did not exist.) "There's only one of him, and all of us."

"We'd only need to take his soul," he murmured to Edward Naughton on Tuesday, his voice hushed but tight with promise. "To sever it, and take control."

"Are you with me?" he asked Andrea Villanova, whispering it on Wednesday, quiet words for sharpened intentions. "Are you in?"

"Yes," they said, and by Thursday, Guy hid a smile of triumph in the side of Persephone's neck.

*   *   *

"So," Hades said, frowning down at Guy in the same courtroom where it had all begun. "Revolt, huh?"

Guy swallowed uncomfortably as Persephone stepped into view, draped in a gold gown and incandescent with jewels that sparkled in the dim light as she took a seat beside her husband. Hades leaned over, offering her his cheek, and she brushed her lips against it, a cool breeze filling the chamber as she took her throne.

"How were you planning to do it?" Hades said, leaning forward with apparent enthusiasm. "Were you going to kill me? Overpower me by force?"

"Something like that," Guy muttered, glancing again at Persephone. She arched a brow, meeting his gaze with a stunningly ambivalent smirk.

"You know, when it came to my attention that you were organizing the other souls to unseat me, I have to say, I was a bit annoyed," Hades commented, twining his fingers with Persephone's. "Luckily for you, I respect it—a little mutiny here and there. Keeps things fresh, keeps things interesting." He kissed Persephone's hand, his eyes still on Guy's. "It's nice to be reminded why they put me on this throne."

Persephone said nothing, and Guy felt sick.

"You take advantage of the souls in your possession," he said to Hades, gritting his teeth and sticking to a now-practiced refrain. "I never deserved to be here, and yet—"

Hades cut him off with a laugh, the sound of it filling the room to slice through the air between them. "You really think you don't deserve to be here, Guy? *Still?* Let's see," Hades mused, looking positively delighted to run the numbers. "You were fated to be a murderer, weren't you? To give in to your inclinations toward tyranny on Earth. And what have you done here?"

Guy said nothing, feeling slightly sickened at the thought.

"You gathered an army of deplorable souls," Hades answered for him, "*immoral* souls, and militarized them to overthrow me. And you were willing to take my life to do it, weren't you?"

To Guy's lack of answer, Hades sat conclusively back and then shot forward again. "*Plus* you fucked my wife, Guy," he pointed out with a shake of his head, "and I wasn't even invited."

Guy grimaced, glancing at Persephone. Wordlessly, she met his gaze with her amber eyes.

"She turned you in, if that's what you're wondering," Hades informed him. "It seems you misjudged her, just as you misjudged yourself. Because *clearly*," he added with a gleeful gesture around the room, "your fate could not have been avoided. You've become in the Underworld what you were always meant to be on Earth," he deduced with a laugh, "and isn't it funny, then, that the consequences are so fitting? Hilarious." With that, Hades' laughter convulsed into pin-drop silence. "You got precisely what you deserved, Guy Carrington."

Guy stiffened, forcing his eyes shut. It was a very *I told you so* moment, which was, if anything, the most hellish experience of all.

"I'm sorry," Guy offered lamely.

Hades waved a hand. "Don't be," he returned. "The Underworld is no easy place, Guy, but I think you'll find it has a different flavor when you know it's earned. It's just something a bit more—" He trailed off, smiling for a moment at his wife. "Savory."

With that, Hades rose, gesturing for Persephone to follow. She took her husband's arm, not looking back.

And Guy understood in a way he hadn't before that this, indeed, was hell.

* * *

"You haven't eaten, have you?" the doctor asked. "For a full day?"

"No," Guy confirmed miserably, lying back on the patient table. "Just clear liquids."

"Well, good," the doctor said. "I'd hate to have to pump your stomach."

"Sure," Guy agreed, closing his eyes.

"So, it's a relatively simple procedure," the doctor explained. "But I will probably make some crucial errors during that time, which will undoubtedly cause undue pain and distress, so afterward you'll likely be meeting with your lawyer to discuss the efficacy of a lawsuit while also trying to submit a claim to your health insurance provider. I'd estimate the whole thing taking eighteen months at minimum."

"Naturally," Guy sighed. "Ready?"

"Quite," the doctor continued. "So I'll just—"

"That's enough of that," Persephone interrupted, breezing in. She snapped her fingers, the atmosphere around Guy abruptly changing as she nudged him over to perch herself lightly beside his ribs. "What were you having done?" she asked, tapping his nose.

Guy opened his eyes to find the doctor gone, and to find himself reclining on her emerald sheets again.

He sat up slowly, loath to meet her eye. "Colonoscopy," he muttered, and she smiled.

"Poor thing," she tutted softly, reaching out to touch his bare chest. "Have you missed me?"

He swallowed, realizing now how long it had been; the six months of her absence must have finally lapsed. "I," he began hoarsely, and paused, clearing his throat. He wouldn't be able to lie to her, not successfully, but still he felt pridefully unwilling to confess the whole truth. "I thought that—"

"I missed *you*," she informed him, sliding closer until their hips touched. She pressed her lips to his collarbone, murmuring into his skin. "Candidly, my mother's nearly as bad as yours."

He swallowed a laugh, refusing to be lured by her charm.

"Persephone," he grunted, as sternly as he could manage, "you turned me in to Hades, remember?"

"Yes," she agreed, not looking remotely sorry. "I wanted to see what would happen."

He frowned. "Then why—"

"I told you," she reminded him. "Nobody's free, and especially not from suffering. Besides," she added, "I'm married. There's sort of an obligation to disclose when one's lover is intent on violent over-throw."

"Ah." The feeling in his gut, it was either shame or disappointment.

"You love him more than me," he murmured, but Persephone shook her head.

"No," she corrected. "This has nothing to do with you. It was a long game before you, and it will be for an eternity after—but *I*," she added airily, rising to her feet, "don't intend to lose."

Guy turned to face her, sliding himself to the edge of her bed. "You're sure about this?" he asked, watching her gaze rake hungrily across his chest.

Her eyes glowed amber, soaking in the view of him, as she gave him her wicked smile.

"This is the Underworld, darling," she whispered, slipping her dress from her shoulders and letting it fall to the floor. "If I wanted morals, I'd go somewhere else."

Sous Vide

The air in New England in autumn is crisp, unconscionable. You can be anything here. By winter it will have fallen away.

*   *   *

It was Gabrielle, a year above her in the program, who first told Chrissy about the job. "Job" already being kind of a misleading word for it, but it paid money, which was the crux of the thing. Gabrielle was graduating and zeroed in on Chrissy as a candidate for her replacement, which was probably recruitment in a more technical sense but didn't feel like it at the time.

Actually, at the time it couldn't have been kinder. The rent on the apartment where Chrissy had been luxuriating in squalor for the last three years was going up—hard times, said the poor innocent landlord, who hadn't repaired the leaky plumbing or the malfunctioning heater due to the aforementioned times. Noah, meanwhile, wouldn't budge on the matter of the future. The separation remained ambiguous and the timing was bad—unexpectedly, Marion's diagnosis had taken a turn for the terminal and their daughter wasn't currently speaking to him, having spotted the Postmates notification on Noah's iPad screen the last time he was charitable enough to buy Chrissy dinner. Chrissy had been subsisting largely on peanut butter and tuna sandwiches since then, which weren't as bad as they sounded.

The problem was that Chrissy's workload did not allow for a second job, or rather, there was a tipping point, where the income from a second job had to exceed the value of dissertation time lost in order to justify it. Tepid math. Gabrielle seemed to know all of this with a glance when she confessed to Chrissy that this job had been her secret to not starving to death—indeed, her secret to being hired out at Oberlin on a tenure track, in a place where the word "livable" might actually mean something.

Gabrielle asked Chrissy three critical questions:

Can you cook? (Yes, Chrissy lied.)

Do you consider yourself, like, an emotional person? (No, Chrissy said, which was true. An emotional person wouldn't have survived the last two years with Noah. Granted, neither would a saner person.)

And finally, are you willing to sign an NDA?

Well, I'm looking to avoid sex work, Chrissy said. To which Gabrielle gave kind of a dark laugh and said yeah, that's exactly how they get us. Chrissy chose not to press her on that.

By the way, what kind of name is Chrissy, Gabrielle asked. She didn't say it from a place of casual curiosity. It was more like a question that was coming from inside the conversation, which was itself happening outside the beautiful stonework of the library. The leaves had just started to turn and the air had a wistfulness, a smell of false nostalgia, because Chrissy had never technically known a happy childhood here, despite being able to conjure up an imaginary one in her head.

Oh uhhhhhh, said Chrissy. It's actually Christabelle.

Oh, said Gabrielle.

Yeah, Chrissy said. As you can see there are no dignified diminutives.

Filipino? Gabrielle guessed.

Correct, confirmed Chrissy, and then conversationally she guessed, Jamaican?

Yeah. Just had to double-check because they prefer a more varied palette.

Who? said Chrissy.

Gabrielle reached into her purse for her phone and AirDropped Chrissy a contact.

Tell Sue I sent you, Gabrielle instructed. And if you can make stuff like, I don't know, ginisang ampalaya or dinuguan, that would be ideal, she added, naming sautéed bitter melon and a stew made with pork blood, respectively.

Wait, so you already knew I was Filipino, Chrissy registered aloud, because those were some pretty deep cuts as far as Filipino cuisine.

Bye, said Gabrielle, reasonably. Because Chrissy so obviously needed the money, and there was no point to continuing the conversation, so it might as well just end.

* * *

For Christmas the previous year, Noah had bought Chrissy the Rolls-Royce of miniature vibrators. It fit into her vagina as well as affixing to her clitoris and it could be controlled remotely, with an actual remote control. The first time Chrissy used it she didn't even think "orgasm" was the right word for it—it was more like a seizure. Her sheets were almost instantaneously soaked.

Noah pressed . . . start? Play? On? And Chrissy rested her head against her pillow, closing her eyes.

Just so you know, I'm going to be busy on Friday nights from now on, she told him over the buzz of the vibrator.

Oh, did you take my advice? (The advice being: Friday night is a great time to work on your dissertation in the library away from the undergraduates, who are full of youthful energy and don't constantly think about death. Instead, the youngs are out living their lives, fucking their unmarried lovers, believing uncomplicatedly that life will reward them for being the chosen ones to seek knowledge here. Lightly paraphrased.)

Chrissy bit her tongue before mentioning that she had gotten a job. Noah didn't like the idea of her working. It sloughed away the sheen of her appeal. (Her libertine youth, her manic freedom, the restless intellect that had driven her to art and poetry, which was now driving her to poverty and madness, just as it had done to all the artists and poets before.) Suddenly, the tiny motor plugging arduously away at her erogenous zones felt like the bright white lights of martial interrogation. Noah kissed the bottom of her foot, switching up the pattern of suction from the remote control. He could have bought her groceries. He could have paid her rent. He could have been more complimentary during her dissertation review, but then of course it would have come off like favoritism, and everyone would have known. She came like a sneeze which meant that now it was his turn. Fair was fair.

She slid off the mattress and onto her knees, viewing her life as an art piece. Later Noah would read poetry to her, his voice low and husky in her ear. She'd say something clever and he'd laugh. She'd covet it like something she'd won. She had always been his most gifted student. Outside the tiny window of her dilapidated studio (she'd have saved on rent if she could have a roommate but that would have meant far less of Noah) the breeze rustled the golden leaves, the russet tendrils. Noah slid a finger under her chin. Pretty eyes, he said. She widened them as far as they'd go. Before him life had been so colorless.

*   *   *

I forgot to tell you, Gabrielle texted her. Do not talk to them.

Talk to who??????? Chrissy said. She had gotten the text while she was driving and now sat alone in her car, headlights off, while she frowned at the screen. The address Gabrielle's former employer Sue had given her was about an hour away from campus, not quite the woods, but on the edge of them, beside a creek. Chrissy had considered crying sketch and not going, but the farm had a Yelp page. It wasn't exactly off the grid. It looked clean and quaint, like a place that might host a pumpkin patch, a petting zoo. There was a lovely detached farmhouse, steps away from the converted barn where Chrissy had been told to check in. The lights were on, friendly and waiting.

Gabrielle texted back: I mean, Sue will tell you the same thing, I just want to make sure you get that it's serious. There was this guy before me who got too attached and I guess it was really messy. Just think of it like social work okay, secure your own mask before assisting others. And then just don't assist others.

What the fuck does that even mean, typed Chrissy.

Gabrielle didn't respond.

*   *   *

The inside of the barn had an industrial kitchen stocked with fresh ingredients and an overflowing pantry, not unlike the kind of kitchens used for television cooking shows. The job, as the owner Sue explained to Chrissy, was to prepare a meal, ideally a complex one. Mac 'n' cheese is not going to cut it, she said. In response, Chrissy made a joke about tuna and peanut butter and Sue looked physically ill. Just cook the food, plate it out there—she pointed into the garden outside the barn, bordered by the creek, where there was a long picnic table, the kind Chrissy imagined seeing in all the hardware store commercials about preparing for summer barbecues—and then leave, Sue instructed. Don't hang around after.

Chrissy couldn't imagine wanting to hang around after cooking an elaborate meal at . . . she checked her watch. 6:30 P.M. Things were getting dark earlier and earlier. Sunset splashed across the backside of the farmhouse and Chrissy thought of Noah, last night's shared bottle of cabernet.

Some rules! Sue exclaimed cheerfully. Don't have sex or masturbate in or around the kitchen. If you cut or burn yourself, attend to it immediately. Are you on any SSRIs?

No, said Chrissy. Wait, should I be?

Make sure you take all necessary medications, Sue said without answering the question. And don't talk to the guests.

Is this, like . . . a soup kitchen? Or something? said Chrissy.

There'll be an envelope waiting for you there when you're done, Sue said, pointing to a ubiquitous plastic invoice tray. Try to clean up after yourself. I don't allow the cleaning staff in here.

Can I just say, it feels like you're being unnecessarily cryptic, Chrissy pointed out. I mean, you obviously know I need the money. Nobody in their right mind would do any of this if they didn't *really need* money. It really seems like you could do anything to me, so could I have some, like, assurance? I mean, you could kill me, assault me, kidnap me, gut me for sport—

You're more use to me alive and silent than you are dead and messy, Sue said. She reminded Chrissy of a matronly judge on an English baking show. She smelled faintly of vanilla and cinnamon and did not seem actively dangerous. Just . . . unreasonably withholding.

Also, Sue added, there's a paper trail. You signed a contract.

Oh! said Chrissy. It was a good point. She decided that when Sue was gone she would furtively email a copy to Noah. Then she faltered, realizing that Noah would probably not launch a full-scale investigation into her disappearance if she did, in fact, disappear, because who would be a more prime suspect than Noah? Chrissy decided that if she survived the night, she would print the contract out and put it somewhere the police would look for her. Assuming they even did. The thought exercise was going downhill fast.

Whatever this is, rein it in, Sue observed, frowning at Chrissy's expression. Then she said bon appétit! and turned away, exiting the barn for the farmhouse.

*   *   *

Here is what nobody told Chrissy before that night:

You can't kill a demon because demons aren't alive in a way that makes sense. You can't kill a demon any more than you can kill a black hole or drive a wooden stake into the concept of monogamy. What you *can* do with a demon is contain the damage, or rather, slake its appetite. A demon is more like a personification or a vessel, a sentience of hunger. So, what do you do with the hungry? Ignore them, if you're the government. But if you care about keeping demons off your lawn in a meaningful, permanent way, then you can just feed them instead.

But you can see why nobody told Chrissy this, right? I mean, who would believe it. Who would listen to that and be like okay, cool. Makes sense. Which is also why nobody told Chrissy that demons can talk, and they can learn and evolve, and if you give them an opening, what they have to say can really make a lot of sense.

Of course, Chrissy was supposed to follow instructions and not to talk to the guests, but obviously she didn't. Which is fair. Nobody ever does.

*   *   *

Chrissy made an easy adobo recipe she'd gotten off an everyday-cooking blog. Despite Gabrielle's advice, Chrissy didn't feel ready for dinuguan, which she had been told as a child was made of chocolate. Even when she'd believed it to be chocolate, she still hadn't liked it, and then when she finally learned it was pork blood, that was the first and last time anything in her adult life had ever made sense. The other stuff—get good grades and you'll be fine, work hard and you'll be able to buy a house, be special and someday someone will love you—only felt increasingly irrational. See! Telling people stuff can be a real mixed bag.

She plated it as nicely as she could—she didn't cook much, being unable to afford the kinds of ingredients Sue's kitchen was packed with—and went back into the kitchen, spotting the envelope that was waiting for her just outside the doorway, precisely as Sue had said. It was almost eight o'clock. Chrissy left the kitchen door open, welcoming in the cool autumn air.

Excuse me, came a voice from the garden. Chef?

Chrissy froze.

This is really more tart than savory, the voice continued. Not to be particular. It's just. It could use some more stewing. Anyway, you're really early. Dinner isn't served until midnight or later, usually.

I know you're not supposed to talk to me, the voice went on. But this is pretty dire. There is a lot of vinegar in here. You're supposed to cook it down? You know, reduce it? The sauce is liquidy too. Did you taste it?

Chrissy hadn't tasted it, no. She remained very still, wondering if the voice would go away.

I'm not supposed to go into the house, the voice continued. But, uh. I can. Just so you know. Because. I can tell you're just right there. I can literally feel you breathing.

Chrissy's heart jackrabbited around in her chest and she forced out an exhale and thought maybe it will make a good story. She pivoted around and walked to the doorway, where someone stood just outside.

Opposite her on the threshold was a teenage boy. His hair was an untidy crop of auburn, a *Mad* magazine–style side swoop. Freckles dappled the bridge of his nose. He was giving her a look she didn't totally know how to read, as it was the expression of a much older man. Noah sometimes looked like that when he was frowning down at his notes and trying to read them.

This didn't simmer for long enough, the boy said, holding a portion of her adobo out for her.

Chrissy had put out the pasta bowls, the big ones that were nearly as shallow as plates. She accepted it warily, saying nothing.

Taste it, he said. You'll see what I mean right away. It just doesn't taste like Lola's.

Chrissy's heart jumped at the mention of her grandmother. How did he—?

Just take a bite, he said impatiently. I'm hungry. I want to eat.

You could just eat it, then, said Chrissy irritably, without thinking. Beggars can't be choosers.

The boy's expression shifted. Suddenly he looked . . . older. In his early forties if you looked closely enough, early thirties if you didn't. He wore a pair of half-rimmed black enamel glasses. He looked like if he opened his mouth, something about Wordsworth might come out of it.

I am not a beggar, the boy-who-was-not-a-boy said in Noah's voice. Now. Be a good girl and take a bite.

Oh, fuck!!!!!!! shouted the inside of Chrissy's head.

She quickly took a bite of the adobo and fought not to openly grimace. The tang of the vinegar was indeed much sharper than it ought to have been. It wasn't *not* cooked, it just wasn't right.

Next time, said not-Noah matter-of-factly, pushing his glasses up his nose, you have to let things stew. You have to really let them breathe.

OhmyfuckinggodfuckingChristholyfuck, said the inside of Chrissy's head.

Okay, she managed to croak.

It'll stave the others off for a bit, said not-Noah. But these things can have consequences. One mistake is forgivable, but a persisting carelessness . . .

A leaf drifted down to the ground below his feet. Chrissy smelled fresh earth, a waft of smoke from a distant chimney. When she looked up again, he wasn't Noah anymore. He was the teenage boy with slightly longer hair, the beginnings of stubble.

See you next week, he said cheerfully, toasting her with a fork before turning away.

* * *

Hey slut, came a message from an unknown number. Slut

Whore, came another message the following day. Homewrecker

Slut. Bitch. Cunt.

It continued at random intervals throughout the week but Chrissy was busy. She had a dissertation to finish. She was so tired her eyes stung constantly but she had no time for a new glasses prescription even if she could afford one. She had a numb spot next to her spine from sitting hunched over her computer all the time. That wasn't getting resolved anytime soon. She thought of the teenage boy who hadn't liked her adobo. Fair enough, it hadn't been good.

The only good thing going for her aside from Noah responding to all of her texts that week was that with the amount of cash she'd made from last week's job, Chrissy had enough in her account now to buy a sliver of parmesan and the canned tuna that was packed in olive oil instead of water. So that week, with the tuna, she had made a one-pot pasta that had stretched nearly four days. She ate it and wrote a few unrhyming lines about things that lurked in the restless autumn night and then paid her rent. It was almost like being alive again.

On Friday, Sue wasn't there waiting for her this time, but she left Chrissy a note saying that the guests had complained and thus Chrissy would have to be more thorough next time or she would be fired. Luckily, Chrissy had already been inspired by her week's brief reprieve from peanut butter. She made kare-kare, a peanut butter oxtail stew. She let it breathe for an hour longer than it strictly needed to, waiting until the crisp air around the kitchen door felt golden-honey warm.

This time, when she brought it out, she nearly stumbled. A teenage girl sat there staring at her with Noah's eyes.

Congratulations, said the girl. This week's dinner looks much better.

Thank you, Chrissy said.

And then she bolted.

*   *   *

Slut
  Whore
  Slut
  Slut

Jezebel!!!

Who's texting you? asked Noah when Chrissy reached over him for her buzzing phone. They've certainly got a lot to say.

Indeed they do, said Chrissy, placing the phone facedown on the nightstand and pulling her shirt over her head. She turned to Noah casually, so casual. Hey, by the way, I've been meaning to ask you—how is everything at home?

Oh, I think Jenna's doing better, he said. She actually smiled the other day during dinner so I think we're on track to being normal.

Yeah?

Yeah, I think so.

She said nothing and Noah kissed the top of her head. Soon, he promised. They had stopped putting into words what exactly would come soon. Chrissy wasn't sure they'd ever technically specified.

Do you think we need to . . . hit the brakes? said Chrissy, chewing the loose skin around her thumb. I mean, I'm not sure I was ever cut out to be a thirteen-year-old's stepmother.

She'll love you, Noah said. She's just going through something right now. You know how teenage girls can be.

SLUT!!! YOU FUCKING SLUT!!! YOU'RE KILLING MY MOM!!!

Oh, sure, said Chrissy. Yeah. That's true.

*   *   *

See, now this is delicious, said someone who looked exactly like Chrissy's father. This mix of tartness and savoriness is really cleansing. Brava.

Chrissy sat in silence while the thing that wasn't her father happily slurped its sinigang and chattered away at her, brandishing the spoon while it spoke.

You know, I've been thinking about your predicament, said the thing that wasn't her dad. To some degree this romance of yours was always going to be a fraught situation. Even under the best of circumstances you probably wouldn't have been accepted into the family. But you knew that, right, so what was the point? Are you *hoping* to be rejected? Like, is that the plan? If it's some kind of self-sabotage I can appreciate that, believe me. It's gorgeous, really well done.

It slurped another bite.

Chrissy was aware that she wasn't supposed to speak. She didn't even have to be there.

It was just . . . really *nice,* though. To sit there amid the rustle of the wind, the creek soothing her mind into a trance. To have gotten the recipe right. To be praised for it. She had made a lot of mistakes while making it. Deboning a fish was really hard, actually. Plus the only person who rewarded her for anything these days was Noah. She was no longer in a stage of academia where things felt like wins anymore. Now it was all just red pen and form rejections.

She loosened the scarf from around her neck. The creek trickled merrily beside the crackling fire that someone who wasn't Sue and certainly wasn't Chrissy had lit. The air smelled like woods and tamarind.

I don't see everything about you, just so you know, her not-dad explained. I know the loud stuff. Pain and sadness and anger and whatnot, that's easy to sense. But I don't really understand it.

You're young, aren't you, Chrissy said before she could stop herself.

Not-her-dad looked up, delight in his eyes at the sound of her voice, the casting off of protocol.

Yes, he said, I'm young. Is it that obvious?

Well—

Chrissy cleared her throat.

It's just. When you get older you finally understand why people do things. Or rather, you understand that there *is* no understanding why people do things. So eventually it just becomes less interesting, the why.

I hope nothing ever becomes less interesting, said the thing that wasn't her father, shaking his head. Then he looked more closely at her. Aren't *you* young?

Not vigilante-teenage-girl young, said Chrissy. When I was thirteen I thought I understood heartbreak. I thought I knew everything.

She paused.

When I was thirteen I *did* know everything, she realized. Jenna already knows everything. She knows more than I do. And yet I bet when she's my age she'll do something just as dumb.

Omg who's Jenna? said not-her-dad, leaning forward.

Chrissy realized she'd broken basically the one rule she'd been told not to break. Well, aside from masturbating in the kitchen, which had seemed to be about sanitation at first but then again maybe not.

I gotta go, she said, and ran.

*   *   *

Slut!!!!!!!!

Look, unless you can tell me where to find taro leaves, I think we can agree the conversation has gone stale, Chrissy typed back.

Fucking whore!!!!! You're a fucking skank!!

You know, your dad isn't that great either, Chrissy thought about typing, only if that was true then what was she doing? So she just kept looking for taro leaves instead, a bluster of wind crackling like static along the blistered window frame of her apartment.

*   *   *

Ta-dah! said Chrissy's first boyfriend Justin. I had to dig around for this form. But it's cute, right?

Not-Justin preened a little, tousling his frosted tips and adjusting his puka-shell necklace.

It's so *decorative,* said not-Justin. Ornamental, you know what I mean? Plumage, that's the word.

The thing is, said Chrissy, when the whole thing started, I thought Noah was *already* divorced.

The laing went down smooth and aromatic. Outside an owl hooted, the creek slurped. It was nearly two in the morning and the whole place smelled like coconut and fresh earth.

The first time was so exciting. It was the best first kiss of my life. And the sex—*god.* Anyway, it just felt right, it felt addicting. It was like chasing a high, I guess. I didn't want it to stop. I still don't want it to stop. The way he makes me feel—

Is this lemongrass? asked not-Justin. I mean the depth of flavors here is just. Honestly. Chef's kiss.

I just can't stop, Chrissy repeated. Then she rethought it. I don't want to stop.

Well, of course not, said not-Justin through a mouth full of laing. If you stop then you'll have to call it what it is.

What is it? said Chrissy.

Nice try, said not-Justin, tearing off part of the taro leaf. Come on. I'm not falling for that.

*　*　*

Chrissy could afford to make herself actual meals these days. She let a short rib simmer all day while she was lecturing and when she came home it fell off the bone, tender as a kiss. She paired it with a garnet-colored wine that she poured into the single crystal glass she'd bought at an estate sale. She'd driven by the sale on her way to the farm, traversing bucolic fields and glassy riverscapes and vermilion trees until the display of vintage glassware waved at her from her periphery like the glimmer of a promising future.

She could afford a little treat here and there, a trinket to make her feel like a person. Still no vision insurance. But she could afford to let things catch her eye.

*　*　*

Slut!!!!!!!

The problem is I used to love all of this, Chrissy said. But maybe you're not supposed to sink your whole life and everything you are and everything you want into just one love. How can anything live up to that? Even literature? Even poetry? How can art ever love you back?

Have you actually made any? asked a polished white woman in a silk headscarf whom Chrissy had never met.

What, art? I'm busy writing essays that aren't good enough and working on a dissertation that's trying to kill me and not replying to a teenage girl who won't stop texting me about my moral failings. And making you dinner, Chrissy added, before looking around. Are there more of you?

Oh, loads, said not-Noah's-wife. But everyone kinda gets it that this is my time.

Chrissy said: The absolute fuckery of it is that I don't get how people can say that money doesn't buy happiness. Because my whole life revolves around money. It has to! That's the system I'm plugged into! You know? You can't be happy *without* money, because in order to be happy you need choices, you need freedom, you need the ability to think and dream and wonder and you just simply cannot do that if you spend all day and night thinking about how you'll pay your next bill. It's unfair that people don't do more to help each other. People shouldn't let other people go hungry. It's so cruel.

Chrissy realized her eyes were watering.

You know why Gabby chose you, said not-Noah's-wife. Right?

Um. Chrissy sniffled. I mean, she knew I needed the money.

Right. And other reasons. This place is so claustrophobic, all these puritanical ideas about virtuous starvation. The food's no good. Have you heard of Miss Manners? Awful. That's why Sue rents out the kitchen. She tried to cook for us for years but we were all just fucking starved. If not for you she'd be dead probably.

Was there a point? said Chrissy.

Sure, if you want. Not-Noah's-wife shrugged, shoveling another heaping spoonful into her mouth. Girl, she said, this is really fucking good.

* * *

Have you been talking to the guests? said Sue the following week.

No, why? said Chrissy.

Sue's eyes narrowed.

(SLUT!!!!!!!!!!!!!!!)

* * *

The air was starting to bite with cold by then. The sky had been gray all week, the ground littered with dimming shades of umber. The creek burbled with tension, like a child faced with the marshmallow test.

I feel like I never see you, Noah said from between Chrissy's thighs. I miss you.

It was addictive, being desired, being missed. Chrissy bought lace underwear. She bought a new journal and new pens. She wrote down words like "ravage" and "sanguine."

The funny thing is I don't actually make these foods normally, Chrissy typed into her phone. Like, they're part of "my culture," whatever that means, but when I was a kid I mostly ate Lunchables and scrambled eggs. I really only started getting better because if you half-ass any of it, you won't get an A in the Care and Keeping of Eldritch Horrors, and then how will you ever know how much you're worth?

You're a fucking slut, came the instant reply.

Chrissy sat up straighter, folding her legs on her duvet, crisscross-applesauce as she typed.

Listen to me. This is important. Someday a man will tell you he's never felt this way in his entire life, that it's different this time, that what you have is real and everything that came before you wasn't love, it was just treading water. He will make you feel special and for a minute your youth will seem incidental, like a forgettable side effect of fate, when actually the only reason you feel special at all is because you're so goddamn young.

But you can have an orgasm on your own, okay? I'm serious. You do not need him. If he says you have talent it doesn't matter. The talent is yours. It's intrinsic to you. It can't be bestowed upon you by him and it never will be.

Theoretically it could be a woman who does this to you, Chrissy typed on second thought. But statistically it is much more likely to be a man.

Her phone pinged back with an incoming text.

Oh my god you fucking slut!!!!

*   *   *

This, said a man Chrissy didn't recognize. Now *this* is food.

It's called dinuguan, said Chrissy. I never liked it as a kid but this one does have a real richness, doesn't it?

It really does, said the man, moaning a little as he ate. My god. It's . . . it's so . . .

Fortifying? said Chrissy.

Yes, very.

Yeah, I thought so. It seemed right. Who are you supposed to be right now, by the way?

Oh, if you don't know then I don't know either. Maybe I'm me? Ha ha just kidding, I don't have a body.

Well, could you be someone I haven't met yet?

Oh, sure! Easily.

Is it someone who will hurt me? All the other people you've been . . . Chrissy trailed off. I mean, except for the first time.

Oh yeah, the first time I hadn't met you yet so I was just fucking with Sue.

Oh. I see.

So will this person hurt you? Of course, to hurt and be hurt is either inevitable or it's the whole point. Really, it's all just a question of why. But then again, you're the one who said the why isn't important, the man said with a wink.

Chrissy fiddled with the dry skin of her cuticle.

So this is my last day, she said tangentially. Sue said she found a replacement for me.

Oh?

Yeah.

I figured that was coming. I knew you were contaminated but I didn't want to say anything because I've been having such a nice time. You're a really good cook.

Thanks.

Do you know what you're doing next?

Not really? But I think I know what I don't want, which is good.

Are you still worried about money?

Mm, I saved enough for a couple of months. And I recently wrote a poem that went viral.

Oh yeah? What was the poem about?

Oh, you know. Girlhood. Exploitation. That sort of thing.

Oh sure, yeah. Meaty stuff, no pun intended.

Ha, yeah, right. Anyway, I'm talking with an editor now about selling a book of poetry. So there might be something there, maybe not, we'll see.

This is really delicious. Sorry, I'm listening, it's just—

No, no, enjoy your meal. Really, I'm glad. I hope I wasn't too trigger-happy with the chili.

No, definitely not, it's perfect. I'm getting a really good balance of spice. What else is in it?

Well, usually it's made with pork blood.

Usually?

Usually, yeah, Chrissy said, and left it at that.

They ate together in silence for a bit, shivering through the sharp scrape of a midnight breeze.

Oh, I remembered what I wanted to say, said the unfamiliar man. When you were talking the other day about hunger.

Oh yeah?

The stranger chewed for a moment longer, frowning into empty space. The night air was a shock of cold, the warmth of the stew evanescing into iridescent flakes of falling snow.

You know what? I lost it again, he said. Sorry.

No worries, said Chrissy. Enjoy your meal.

* * *

Chrissy bumped into Gabrielle while she was on tour promoting her book of poetry.

You know, a few more details might have been helpful, Chrissy said as she signed her name with a flourish, handing the book back to Gabrielle, who knowingly shrugged. What was the last meal you made, by the way?

Caribbean black pudding, said Gabrielle. Yours?

Oh, I made the dinuguan you suggested.

Nice. Hey, did you break it off with whoever it was you were sneaking around with?

Oh. You knew about him?

Yeah. No offense but you're not . . . you're not the first person to fall down that trap, you know?

Oh. Yeah, ha, well—Yeah, that's over.

Great, that's great. It didn't seem like a good situation. I'm glad you got out.

Right. Yeah, me too. Thanks.

Yeah. So anyway—

So is your job . . . going well, or—?

Oh, yeah! Yeah, loving it, but you were honestly smart to get the hell out of academia.

Oh gosh, I mean, I don't know about that, I just had such a lucky break—

Don't call it luck, Chrissy.

No no, I just—I just mean, you know, obviously my timing was good. But everyone in that program was talented. And I mean, if I could have gotten your job . . .

Sure, sure, I hear you. Well, anyway, I'll let you get back to your adoring fans. It was really nice to see you, Chrissy.

So nice seeing you!

We should get a drink next time you're in town.

Yeah absolutely, I'd love that!

Bye now—

Bye!

As Gabrielle walked away, Chrissy's phone buzzed with a text. She pulled it out of her pocket, glancing quickly at the screen.

WHERE IS MY DAD YOU FUCKING SLUT!!!!

Teenage girls! It was really too bad that no one took them seriously. Which was honestly what the whole book was about.

Chrissy shook her head, returning her phone to her pocket. Then she gestured to the next person in line, smiling the smile she'd practiced for so long, the smile of the no longer hungry, the pacifying calm of the adequately fed.

IV

Winter

the horrors may be unrelenting
but motherfucker so am i!

Tumblr user helloitsbees

For you I will choose life.

Sensual Tales for Carnal Pleasures

Prelude

My mother brushes an ivory comb through my hair, as she used to when I was a child. I am grown now, but tonight she sits behind me on the bed and gently coaxes the tangles out, her fingers running deftly over the tendrils of my hair as she gives me a long-familiar warning.

Someday you will meet a man who is tall and dark and handsome, she says with a steady rhythm; almost as if she is casting a spell or weaving a delicate fabric. I, who have seen her do both, know that either could be true. *Beware the lure of a handsome stranger, my darling,* she warns, *for nothing beautiful is ever as it seems.*

She tells me I am proof of this. She says that I, in my beauty, will tempt and be tempted, and that such things can so easily be my undoing. I believe her, as I always have, and I heed her warnings, but still I am restless tonight, as I am on all nights. As I have been since the night I was born.

"Do you think it will be tonight?" I ask her softly, uncertainly, and her fingers pause their wandering.

"Yes," she says, and nods. "I'm quite certain it will be tonight."

I manage a careful swallow, my throat suddenly dry and tense, and feel my mother's lips press against my hair.

"Remember what I've taught you," she murmurs in my ear.

I always remember.

I can never forget.

The Night Castle

I open my eyes a sliver to note the glow at my window, golden and warm. I can't quite see what's beyond the pane, but its arrival prompts a drowsy procession of ritualistic movement—sliding my feet out from beneath my heavy duvet, uncurling my toes in the fabric of the rug, finding the ridges of the cobbled stone beneath—as I make my way toward it, scrubbing my hands over the thin veil of my eyelids. When I reach the glass, the glow outside pulses brightly, waiting. I undo the latch with meticulous deliberation, careful not to make a sound, only for a winter breeze to take hold of the window's edge and draw it free from my fingers like the tug of a lure.

Outside my window there is a castle, floating, with five illuminated towers, each forming the apex of a five-pointed star. Each of the towers shimmers with gold, irradiant in waves, and there is a pulsing, gentle warmth from within the castle's battlements that beckons to me, coaxing me forth like the crook of a finger. The castle hovers, as if manifested from nothing; a thick, entrancing fog spreads out from its base in eerie, alluring tendrils.

The draw of it is tempting. I reach out a hand, my fingers drifting helplessly toward it.

"Hello," says a voice from behind me, and I turn with a startled gasp.

Inside my bedroom is a man who is all dark shadows, his hair a gleaming black, with eyes as dusky as the thick fog outside. His clothes, from what I can see beneath a heavy cloak, are a black so inexplicably midnight the fabric couldn't have come from any human dye.

When I first see him, my attention initially snags on the ornate gold mask that obscures the top half of his face, but then my apprehensive study is drawn elsewhere by the light that glimmers in flashes behind and below it—by the white of his teeth that cut against his lips as he smiles, and the glint in his eyes as his gaze settles knowingly on mine. He inclines his head, a slow, syrupy smile still pulling at his lips as he sweeps his cloak aside to accommodate a subtle bow.

Beneath it, I can see the underlying pattern of shimmering stars, and I feel as though he contains the entire galaxy in the bend of his arm, drawing my breath along with it.

"How did you get in here?" I manage, stifling my nerves, and his smile broadens. It's a bit crooked when he smiles; discordant. As if a part of him wishes not to show amusement at all, but under the circumstances mirth cannot be prevented.

"Never mind that," he tells me, and he is handsome, and he is

tall, and strangely, all of my bedroom and the entirety of the night
are awash in darkness except for him—except for the light catching
and dancing around him as though he commands it, toying with it
in the palm of his hand. "I don't suppose you'd like some company,
would you?"

I feel my brow furrow.

"Who are you?" I ask, though I think I know the answer.

"I am the prince of the night castle," he replies. "Tonight, the castle
is for you."

I pause, fighting back the lurch of my recalcitrant tongue. "And
what exactly do you have for me in your castle, Your Highness?"

My tone is not especially deferential. Again, though, he only
laughs.

"So formal," he tells me. "Call me Noctus."

"And what do you have in your castle, Noctus?" I repeat.

He beckons me forth with a smile I know will be my undoing.

"Anything you wish," he promises, just as my mother said that he
would.

Beware the lure of a handsome stranger, my darling. She has warned
me many times, but now I find her lessons immaterial. For this, the
night prince before me, is more than a handsome man.

He is a dangerous, beautiful thing, and I know it already.

"Show me," I whisper, embracing the devastation ahead.

The Dining Hall

The castle's portcullis is solid gold and opens at its prince's touch, an
indulgent pet greeting its master. I'm not unused to finery, but even I
confess to being awed by the way the inside of the castle gleams. The
entry hall is grand—*too* grand, actually, considering that only the
two of us seem to occupy it—and a low, tempered hum of phantom
music plays from nowhere as he leads me past an opulent set of stairs.

"Where does it go?" I ask, my fingers resting daintily on the angled
plane of his arm as I tilt my head toward the staircase.

"You'll see," he assures me, sweeping through his castle so gracefully that he, too, seems to float on air.

He takes me into the dining hall, proclaiming I must be hungry.

I suppose I am; it's the middle of the night, after all, and dinner feels a long way off, but my misgivings give me pause. He seems to know this but does not move to reassure me. I suppose this is fair. Why have I come at all, if not to partake?

He eyes me closely as I lift a proffered goblet to my lips, taking a tentative sip.

I expect the glass's contents to be wine. Immediately upon raising the goblet to my lips, though, I understand that it won't be. It has a similar texture, even a similar smell, but the sensation of drinking it is foreign and misplaced. At first it tastes like something simple, something berry-flavored and sun-ripened and sweet, but as it makes its way down my throat, I feel a tingling of something that warms me from the inside out.

"Do you like it?" Noctus asks me, and I glance at him, uncertain.

I want to say yes, but I can't, not quite—something is discomforting. Something about the feeling both floods me and ignites me, but it tastes a bit wild, a touch sour at the end.

"It's unsettling," I eventually manage, and he laughs as if I've told a joke.

"The castle's wine is meant to make you feel as if you're tasting love itself," he explains, and now I see why he found it so funny.

"I wouldn't recognize the feeling," I say without meeting his eye.

"Pity," he replies, and slides another goblet toward me. "And this one?"

I sample this one just as hesitantly to find it is another flavor altogether. It bursts and cascades on my tongue, and if the love elixir was meant to be sweet, then this is exquisitely savory, a tremor that rattles up my bones.

"This," I realize, "tastes like madness feels."

His dark eyes glint with appreciation.

"It's meant to thrill you," he says, "as fully as desire."

I shudder.

"Don't tell me you don't recognize that either," he tuts in sardonic disapproval, and I fight the urge to roll my eyes.

"So what should I expect the food to do, then?" I ask drolly. "Submit me to lust? Dissolve me to devotion?"

"Neither," he says with a shrug. "Unless you feel given to such things already."

At the look in his eye, I think it would be catastrophically unwise to sample any more of the castle's offerings. I let my gaze skate over the feast that lines the table and mimic disinterest, going so far as to spare the artful, crystalline tarts a sniff of disdain.

"I'm not hungry," I tell him.

He seems unsurprised, though not disappointed. "Would you like to see something new, then?" he asks patiently, almost patronizingly, though I suppose my pride might be doing funny things to my ears, and the wine-that-isn't-wine still coats the inside of my stomach with warmth.

"I would," I say, cursing the way my voice suddenly sounds so breathless.

The Room of Truth

He guides me back to the staircase in the entry hall, leading me up the marble steps. I watch my feet as I walk, careful not to stumble, and eye the gold filigree that swirls amid ivory stone.

"This is a lot of excess," I comment. Under his breath, Noctus chuckles.

"It is," he agrees, "but with all privilege comes a cost."

"To whom?" I muse aloud.

He glances sideways at me, determining whether I am worthy of an answer. "We'll start with the room of truth," he says tangentially, so evidently not.

"Truth? Ironic," I murmur.

"More hypocritical, I'd say," he replies, unfazed.

I catch him hiding a smile, though he says nothing as he leads me down a corridor, the plush crimson of the rug giving way beneath my feet like grass that rustles on a breeze.

The door of the room he leads me toward is unadorned, which I find something of a disappointment compared to the rest of the castle's opulence. Still, I can sense why he took me here first. It has an energy to it, a frequency that coaxes me as much as it repels me.

Noctus pauses, resting his hand on the door where its heart or lungs would be. A purple-tinted eye materializes from the grains of the wood, fluttering open as if from dormancy or sleep to stare directly at me. Noctus, meanwhile, disappears into my periphery.

"What do I do?" I ask him uncertainly. The eye follows me as I fidget in place. Whatever the room wants, it clearly has to come from me.

From behind me, Prince Noctus places a steadying hand on my shoulder.

"It's the room of truth," he reminds me, as if this is enough to answer the question.

"So . . . I have to offer it something?" I guess, glancing over my shoulder at him, and he gives me a somber nod.

"The closer to you, the better," he says, and I sigh.

I consider it for a moment.

"I sometimes feel I would like to be freer," I carefully confess, and the eye blinks.

I feel Noctus come closer to me, his hand tightening where it rests on my shoulder.

"More," he suggests in my ear, and I sigh again.

"My mother has such high hopes for me," I explain, closing my eyes so as not to be perceived by the door's expectant stare, "and my father has such immovable expectations that I feel sometimes as if I will be crushed by the weight of them both. I feel as if I'm in a cage. I feel lonely, exhausted, lost. I feel—" I exhale. "I feel that I crave my own freedom so much that someday I will shatter everything around me just to conjure enough space to breathe. I feel capable of destruction, and I think sometimes that if I were freer, then perhaps I would find it easier to . . . exist."

By the time I finish speaking, I feel as if I've had the wind knocked out of me—I suppose I should have measured the truth before I gave it, but I haven't quite gotten my footing here, and the expulsion of it is almost too much. I double over, still avoiding the door's discomfiting eye, and when I straighten again, after heaving a couple of steadying breaths, I find that there is no longer any barrier to entry. I step forward without waiting for Noctus to follow, though I hear his steady footfall behind me; inside, the room is bare and generally unremarkable, save for a spinning wheel in the corner.

"Is this all?" I ask dully, wondering if I've spilled my secret for nothing.

"Yes and no," Noctus replies, removing his cloak of stars and draping it on a hook that stretches hospitably out from the wall before he settles himself at the spinning wheel. "This spins threads of fate," he explains, gesturing to it. "With it, I can spin your truth into a veil of sight."

"Sight?" I echo curiously, moving toward him as he begins to spin.

"Sight," he confirms with a nod. "A glimpse of something you truly desire—but only just a glimpse."

My gaze drifts over the motions of his hands while he works. I wait while he conjures a thread that seems to manifest from nothing, then watch while he lets it float in the air between us, spinning and twisting and drawing from his magic to form a thin, translucent fabric. When it is whole, Noctus plucks it delicately from the air, balancing it on his fingertips.

"Try this," he offers softly, and I close my eyes as he drapes it over my forehead. His fingers brush my temples and I nearly sigh in longing, a shiver of anticipation coursing through me like the wine I drank downstairs as he leans over to speak in my ear.

"Now look," he beckons, and my eyelids flutter open.

Where the room once stood, I see the bars of a golden cage, and for a moment I panic that he's trapped me—that by defying my mother's warning, I've sealed my own bitter fate. But then I notice a door, and a latch, and the moment I reach out to press my hand against the woven, braided gold, it gives way easily beneath my fingertips. Like the gossamer thread of a spider's web.

"What do you see?" I hear Noctus ask me from somewhere far away, and it startles me, because I see him now, too, clear as day. He stands before me, hand outstretched, and even I can guess what this means.

"I shouldn't have come to this castle," I tell the figment-Noctus, who takes my hand. I let him, though I sound like a child, my voice struck through with stubborn indignation. "I should have stayed in bed."

He laughs, a storm of something I don't yet understand brewing behind his clever eyes.

"I have a bed," he tells me softly, his grip tightening around my fingers, and in that moment, I know as if from another life that I will be the fool who ignores my mother's warnings.

But then I remember that this is only a vision, and so I reach up, tearing the veil from my eyes, to find the real Noctus facing me with a worried frown.

"Do you not like what you've seen?" he asks me, looking anxious for the first time.

I find within me a tender softness that wants to comfort him. I hold firm to my better judgment, though, and my sharper edge.

"It isn't the future," I reply bluntly, "nor is it the truth."

He seems to understand.

"And if it is?" he says quietly, but I have already let the veil cascade from my hand to the floor.

"It isn't," I say.

His gaze falls slowly to the veil.

"Let's try something else, then," he says, clearing something from his throat.

The Hall of Mirrors

"What is this?" I ask as he leads me down a new corridor. This one is lined with reflective glass of varying shapes and sizes, each frame more elaborate than the last.

"The hall of mirrors," he replies, aptly. "You said you wanted the future," he remarks with a sly glance at me. "Each one will give you a glimpse."

"Always with the glimpses," I comment, making a face. He laughs.

"I suppose if you stood here long enough, you could find a series of mirrors that would let you watch it all," he amends. "But as there's so much else to see, and the night is only so long . . ."

"Fine," I sigh, pretending as though I have no curiosities at all. "What's this one?" I ask, stepping toward a thin, vertical mirror that stands at my height. I can see the length of my body in the glass; from behind me, I catch Noctus's gaze lingering briefly on the curves of my hips, though his expression remains hidden by the mask he still wears.

"The mirrors won't show you anything for free," he cautions, his eyes on mine now in the reflection. I wonder if I imagined that they ever strayed elsewhere, or if it was only what I wanted to see. "They will force you to make a choice."

"What choice?" I ask, though the moment I do, two of the mirrors in the corridor illuminate. One of them sits within an ebony frame carved from bone, the other in gilded bronze lined with polished filigree. I consider the bronze frame, chewing my lip as my eye travels over the pretty, artful engravings, but I opt for the bone instead, sensing a pull toward it.

"Ambition over romance," Noctus observes. "An interesting choice."

"Do you see what I see?" I ask him, reaching out for the scene that plays within the mirror's frame like a daydream.

"No," he says. "I wasn't the one who made the choice."

"Hm." I force a swallow. "And if I want to see more?"

The light in the bone frame goes out; beside it, two more mirrors pulse with light.

"Choose carefully," Noctus warns, but I'm immensely tired of warnings. Rather than lose myself in the mirrors, I turn to him.

"What did you choose?" I ask Noctus, and he blinks, startled by the question, though he conceals it quickly.

"What makes you think I chose anything?" he asks, his voice carefully ambivalent.

"This is your castle, isn't it?" I prompt, turning back to the wall of mirrors. "So surely you must have tried all its offerings yourself. Or does it not present you with choices at all," I amend, "since you are its rightful owner?"

He hesitates.

"Yes, I've tried the mirrors," he says, "and yes, this is my castle."

My attention snags like loose thread on the things left unsaid. "But?"

I catch his reflection as he grimaces.

"*But*," he allows, "I made it with someone else's help, and not everything is my doing."

"Then who did you—?"

"Didn't you want to see your future?" he interrupts me, gesturing to the mirrors that still await my choice, but I can't be deterred so easily. My mother has always said so, and she is never wrong.

"What did you choose?" I press him.

He considers me carefully before answering. "Does it matter?"

"Yes," I reply, and then, for fun, I give him a clever smile of my own.

He sighs.

"I also chose ambition over romance," he says. "And I chose it over loyalty, too. I chose magic over love, and power over everything."

I let the words linger; imagine them settling weightily at my feet.

"Was it worth it?" I ask him.

He clears his throat, turning away.

"Maybe we should get some air," he suggests, his gaze already drifting down the hall.

The Wishing Fountains

The castle's grounds, forming the centerpiece of the five-pointed star, are equally ornate. Flowers with velvety-soft petals bloom close to the ground, all in shades of purples and reds so rich they would almost be black if not for a hint of softness, like the inside of a currant. He leads me past a line of flowers that reach out for my ankles, brushing them like a caress, and toward a series of fountains.

"Fountains are for wishing," he tells me. "Make a wish, and watch it come true."

"There's a price, though," I assume aloud, and his mouth quirks slightly.

"Yes," he says, "there is always a price. But for a wish, isn't any price worth paying?"

"Depends on the value of the wish," I remark.

His mask glints when I look at him, as if beneath it the expression on his face has changed.

"Somehow," he murmurs, "I don't think you'll err too small."

I walk toward the closest fountain, finding the others too gaudy, and run my fingers along the lip of the cold stone basin.

"Will it ask me for something?" I say to Noctus, then immediately leap back from the fountain's edge, finding that the reflection of the water has changed the moment I've spoken. A ripple surfaces from nothing, spreading out in waves, and the glassy reflection of the fountain's heart rises up, like a tiny hurricane on tiptoe, to form the shape of a faceless woman.

She beckons to me with the crook of a finger.

"Every wish has a price," she warns, her voice as harsh and loud as rushing water.

"So I've heard," I reply. For a moment, she only stares at me.

"Your price is this," she hisses without warning, darting toward me like a snake. I leap back in alarm, my back colliding with Noctus's chest. He grips my shoulders, holding me steady, and I hold my breath as she faces me with an eyeless, disquieting glare.

"For your wish to be granted," begins the fountain-nymph, "another will suffer a curse upon their head. For your happiness, another shall grieve. For your fulfillment, another shall wade in malcontent. Do you agree to the terms?"

I pause, considering it.

"Do I know them?" I ask. "The sufferer."

"Perhaps," she says. "Perhaps not. That result is not ours to choose. Only an action and reaction. A tide must always return to shore."

I twist around to look at Noctus, who still rests his hands on my shoulders. "Did you make a wish?" I ask him, and he bristles.

"What does it matter what I chose?" he counters gruffly. "Tonight the castle is yours."

But I can see the question settles irritatingly under his skin, and that he will eventually answer me if I play my cards correctly.

So I shrug, facing the fountain again. "It doesn't matter," I say. "I'm just curious."

He braces himself, the pressure of his grip changing as he wrestles with himself.

"I accepted the terms," he ultimately admits, as I knew he would. I hide a smile.

"Then I accept as well," I tell the fountain-nymph. "Let your justice fall as it may."

She nods, neither approving nor disapproving.

"Your wish?" she prompts.

I turn to face the prince of night, watching him gleam against the backdrop of the golden castle he set among the stars.

"I wish to see your face," I say.

I can see his eyes narrow behind his mask.

"That," he tells me, "is hardly a proper wish, given the price."

"I do not mistake the price," I tell him. "I know the value of a thing I wouldn't otherwise have."

His eyes change again. I suspect that beneath the mask, his brow is furrowing.

"Are you certain?" he asks me, but he knows, as I do, that it's too late. The arms of the fountain's spirit rise up from behind me as if they will crash atop my shoulders. I flinch, but they alight instead on the sides of Noctus's face, stroking the bones of his cheeks as if to comfort him through the loss of his gilded facade.

"Grant it," I say as if everything here is mine to command, and she—the fountain—obeys, withdrawing the mask from his face. Noctus, shuddering in its absence, brings his hands to his cheeks, touching his fingertips to the edges of his eyes and obscuring them from view.

"Elsewhere, a young woman sleeps alone," the fountain tells me. "For your wish, her sweetheart will not make it through the night."

I wince, but hold my ground.

"I knew the price when I paid it," I say tartly, and then as she retreats, I lean forward, gently taking the prince's hand from his face.

The rest of him is as handsome as his eyes suggested, as finely crafted as I would have guessed from the shape of his mouth, but there is a jagged scar that slices across his nose and down the side of his face, splintering like lightning over his cheek. I run my fingers across the fractured white lines, tracing the crevices with the warmth of my touch.

"Who did this?" I ask quietly.

"I did," he replies, and hesitates. "Well, not exactly. The dream lords took it upon themselves to punish me, but the crime that earned it was my doing."

"Dream lords?" I echo. His eyes cut away from mine.

"There is a king," he explains. "A dream king, who commands the lords and their powers. I was a lord once, a long time ago, but I desired too much. I used more than the magic I was given because I believed it was earned, and I was punished for my pride."

He waits for me to speak, as if he's waiting for judgment.

I let a few breaths pass.

"So you are a fallen prince, then," I say eventually, my hand cupping his cheek, and he leans toward me with something like gratitude, his eyes briefly falling shut.

"I'm a prince," he says, "just as I wished to be, and the ruler of an entire domain. Of more than dreams; of waking consciences. It's not enough, for me, to command a sleeping mind. I wanted to lure something more. To possess something else. To *find* someone else—"

"A companion," I guess softly. He looks surprised, but nods.

"Yes," he says, after a moment of pause. "A companion."

"An equal?" I ask whimsically, and the corners of his mouth tilt upward.

"I suppose," he permits, "though I have found no one worthy of the title."

I turn to face him. "What happens then?" I ask him. "When you find someone unworthy, I mean."

His dark gaze fixes on my face, on the curve of my lips.

"Better you never find out," he tells me, and leads me deeper into the garden.

The Labyrinth

He leads me toward the labyrinth, a maze that looks much as I might have dreamt one if prompted to do so, though I know for certain now that this is not a dream. The scar on the night prince's face proves it—it is a wound caused by magic, and even I can tell as much. It's less a mark of injury than a brand of retribution. He has been claimed by the dream lords as an enemy, and I think perhaps that's why he's built this castle with its many battlements, fortifying his kingdom even as it floats so high above the ground.

"And what will I find here?" I ask, reaching out to touch the hedge that forms the first wall of the maze.

"The labyrinth," he tells me, "will destroy your fears."

I study him for a moment, wondering what I will have to choose for this; surely the loss of fear is worth more than the granting of a wish, though I'm distracted now. Noctus is more handsome than ever in the dim light of the garden, and the scar does not diminish his beauty, but heightens it. The dream lords who sought to punish added their carvings of pain, and now he shines at every angle of the moonlight, refracted like the planes of a many-faceted jewel.

"Why me?" I ask him.

He doesn't answer right away.

"Perhaps I'm drawn to you," he says guardedly, "though I don't know why."

"But you must have seen your future many times," I remark, thinking of the mirrors, the veil of sight, the fountain of wishes, the magic of dreams that answer so loyally to him. "Have you seen me in your castle before?"

He doesn't want to tell me the truth, but without the mask, I can see it plainly enough. Counterproductively, the more I see of him, the less mastery I have over my own sense of caution. I find it increasingly difficult to look away.

"Will you enter the maze?" he says without answering, staring down at my waiting face, and I shrug.

"What will it cost me?" I ask.

"A piece of your soul," he replies, as if this is nothing.

"Which piece?" I counter, and he laughs.

"Your soul is not a cake to be sliced apart at will," he tells me. "You can no more choose which part of it leaves than I can piece mine back together."

This catches my ear; I hear it as a lament, and I follow the trail of remorse to the truth.

"How many times have you been in the maze?" I ask him.

"Only once," he says, and hesitates before adding, "At one time, only the labyrinth existed."

This is a surprise to me. "The labyrinth came before the castle?"

"Yes." He nods. "The castle only exists as a result of discarding my fears. I would be nothing without the maze. Nothing, that is," he amends with a laugh, "but yet another soul lacking caution."

I know he means me. I ignore it.

"You betrayed someone, though," I point out. "So weren't you fearless enough already?"

"To turn on a king is not bravery," he corrects me. "To simply suffer an insult to one's pride is not courage at all."

"Insult to one's pride?" I echo curiously. Too curiously, and he stiffens.

"Yes" is all he says.

I can see I've miscalculated. He doesn't meet my eye, and I suspect I might have gone too far.

"And now?" I ask.

He glances down at me then, contemplating something. His gaze travels over my face with a softened look of longing before it's disrupted, abruptly, by the crispness of his voice.

"And now it's too late," he replies, "and the night is slipping out from under us." He gestures me forward, and the moment is long gone. "Will you try?"

I give him a searching glance before nodding.

"I will," I agree, because it seems like my turn to be agreeable, and the labyrinth shifts instantly beneath my feet, giving way for my entrance.

I walk slowly into the greenery, following my feet until I spy a set of silver scales from afar. I chase it through the twists and turns, heart thundering as I grow closer. When I reach it, it seems clear enough what to do, so I take my place on one side of the scales; on the other side, a mirror image of myself appears. She, like me, is dressed in her silk nightgown, her eyes wide and hair mussed from sleep, and she lifts her chin to stare defiantly at me.

The moment her eyes meet mine, I feel a sharp prick in my chest, like a stab from a narrow syringe, and then the scale gives way beneath me; I see the other version of me glance sadly in my direction, hovering above me with sorrow and pity as I land with a grunt of dismay on the softened ground.

"Hello?" I call, the maze suddenly gone from around me as I struggle to sit up. "Prince Noctus?"

He flickers into being beside me.

"You summoned?" he asks wryly, and I think perhaps he's not real.

He seems different, as if I'm looking at a reflection of him rather than at the man himself.

I stand, dusting myself off, and turn to face him.

"Why are you here?" I ask bluntly, and he shrugs.

"It appears that what you fear is me," he replies, and belatedly, I remember that this is the entire purpose of the maze.

"I don't," I lie.

"Maybe it's something else, then," he suggests. "Something I represent? Risk, perhaps, or even—" He hesitates. "Love?"

"That's quite an estimation of yourself," I mutter under my breath. He gives a hearty, affectionate laugh before sobering, the humor in his voice settling shakily to something molten; something darker, more sincere.

"I've seen you in my future," he confesses, his eyes changing in the light. "Someday, in another time, I've already given you my heart."

He takes my hand, brushing his lips against it.

"I've been waiting for you," he tells me, gesturing to the castle that gleams in starlight.

I consider, as I have all evening, the tempting promise of his offer. The glimpse of something, of the freedom I so quietly, achingly crave. Of everything that could be mine if only I said yes.

I consider the words my mother taught me, too; that nothing beautiful is ever as it seems. Not even a beautiful promise, or a set of beautiful words.

"What have I lost?" I ask him. "In my soul, I mean."

He glances down at me.

"I can't possibly know that," he reminds me, but I can't help but wonder what's been severed from me.

"What if what I lost," I begin to say, "makes me something less than what I was before?"

"What if what you've gained," he counters, "makes you something greater?"

I sway toward him on a breeze, as much in his grasp as the magic that floats through the night's winter air, and I shiver, suddenly noticing the chill that embalms us.

"Take me inside," I suggest, "to somewhere I can know you."

The game changes. We both feel it happen.

"I'm already inside," he says, proving that I was right, and this was only ever his reflection. "This was my last chance, and I am waiting—none too patiently, I'm afraid—for your return."

Ah, so he hoped I would be braver, less careful, more foolish.

I hoped he would be wrong, but I can't stay away much longer. Curiosity tugs at my wayward tongue; yearning pulls at my knees.

"I want to be with you," I confess, and then he disappears, and the maze is back again.

Beyond the walls of the labyrinth is the pulsing glow of the castle as it calls me along a rose-lined path, the petals withering to ash as I begin to walk.

The Prince's Chambers

I take my time making my way to him—my fear may be gone, but my curiosity about his castle stays with me. I walk past the ballroom with its earthly delights and through the corridor lined with jewels, with vices and virtues, plucking them from the walls and replacing them, just to see how they feel in my hands. Guilt feels fine and light, joy feels heavy and frantic, patience pulses comfortingly as though taking cues from my own heart. I have no trouble lifting honor, and duty, too, slips onto my finger like a braided ring, but pleasure burns my hand when I try to cuff it around my wrist. I reach back with a hiss, pressing my thumb to the red welt that's already forming, but when I return it to its rightful place, a set of double doors opens up ahead.

I know the moment I see the doors—I can tell even without looking at the scripted letter N that's carved in the hearts of them, though they're difficult to miss—that these are the prince's private chambers, and I know they're where he's most comfortable. Where he's most vulnerable. Where he's most lonely, and most alone. I remember that my evening started in my own bedroom and I wonder what it will be like to end the night in his, though the question skitters from my mind as I enter.

From the moment I stand in the doorway, there is only him.

He's without his cloak and mask now, and so he's just a man, though I can feel the magic still pulsing from him that matches the walls, the floors. The heartbeat of this castle, which I can tell instinctively, even if I had not been told, belongs solely to him. This is his creation, his project, his pet. This is what he built with his betrayal, and what I'm sure he will die to protect.

He turns to me as I walk; he's alerted to my presence by the weight of my footfall on his castle floors, feeling it as surely as if I've swum here through his veins. He knows where I've been within the walls of his castle, and he knows what I've touched. He doesn't know what I've seen, though, and for all that he thinks he knows me, he doesn't know who I am.

He doesn't know what he's let inside his doors.

"How do you feel?" he asks me, almost fearfully. As if he worries his efforts haven't been enough.

"Fearless," I say, stepping toward him.

He lets out a harsh, sudden breath. A man with a last, final hope.

"Do you understand," he asks slowly, "why I brought you here? You have to choose me," he says, almost desperately. "You have to choose me, or you can't stay."

I pause. I'm fearless, yes, but not stupid, and my mother's warning still echoes in my head.

"Tell me more, first," I suggest, though I step closer. "Tell me about the king of dreams."

He takes me in his arms, though his smile darkens.

"The king of dreams has a court of lords who do his bidding," he says, his hands hovering above my waist. "He has a queen, too."

"A queen of dreams?" I ask, and he shakes his head.

"A queen of destiny," he says. "If you ask me, she has the worse end of the deal. She gives dreams meaning," he explains, his fingers floating up my spine. "*He* only gives fate a flimsy shape."

"You don't like him," I note. "The king."

"I didn't enjoy being one of his lords," he agrees. "I was the youngest, the least trusted. The least powerful, or so he assumed. I proved otherwise."

"You used his magic to make this castle," I deduce. "And what do you do with it, now that you have it?"

He gives a bitter laugh, as if the words spilling from his lips are poison.

"I tempt the waking," he says. "I lure the sleepless."

I tilt my chin up, my lips curving into a smile.

"You're a siren," I murmur, and he leans down to stroke my cheek, letting out a sigh.

"The castle is a function of choices. Of free will," he clarifies. "I needed someone to choose in order to make the mirrors. In order to see you." I lean into him, letting him brush his lips over my brow. "I needed the fountains, too, to find you."

"All of this." I clear my throat. "All of this was for me?"

"Can't you feel it?" he whispers, his lips close to mine now. "Can't you tell?"

I press my palms to his chest, feeling his intake of breath beneath them.

"What happens to them," I ask again, "if those you lure are unworthy? If they make the wrong choices?"

"They never leave," he says, and I think of the eye at the door of truth, the fountain-nymph who granted my wish, the haunting music that played from nothing.

He is a beautiful, dangerous thing.

"The dream lords," I murmur, drawing my fingers along the hollow of his throat. "Don't they carry some sort of emblem?"

He takes my fingers, slowly guiding them to the buttons of his shirt. I hold my breath, peeling them away, one by torturous one, until my hand alights on a tiny hourglass that hangs around his neck, with iridescent, shimmering swells of sand contained within it.

"All of our magic," he explains, "comes from this, born of the dream king's power. So long as this exists, so will I. So will everything I create."

My fingers close around it, and in a flash I see again my vision from the mirror of ambition. I see the sand engulfed in flames, and I see my own bare feet as I float peacefully back to my bedroom, rubble and ruin in my wake.

The chain breaks easily in my hand the moment his lips meet mine, and in the pressure of his kiss, he doesn't notice how deftly I slip the hourglass from around his neck, nor does he sense the hazy catch in my lungs as I take the source of his magic in my hands. Maybe he's distracted by the feel of it; after all, even I am not immune to the way fate circles around and meets us where we stand, trapping me like the snare of a spider's web. My breath nearly escapes me; nearly flees the grasp of my decision.

But I do not forget my mother's warning. *Beware the lure of a handsome stranger, my darling,* she has said so many times, *for nothing beautiful is ever as it seems.*

He knows I have the hourglass the moment I push him away, breaking the kiss with a gasp of finality. I see his eyes widen as he processes that I hold it, and I see the flames flicker behind me from the hearth in the fear that floods his gaze.

"I know now," I tell him hoarsely. "I know which part of my soul your castle took from me."

He swallows, unable to look away from what I now hold in my hand.

"When I first saw you, I thought this would be much harder," I admit. "I was burdened by the control of my mother and father, I was weakened by my conscience, I was tempted by the sight of you—but all of that's been stripped from me. My soul is unencumbered now, and now I am fearless, and so you've miscalculated your wish."

He stares at me.

"Who are you?" he rasps, but still—even in his horror—one hand reaches out for mine.

Still he longs for me, and I for him, though my purpose is much greater.

"I am the daughter of the king of dreams and the queen of destiny," I tell him, though I know, at last, that I am so much more than this. "I am a storm," I say, "and I am a flood. I am a force, a crash, a reckoning. I am the sum of all who came before me; I am the master of my fate.

"I am Nightmare," I tell him; revealing, at last, that I am a princess in my own right, "and I was born to burn your kingdom down."

The Past

There is always a cost, my mother tells me, brushing her fingers through my silken hair. *He will come for you; you will always find each*

*other. But remember, my darling, that there is always a price, and all you
can do is pay.*

What will I do? I ask her, and she tells me how to find my father's
magic, how to take back what is rightfully ours.

But what if I give in? I ask her, and she warns me not to falter, not
to lose sight of what has so long been foreseen.

Why must I do this? I ask her, and she reminds me that this is my
birthright; that she had seen it on the night that I was born, and had
sewn it as my fate when I was a child in her arms.

I am the daughter of the king of dreams and the queen of destiny.

I was born as much for love as I was made for destruction, and
now, at last, I understand.

There is always a price, my mother tells me sadly, *for nothing beautiful
is ever as it seems.*

The Future

It's difficult not to remember my prince's face as I destroyed his
life's work, letting the sands of magic that belong rightfully to my
father—and thus, to me—coat the flames that swallowed up a lifetime's worth of plans. There was a price, my fated love for him that
was as unknown as it was certain, and I paid it; in return, my father
stands uncontested, unopposed, and rules his realms once again.

But not for long.

Each of the towers shimmers with gold, irradiant in waves, and
there is a pulsing, gentle warmth from within the castle's battlements
that beckons to me, coaxing me forth like the crook of a finger. The
castle hovers, as if manifested from nothing; a thick, entrancing fog
spreads out from its base in eerie, alluring tendrils.

The draw of it is tempting. I reach out a hand, my fingers drifting
helplessly toward it.

I remember my mother's warning. *You will always find each other.*

I see now that it was a blessing as much as it was a curse.

I couldn't let him go; not fully. I wear the precious few remaining
sands around my neck—the ones I couldn't burn—to remind me of
what I've paid, and what I must always pay for the keeping of my

heart. I am the daughter of the king of dreams and the queen of destiny, but my mother and I have always known it was my fate to live with a conscience torn.

So long as any dream remains, a magic prince can always be reborn.

"What have you brought for me, my love?" I ask the wind, knowing that the castle he has built for me will stand in ash again before the night is through, but at least we'll have these hours together. On these nights, elsewhere, children sleep soundly, and tired minds will finally find rest.

Because on nights like tonight, Nightmare is with her prince.

At the sound of my voice, Noctus materializes beside me with a smile, the scars of his betrayal refracting the light from the castle's golden walls as he reaches out, touching the hourglass I wear around my neck.

"Oh, a number of things," he says. "The hall of mirrors will reveal your future. The courtyard of fountains will grant your wishes. The labyrinth will destroy your fears. The dining hall is just a dining hall," he admits, "but it serves the finest food you've ever tasted. Flavors that haven't been invented. Feelings that can never be reproduced. In fact, one sip of the castle's wine," he murmurs with a step toward me, "will make you feel as warm inside as love itself, or thrill you as fully as desire."

"And what if I simply want a good night's sleep?" I ask.

He smiles.

He is more than handsome.

He is a dangerous, beautiful thing.

"I have a bed," he whispers to me, and at least we have this.

Chaos Theory,

or The Free Agent's Guide to Transitive Thermodynamics

> Do I contradict myself?
> Very well then I contradict myself,
> (I am large. I contain multitudes.)
> Walt Whitman

NAOMI
New York, New York

He's late. I know I shouldn't be surprised. Over the two months we've been dating—if dating is even the word—he's literally never been on time. You'd think I'd either give up or get used to it, but somehow he destabilizes me just enough that saner options simply do not occur to me. Instead I just sit here, stewing, hating the day I swiped right on his stupid beautiful face; hating the moment I decided that not wearing underwear would be sexy; hating that now everything feels sort of damp and not in a sultry way; hating that I've chosen a dress so tight that even if I *did* just give up and go for a cocktail and wings at the bar like I normally would with a friend or even a different date that I didn't long so pointlessly to sleep with, I'd ultimately regret it on the waddle home.

Though, of course, if he *does* show up—nearly half an hour late, mind you—the last thing I want is for him to know I've just been sitting here, pathetically waiting for him with my back to the door (so as not to seem too eager), jumping at every person that passes by on their way to the toilet (because I am extremely fucking eager). God, is any orgasm worth this? I've got a vibrator, haven't I? Admittedly I haven't charged it since I met Charlie—these days I just come spontaneously, at any meandering thought—but the important thing is that I have two hands and what the *Post* calls "a truly sparkling imagination." Surely nothing is worth this kind of shame. And I'm a feminist!

I jerk upright, having landed definitively on my course of action (sweats, a bodega pint of ice cream, and furious masturbation) and instantly collide with someone who was passing by me for the bathroom. I manage a flustered apology, but of course it's no use.

"Naomi, my god, you look incredible." Charlie Miaza smells like sea salt, a fresh shower, and the way it feels to drive too fast on the freeway at night with all your windows down. His shirt is parted as if he doesn't understand shirts, although I know—oh, *I know*—that it's actually proof he understands shirts with a gravitas so profound it's as if he came up with them. As if he personally invented little collarbone dimples and the kind of oral sex that should only be bestowed upon mortals by gods. "Sorry, did I keep you waiting long?"

"I—" I feel dizzy just from his proximity, which is precisely what I meant when I said he destabilizes me. The answer is yes, Naomi, yes, he kept you waiting for what is socially considered *a very long time*, it's frankly unacceptable, at this point the maximum amount of joy you could possibly salvage from this fucking night now rests solidly in the hands of Ben and his esteemed colleague Jerry! Tell him, Naomi! Tell him no amount of casual sex is worth the endless humiliation! Does. He. Not. Understand. Phones! Tell him it's actually *very easy* now to use voice-to-text, almost insultingly simple actually, so that even if he was physically unable to type very brief, informative phrases into the thread of messages which—dear god—currently consist of a series of artfully shot photographs of your erogenous zones without inculpating your face because YOU, Naomi, ARE NOT AN IDIOT, he *still* could have found a way to—

He kisses my cheek, right by my mouth, so casually it's like he did it thoughtlessly, by the grace of pure accident. "I owe you one," he whispers, and the picture we make as his mouth scrapes by my ear is so viscerally sensual I see at least four women look my way, transfixed.

I shudder a little as he guides me into my seat, the perfect gentleman. He calls something to the waiter that I can't hear because my blood is hot and fast in my ears, his hand smoothing idly down the back of my neck. It's all so powerfully sexy, like his competency is something he wears, or like oysters or something, I don't know. He hands me the menu, strokes the back of his knuckles across my cheek, scrapes his stubble with one hand like he knows perfectly well I'm going home tonight with bite marks on my thighs. He orders a bottle of wine and says he hopes I'll like it, this place is known for its rack of lamb, suddenly I don't remember how to do things like order. Perhaps I've never actually known. What do I like?

Charlie Miaza looks at me like he's never seen me naked before. Like maybe tonight if he behaves himself very well I'll give him a prize. A *reward*. His tongue passes slickly over his teeth and he says, "Naomi. Not to be too terribly forward, but should we skip dessert?"

Yes, I think. *Oh, god, Charlie. Yes, yes, yes.*

VIOLETA
Neustadt, Saxe-Coburg

I suppose I have known that I would one day be royalty from, well, birth. It always seemed a sort of eventuality, even when my figure was at first so boyish and my front teeth almost comically large. But amazing things can be done with time and proper dentistry. My main difficulties were always going to be the preservation of my virginity and the meddling of my mother, but thankfully I was born at a convenient time, solidly ten years Karlo's junior and incidentally unexposed to temptation while the women his own age were armed with newly progressive politics and a radical fondness for contraceptives. Mama was a greater obstacle, of course, but I am not lazy, and I can even be quite smart when properly motivated. There is almost no reason to be smart, obviously. Karlo doesn't like intelligent women or he would have set his sights somewhere less impressionable. Really, it was me and four or so other heiresses barely out of finishing school, and Karlo only wants what all men secretly want: a listener. And someone functionally a child, because what else is purity if not the remnants of girlhood delicately plated for his sole consumption?

Which is why I learned my particular laugh, of course. I learned to blush furiously when other people swore in my presence or made lewd jokes at my—laughable even to say it—expense and to look as innocent as possible when glances began to stray below my neck. I can't say when I knew that I was pretty. I think it probably happened much later than my certainty of what I would someday be, because my prettiness always seemed totally incidental. If anything it was proof I was always on the right track. Because it's so very easy to be pretty with money! The right clothes, the right products applied in the right light, anyone could do it. Ask Vivienne, who looks like her horse-faced father but still married a Bonaccorsi—and the handsome older one, too, not the gray-faced Horatio that my mother once considered the ceiling on my prospects. Mama was terribly mouthy before she had her accident. I don't really resent her for it because to me it seems very simple. She hated me because I had ambition and all she had was duty. Imagine having to marry my father, to pleasure him all night and day without complaint! I'd have liked us to be friends but what would have been the point? I'd have liked to be friends with Regina, too, but sometimes older women make things quite impossible for any young thing they perceive as a threat. I can only assume they are very sad and jealous.

In any case Karlo was quite taken with me right away. I was wearing the lilac silk that makes my skin look very dewy and fresh—the word "unplucked" always comes to mind, personally. I had made sure our first meeting was very casual and innocuous, as I don't believe a man's attention is best won in open warfare, where everyone can see. It's not a gladiator fight, this war. Maybe if Vivienne had known that she might have aimed higher than a Bonaccorsi, which still requires her to kneel to me. The point is Karlo was fresh off his horse, having come hunting at the behest of my father (I have always been a keen mimic and Papa's lazy shorthand is almost upsettingly simple, truly a security risk). There was blood on his cheek, which made him very beautiful to me, beautiful in a way he would never be to me again.

I feigned shock of course to see him. I lowered my eyes and made myself small as if my father would be very angry with me to learn I was underfoot. I could tell Karlo felt very sorry for me, and I kept my voice very quiet and my eyes very large, so that he didn't realize he was leaning toward me until I let my gaze stray to the smear of carnage on his cheek. "Poor thing," I said softly, tracing it with the pads of my fingers as if it were an injury. I could practically smell the double act of paternal sympathy and lust for me, a silly girl who saw a heroic man as a wounded boy, because that's the real sweetness of devotion.

Now, of course, Karlo hardly looks my way, but it doesn't matter now, does it? My wedding dress cost more than Mama's entire fortune and the tiara I wore was Regina's own. I chose it for sentimental reasons, obviously. So that she would know that everything she had would ultimately be mine.

"Violeta," Regina says when I offer her a doting curtsy. She always says my name as if she'd like to spit it out. It cheapens her, which I relish. By contrast I am unfailing in my mirage.

"Mother," I say, and clasp her hands once the drudgery of protocol suggests we may be intimate. "I am so worried about poor Karlo. He works so hard."

"Yes," she says, looking away. She and I both know Karlo is off fucking a maid somewhere, or maybe gallivanting on one of Regina's other estates with his usual favorite, the Duchess Spiros, who viciously unmans him every time they see each other. I cannot remember whether they are speaking right now, though I do keep an eye on their correspondences. Gaiana Spiros is a breathtakingly attractive woman about fifteen years my senior, which means her breasts sag from nursing her four Amazonian children (mine have a wet nurse because I may be of average conversational ability but I am not a fucking fool) and her eyes have become quite hawkish over time. Still, based on her letters to Karlo I can tell she is immensely talented in the bedroom. I sometimes pleasure myself to the things she says— her prose positively sparkles—although Karlo's responses are horrifically dim and uninspired. I cannot imagine what she sees in him.

"I was thinking, Regina, perhaps we could take the boys to the summer cottage for a couple of months at week's end? Just to give my darling husband a rest." I widen my eyes as sweetly as they will go, which is very sweet. I have practiced hard, which is why Papa has never asked me where I was when Mama fell. "I think the sea air will refresh him."

Oh, he will hate it! He loathes the summer cottage, it has hardly any fuckable maids, but I adore it. It's not really a cottage, it's actually an enormous medieval castle, and though certain parts are in relative disrepair (it's more crumblingly antique than properly posh), it happens to be Regina's most precious property—the place she felt safest in her youth. But someone has made sure the reporters all know the sordid details of Karlo's recent string of infidelities and if I'm to have any fun at all this year, I'll need to strengthen our family image first. And the stables at the summer cottage are managed by a most wonderfully attentive groom.

Regina knows, of course, that if she does not agree then something mysterious will happen. Perhaps one of her little dogs will disappear for a few days. Perhaps she will find herself slightly ill, just slightly, with an exhaustive fatigue that won't go away for several months. Perhaps her heir will be caught disgracing his family name yet again. Or perhaps nothing will happen! She is welcome to find out.

I smile adoringly at her and wearily, she relents. "Very well, Violeta."

"Oh, Mother! How did I ever get so lucky," I say, kissing her hands. Her rings will all be mine someday, and won't that be lovely! I have ever such elegant fingers. I practically skip back to my room, delighted with my good fortune.

I can't wait to tell Karlo that for the rest of the season, he is mine.

JESSAMYN
The Temple of Benevolence, Glorious Homeland

Today. The enemy grows. Ever nearer. The anticipation. Coats my throat wets my silken skin unfurls within me a deep vibrato that sings in my mouth frantic beats of time pass like raindrops dripdrip-drip he comes. He comes.

From behind the glass veil I see him closer now, closer. It will not be today. This day which is hung low with wetness. I dare not venture. No patch of sun from which to hide on sweeping wing though I see him. I see him. My shoulders strung like a bow tightly locked I imagine my teeth around the delicacy of his throat. He will be mine it is only. A matter. Of time.

Look at him there twitching as if to say he knows I am watching. I am watching always watching. I am stretched long and low as if! To pounce. You come for me again my nemesis, my monster. One day soon I shall paint my walls with your shining coat I will hang your insides like velvet drapes along the eyes of my opulent prison.

I will present your heart to Mother as a gift a token of war a badge of devotion I am the huntress I never fail. I wait. I watch. You trill something calling out to the sky and I laugh hahaha in the face of your shrieking panic. You fool you will never outlast me. This day is not the day of your demise but there will be other days. Other times.

"Look at that bird, Jessamyn." Mother attempts to stroke my head while peering beyond the glass veil. "Isn't he beautiful?"

Mother is benevolent. And a fool. I swipe admonishingly at her wrist as if to say you will die without me. This is why I stay with her. Both because she is a goddess of the harvest and because without me. She would be. Quite dead. She breathes out very swift and harsh like the wind and seems angry. Mother can be. How shall I put this. Mercurial.

It is no matter because there is no rest for me my vigilance is eternal. I watch not just for Mother but for the others of my clan of which there are here four others, Daisy Araminta Olympios Irene. The others amuse themselves with opiatic distractions. Balls of string silly toys for silly fools. Breathing only because I allow it. Because I protect them because I am ever vigilant ever watchful. I know there is darkness in this world for I have seen it. And I do not allow it inside this sacred place.

Occasionally there is a large hairy version of Mother who sleeps in Mother's bed but he too is watched closely very closely. Only these members whom I permit within the realms of this glass castle are permitted to come. To go. To live.

I sink deeper into the cloud-covered softness of my post. Rest is needed at this time. Outside the enemy bleats again. A warning. A threat. I offer no reply.

When it is his time he will know. Oh. He will know.

And so will I for I am the arbiter. The protector. I alone will decide.

HADIA
Outskirts of New Asheville, North Carolina

My stomach is a little sore around the injection spot. I'm praying this time it will work, because if it doesn't, I don't think I can take another round of this. I'm finding it difficult to keep from crying this morning. I don't know, I think maybe I'm just tired, or possibly the hormones are making me crazy again. I ring Lottie with a single push of a button, almost by habit.

"Oh, honey," she says when she sees me on the screen. Damn, I think, because it must be more obvious than I thought. No doubt the Holomoji is flatteringly deceiving. It's a flaw in this new update, the full-body holograph they just added to the messaging app to make it, I don't know, more fun I guess. It extrapolates and therefore can't possibly guess I'm doubled over on the kitchen counter. I miss when the Holomoji were only from the neck up, though when Carl is feeling mean he likes to tell me that that's how I tricked him.

"Bad day?" asks Lottie. Her Holomoji is set to the salsa dancer but mine just stands awkwardly like a stick figure. I tried to set it to something more interesting but my phone keeps freezing up. I have bad luck with things like that.

"Not really," I say, because it's not any worse than all the others. "Just wanted to see what you were up to."

Of course my timing is shit, though, because I hear the door bang open downstairs. "Fuck, Carl is home," I tell Lottie. "I'll call you later."

"Love y—"

I shove my phone into my pocket and straighten just before Carl enters the kitchen, eyes frantically roving around for who knows what, a miracle I guess. Sometimes I think he still expects to come home to a spread of fresh bread and an assortment of homemade jams like when we were still courting, before my father secured the marriage and back when I still had the energy to drag myself out of bed. The hormones really make things difficult. I'm just so tired all the time.

"Anything to eat?" Carl asks without looking at me. He has this amazing ability to look through me these days, which I'm thankful for a lot of the time. Most of the time, really. The hormones have made me softer around the middle and even I don't want to look at myself. I've perfected this silly little dance where I leap from the shower to the bedroom closet with my eyes closed, just to avoid seeing the way time and failure continuously march across my midsection. And probably my face, too, although I've been going to the place Lottie recommended and that's helped tremendously. Apparently the other playground mothers swear by it, so I'm lucky Lottie told me (she doesn't need it herself, being naturally flawless).

I already feel bad enough when Carl's colleagues come over. At least the house is always spotless, but of course it is. There's nothing underfoot.

"I can make something if you're hungry," I tell Carl. In the past he used to appreciate my inventiveness, or at least have the patience for it.

"Oh. I came home because I thought—" His eyes meet mine accidentally and then skitter away, leaving us both a little remorseful. "Never mind. I'll grab something at the office."

"Why did you come home?" slips out of my mouth and I wince. Idiot. This time when Carl looks at me I know I've fucked up. He won't be home for dinner now and it'll be all my fault when I'm sitting alone again. Maybe Lottie will come over? Sometimes if Carl isn't home it means Lottie's husband Vitaliy is out with him. They are each other's favorites even though Vitaliy is an idiot—or perhaps that is what endears him to Carl, I don't know. They like to hunt together in the woods just down the road, or do whatever they do. Wherever they go.

"I didn't realize I needed to have a reason to be in my own house," Carl says coldly, which is about what I expected. I only meant to ask—Well, it doesn't matter what I meant, of course, it's what I said. Idiot.

"Sorry, it's—the hormones," I manage to say. "You know they make me . . . difficult."

His look softens a little as his gaze drops to my stomach. Maybe he will see my bloat as a promising sign? I don't know what would be more offensive to him at this point, me getting lazily soft or me staying selfishly thin.

"Forgetful, too," he adds with a teasing lilt in his voice.

Oh no. What have I forgotten? Fuck, I'll be thinking about it the rest of the day. This is worse actually, because now he might come home and then there will be no chance of seeing Lottie. I'll just have to wait and find out what happens, either way I'll have to put something on the table. Fuck! Fucking balls. The injection spot aches a little again and I bend over without thinking.

"Poor Hadia," says Carl, brushing the hair back from my cheek. He smells like perfume. Not mine, obviously, because I can't wear any these days—the smell of almost anything nauseates me. Son of a bitch. If this round doesn't work what will happen? Illegitimate children can't inherit, thankfully, but neither can imaginary ones. For a moment I panic. Will Carl leave me? Kill me? It's been known to happen. Is he capable of that? Not himself, surely, but he could hire someone. No, my mind is spinning out, it never used to do this so often. It must be the hormones.

I exhale jaggedly and then a faint burst of clarity. Lottie will think of something.

Of course. Lottie will know what to do.

After Carl kisses my cheek with what I wish I could call thoughtlessness (when we touch now it is almost too calculated, as if he has to practice several times in his head before he makes contact with me or else he will never stomach the effort) I ring Lottie quickly. I can hear her girls singing in the background, a song she made up for them when they were babies. She is such a good mother. Even her boys are so thoughtful and kind. They all seem to sparkle with health, I can't explain it. When Carl and I come over I know he hates me all the more for the comparison to her, but I don't mind. She is too good to hate, too thoughtful, too kind. I don't envy her because I know if I asked her to cut out her own uterus and trade it with mine she would do it in a heartbeat. Imagine wasting my energy on badness when there is sweetness like that?

"I can't talk now," she whispers. "Tonight? Our spot?"

Relief washes over me. Lottie will save me. "Okay," I whisper back even though my house is empty like always. "Tonight."

VIOLETA

Ha! Karlo is furious. He's been storming around our bedroom terrifying the servants for almost an hour now. I wonder if one of them can be made to tell a reporter? Hm. Eustaquio does have a weakness for drink and I know he thinks I'm pretty. I shall flirt a little before we go, make a gift to him of one of Karlo's bottles. Oh, and then when Karlo discovers it's missing, I'll tell him Regina suggested giving it away because she is worried he's drinking too much. Oh heavenly host, can you imagine?

Karlo shatters a vase but then seems spent, sagging a little when I touch his shoulder. "You really must control your temper," I tell him. "You know how I worry about your heart."

"For fuck's sake, Violeta," he spits at me. "I am barely forty."

I read in Karlo's most recent letter to his lover the Duchess Spiros that he is feeling much aged these days. As he should! He married a much younger woman and I am holding up beautifully. I actually think my looks have improved with age. I worried a little bit when Olympios was born but I think the widening of my hips was an improvement. Now I am a proper womanly shape instead of slightly coltish, and of course I am saintly in the glow of motherhood. Regina only managed one boy. I am literally twice as fertile.

Once Karlo is calm he is very boring to me. We do still have sex quite often because I am very attractive and I know what to say to him that the Duchess Spiros won't. I assume she finds such submission to be shameful. But what shame is there in securing my marriage, and therefore my place in the world? What she considers personal indignities I believe to be more transactional in nature. Besides, I would never do what she does, fucking him with toys and such as if she is the man. Not because I dislike such things (I like to do the fucking on occasion because power suits me) but because afterward I would never be able to look at him without laughing. If I ever allowed myself to leave him keening desperately beneath me I would never be able to stop seeing him that way, and then how would I do any of this? Any of it at all?

I like it when Karlo is a little angry, and so I provoke him again after dinner by telling our older son Artem that he is getting so broad in the shoulders. Karlo is notoriously sensitive about his lankiness. I actually think it lends him his only attractive quality—which aside from his inheritance is his elegance—but why say so? He has dozens of women on staff to tell him how very masculine he is. Only I can withhold approval in such a way that he makes any effort in bed. I hear with the others he almost never gets on top.

After I make a little theater with my orgasm—I do tend to have them with him, I think because I find the initial provocation to be at least 80 percent of my arousal—we pretend we are a normal couple and read together in bed. He gets a very mysterious letter that he's extremely secretive about. I'll read it later, I know where he keeps his things like this. I wonder if it has to do with his coup? I know he is planning one. I cannot dream he will be successful. I know he's tired of his mother ruling over him but she is endlessly smarter than her son. I think probably because Regina never expected to be queen and assumed the throne only by necessity. After her husband died and the nobles rose up against her, she barricaded herself in the palace with nothing but five loyal guards and her son. Karlo was ten, old enough to remember that Regina secured her reign with her own negotiation tactics and the antique rifle she snatched up from the wall in a fit of divine-handed fury—the story is she fired four rounds successfully into the four heads of her opposition, but I think probably it was more of a prop—and considering that Karlo has still not done any military service nor even been struck playfully, he cannot think to actually defeat her. She had five guards loyal to her then— now she has hundreds of thousands. She is beloved by all but the nobles who opposed her in the first place, a scant dozen who think Karlo can rule. Imagine!

But of course if Karlo commits treason then I am not in a very good position. Regina seems fond enough of my son Artem but I cannot know if she would choose him as her heir if Karlo fails. I shall have to spend some time talking Karlo down from whatever he is angry about—probably his mother betrayed him in some way by suggesting he put his overactive cock away or for god's sake set down the bottle. Tranquilizing Karlo's temper can be a very lengthy process, as it involves a great deal of flattery and hours upon hours enduring the ravings of a hypocritical madman. Perhaps Regina will have to go if this keeps up. Oh, how exhausting it all is! You cannot say I haven't earned my crown.

By the next morning everyone is packed and Karlo, sliding cheerfully into a separate car from the three of us, seems a bit too delighted. Has he sent a girl to the summer cottage? Or maybe it is political which would be worse. Yes, I think it is probably politics. He can plot quite safely from the summer cottage which means— alas—that I will have to work.

I sigh aloud, and Olympios—my livelier boy, Regina's favorite, quite monstrous to his tutors though—looks up at me. "Are you unwell, Mama?"

Artem looks up at me as well, waiting to see what I will say. Artem is my favorite because he doesn't say unnecessary things. Actually, Artem hardly ever speaks, but I know he is watching. I know he sees his father for what he is, and me for what I am. And Artem was my savior, really, by coming easily and quickly. Olympios is more like a puppy, his loyalty sweet but extraneous. I don't have plans for a third but if I do it will only be because one of the other two are gone, or if maybe Karlo does something stupid and I need to sway the press in my favor.

"Mama is always thinking of what's best for our family," I tell Olympios, tapping his nose gently. I am a good mother, I think! I like them more now that they are older. I have to pretend a bit with them sometimes but it isn't hard. They both have my bright eyes, which is good for them. Karlo's heavy brow makes him look perennially confused, as if he might have misheard you. "Nothing for you to worry about, darlings."

Artem doesn't believe me. Clever boy! I'll tell him later why he is dressed in Karlo's old clothes. The media loves it when we echo the past. It reminds them of a time when they had power and relevancy. Also the economy is not so good these days and we cannot appear too privileged. Hm. I will make sure to release more details than usual, as if I have only come to the summer cottage to be hard at work, mothering and such. What drudgery.

Olympios snuggles into my side which I do not love, but it makes a pretty picture. I think I will have a party and invite the Duchess Spiros. She will help get Karlo in line and he will be dizzy with distraction by the mere fact of her presence. They will think they are getting away with something, too, which will make them both even sillier than usual. Problem solved!

Artem sits back in his seat, at ease now that I am smiling. He can see I have a plan. I lean over Olympios and chuck my elder son's chin lightly. When Artem smiles he reminds me of an imaginary version of his grandmother, if Regina had ever realized that she and I could be allies. I was so profoundly disappointed when she began to distance herself from me. But never mind! I make my own allies.

"Maybe we will see your other grandmother while we're gone," I tell Artem, which is always a treat. I like for Mama to see that her sacrifice was not in vain. Locked-in syndrome, they call it, from a spinal injury in her fall. It means she can probably see and hear me, which is wonderful news. After all, my life is so charmed, and don't we all want better things for our children? I would hate for her to miss it.

JESSAMYN

He comes again this day. Outside the glass veil he builds his nest with such effort it is clear he thinks he will outlast and conquer what is mine. He thinks he really thinks he will suckle his progeny to greatness from this sacred place where I have now ruled for moons and moons. He really thinks. That he is safe. The enemy is weak-minded and that is to my benefit. As always I wait and watch wait and watch I am ever so careful. Mother and Man-Mother are talking in the bed as I wait and watch from my perch on high. They do not seem to understand as the enemy does. As I do. That the victor takes the high ground.

"Jessamyn's in a mood again," Mother says. "She seemed sweet this morning. I really thought she was finally warming up to me."

"It takes time," says Man-Mother. "The shelter said she was skittish, right?"

"Yeah, apparently she was living under a freeway overpass, poor thing. She doesn't seem interested in socializing with the others."

"Well, you knew that when you took her in, right?"

"Of course, of course, and it's not like animals are put on this earth to please *us*, or to be friendly just because *we* expect it—it's just that it would be, you know, *nice*, I guess, and since the other cats are so social I guess I thought—"

"Just give her time. I'm sure that once she realizes she's safe here she'll warm up to the others. And you're so patient with her."

"I mean, she's generally pretty quiet—"

Their prattling. It is ceaseless. I groom myself to obscure the fact that I grow tense very tense from the continued construction of the enemy just outside the glass veil. I do not know how easily these walls will hold. The others are vacuous and stupid. Olympios in particular is showboating around and Irene the idiot is falling for it. They distract themselves with delights of the flesh it is almost unhinged a sort of anesthesia. Sometimes it is very clear to me they do not deserve my protection but I am not a protector only of the worthy. Still if my enemy comes for me. I will not mind if Olympios is in the way.

Daisy asks me if I will play with her and I say no I am busy.

"Did you see that? She just hissed at Daisy. And Daisy is the sweetest one!"

Mother sounds apprehensive but I do not see the source of her concern. Is she dead dismembered lying gutted somewhere crying for help? No. So I should think. That she is fine. Meanwhile the enemy continues his plague of homesteading laughing at us all the while. Maybe Mother is more perceptive than I give her credit for. Just kidding. She is very stupid and her coat is pale and unwashed. She is lucky she has me the alternative would be unthinkable.

The enemy trills again a song of victory like war drums. Thundering. He will come for us I know he will come. I ready my claws and Daisy tells me to come play and I tell her to fuck off out of here is she not. Paying attention.

A wise cat knows better than to court doom, says Daisy obsequiously.

Perhaps I am not a wise cat. But I am an alive one and I intend. To stay that way.

NAOMI

I am an award-winning journalist and have been one since the ungodly age of nineteen. I have an absurdly unnecessary MFA and no debt because multiple institutions fell over themselves begging me to come write for them. I can afford to live in a one-bedroom apartment in a high-rise with a balcony and a doorman and I have serviceable health insurance, including my eyes and teeth. And I am texting Charlie Miaza again, because I am coincidentally also the dumbest girl on earth.

Things pretty much instantly devolve into sexting because the man is nonstop. And apparently I am too, which is insanely unhelpful. I turned my camera off during our weekly Zoom meeting for the magazine I'm currently on contract with, which I never do, because I actually take my job seriously. Except for right now, because Charlie is asking me to relive last night in devilishly, grammatically impressive ways. I routinely forget what Charlie does for a living—I know he's a lawyer, but I can't remember what specifically he works on. Or wait, is he in finance? Jesus, even my confusion is somehow arousing. I know he wears ties and I also know what he uses them for. Only when I've been—and here, a gritted sigh on behalf of all women—a very good girl.

Did you come? Charlie texts me.

Yes. Luckily Maureen hasn't stopped talking for the last five minutes and that's really all it took, though I let him keep going so as not to seem unathletic. Did you?

I'm in a meeting.

This motherfucker. You're joking. I pause for a second before adding you motherfucker.

Language. So I haven't been a very good girl. I wonder what the consequences will be for my profanity. (Maureen starts up again, so I can and will imagine.) It would be highly unprofessional to whip out my cock right now, Naomi.

Someone asks me a question so I type something in the Zoom chat with my left hand about the inadequacy of my Wi-Fi. Did you do this just so I'd owe you one?

Yes. I'll collect at your place tonight. Around 9?

Abnormally late for dinner, which suggests sex and nothing else. I'm a booty call, right? This is me being a booty call. Ah sorry, I have plans tonight. I'm still typing some half-hearted lie when I get a response from him.

No you don't. See you then.

I come for the fourth time on the strength of my own self-loathing, because he's absolutely right. And to nobody's surprise, after I've shaved absolutely everything and applied a reasonable amount of feminine marinades to my naked body, nine o'clock rolls around with no Charlie in sight.

I flop backward on my bed and go through our old messages before realizing that's a mistake. I should go out! I sit up abruptly. Of course that's what I should do. I told him I had plans, so I should immediately seek out some plans. I feverishly text my friends, who all remind me that it's Wednesday. So??? Since when has anybody cared about the nature of linear time! I'm on a rampage now, trailing sparks as I stomp over to my closet. I pick out the most obvious thing I own, a shiny black bandage dress from the era of Hervé Léger knockoffs that is all but begging for someone to proposition me. My highest heels, too, so I can tower impressively over my paltry convictions. It doesn't even matter where I actually go, what matters is *the plan*, which I have! I'll just order fries and drink a dirty martini at the bar and then who knows! Maybe I'll feel alive in a way that's independent from Charlie Miaza's inexplicable effect on my vagina! Maybe the spell will be broken! Maybe I'll bring a book! I double back and grab one off the shelf because you know what, waiting for a miracle might take a while.

I'm out the door by a respectable 9:27 when I collide with someone in the corridor. "Naomi," Charlie says, chuckling a little as he says my name. "Going out?"

I can't imagine how he got in. I bet he's befriended the doorman. God! He would.

"Yes," I say stubbornly, and a bit stupidly, if I do say so myself. "I told you I had plans."

"Mm." He tucks my hair behind my ear and seems taller, somehow. He's wearing a suit and smells divine, like how it felt the first time I was away at college and realized my father had no idea where I was, that in fact nobody knew where I was and I could make use of that, capitalize on it. He smells like the freedom to make unwise decisions and looks rare, like the attentiveness of a man who only replies to every other text. My god I am diabolical! Do I even hear myself? This isn't magic, it's—it's—

Charlie kisses me and suddenly, through no fault of mine I am sure, he is pinned between my chest and the wall. He looks amused and also a little . . . fond? What is his plan? Is he trying to kill me? Is he trying to MURDER me?

"Naomi," he says, and oh, I am his, I am so very, very his. I've known this for a great deal of time now but only passively, as if it were something that could still be denied. I should probably wonder things occasionally, like . . . have I ever been to his apartment? Do I even know what neighborhood he lives in or what he does during the day? Does he ever explain why he's late? Does he even *like* me?

"Naomi, open the door or your neighbors are going to file a complaint with the building." His hand is nearly up my skirt, which is admittedly not very difficult with the degree of skirt I have selected for the evening.

The last reserves of my dignity rear up in protest. "I have plans," I inform his neck. He definitely works out frequently, probably every day. Maybe that's why he's always late? Is it possible he's always at the gym for hours, losing track of time because it's an underground gym like the casinos in Vegas, where maybe they don't allow phones and he doesn't own a watch? I could buy him a watch. I could buy him ten watches.

"Mm," he says, and takes my keys from my hand. He unlocks my door with my hand now in his, giving me a furtive glance over his shoulder like we're lovers, or children getting away with something. Like we're spoiling dinner with dessert. The words I LOVE YOU flash wildly across the front of my brain and I know it's a lie, I know it can't be true, it must be socially conditioned by Hollywood films and their sexy montages. And yet if he asked for my kidneys or the pleasure of his babies I would have? To think about it?

Somehow I reenter my apartment with the world tilted sideways below my feet. Charlie Miaza undoes his tie and my legs are no longer legs, or at least not doing what legs are meant to do. He laughs and tosses me onto my sofa as if I'm a tiny, lovely doll.

"This is fucking satanic," I say to my ceiling.

Charlie steps over me.

"Language," he blithely remarks, and for nearly four hours I don't reply coherently at all.

HADIA

Lottie joins me in the usual spot, down where the edges of our properties meet. The totality of the land was a gift from the State after

all the reassignations, but it was always too much work for just Carl.
The soil has been overworked and yields almost nothing, the entire
ecology of it basically starting over as if from ash, and though things
are improving—there are predators now to hunt the infestations of
rodents that have been eating the earliest crops, so maybe in another
generation or so the soil will yield again—it was still most beneficial
to parcel it up and sell it, minus a few patches here and there. Carl
chose this plot for Vitaliy specifically, because—Well, it's the worst
part of the land, without question. Nothing can possibly grow and
it borders the woods that were protected by law under the old federal administration, which means the area north of Vitaliy's parcel
will likely become a housing development or something. It would be
difficult because the land is so rocky, with steep cliffs eroding at an
ungodly pace into the dry and brittle canyons below, but with housing prices as they are I can't imagine those woods will stay protected
for long.

It's about a five-minute walk from our edge to theirs at a brisk
enough pace. Carl thought our children would play together here,
and maybe they will someday. For now, though, it's where Lottie
and I used to hide the joints she'd steal from Vitaliy and where I'd
bring us snacks, usually whatever it was Carl didn't want that day.
Sometimes I'd purposely make things he'd like but not love, just to
be sure I'd have some extras to split with Lottie.

Tonight our time is pretty limited. That's been the case for a while.
I'm not sure what changed, exactly, just that Carl is losing patience
with me and seems somehow more *and* less interested in what I'm up
to, in that he wants to keep an eye on me but doesn't require insight
as to why I do anything I do. This seems to have infected Vitaliy as
well. (He is fond of Lottie and indulgent as husbands go, but Carl
has a tendency to inspire meanness.) Vitaliy is a deep sleeper, at least,
but Carl keeps inconsistent hours—there's no telling where he went
after dinner and when (or if) he'll be back. I did manage to turn one
of the security cameras toward the garage some months ago, though,
so my phone will alert me to movement with enough warning to get
back to the house. I missed it a few weeks ago because Lottie and I
had been laughing so hard about something one of the other playground mothers said to her in the grocery store, but I just told Carl

I'd gone for a walk because the doctor recommended it. He didn't ask further questions, so either he bought it or he didn't really care. The latter isn't really like him, but neither is the former. I think I just got lucky and he happened to be distracted at the time.

Tonight Lottie and I are both empty-handed, but it doesn't matter. We spread out a blanket and huddle together. The nights now are often cold.

"You could find someone else," she whispers to me. "It could be Carl's fault, not yours."

"Shh," I say, purely as plausible deniability, in case he's somehow magically watching. "Of course it's not his fault, it's mine." The medical records say so, and who am I to argue with the State?

"Still, statistically speaking . . ." She trails off. "And all you have to do is carry it."

"All," I murmur like a fading echo. She shudders. We both know what happens if I get caught—I'm not the first woman to think about padding the numbers, and DNA testing is now standard when the baby is born unless the father specifically declines. There *is* a slim possibility that Carl might not care if the baby is his, or that he might forgo the test because any child is better than nothing. I never got the sense that Carl cared much about his legacy, but he doesn't want to be emasculated in front of his friends—Vitaliy for example has five children without even trying, as if he gets Lottie pregnant just by wishing on a star, and Carl's brothers have at least three children each. Carl does not like to feel excluded.

I dislike even thinking about Carl in this way. He's not exactly the dream but he's not a nightmare, either. When I first met him I really thought we could be happy together. I thought, actually, that he was the first real bit of fortune I'd ever encountered in my entire life—certainly the first since Mom got sick. He's a bit older but not old; a little impatient but not usually unkind, or at least he wasn't then. Most of my problems aren't technically Carl's doing. They're just . . . the world. The cards we all got dealt after the war.

Sometimes, yes, I do resent that things aren't different, or wish that someone along the way had cared more or acted faster, before things took such a turn. But does it matter? Now I know the only luck in my life to be Lottie, and even on very dark days, I don't particularly wish for more.

Lottie and I sit in companionable silence for a long stretch of time. Her fingers are laced with mine, both of us shivering and shot through with cold but neither of us offering to leave. I wonder, as I sometimes do, what it would be like to have no Carl, no Vitaliy. Just Lottie and me, singing songs she invents, dancing together in our kitchen, tucking the children into bed and saying sweet things just because they cost nothing. Just because they feel good and kind to say.

"You could run," Lottie says. The words create a little puff of warmth in the air like a ghost.

I say nothing. Lottie continues, "The truth is he might kill you to be rid of you either way. If you don't have a child, he could kill you. If you do but the child isn't his, he could kill you. Everyone will say it's an accident because it's Carl. The police might look into it—"

But the police are paid by the State and the State owes a debt of gratitude to Carl. Without him, they might not have won. Thanks to him, everything is . . . better now.

I shiver a little and Lottie pulls me closer, as if I'm one of her babies. As if I'm Gaiana or Artem, the little twins who just started school, just started saying the pledge of allegiance with a look of pride in their little twin eyes, waiting for Vasiliy and Lottie to praise them. They are clever, sweet things. I wish someone could tell them some different words worth remembering.

"Would you consider it?" Lottie asks me. "If I could . . . find you a way out."

Again I say nothing. What can I say? That I would rather take my chances here where death is certain than out there where death is uncertain but alone? If Carl kills me, at least I know Lottie will attend my funeral. I know that my friends—the friends Carl has chosen for me—will say kind things about me. If I run they'll only spit on my name. Only a selfish woman runs. I am already a bad woman, something inside me is broken, not even all the medicine in the world can make this valley run green. Barren, isn't that funny? I am quite literally dead inside.

Time moves so differently when every day is part of a cycle. There is hope and dread and failure built in—victory, too, I assume, if I ever get that far. Though there is so much more after conception, isn't there? If I cannot make the spark that becomes the baby, then who is to say I can carry the baby, or that the baby will not one day succumb to an accident, or that I will fail in some other, more painful way? If all I am is a mother or a mother-in-waiting or a failure to become a mother, then where exactly does it end? It all just undulates, up and down, more like a pendulum than any sort of velocity. Like bobbing on an ocean, barely afloat.

Lottie turns her head so her lips brush my cheek, her breath warm on the side of my mouth. If I smiled right now the edge of it would slip into her mouth, maybe land on her tongue. I like that. The image in my head of something anatomically impossible is glowing and golden, and for once I don't think about the raw skin around my stubborn middle, the tired injection site.

Lottie lifts a hand, long fingers outstretched as she gently, like the bristles of a paintbrush, like the way it must feel to bathe in starlight, turns my chin. She and I stare at each other for a long time, her nose touching my nose, her chest rising and falling as mine rises and falls. She has to know I would never run because I could never leave her. She must know that she wants me to run, to thrive, for the very same reason I will always remain.

When she leans closer I know she is smiling. I'm not. My day is not like hers. My mind has too much time to invent. I will drive myself mad if she brings her lips to mine because I have no other pressing things with which to distract myself. There is no life in my house, there would be no division between the self when I am with her and the self when I'm without. I am only this one thing, this one fragile thing, so easily crushed, and—

My phone screen lights up in the night, startling us both. I grab for it quickly, heart pounding unevenly in my chest, flailing like a rabbit in a snare. "Carl's home." I can't catch my breath. I shoot to my feet, nearly tripping in the process. "I have t—"

"Go. I'll take care of this." Lottie moves quickly, efficiently, like all mothers I know. She has a gift for it, the muscle memory. "Hadia, I—"

I shouldn't stop. I don't have time. I do, though, and reach for her outstretched hand, smashing my lips to her knuckles.

"I'll die before I leave you," I say, and sprint through the night as if each step will be my last.

AYA
Washington, D.C.

Blood is almost impossible to get out of synthetic fabrics. I watch the clothes spin round in the dryer like they're some kind of hallucinogenic, letting the motion transport me even though I know the stains won't come out. They never do. And it was such a good shirt! Overpriced like everything is these days but soft from the moment I first bought it. Just as well, though. There were sweat rings and oil flecks on it, too.

My phone rings and I watch the clothes go around in the dryer again, another full rotation before answering. "This is Andreev."

"Aya! You bitch! I can't believe it!" Daisy is shrieking into my ear, so I pull the phone away, smiling apologetically at the elderly man waiting for his laundry beside me. "We just heard from headquarters. Holy shit, you got Charles McCabe!"

Yes, and now I've lost my favorite shirt. "Venkat is a mastermind, you know that. The plan was flawless and really, I owe it all to Bischoffs." Our surveillance guy. Without him I'd have gone into that building blind. I'd be dead, just like Charles McCabe, and he'd be the one trying to get my viscera out of his tux. The victor is always the person with a plan.

"Shut up!" Daisy is positively gleeful. "You *bitch*," she says again, admiringly. "I can't believe you're not in the office right now. I mean seriously, did Slavomir give you a raise on the spot? He better have. You've been owed a promotion for a fucking *age*."

It's true. That's what I was thinking about this morning, actually, when they first told me about the tip that Charles McCabe was—of all things—attending a courthouse wedding. I was absolutely certain when I heard my mark that it was a trap, that there was no way in hell an internationally renowned assassin would do something as completely boneheaded as to be in city hall on a weekday. It was too late to say no when Venkat gave me the dossier, plus I'm too low on payroll to have a choice in the matter, and I thought oh fuck, McCabe knows, he knows they're going to send me because I'm exactly the operative they'd send for something like this. He's finally going to wipe me off the board like he promised to do nine years ago when we graduated from the academy and got our assignments. Never mind that we'd fucked in his dorm room like five minutes earlier and were still a little drunk from celebrating with our cohort the night before. He just slid his assignment out of the manila file, swept a glance over it, and gave me a look I already recognized as one of abject pity. *Looks like I'm gonna have to kill you, Andreev,* he said to me, *but for the record, I'll fucking hate to do it.*

But I didn't have a choice, I never had one, and I guess in the end that was probably best. When I opened the door and saw him standing there in his tux—when I took it in, black tux, white dress, nobody else but the judge and a witness and my brain did the math, fucking shit, he's not *attending* a wedding, it's *his fucking wedding*—I didn't get a chance to make a decision. I pulled the trigger and he went down. The bride, whoever she was, she pulled out a pistol from god knows where, and—

Anyway, the shirt is ruined.

The buzzer on my laundry goes off and I reach inside just to confirm that yep, that's a goner. I toss it into the trash and realize I just spent over five dollars on laundering one fucking shirt.

"Hello? Aya, you still there?"

I blink myself back to cognizance. "Sorry, I'll be right in. I was just—I just had to do something but I've got paperwork, so—"

"Dude, *fuck* the paperwork. Aya fucking Andreev! You just pulled off the mark of the *century*! I'll do your paperwork, Venkat owes you a fucking car, Slavomir's so drunk I think he just asked me to do a threesome with him and his wife—"

"Slavomir has a hot wife," I admit. "Regina keeps it tight."

"Dude *I know*, get over here before I eat all your cake and hers too, I'm calling you a company car right now—"

It arrives about four minutes later. We're not chipped like McCabe's people because if the company can find you, so can the enemy, but since nobody alive wants me dead tonight I give Daisy my coordinates over the phone. I slide in and the car takes off, playing the usual jingles on the screen about the latest food delivery app or self-diagnosing healthcare chip. I wave a hand over the screen and turn off the noise. I wish I could turn it off inside my head.

Charles McCabe. Today was supposed to be his wedding day. Who the fuck was he marrying? She must have been fantastic in bed. And funny and smart and interesting. I always liked that about McCabe, that he only wanted the girls in our cohort with a sense of humor. He always came back to me, which I try not to brag about, mainly because in the light of day we were just friends. *Just friends,* I can't even think those words now without seeing the lift in everyone else's brow, the doubt that was so annoying because can't friends get each other off from time to time? The academy was hard, and the thing nobody wanted to say out loud was that it was sad. Tactical psych was the worst. We had to play both sides every day, the person doing the torment and the person surviving the torment, because you never knew which one you would be. You never knew from day to day whether you or your roommate or your study partner or your TA would be the one holding the knife. Proverbially. I only joined the academy because Mom was so sick and they covered everything, healthcare, food, they even gave me a stipend to use on things like books and clothes, even though we had a uniform. Anywhere else I'd have gone I would have drowned in debt.

We weren't supposed to tell each other our stories. Nobody was supposed to know how to hurt us, what weapons to use to cut our hearts out of our chests. But I knew McCabe's and he knew mine, and then I killed him on his wedding day.

"Andreev!"

I blink when Slavomir claps a hand on my shoulder. "Sir?"

"Come on, come in." He beckons me into his office and I'm grateful, because now that I'm walking into the office—my desk is in the bullpen like everyone else's, back in the corner with a stack of unfinished paperwork because I was planning to use today to catch up on my old reports before I got The Call—people are crowding around me. Someone shoves a plastic champagne flute into my hand and I raise it to my lips without thinking, coughing a little when I realize it's filled to the brim with vodka.

Slavomir ushers me in and hits the window tint so no one can see us, which makes everyone outside his office hoot lewdly at us like the deviants they are. "Shut up, you animals!" bleats Slavomir, slamming the side of a fist against his window before turning to me with a tipsy grin. "Animals," he says again with a shake of his head, then falls into his desk chair. It has incredible lumbar support. We're all jealous. This morning I just kept thinking, If McCabe doesn't kill me, I'll ask for Slavomir's chair.

"Andreev, you're a star, I always knew it." Slavomir grins lopsidedly at me again. "The moment I saw you at the trials I thought, that girl has *it*. Efficiency, adaptability, the whole shebang. You took out your partner in three minutes flat and didn't even break a sweat. The second the other one hit the floor I thought: I have to have her. I've got to have Andreev, the girl's a star." His smile turns doting, like I'm a favorite daughter or one of his pets. "And you know I don't say that lightly."

"Yeah," I manage. Slavomir's favorite operatives are usually the women, but funnily enough they don't get promoted at nearly the same rate as the men. He just likes to spend time with them. I believe he calls it mentorship. Hates to let go of *talent*. It's why the partner I took out at trials in three minutes flat works out of headquarters now, a tactician instead of cavalry, comfortably sat behind the walls of an office with a mortgage and a marriage and a dog. Because Slavomir likes my efficiency.

"Now look, I know I owe you a promotion." My chin snaps up. "I've owed you one a long time," Slavomir says, looking oddly sincere, "and I've got the paperwork right here. There's just one thing we've got to do first to get all the loose ends tied up, and then—"

"Loose ends?" I blink at him with confusion. "Sir, I don't think McCabe's getting any more dead."

Slavomir barks a belly laugh at me, his face turning red with effort to rein in his apparent amusement. "There's that wit, Andreev." He wipes away tears and I become concerned he's drunker than I thought. "No, no, nothing like that, it's more administrative."

I sit up straighter. "Administrative? Does this mean—"

A desk job. Oh god, a desk job. Maybe even management? I could cry with relief. No more ruined shirts, no more encrypted dossiers at ungodly hours, maybe even a goddamn day off to visit Mom—

"Whoa, whoa, slow your roll, superstar." He slides a file across the desk to me, the front flap open. It's a dossier, although it looks more like an employment record, like something from HR. For a second I think I'm being disciplined, or commended? My picture is looking up at me, unsmiling, but—

I never took this picture. It's me, but I'm wearing some kind of shapeless linen shift? I take in the name *Hadia* and nudge it aside to find another picture of me, but I'm . . . hot? Not that I'm currently ugly, I guess, but I've worn my hair in the same basic crop for years. I keep it in plaits just to keep my hair out of my face. Never a ponytail, never long like this, too easy to grab. The name next to my picture says *Naomi*. The third page is a picture of a cat, an unremarkable shorthair in what looks like a shelter mug shot. *Jessamyn*. A stupid name for a cat, but I've never liked cats. I respect them just fine— they make sense to me—but I'd never have one myself. The final file is me but I'm wearing an off-the-shoulder gown and a tiara and I'm stepping out of an enormous black SUV. It's not a headshot like the others, more like a paparazzi shot. *Violeta*. I'm looking shyly away from the camera with my hand protectively near my face, but there's something in my eyes that tells me I know I'm being photographed. I not only know, but I actively don't mind it.

I inhale sharply. "Sir, is this—?"

"Now, look," Slavomir says as if I've interrupted him. "This is very confidential stuff, very high level. Normally I wouldn't share this much with you, but given everything—and I know you should be celebrating right now," he adds, as if my main issue is that I'm not currently drunk off my ass with the others, "but this can take some time to digest."

"I don't understand." I'm shaking my head and clutching my little plastic flute of vodka. "Are these . . . Am I a mark, or . . . ?"

"Oh, bloody fuck, no." Slavomir laughs again. Clearly I am on fire with the jokes tonight. I should contemplate a one-woman show. "No, no, listen. You know that what we do here can be . . . complicated."

"Complicated" is one word for it. Nobody ever knows the full scope of any given plan. This morning, for example, I was called into the office by Venkat and given five minutes to memorize a schematic, a route, and a passcode that he then took from me and burned. Then I was transported by another operative and given an earpiece, on the other end of which was Bischoffs. He knew the route but not the target. That was given to me only when I was placed at the drop-off point. *Your target is Charles McCabe. Best of luck, Andreev. Operation begins in five seconds. Five, four, three, two—*

"—what is called the Omega Universe," Slavomir says. "Basically, there are multiple parallel worlds that have diverged from a single point along the Omega Timeline. We oversee the others, because we were the first to develop a window that our operatives can pass through. Other 'verses have since developed the technology themselves, but, you know, we keep an eye on it. No antitrust legislation here." Another Slavomir laugh and the deafening sound of rushing water. "—aware of the second principle of chaos theory? I like to think of it unofficially as a sort of vacuum principle, you know, where nothingness in one universe releases a burst of chaos in another, so ultimately it has to be a sort of controlled explosion—"

I feel a fogginess in my brain that makes it hard to concentrate. His words pass in and out, mixing with the blood on my shirt. The image of Charles McCabe on the floor, in my bed, on the floor, in uniform beside me, so proud to stand before the academy that day and take his vows, in his tuxedo promising his life to someone who isn't me. *Just friends.*

Slavomir's voice resurges like the burst of a dam. "—other versions, you know. Other McCabes, other yous, and now that the balance has been offset between the two of you it's rather . . . precarious. An unusual situation really, very unusual—not many cross-universe rivalries like this one. But we've targeted these four multiverse threads, as they are the largest threat to the stability of our own."

He looks at me and I realize I've been sitting here too long without talking. I nod.

"The point is," he says, leaning back in the chair that Charles McCabe unknowingly bled for this morning, "there are four other McCabes and four other Andreevs. That means four chances to really get this right, with every other Andreev taking out every other McCabe. That's the neatest way to make sure entropy remains controlled, systemic. If the same thing that happened in this universe happens in all the others it creates a domino effect—very thermodynamically ordered. That's what management is looking for."

"So then—" I swallow heavily. "He *can* be more dead, is what you're saying. I have to kill Charles McCabe again?"

"Not *you*," Slavomir assures me hastily. "In fact, *you* can't. That would be messier, it involves a lot of paperwork. No, no, *you*," he says, pointedly shoving the file at me again. "These versions of you. You simply have to distribute the dossiers and make sure each of these operatives is informed of their mark. Very simple. Yes?"

I look at the four other versions of me. A cat? A fucking cat. I skim the file. My target is—Jesus fucking Christ—a bird.

"Oh, that's an interesting one," says Slavomir in a sort of clinical voice, as if it is objectively fascinating, like a research project. "The bird is carrying a disease that could wipe out the entire population. The political environment there is a little unstable, vaccine protocols are down, it's basically ecological terrorism. You'd be saving thousands, millions of people, just by delivering a message."

Charles McCabe is dead. And he is also a bird. And a crown prince.

And an arms dealer.

Fuckety fuck. I lift my glass to my lips and drain it in one swallow.

"There she is!" Slavomir cries, delighted. "Aya Andreev." He shakes his head, teary-eyed. "I always knew you were a star."

NAOMI
Universe Sigma-Gamma

My phone is burning a hole in my pocket. The message is burning a hole in my phone. The entire universe is in flames and my brain is smoldering. I can't think properly, I can't even hear properly, this entire meeting—in person for once—is lost on me. Holy fuck. Holy fuck. Holy fuck.

Omg so funny you'll never believe what happened today, said the text from my friend Daisy, who is honestly not even my fucking friend. Isn't this your dream guy that you've told us basically nothing about??? I, like, DIED.

It was a screenshot of her latest match. Charlie M., age thirty-four, who wears shirts like he doesn't understand shirts and yet *very obviously* understands shirts in a way I never will. *You have matched with Charlie M.!*, and a sexy little wink face that suggests sex is on the table. Daisy's face right next to his. Daisy, tits out, matched with Charlie. Charlie seeing Daisy's tits and saying fuck yes I love tits. Charlie Miaza. *My* Charlie, who was late again to drinks last night. He made up for it—I fucking hate when my dad comes to visit, his new wife is unbearable and all I do is miss Mom horribly, like someone cut her out of my stomach—and if it weren't for Charlie I think I would have slapped Regina clean across the face. But Charlie kissed me and doted on me and slipped me caring glances and told Regina not to talk to me like that and stood up and coolly paid for dinner and told my father I was the best thing he'd ever done, the only good thing, and then he kissed me again and even though I know it was a performance my knees still went a little weak. And I thought again, dangerously, how profoundly and acutely I couldn't possibly love him, but did.

And now I'm underwater in a conference room. My phone is burning a hole in my pocket, and I'm about to psychologically snap. In. Half.

"Naomi?"

I try to shake myself back to the present but don't really manage it. The clarity I aim for still feels a long way off, but I look up at the receptionist. She's a new hire, I think her name is Patricia. "Yes?"

"There's someone here for you." Patricia steps back from the doorframe with the expectation that I'll follow her, and I realize I haven't written a single word in my notebook. I gather it up anyway, and my pen, and the croissant I've been tearing to shreds and I follow her without checking if I should. Slavomir, my editor on this assignment, doesn't seem to notice or care.

"Here you are, conference room A," says Patricia, delivering me to an empty room like a mediocre pizza. There's a screen pulled down, so a video call I guess. I take a seat heavily—think a fourteen-year-old being told they can't go out. Then the screen flickers, and the image of someone fills the screen.

"Naomi. Hi. I'm Aya Andreev."

I blink because I am hallucinating. Clearly I am having a very strange dream. "Hello," I offer vaguely in reply.

"Yeahhhhhh," says Aya Andreev. "I can't tell if you're—" She frowns at me. "Are you seeing me?"

"Hm? Yes, the connection is fine." It's probably a bad sign that I leapt to anger at Daisy when this is clearly Charlie's fault. It's just that Daisy was so smug about it. She could have approached it differently, you know? I've never had very good relationships with women and honestly, I don't know if Daisy and I even speak the same language. Like, was she trying to be mean? Was she just . . . Did she actually think it was funny? *Was* it funny? I think back on what I've told her about Charlie. I think I downplayed his significance to me, saying he was great in bed but there was no future there. . . .

Maybe she thought it was funny.

"Naomi?" asks Aya Andreev. "You get that I'm, like. *You*, right?"

Yes, I do get that. Her hair—my hair—is in short French braids and she's not wearing makeup. It's close to what I look like at kickboxing when I'm hungover. I guess it could be altered footage? I don't know. What a weird prank.

"Look, are you familiar with the second principle of chaos theory?" Aya stops. "No, that isn't right. Let me start over. Do you know who Charlie Miaza is?"

My attention rockets to hers. "What?"

"Charles Seang Miaza, alias Charlie Miaza, private equity manager for Miaza Capital, age thirty-four. Currently resides in Manhattan—"

"What's this about?" I interrupt, because this is the first I'm hearing about Charlie's full name or where he works or the fact that he apparently works for himself (why, then, is he always late?).

"Well—" Aya looks over her shoulder like there's someone there coaching her. "Look, I'm gonna level with you. I don't have a fucking clue how to deliver this message but basically I'm you in another universe. I just killed an assassin named Charles McCabe who is Charlie Miaza in your universe. And because I killed my Charles—" She stops abruptly, her face going slightly uncomfortable in the way that I recognize, because I had to train myself to stop doing that early on. It's best as a journalist to maintain an expressionless look I like to call my *attentive listening face.* "Because I killed the version of Charlie in my universe, you now have to kill the version of him in yours." Aya pauses again. "Because of the second principle of chaos theory."

"I guess you could tell me what that is?" I suggest.

"Well, it's, um, thermodynamic-y," she says. "They didn't cover it at the academy so I only kind of understand. But basically since there's a bunch of nothing now where Charles McCabe used to be in my universe, that means his . . . entropy? Or something? Is going to increase in yours." She looks embarrassed, the way assistants do when they need me to change the date of an interview at the last second. I recognize the look of someone who is just doing what they're told. "It's like there's been a vacuum created and, like, things could get . . . bad."

I feel very sorry for this version of me, which isn't helpful. Because I've just remembered what she told me to do. "I'm sorry, what?"

"You won't get in trouble," she says quickly. "I mean, we'll assign your case a tactician and you'll get a dossier and all that. You'll barely have to think at all."

"You think my concern about murder is the logistics?" I ask her, genuinely flummoxed.

"Oh gosh, I—" She looks hugely upset. "I'm so sorry, I . . . I forgot."

"You forgot? That murder is bad?"

"No, but I'm—like, I was trained for this?" Her glance is both defensive and pleading. "I wasn't given a choice. I didn't want to kill McCabe, I didn't want to do any of this, but he was my target and Mom was sick—"

I can't help it. "She's sick there too?"

For some reason I thought it would be different. For some reason I thought—

I thought it would be better.

Aya looks sadly at me. "She's dead here," she says. "Actually."

I inhale a sharp breath, then push it out. "Sorry."

"It's fine."

"It's not fine—"

"I don't have much longer." She smooths over a much more effective facade and I almost want to applaud her. I know how difficult that is. "The point is you've got to kill him."

"Why?" I ask. "Is he dangerous?"

"Not yet," she says. "Not at this moment. But he will be by the end of the week."

"Why? What's going to happen to him?"

"Well—" She's getting better at this, but her face still turns rosy. "Because by Friday, he'll either become a war criminal or—" She cringes. "Host to a malevolent spirit."

"What, like a demon?" Wait, that's not the important question here. "Are you saying you don't know which one it'll be?" Oh, I can tell by the look on her—my—face that she knew I'd be pissed about that. "Then how do you know it's going to happen at all?"

"Well, a lot of this is statistics—"

"Statistics? You want me to kill someone based on what they *might* do?"

"It's definitely one or the other. Well, there's a minor third option, but—" Aya stops. "Basically, what happens to Charlie depends on what Violeta does to Karlo."

I thought I was incapable of cogent thought before. Now I am just a meat sack of confusion. I'm three brain cells in a trench coat.

"Who the *fuck*," I demand, "is Violeta?"

VIOLETA
Universe Kappa

The woman who is me is very nervous. She has many noticeable tics of apprehension which make me doubt she could really be me, though she does look very like me. Like a version of myself I might imagine in a dream of a different life, or like how I might look in a nightmare where I have somewhere to be but my feet are trapped. Oh! Like how Mama must surely feel, locked snugly inside her mind.

I appear to have drifted a little in thought, because by the time I remember to listen to what the other me is saying, I have lost track of the point. The other me doesn't seem to have noticed, which makes sense. I have a very attentive listening face, especially when I am not paying attention.

"Basically it's the second principle of chaos theory," the other me concludes.

"Self-similarity or interconnection?" I ask.

"Er, the . . . second one," she says uninspiringly.

"Interesting, because I would have guessed it has to do with feed-back loops. But of course this sort of thing is really beyond me." Without thinking I have begun to flirt with her gently. It is really a survival technique, I don't know how else to explain it. You'd think that I could be myself around myself, but actually, all I feel is a very strange need to leap out of my chair and into the screen, into what-ever world she occupies. She won't say she is an assassin but I know she is. I can tell. "Anyway, what is it you need me to do?"

She seems flustered, as if she expected something different. "You . . . you don't have any more questions? Or need, like, proof?"

"Do you have any?" I pose neutrally.

We look at each other for a long time.

"Right, well, Charles McCabe—the version of him that's in your world—is your husband, Crown Prince Karlo." I nod because this is very simple. "In my world he was a . . . sort of a complex multilay-ered criminal. In your world he is royalty, and currently he's—"

"Is this about the coup?" I interject. "Because I have that under control."

"Oh. Well, yes. Sort of. The thing is, before I killed McCabe, your husband might have turned out all right," the other me says. Her name is apparently Aya but I think it's a silly name, more like the sound of a cat complaining. Violeta is much better. I'll call her Worse Violeta. "But now he's much more dangerous. The coup he's plan-ning, it'll set your world on track for wide-scale military takeover. Martial law that gives way to a fascist regime."

Worse Violeta stops talking for a long time as if she is waiting for me to speak. "And this is . . . bad?" I prompt eventually.

She looks at me like I'm an idiot, which I'm used to. Karlo looks at me like that all the time, and so does the Duchess Spiros, and so did Mama. But that look is precisely why I'm able to live as freely as I do. Imagine if I actually cared who mistook me for an idiot, and to their own detriment, too! What an incredibly foolish way to live.

"Fascism is generally bad, yes," Worse Violeta parses out for me as if I'm a child.

"Theoretically, sure, for the world at large and presumably most people," I point out. "But I would be the wife of the fascist in question, which as I understand it is quite different." If Karlo controlled the state then I would no longer have to worry about silly things like my relatability to the public. If he controlled the media I might lose my upper hand—I am much savvier about my image because Karlo does not consider the cruciality of optics—but what would it matter?

Worse Violeta looks slightly green as she pauses to consider this. For a moment I think she will have no argument. Then I begin imagining what would happen if Karlo were to ascend the throne. Or would it be an empire? Would I become an empress? Of course, without the threat of public disapproval perhaps he might be rid of me. Omnipotence may not suit him. He already wears privilege so irresponsibly. Suppose he were to replace me with the Duchess Spiros? It would not be unheard of. He could not turn Artem against me but Olympios is young still. Things could still go awry. Hm.

"Well," Worse Violeta manages as I begin to see the virtues of her concern. "Historically, wives of tyrants meet the same fate as their husbands. Do you think Karlo would be able to hold his regime? Because if not—"

"No, I understand," I say, because I've already arrived at this conclusion. "So you want me to kill Karlo?"

"Yes." She looks relieved. "You don't have any moral opposition to that, do you?"

He is the father of my sons and my partner in life. "Of course not. As you say, fascism is bad."

"So true," she exhales. She seems fonder of me now than she was a few minutes ago. I like it, having an ally. I will call her Other Violeta now. "And so you know, we'll take care of everything in terms of the police."

Hm. She seems to be underthinking this. "Karlo cannot simply fall dead," I point out. "Someone has to kill him, and it cannot be known to be me."

"Oh." I recall that she is an assassin, so she is probably excellent at killing but inexperienced with the delicacy of statecraft. It is lucky we are on the same team. "Well, who is the best person to kill him?"

Oh, what a delightful question. I consider my options. His own nobles could turn on him in an instant of course but that would not

endear me to them, and I plan to keep my crown. His mother is an
option. Perhaps he could be caught for his part in the coup and tried
for treason? But I would be implicated. I could protest innocence but
Regina will know, she'll suspect me. Perhaps she'll decide to play
regent and try to turn Artem against me, or find a way to ensure
that Olympios inherits instead. Oh the trials of having a dim but
charming second son.

It will have to be personal, then, not political. "His lover, the
Duchess Spiros, in a murderous rage."

"Ah. I like it." Other Violeta nods and I see that she is very comfortable with tactics. "Do you intend to frame her?"

"No need," I say cheerfully. "I do not think it will be difficult to
achieve my intended result. Karlo is very hotheaded and Duchess
Spiros is a woman of fiery passions." I had always intended to have a
party at week's end. I'll add a hunt so that Karlo will be particularly
irrational. He has terrible aim. Ah! I know. I will join the hunt and
bag his prize, claiming beginner's luck of course as I am usually so
careful to appear unskilled. He will be mortified by his loss. Then
when the Duchess Spiros begins their little sex games he will want
the upper hand, and she will refuse because she is herself and not me.
Oh. Things will get so messy. I do love when a plan comes together
very simply. Almost elegantly! I am ecstatic.

"I think you've got this taken care of," notes Other Violeta, observing the change in my expression. Alas, I must have unintentionally
gotten too comfortable. The last person to make such an observation
was Mama. But there would be no need to hold anything against
Other Violeta! She is myself and I am her and we are one in all
things.

Sublime. "Is there anything else?"

"No, that's—"

"Who else are we?" I ask curiously, because it's very interesting,
isn't it? This idea that there might be a partner in life for me after
all. I thought I was alone but I'm not. I could cry with relief. I've not
actually cried in the past but I've observed it and found it to be the
right reaction for certain occasions such as this. Relief.

"Oh, well—" Other Violeta looks away, her eyes temporarily leaving the screen. "I don't really know if I'm allowed to say."

"Oh." There is a small deflation in my chest. "I understand."

She looks back at me very seriously then. "Can I ask you something?" I nod my assent because of course. I am happy to help. "What happened to our mom? In your world, I mean. Is she dead?"

"Oh, no, don't be silly!" I laugh. "The doctors assure me that she can still hear and see and process information. So it's even better, really, because she still exists but she can't disagree or disapprove or tell anyone what actually happened. I didn't want to, you know, not at first," I point out, as Other Violeta holds her expression very still. It must be her version of attentive listening. "I thought even if she didn't like me very much she would still see the beauty of my success. I'd have made a very good life for both of us if she'd just been a little more—" I bite my lip girlishly as I think of the word. "Compliant. Generous, even! It's very uncharitable what she was going to do. She would have poisoned Regina and Karlo against me, and for what reason? So that I would marry lower? Is that what she wanted for me? I never did get to ask her." I pause to think wistfully about her fall. There was a little flame in her eyes, so I think she knew it was coming. I like to think it was the moment she gave her approval to go on and live my life. Though I have a tendency to be overly poetic.

"Oh. Okay." Other Violeta coughs. "Well, I wouldn't worry about the others. You're in the best situation out of all of us, actually. Probably."

"Oh!" That's nice. "But of course I'd love to help the others if I can. Is there anyone who particularly needs help?"

There is a flicker from her then that I recognize at once. I've seen it many times on Regina's face.

"No," says Other Violeta. Which is obviously a lie.

HADIA
Universe Omicron-Delta

The Holomoji of the woman who claims to be me is hard and muscular. Even her face is more angular than mine. Her cheeks are like arrowheads or something. She's broader in the shoulders as well, and more masculinely dressed. She seems tired. I can relate. I am only having this conversation at all because she assured me they took care

of the surveillance inside the house—but I can't help looking up at
the camera anyway. The red light that signals recording is off, but I
find that only marginally comforting. There are many, many more
imaginable impossibilities than the one where a camera keeps working even when it should cut out.

I should know. I am living one of them.

"Because I killed Charles McCabe," she says, "you have to kill
the version of him in your world. Over there he's an arms dealer for
a totalitarian regime, very dangerous. Those weapons are also being
trafficked internationally, to fund guerrilla warfare in other countries. Including countries with rampant human-trafficking offenses
and major violations of human rights."

I hold my breath. I have always known the State owes its debt of
gratitude to Carl's family for funding their side during the war. They
would have lost without his fortune.

Before the State consolidated the properties and assets of the opposition, Carl's family was already very significant. He doesn't like
to talk about it because it's unrefined—*very* unrefined compared to
what he does now, which is essentially chair the board of military
operatives put together by the State. It's ceremonial. But his family,
in a previous world, made fried chicken sandwiches. I'm belittling
it—it's difficult to put it another way—though I suppose I could say
they owned a fast food corporation that specialized in . . . well, fried
chicken sandwiches. You see. There is no getting around it, which is
why Carl does not discuss what he did before the reassignment. And
it is ultimately not relevant. War is won by geography and commerce,
and when the two sides shared equal right to the same land, money
was the victor. Something Lottie's twins will never learn, because in
school nowadays I hear they are taught that our heads of state were
simply heaven-blessed.

"So I have to kill him," I say, glancing down at my hands. This
concern—this despair—is not false. I am shaken to some extent,
definitely, but could I honestly say I've never thought of killing Carl
before? This is the solution to my problems. It always has been. The
reason I've never thought seriously of doing it is because I don't believe there is actually a way. There are cameras everywhere. Everyone will know it was me, and they will all know why. I have no life

if Carl is dead. I can't marry again—no one will have me, they'll know of my barrenness, the State is my doctor and the hormones will be widely discovered—and given the State's general suspicion of women, who as a demographic sided predominantly with the previous federal government only scant decades ago, the property will transfer from Carl to our heirs, of which there are none. If Carl dies I lose everything. If I kill Carl, then I will be rid of Carl, but I will have nothing else.

"Maybe there's someone else," suggests the other me. Her name is Aya, which is lovely. It sounds like a little song. "If someone else appeared to commit the crime, would that be better? Would it give you a better shot?"

A small flame of something ignites in my chest. Hope, maybe. I am reminded again of my silly little dream—the kitchen I share with Lottie, with her children that love me as if I'm their mother too, the songs we sing together with the pretty words Lottie dreams up for us all. What does this dream not have? Carl, of course, but also, no Vitaliy. I must be rid of him, too. And what a simple thing, if Vitaliy is the one who kills Carl. No, no, I mustn't put this in the hands of the State—who knows if that trial would end justly. But if Vitaliy and Carl were *both* to die, perhaps of a tragic accident, then yes, Carl's brothers and their children would inherit my house and Carl's fortune, but so would *Lottie's* children, and since she is their mother she could continue to live in their house. It would appear more than charitable for her to invite me into her home, as we would be two widows. . . . Perhaps she would not even have to remarry. Her eldest will come of age soon. He is already nearly thirteen and he adores her, as everyone does. He will care for her, and she will care for me.

I start to cry then, unwillingly. The hormones, I assume. This feeling, I don't know what to call it. The exquisite danger of happiness I don't yet have, which isn't guaranteed. But how can I ever look away from it, this ending? This is the ending! I want to run straight for it with relief.

"I could do it," I whisper. "With Lottie's help, I could do it. They could take a hunting trip together in the woods—they often do. They could . . . fall. Stumble." I prepare Carl's food and Lottie prepares Vitaliy's. Many ordinary household items can cause temporary paralysis.

Even intoxication might be enough. Lottie will have to stay above suspicion of course, she'll have to stay home, but I could follow them. I may be soft around the middle but I'm not incapable of stealth. They would never suspect it! Carl knows I can't kill him and he'd never dream of anyone having designs on Vitaliy's death. Vitaliy is significantly less powerful and infinitely more likable, on account of being an idiot. "And if Carl were gone—"

"Oh, Hadia." Aya looks impossibly sad then. "Hadia, I'm so sorry, I should have clarified—it's not Carl."

"What?" My brain short-circuits as I look at her Holomoji, which is definitely wrong. Her posture still looks erect but I can see from the expression on her face that her shoulders have slumped forward. She is holding her head in her hand as if she's sitting at a desk, hunched miserably over it.

"I'm so sorry," she says again. "The version of Charles McCabe that exists in your world isn't your husband. I'm so sorry."

Her apology glances off me. I barely flinch. I hardly feel anything now that my silly ending has been ripped from me yet again. I should really stop replaying it for myself. Sometimes I see it at night, to help me fall asleep. I always rewind and start over to try and play it slower, so I can enjoy it for longer. It never works. It never lasts. "Then who is it?"

"Your neighbor." Aya is looking at me as if she worries I am catatonic. "Hadia, I should have said right away, I'm so—"

"Vitaliy?" I ask, because like I said, Vitaliy is an idiot. How dangerous can he possibly be? "I know you said he would get worse over time—" I don't understand chaos theory. I don't know the first thing about chaos theory. My life is so fucking ordered, every minute of it. I am the only chaos in this world. I and my thundering heart. "But still, I wouldn't think Vitaliy capable of—"

"It's not Vitaliy," Aya says. "It's a woman. Charlotte McCrary is her maiden name."

This time I thunder backward as if she struck me. I'm reeling as if she shot me. "What?"

"I'm looking over your file again just to be sure, Hadia. I just want to triple-check, I should have been clearer. Okay, next door is Vitaliy Bures. His wife is Charlotte Bures, born Charlotte McCrary, who goes by—"

"Lottie." I don't mean to whisper it. Really, I don't. I think I mean to spit it out or choke on it but instead it slips out. Not a spiteful whisper, not shock. The whisper of one lover to another. Sweetness meant for closed doors and candle flames. "You want me to kill Lottie."

"Hadia, I'm so—"

"If you apologize again I will kill you. I will pass through every world to find you and slit your throat." Hormones. It must be the hormones. I stand straighter because suddenly my stomach no longer hurts. I feel no softness, no sagging devastation, everything is aflame now, everything in me rages. It's not fair. It isn't fair. It isn't fair.

None of this was fair. It was all wrong from the beginning. I never had a chance. My ending is being ripped from me. If I kill Lottie, nobody will notice. Her body will fall without a sound. Her husband and children will mourn her but Vitaliy will remarry and her babies will pledge their allegiance to the State. It isn't fair. I will have nothing. Without Lottie I have nothing. It isn't fair.

How can anyone ask this of me? I want to break down. I want to break into pieces. I want the shards of myself to lie here on the floor, to pierce through Carl's foot so he remembers I once existed. That I was here and I was dangerous. I am dangerous.

This me, this person in another world who has never lived what I have lived, she wants me to kill the only goodness I have in my life because it is bad. Because all this time I thought Lottie was sweetness and instead she is something more. But I can also be more.

Maybe the truth is that I am a vessel of chaos. Touch me and I will explode.

"What do you want me to do?"

JESSAMYN
Universe Beta-Pi

There is a voice. Coming from the box. I pay it no mind for I am. Very busy. Outside the enemy is brazen. There is bloodshed in his song. I feel it. Notes of war. He mocks me but I do not mind it my vigilance is not conditional. It does not turn on his acknowledgment it is not lessened by his ridicule it is Eternal. I am. Blessed.

The voice is very distracting. I bat my ears I dislike it. The voice says my name many times Jessamyn Jessamyn Jessamyn.

"A ridiculous name for a cat. Jessamyn, can you hear me? It's . . . I'm you, I guess. I don't . . . this is so fucking absurd, all this for a chair with lumbar support. Jessamyn, there's a bird outside, I'm like forty percent sure it's a lesser goldfinch—You don't know what different birds are. What am I doing. Look, there's a bird and I need you to kill it. Fucking Christ. This is ridiculous. You're a cat. Isn't this your natural instinct or whatever? I don't know how to make sure you kill *this specific* bird—"

Daisy begins to paw at the screen. Mother will not like that. GET DOWN I tell her with the full weight of my authority because I am the overseer and I oversee. I ensure that there are no. Offenses. GET DOWN FROM THERE YOU IDIOT.

The enemy chortles. It watches over its young and then turns as if to say. Fuck you. I do not like this at all. I am. Mortally offended. Of course I do not show it because I do not show weakness and it is weakness to tell the enemy when you have been injured or where there are flaws. I know there is a flaw because Olympios is also looking at the bird and he sees this behavior but still he looks away and is not offended instead he looks at stupid Araminta who is playing with feathers in the patch of sun on the floor. I dream sometimes. About that patch on the floor. One of the others is always in it. It is also not safe. It is right beside the glass veil. I do not think. It is meant for us. One day the others will be punished.

Every day except for some days Mother goes to the altar of the gods and returns with the harvest and today is one of those days. It will be some time before she returns I know this because Man-Mother brought us food today and got very close to me as if to touch me. He reveres me I know that much. Not properly he is not a talented worshiper but I can see that. His devotion is real.

The enemy plies its young with lies. Here is food I have made for you. No. It pretends to be a goddess of harvest like Mother. It is not. The enemy is a thief. His nourishment is stolen. I know too why he feeds his progeny. He builds an army right before my eyes. It is shameless.

The voice on the screen continues to speak. "You know what—let's just try something, okay? Here you go, other me. Have at it. Jesus."

Daisy gives a loud cry of joy as the glass veil vanishes. As if by magic it is whisked aside. For a moment I stare in disbelief. Then the enemy's eyes meet mine and I know.

This is a calling. From the heavens I have been called. My mission is Divine. It is Blessed.

I soar from my tower on the wings of destiny. Behold the enemy shall quiver! For I am the harbinger of wrath. On this day Vengeance is risen. Chaos is upon him.

For at last my time has come!

AYA
The Omega Universe

When I finally step away from my desk, I feel a hand on my shoulder. "You did good, superstar," says Slavomir, patting my back. "Get on home."

I nod. My back hurts. I haven't been on desk duty for a long time, maybe years. I wonder if I'll be able to take a vacation? There are rumors that management gets vacation days. I try to imagine where I'd go if I could take a vacation but all my brain will offer me is images from my past, various shots of Charles McCabe like my own personal in memoriam.

I haven't been able to sleep these last couple of nights. Every time I close my eyes, I see that look on his face—the thing that isn't surprise, but also isn't really anything because I do have an unnaturally good trigger finger. I always scored highest in marksmanship, which was a surprise to me. Mom hated guns. I can't say I like them, either. In another world, would this have been a different sort of talent? I mean, what is this skill, anyway? Hand-eye coordination? Motor control? Maybe there's a universe where I do embroidery or something. Or nurse baby squirrels back to life with my hands.

McCabe always wanted to know more about Mom. I admit there were moments when I wondered if he was actually just being clever about it all, warming me up because I had no other friends and I was his only real competition. We didn't see each other as competitors yet—school has a way of making the future seem imaginary, like some horizon we can't actually touch, but maybe McCabe was smarter than me. Maybe he filed it away, all my little childhood wounds. Maybe he kept a file somewhere in his head, a dossier like the one I received the morning I killed him on his wedding day. Aya Andreev. Abandonment. Weak left wrist (a fall that never healed properly—it pains me sometimes when the weather turns cold). And, of course, a disemboweling desperation to be loved.

I shake myself as I walk out the door. Stupid to wonder these things. To mythologize my significance in his life. Of course he never cared about me. And even if he did, what would it matter? I killed him. Even if he had a file about my weaknesses somewhere in his head, it wasn't a very good one. I had one for him, too, but it wasn't even relevant. It was things he found funny. Foods he didn't like. Nothing that would have helped me kill him. In the end, that thing was always intrinsic to me. It had nothing to do with him. He was just a body, not a sweet tooth or a sense of humor. If he had ever been anything more, it vanished the day we both got our assignments. The day that someone else—the academy on high—chose our sides.

I think around the thought I actually want to have, which is like a golden orb of something, sadness and loss and the feeling of once having held something in my hands, only for it to disappear when I wasn't looking. Instead, I try to picture the other McCabes out there; I wonder what they're like. They're marks, just like all the marks I've targeted over the years, and like them, the other McCabes are bodies that I will never actually get to witness.

Still, my files are detailed. Prince Karlo is a real piece of work. No loss there, and much as I hate to draw a line around myself and Violeta, she obviously has this well in hand. I shudder a little, recalling the way she talked about Mom's death. Well, *her* mother, which, okay, is a very different version as well, maybe not even the same person, but it was still murder, or at the very least attempted murder. God, to think, if Violeta were in my universe—

Well, she'd have killed Charles McCabe without blinking, wouldn't she? But I already did that. So ultimately the point is moot, and there is no difference between us after all. Nothing that matters, anyway.

Jessamyn will be fine. Cats hunt birds, it happens. The two I'm worried about are Naomi, the pretty journalist version of me, and Hadia, the dystopian housewife who can't have children. No, strike that, I think there's more to Hadia than meets the eye. I think she's tougher than she looks, and even though I feel impossibly sorry for her, I also think she's resilient. It's weird, isn't it, to compliment myself that way? But I'm an assassin, Violeta's a psychopath, Jessamyn's a . . . "hunter" is a generous term, but still—all of those things have a certain cold-bloodedness in common. They have necessity for common ground. If it's inside all the rest of us, it's probably inside Hadia, and that means she'll find it in herself to do what she has to do.

But Naomi's life is pretty cushy, actually. She does well in her career. She has some friends the same way I have friends, which is to say superficially, as a result of the workplace. What *she* has going for her is that her relationship with McCabe is already tenuous. She wanted to know why her version—Charlie Miaza—still had his online dating profile up, and why he's always late for their dates. The answer to both is that he has a young daughter who plays with his phone and a difficult relationship with his ex-wife, which means his plans are constantly changing at the last second. But if he won't tell Naomi that, then neither will I. I'm not about to make this harder.

My mind sees a toy and grabs it: Charlie Miaza's ex-wife is the same woman McCabe was going to marry. I recognized her the moment I saw her picture in the file. Her name is Gaiana Spiros and she's beautiful. Really beautiful, glowing almost, even in a photograph.

I wonder, if in Naomi's universe McCabe is miserably divorced—if in that universe he really does love Naomi, and she's me—then does that mean . . . ?

I shouldn't wonder, but the thought is grotesque and comforting. Beautiful in its contortions. I want to live in it as long as possible, as long as I can.

I pull my coat tighter around me, bypassing the fleet of company cars and choosing to walk the few miles home.

VIOLETA

I have never shot so beautifully before! What a rush. The stag goes down with barely a sound, a perfect puncture through the eye. When it happens of course I proclaim my astonishment, going so far as to swoon into the arms of Vitaliy, Duke Spiros, whom Karlo particularly dislikes for obvious reasons (being married to Karlo's lover and, more importantly, taller), but inwardly there is a sense of tranquility, as if a restless creature inside of me has finally found the motivation to lie down. I generally find hunting stupid, given that it is a silly game played mostly by men who cannot find a clitoris, but on occasion I will concede it can be quite stimulating. It's a very convenient way to commit fully sanctioned violence. And to think it's only my first kill of the night!

Dinner is flawless. My menu choices are excellent, particularly when I have caught the venison for our stew. There are many men who flirt with me this evening as always, though I only have eyes for one guest at this table. The Duchess Spiros, who sulks into her wine. Beside her—because Karlo is never discreet—my husband is slumped in a childish sulk, his arms folded tightly across his chest. He caught nothing today, and he and Gaiana Spiros have already had a row over something silly, him being too gruff with her in public and mocking her too intimately, in such a way as no one else should know. The table is abuzz with rumors, and the nobles present—all pieces in Karlo's intended coup—are beginning to murmur among themselves about whether Karlo would be any real improvement over Regina. Thrice now a conversation has stopped completely just as Karlo has approached—a sure sign that he was the subject of gossip. How embarrassing for him. His ego, fragile as it is on a normal basis, seems ready to explode.

As for the Duchess, I've made sure to make a comment about Gaiana's figure being "full" (I myself look fashionably thin, whereas she considers country living to be an excuse to dress casually—by which I mean dowdily) so she has drunk far too much wine and hardly touched her food. Meanwhile I am the toast of the party. If only I could host an assassination every weekend! What fun that would be.

As guests begin to trickle to the drawing room for cards and di-
gestifs, I see Karlo pull Gaiana Spiros too roughly by the elbow, and
she jerks away from him, incensed. Ah, he is treating her as he treats
me. He thinks the worst that could happen is that they might quarrel
and not speak for some months, but I am of course ready to ensure
that this night plummets to its messiest conclusion. I have been making a point to be a bit silly, so that the Duchess Spiros thinks I am
quite drunk, and I've been flirting outrageously with her husband
Vitaliy, such that even Karlo seems to have jealously noticed. It isn't
unheard of for Duchess Spiros and Karlo to disappear together, so
once they do, the rest of the party continues on. Perfect.

I feign illness and sneak after them. Karlo and I always stay in
separate rooms at the summer cottage and his room is nearer to the
woods. It is a lovely room with a balcony. As I've said, the summer
cottage is actually a castle dating back nearly a thousand years, and
Karlo's favorite room—the one his mother once told him he could
not have because the balcony was dangerous and needed reinforcing,
something Karlo has infantilely claimed to be an excuse for Regina
to retain the best room—is one of the oldest parts of the building.
Beneath it is a courtyard that has been marked off for several years,
owing to some protrusions of rock where tree roots have forced up
the stone tiling like the jagged canines of a rabid dog.

By the time I approach quietly from the corridor, I can hear the
argument has escalated to shouting. The Duchess Spiros is not hotheaded by nature—rather, she's very levelheaded, perhaps even cold-
hearted in her anger, which is the very worst thing for someone like
Karlo, who loves to throw tantrums and provoke a reaction. Gaiana
is becoming increasingly put off by him, I can tell. All night her
eyes have flashed coldly as she becomes more condescending. Good!
Karlo will not stand for that at all, he hates to feel stupid. Hm, I
wonder how to push this along? I have to make sure Gaiana can't
leave, of course, as that is her tendency—her letters are a constant
stream of apology for leaving a lover's tryst early to end a fight. I
pull a wrought-iron key from my pocket, locking the door to Karlo's
room from the outside. There is a servants' entrance through which I
can sneak in and watch from behind the wardrobe screen, but neither
Karlo nor Gaiana know about that. Imagine how freeing it would be

to never wonder how things like fresh laundry enter your room while you sleep. As if all tasks are performed by angels and elves.

"—dare you speak to me this way! You forget to whom you speak, Gaiana!"

"Oh, I know very well to whom I speak, Karlo, but you forget the terms of our relationship. You forget that it is *you* who has always wanted *me*. If I wanted a life submitting to your hysteria I would have chosen you when you asked me to marry you all those years ago!" (Oh, what a blow!) "Luckily you've already got an airheaded bimbo for that!"

She means me, but I am not offended, of course. Gaiana believes this of me because it is what I want her to believe. But Karlo is positively incandescent with rage. From behind the screen by the servants' entrance I have to suppress a cackle at his expense.

"Don't you dare speak of Violeta that way!" roars Karlo, which would be sweet if this had anything at all to do with me.

"You simply can't be reasoned with, Karlo." Gaiana stalks to the door, yanking it, to realize it has been locked. (Again, the urge to laugh sweeps over me in a wave. What! a! rush!) "Have you locked us in here?"

Karlo grabs her arm and I watch a dangerous look of cold fury alight in Gaiana's eyes. "You're not leaving here, Gaiana. You came to my house at my invitation. You answer to me."

"This is your *mother's* house," Gaiana spits at him. What a horrendous thing to say! I am giddy with excitement. "And if you still think you have a shot at the throne after everything everyone is saying about your behavior this weekend—"

"What's that supposed to mean?"

She tears away from him, looking for another exit. But of course there is none—none but the one I'm standing in, or the balcony. "Never mind. I need some air. We both need some air."

Karlo follows her to the balcony, a drunken flush in his cheeks. "Where do you think you're going? I asked you a question. *Answer it.*"

It is harder to see them now, so I creep out from the servants' entrance to conceal myself behind an antique armoire. Gaiana is silhouetted by moonlight and I regret telling her she looked full as if it were an insult. She looks womanly in a way I never have, me with my careful, delicate ingenue's smile.

"You do not *command* me, Karlo—"

"Fuck you, Gaiana!"

"Fine. You really want to know? The truth is you've embarrassed yourself so thoroughly the nobles are considering putting *Vitaliy* on the throne," she says with a neutrality that is so obviously glee. This is not true, of course. Perhaps Vitaliy might think it is, but no, the nobles will only succeed with Karlo. They know he is mercurial, but better a mercurial man than the puppet of a rational woman. I know how they think and so does the Duchess Spiros, when she is less drunk.

"YOU LIE," shouts Karlo, slamming an open palm into the balcony railing beside her. He does this to me often, hitting things because he wants to see me jump, like a mouse. I do, of course. Gaiana does too, but her reaction is genuine. She is the dominant one. He has never threatened her before.

Briefly, a different look appears in Gaiana's eyes. I know it. I think fleetingly of Mama, and those moments before her fall. The knowledge of what is coming, and that it is inevitable. That it is already too late to stop.

"Don't you raise a hand to me—"

"I'll do what I damn well please—"

"Get off of me!"

"Listen to me, you raging bitch—"

"I said *get off*," Gaiana snarls, and then there is a scuffling sound, and something like a muted thud. And then—

Well, I can't really see anything from where I'm standing, so I tiptoe forward a few steps, still concealed in the room to catch a glimpse of Gaiana standing alone on the balcony. Oh, this must be it! Part of me is very excited, so excited that I almost want to tap her on the shoulder and kiss her full on the mouth, but at the very last second I remember there is no good reason for me to have appeared inside of a locked bedroom where I never go. The Duchess Spiros gives a shriek, and then I hastily sprint unseen to the servants' entrance, unlocking the bedroom door as quietly as possible before racing downstairs,

mussing my hair and cheeks to look as if I have spent the last twenty
minutes vomiting in the powder room.

By the time I reach the other nobles, swaying a bit in commitment
to the evening's theater, they're crowded around, looking at something. One man—by god, it's Vitaliy—is braying like a wounded
dog. I push my way through the crowd, trying to make my ecstasy
look like concern.

"Your Highness, don't, you shouldn't see him in this state—!"

I witness only enough to know I've done quite fabulously. I wonder
if there is chaos elsewhere in the universe I may yet have the chance
to control?

"Karlo!" I wail, and fall to my knees as the others look up, spotting
Gaiana on the balcony where she stands frozen, her face an ashen
white. I feel badly for her, a little, except she did call me a bimbo.
Sometimes the execution of justice can be all too swift.

NAOMI

I still haven't decided what I'm going to do about all this. Murder
just doesn't seem plausible, really. It feels like a poor career choice,
to tell you the truth. And I'm not entirely sure Charlie deserves
it, even though I don't personally feel too thrilled with him. For
one thing, he's late again. This time, luckily, I don't bother fussing
over my choice of lingerie or determining how to appear uninvested
when I have never been so invested before in my life. Instead I pace
the floor of my living room, pondering weapons. I live on the thirti-
eth floor of a high-rise, so a fall is always an option. I do own knives,
most of them in good shape, one or two of them perilously sharp.
I know Aya said her agency would cover for me if I went a violent
route, but surely there has to be something more . . . coincidental?
Could I possibly choke him? Tie him up and leave him to die of
dehydration?

I shudder so violently I nearly drop my glass of wine. I take out my
phone and search *how long does it take to suffocate someone with a pillow*
and then before I can read the answer I throw my phone across the
room. Jesus fucking Christ.

Another ten minutes goes by and yeah, okay, I'm feeling more hospitable to the idea of murder. I'm, shall we say, less than thrilled. Is there a way to murder someone sexually? I once read something about embolisms caused by oral sex, something about blowing into a woman's vagina. Is there an equivalent for men? Is this something I can pitch to my editor? I lose my train of thought for several minutes and then the buzzer goes off. Someone downstairs to see me.

I drain the remainder of my wine. Charlie Miaza, this is it.

As I set my now-empty wineglass on the coffee table and hurry to the door, I think again about what Aya told me. So, Charlie will either do something horrible to the global economy (?) or he'll . . . become possessed by a spirit (??). It seems like the latter would be easier to deal with, potentially not even worth murdering for. The former seems bad, but how would I even know? I'm sweating, it's a bad sweat, I smell terrible. I sniff my armpits and recoil in horror but it's too late.

Charlie Miaza is already here.

"I'm so sorry I'm late," he says as usual, leaning in for a kiss. I dance away almost comically, then try to play it cool, as if that was just an invitation to come inside. He does, and shuts the door behind him. He steps inside and politely takes off his shoes and I want to run my fingers through his hair and whisper to him softly about my dreams. Then I snap to cognizance again, turning away so he can't see the madness in my eyes.

"Should we get some air?" I ask with an undertone of hysteria, struggling to reach the sliding door of my tiny, nearly nonexistent balcony over an obstacle course of mislaid books and a gigantic floor pouffe I once bought because I thought I might read on it.

"Naomi, it's thirty degrees outside," says Charlie, sounding amused. Oh dear. I think I might genuinely want to bear his children. It's also very possible I'd like to gently caress his naked body with a lightly dampened sponge when we're both wrinkled beyond recognition. (I! am! an! award-winning! journalist!)

"Yes, but, you know, I worry about the sanitation of buildings with so many tenants," I say, and begin to recount a story about avian flu, or am about to, anyway, when I turn to find that Charlie is standing directly behind me—so close I jump. "Jesus, what are y—"

I turn to find him laughing silently at my expense, a little smile on his face that says things like hello, in this moment I am yours, and maybe if you're lucky the next, and the next, and the next. His hand slides up along the back of my neck, a flutter of a touch. A lovely hello. Looking in his eyes reminds me of the way it felt to wait for my birthday when I was small, and then I know it doesn't matter. It doesn't matter what he does, what chaos he causes, who else he looks at like that. I can't make those things feel important, and I know it's terrible, and I know my doom is written on the wall, whether in big ways or small. Inevitably we will fight, he will disappoint me, the glow will start to fail and maybe that will be a month from now, a year, maybe we'll part ways in our fifties, amicably dividing the crockery we never use. It will end, definitely. It will end, absolutely. But right now, as far as I'm concerned, the universe can tear Charlie Miaza from my cold dead hands.

His thumb rubs gently over the soreness of my neck, where I bend too long over my keyboard, writing. He smells like laundry detergent and the advent of the female orgasm, and when he leans toward me, I can feel myself throwing all my reservations away. And probably my morals. Maybe it will make a good story, I think. Maybe I can call this a lead instead of what it so obviously is, which is a delusion.

"Charlie," I whisper to him, wondering if he can hear the echoes of my decision. If he can taste the detritus of my willpower from the tip of my idiot tongue.

He leans into me, matching me pulse for pulse, and there's that smile on his face. Like he's in on the joke. Like we *are* the joke. There's a little flicker of something, a slight change, and for a moment I can't tell if it's desire or something else. Longing. Either way, I'll take it. Either way, I close my eyes. The distance between us lessens to nothing, his mouth breaths from mine.

Then his hand shifts, closing around my throat so suddenly I choke.

What the—

"Andreev," Charlie says in a funny voice. "What, pray tell, the fuck."

When I open my eyes again, the look on his face isn't laughter. Nor is it longing.

It might be desire, but it doesn't look right.

And it's hard to call this kind of thing ambiguous. Strangulation kind of only goes one way.

Okay then. My vision blurs a little before survival instincts kick in. Fight or flight? My options are lamentably scarce.

Luckily, five years at the same kickboxing studio gives me better reflexes than I thought I had. I somehow shove a knee into or around his ballsack, giving myself just enough time to dive elsewhere, toward the kitchen. (Never mind the thing I said before about love or whatever. Aya had a point, it seems. Knife it is!)

Unfortunately Charlie's reflexes are even quicker, and he grabs me around the arm.

"Andreev," Charlie says again, still in that voice, which is technically his but not really, not quite. This voice is quieter and more mechanical, like it's unaccustomed to speaking. "You can't seriously think you can get away from me, can you?"

Oh! This seems! Very bad! I twist and pull as hard as I can but his grip is deadly, insane, and I'm wearing the fluffy socks with no traction that I *delight* in on most days. I don't technically know what the options were—whether Violeta killed her mark or didn't—but it seems the universe went the hostile spirit route. I really thought that was a joke. Not that I thought the other option sounded better, but the paranormal . . . that always felt particularly unlikely. Supremely, profoundly fake.

I kick him as hard as I can in the quad, hoping that throws him off a little. It does! *Great.* I know I won't be able to get to the door— even if I did, what am I going to do? Run down thirty flights of stairs? Bang on a neighbor's door, I guess, but since when has any neighbor rushed to help in any situation?—but there's a wineglass on the coffee table. My trusty wineglass. My *beloved* wineglass. I fumble for it, banging my chin on the coffee table when he yanks me back.

"You really thought you could kill me and get away with it? Jesus, Andreev, when I saw it was you—" He lets out a growl when I turn and bite his hand, this time scrabbling madly away on hands and knees. "*Fuck*, Aya—"

Aya? As in the other me? That's . . . strange. I didn't realize the spirit thing would be so specific. "I'm not Aya," I manage to pant, because I've already worked much harder than not–Charlie Miaza. Who did Aya say she killed, the other version of Charlie? Charles? "I'm not Aya, I'm Naomi, I've never even—" I cut off in the middle of my sentence, trying to find another weapon. I'm not sure a pillow is going to work under the circumstances. I had no idea the element of surprise wasn't going to be in my favor, though at least this is kind of a relief. There isn't a lot of moral ambiguity to fuck around with *now*. "I'm—"

I reach for the wineglass again, this time snatching it up successfully from the table. Almost immediately, though, I drop it, the bell of the glass shattering on the floor. I let out something of a whimper when he yanks me back by my hair, grabbing for my chin. I'm not an expert, but I'm pretty sure there are a few critically perilous maneuvers he could pull from here.

"Listen—" I can hardly get a word out. *"Listen to me—"*

"McCabe," comes a disembodied voice, out of nowhere. It's coming from . . . Jesus, it's coming from my fucking HomePod.

"McCabe," says my voice again. Only it's not my voice, because it sounds sad and exhausted and a little bit girlishly sweet. "It's me," says Aya Andreev, the same way you might say good night to a lover, or offer ice cream to a child.

And for just a moment, the man who is no longer Charlie Miaza falls rigidly, perfectly still.

AYA

It isn't strictly protocol to interfere. I'm just supposed to watch. I watched Violeta, too, but she didn't need my help. Naomi does, and even if she doesn't—

Under the circumstances, it seemed a calculated risk.

"I didn't realize it'd be you," I say quietly into my mic, my hands shaking as I watch McCabe's eyes swivel to the places a camera might be. He knows the tricks of the agency. He worked for one very like mine. "I didn't know, and when it was you, I didn't . . . I couldn't. We never got a choice, but if I'd had one—" I stop as he locates the camera, his eyes finding the lens where he can't see me, but I can still

look him in the eye. I take a deep breath just as Naomi's fingers close
around something, her form quietly looming behind McCabe's temporarily frozen body as he stares accusingly into the camera, blindly
looking back at me.

"I love you, McCabe, you know that." I let it out on an exhale,
urgent but not rushed. "I've always loved you, ever since that first day
at the academy. From the first day I met you to the last breath you
ever took. I swear, I loved you for every single second of it."

His lips part. He hesitates just long enough.

Then a splatter of blood covers the camera, but I'm too much of a
professional to jump back in my chair. McCabe—Charlie Miaza, in
this universe—jerks to a halt and then begins to fall, landing with a
thud I can hear but not completely see. There are patches of visibil-
ity, of course. From the corner of the camera lens I see the stem of a
wineglass sticking out from his carotid.

"Aya?" asks Naomi. She's heaving in breaths.

"Yes?"

"Thanks. For the distraction."

Right. The distraction.

"No problem." I lean back numbly in my chair, closing my eyes
for a moment before sitting forward again, recalling that my job isn't
yet done. "Naomi? We'll have someone in there right away to clean
everything up." I don't want her to think she has to go to sleep in
the same place as a body she just killed. "You might want to, um—"

"Alibi," she says suddenly. "I need an alibi."

"Oh, yeah—"

"I didn't really have a motive, right? Not a good one, anyway. Not,
you know, beyond a reasonable doubt." She's babbling.

"You're not going to need a defense, Naomi." I can tell she's not
really listening. I think running through logistics is helping her,
keeping her calm. "Naomi, just—take a breath, okay? Everything's
fine. He's gone now, you did what you had to do, you're safe. I've got
you and you're safe."

She giggles then, a little shrilly. I can't see her through the blood
flecked across the lens.

"Naomi, are you okay?"

"It's just funny," she says. "I always wanted someone to say that to me. To make me feel that way, like I'm actually safe. And it turns out I didn't need a boyfriend—I just needed to hear it from myself."

She laughs again, harder this time, almost howling. Then things change, and I hear sniffling, and I know she's not laughing anymore.

"It'll be okay," I say again, because I know the agency is sending someone in right now. I've never known how they do it. Maybe I'll learn soon, once I ascend these ranks. Only two more to go and this file is closed. Only two more.

I close my eyes and see McCabe staring blankly at me.

I love you, I've always loved you.

"How did you know that would make him pause for long enough to give her an opening?" Slavomir asks me later, when I turn in my report. He's chuckling, probably because it's so funny. How hilarious to let your guard down over the love of some girl you haven't seen in almost a decade. To let her kill you for the second time, all because you can't move, can't breathe, over something that can't possibly be true, and certainly isn't relevant.

So I don't bother telling Slavomir that I knew it would work because it would have stopped me. If McCabe had said those words to me the day I'd walked in to kill him, I would have let the gun fall to the floor. I would have let him cut me open. I would have let him burn me alive.

"Well, you know men's egos" is what I actually say.

"Too true," says Slavomir, shaking his head as he slips the report into my file.

JESSAMYN

From the moment I leap. I know my aim is true. It does not happen instantly. This hunt is a patient one. I am vigilant and vigilant and vigilant. When the opening arrives I see it written on the pages of my destiny I become one with fate. What sweet Carnage.

Behold—

The blood!

The blood!

The blood!

HADIA

Now that I know all my daydreams are nothing, it's almost easier to get through the days. I should have given up a long time ago. I throw away the needles, the hormones, the clothes I've clung to "aspiration-ally," as if I will ever be anything but round about the middle again. Who is left to be beautiful for now? Carl will be rid of me somehow, and without Lottie there is no one to help me. Worse, there is no one to care. So I give up, and it is so freeing I could cry. Of course, that could still be the hormones. It's not like they can so easily come and go, or that mentally being rid of them clears my body of the wreckage.

I know I behave abnormally on the day, because again, I'm not wor-ried about whether there will be consequences; whether someone might intervene or drag me before a jury of my (likely Carl's) peers. Aya told me her agency will take care of it, so . . . good! I don't know whether that includes Lottie's children, but what is there to do, worrying about that? What hope is there for them in this world? They would only be sycophants like Carl and Vitaliy, or criminals, traitors like Lottie. They could be tools of the empire. They could be objects of the regime.

Or worse. They could wake up one day and discover they're me.

I do know how to drive, and it occurs to me that after this is over they'll probably stop letting women get their licenses. It's a little surprising they haven't already, but maybe my generation was grand-fathered in. It's still alarming, though, to see a woman driving alone, so I tuck my hair into one of Carl's hats when I pull into a turnout on the edge of Lottie's property, where the various farm equipment is usually delivered.

She hurries in so quickly her cheeks are rosy and bright. "I can't believe you stole a car!" she says, breathless, and then she turns to me with a look of pride. "Look at you," she says, and holds out a hand, brushing her thumb across my cheek. "Beautiful."

I'm not beautiful, of course. I've grown another chin over the course of the past week and the evidence of time is all over my face. I've never looked older than I do right now, and Carl's hat isn't doing much for my palette. Red has never been my color. But oh, that flush of pink on Lottie's cheeks. I do everything in my power not to kiss it away.

We didn't discuss the implications of our conversation the other night, when it seemed like Lottie was offering me something I never dreamed I might actually have. Instead, I stole Carl's network passcode and drew up the building plans for Vitaliy and Lottie's house. There's an extra room not accounted for on the blueprints. Then I drew up Lottie's bank statements. They were mostly blank, but then I remembered that Vitaliy complains about having to manage the household, and I realized Lottie would do everything in Vitaliy's name. Which is when I found the money.

"So where are we going?" asks Lottie in a hushed tone. I know she thinks she and I are doing something silly and dangerous, but only dangerous to me. I understand now that Vitaliy not only adores her, but trusts her. She gave him what he wanted for long enough that she now can do what she wants, and apparently what she wants—according to the transfers I found in her private account, which is only private because it's in Vitaliy's name, and the reassignation left certain men their privacy—is to turn her arid, ungrowable farmland into the perfect place for the manufacturing of biological weapons. Like smallpox blankets, part of a history we're no longer supposed to know. Something to subdue the detractors—to wipe the dissidents out.

Where is the money going? What outcome is she plotting? It doesn't matter, because she's already been caught. It can't matter, because now I know, and I'm right here.

I pull into the main road and start driving. "Not far."

We have a few hours before Carl wakes up. Turns out roofies are still easy to order on the internet as long as your name is Carl and your financial ID password is "password."

"This is so *exciting*." She looks giddy. "Does this mean you've considered, you know . . . ?"

She thinks that one act of recklessness means I'll be more inclined to choose another. "What would be the point, Charlotte?"

She looks at me with a frown. "What?"

"Sorry. Just trying something out. Your full name is Charlotte, right?"

"Yes," she says slowly. I can tell she thinks I'm acting strangely, and I am. I most definitely am. "What would be the point?" she echoes. "The point would be your life, Hadia. The point would be a world where you and I raise our babies together. Where *we*," she meaningfully amends, "are together."

I keep my eyes on the road when she places a cool hand on my arm. "Hadia?"

I say nothing. At first.

Then I shake my head.

"Oh, Hadia." She must know she's making it worse. "Hadia, pull over."

A tear slips out. "I'm fine."

"Hadia, please, just—over there." She points to the edge of the woods. "Nobody will see us if they drive by."

"Lottie—"

"Just do it, Hadia, please. I need to tell you something."

I want to keep driving. I have a plan, after all. I'm going to keep driving. But her hand is still on my arm and I jerk the wheel, pulling over at the very last second to drive the car into the trees. "Lottie, I'm so—"

Her mouth is hot and wet on mine the moment I cut the ignition. I'm so startled I don't exactly know what to do with my hands, but then she climbs over me, reaching blindly for the levers of the seat to push me backward, to put distance between herself and the steering wheel. Her kiss is molten and deep and I tell her everything, everything. I pour my loneliness, my love, and my devotion into her mouth like honeyed wine. I want to touch her, I want her to touch me, I want to hold our bodies close together, I want to sing her love songs. With her and for her, I want to sing.

"I can't do it." My voice is hoarse and broken as she mops up my tears with her palms.

"I know, sweetheart, I know—"

"No, Lottie, I mean—" The words are unsteady until suddenly, they aren't. "I know," I tell her. "I know about the money. About the injections, the lab. I . . ." Another shuddering breath. "I know."

She leans back, her face carefully empty.

"I never understood how you could seem so . . . so satisfied. So happy." I swallow. "But then I realized—of course. Of course you're satisfied. You have everything you could ever want. Your husband is a handsome idiot who lets you do whatever you like. You don't mind having children, you like it, you like the power it gives you, being saintly Madonna Lottie with the other playground moms." Her kiss lingers so sweetly on my mouth, strawberries dipped in cream, alternate futures. "You like being secretly clever, openly adored. You're being paid well, *so* well, and it's not some glorious revolution you're funding. Change wouldn't win you anything, because all that freedom means to you is fewer rewards. You have everything you want, everything you need, and you secured it even on that disastrous land that Carl gave you—you managed to turn shit into gold for yourself when Vitaliy couldn't. There's only one glitch in your plan, isn't there?"

She looks hard at me, as if daring me to answer.

"Me," I tell her, and this time, my voice is steady. "If it weren't for me, you could convince yourself that the other mothers are happy too, that this is what's best for them. The real pain, the real suffering— you can ignore it because it lives far away. Because it doesn't look like you. But me? You can't live next to my misery, Lottie. I remind you of everything that's gone wrong."

To her credit, she doesn't pull away.

"Are you going to deny any of it?" I ask her. According to Aya, Lottie will only get worse. The chaos theory of it all means that Lottie's absorbed the echoes of Charles McCabe, that she's become more dangerous, and that she will do exactly what Carl's done and use her position of privilege to make the ladder harder to climb. To make it disappear from view entirely. No other woman will ever be as beloved as Lottie, nor as blessed. She bought her right to a perfect life; to the assurance that she and hers will be marked for special treatment while everyone else slowly circles the drain.

She considers me a long moment before opening her mouth. "You're right," she says, and her voice sounds stonier now. "But you never asked me if I agreed with them. I think it's good for everyone, for families. My family means everything to me."

"Not enough to keep you off my lap," I point out.

"They wouldn't have to know." Her eyes have gone thin with calculation. I thought I had seen all of Lottie before, but I hadn't. I still haven't. "Give me some time and I can bargain for your safety. I can make sure of it. For now Carl has the State's ear, but I know I can win them over. You can keep your house, we can keep things exactly as they are, and—" She shifts away just slightly, though not far enough to part. "We can be together, Hadia." She takes my face in her hands. "I can keep you safe, and no one will ever have to know."

I realize then that she's not just toying with me. She genuinely does want me. Oh, what a fucking hypocrite! I want to laugh. I want to cry. I want to scream. What a fucking hypocrite she is, she in her gossamer dress, the lovely swell of her breasts, her bitten lips, her friendship that was—that is—my only lifeline. My only anchor to this life.

I tip my chin up and she reaches down hungrily, relief flooding from her mouth to mine. Remorse pours from her like nectar. "I'll fix it, Hadia, I'll fix everything for us. I'll make everything right for us." Her nails scrape gently over my throat and I can't help a whimper, reaching behind her to unzip her dress. She moans appreciatively and leaps to help me, tugging me closer as she reaches one hand around, searching blindly for her zipper. I find it at the same moment she does, my fingers covering hers as we both tug it down. She laughs exuberantly into my mouth and I die a little, wondering just how far her happy ending can take us both.

I drop my lips to her neck, to the top of her breasts, and she whines for me to hurry up, to press her bare skin to mine. Her arms lock behind her as she fumbles to tug down her sleeves, these modest sleeves that good women wear. We're not sluts. We're not deviants. We were put on this earth to raise our children, to please our husbands, to pledge our allegiance to the State that just wants to keep families safe. It's why we were born. To suffer because we are so adept at suffering. To feel pain because it is holy and good.

She mistakes the jerk of my hips for something else. She's grinding lower on my lap, she's gone breathless, her mind is on other things as I start the car, slamming my foot on the pedal. She rockets forward, unable to brace, her arms still locked behind her as I careen backward, my head smacking hard against the headrest.

"What are you doing?" she shrieks, but I can't hear her. My vision is blurred with tears. Oh, I love her, I love her so deeply, so disembowelingly, that for a moment I almost want it, the future she promised

me. I don't care whose secrets I have to keep to have her. I want it, my
ending, the one where she is mine and I am hers, where she knows
the beat of my heart and accepts it, and loves it. I want space in her
life, I want to cradle her body with mine, to consume her inside me,
keep her there, locked safe in my chest. For a moment, every beat of
my heart says only Lottie darling, Lottie mine.

But then I remember that she can love me and still think I am
only me. That I am only one person worth loving and not a thousand
women, a million. That I am not every woman who was born without
her fortune. That somehow she could watch me dry my tears and
make no mistakes and still believe that I alone am owed the privilege
of her lucky stars.

It is difficult to drive with Lottie on my lap scrabbling for the car
door, for the window. I had the element of surprise and the benefit
of feminine clothing to keep her restrained, but she's already seen it
in my eyes, what's coming. Luckily it isn't far, and there isn't much
she can do.

When the car flies off the edge of the cliff, Lottie's screams shrill
and bright in my ear, I find that I am laughing. The second principle
of chaos theory, how funny it all is! I only wish I could ask Lottie
one question.

How do you like my chaos now?

AYA

I watch the car fly over the edge of the cliff and turn off the monitor.
I don't need to watch the impact at the basin of the valley. I don't
need to watch the combustion, the unsurvivable explosion. I have
seen this kind of death before and the physics are pretty guessable.
In fact, they're pretty undeniable.

"Hey." There's a knock on the edge of my desk and I look up
sharply to find Daisy frowning at me with concern. "You okay?"

"Hm? Yeah, why?"

"You're crying." She looks bewildered as I raise one hand to my
cheek, finding it wet.

"Oh." The concern on her face is for my sanity, I see. "I'm fine."

"You sure?"

"Yeah, definitely." I scrape my palm against my cheek until it's dry, not bothering to offer an excuse, and Daisy lingers. "Did you need something?"

"Oh right, yeah. Slavomir's looking for you." The look on her face shifts readily from concern to conspiracy as she leans toward me. "I think it's promotion time, baby!"

Her excitement strikes me as . . . I don't know, strange. It seems like something that was enough to motivate me to kill a man a few days ago and hunt down every version of him in the rest of the distant universes would now be enough to get me out of my chair. But I don't know, for some reason I just can't summon the enthusiasm I should be feeling.

"Right. Thanks."

Daisy's look of bemusement is back. "You sure you're okay?"

I guess it must be a little selfish, feeling melancholy about something that won't be Daisy's for another few kills. That could take years. "Yes. Yeah, definitely." I rise sharply to my feet, forcing a smile on my face. "Should we celebrate later? Drinks on me?"

"Yes!" She gives a little fist pump of excitement. "Perfect, just what I needed to get me through all this paperwork." She mimes hanging herself and I try not to think about Hadia's car careening off a cliff.

I knock on Slavomir's open doorframe and he looks up, beckoning me in with a broad grin. "Superstar! There she is. Come in, come in." He gestures for me to shut the door behind me, so I do.

I take a seat as he exits out of something on his monitor and turns his attention to me. "I got the alert from the top that your file just closed!" he exclaims, theatrically flipping the front cover shut on the thick manila folder I realize is marked with my name. "Beautiful work, Andreev. Efficient, neat, timely. You really are a star."

He winks at me and I force another smile. "Thanks."

"It's the fastest we've ever dealt with a chaos case. Obviously, I'm thrilled whenever my best agents make me look good." He's smiling at me, though I'm not really sure why we're still talking. I guess he wants to ramp up to it. "A performance like that deserves a reward, don't you think?"

Oh good, not too much ceremony, then. "Sure."

"All right—excellent!" He reaches under his desk for a bottle of champagne and unwraps the foil on top, then grips it. "Ah, better aim it this way—safety first, as we always say." He babbles and winks some more, pops the bottle, pours some into two glasses and hands one to me, licking some of the spillage from his fingers. "A toast," he says.

I dislike having to run through the motions here, but I do it. "To the best agent I've ever had," he says, and takes a long glug from his plastic champagne flute.

I flash back to the moment those days ago, learning about the other versions of Charles McCabe. The other versions of me, the ones I could and couldn't save. I can't bring myself to take a sip so I fake it, but Slavomir doesn't notice. He finishes his glass and then shifts to sit on the edge of his desk, looking down at me as I fiddle with the plastic stem. I remember, viscerally, the one sticking out of Charles's neck.

"What do you think about a couple vacation days?" asks Slavomir, and I look up at him. He seems to be expressing something with his eyes that I can't parse. "We'll want you back, of course. McCabe's team is down an operative, so might as well get 'em while they're reeling."

"What?" My mouth is dry. I don't think champagne will help.

"Well, tactically speaking, when any agent goes down—"

"I thought I was being promoted," I blurt out. "To management. A desk job?"

I don't know why I phrased it as a question. Slavomir gives me a sympathetic look, reaching down to take the champagne from my hands and set it beside him on the desk.

"Listen, I know you were hoping for a promotion, kid, and believe me, you're close. You're close! But you're the best I've got, Andreev, the biggest star in that bullpen, and there's just a few more t's to cross before we move you up to management." I barely register the words until he leans down, resting his hand on my knee.

"Andreev," he says. "You can't really think I'd let you go now, can you?"

I say nothing. I don't move.

He shifts his hand so his palm rests on my thigh.

"You're gonna do big things one day, hotshot," he says in a low voice. Even with my eyes down I can see the crease in his trousers. "I'm gonna get you there soon, I promise."

His hand moves and I catch his wrist. He startles—it's been a long time since he's been in the field. His reflexes are slower than mine. "Don't."

He gives a false laugh. "Sorry, sorry. Just wanted to comfort you, that's all. I know you've been wanting to get out of active duty. But that kind of promotion is earned, Andreev. It's not given."

I want to scream. I want to break the bones of his wrist. No, I want to cry. I want to fold in half and sob into my hands. I hate that if I cry, it shows weakness. He'll put it in my file, I'm feminine and soft, I'm a problem, I'm disobedient, he could write anything down that he likes. It doesn't matter how much blood I spill for this agency, or for him. I paid this price because it was what I had to do for freedom, but all it bought me was pain.

When my gaze locks on Slavomir's, I know he knows what's coming. They always do. Even McCabe.

In the end it only takes a couple of motions. Standard-issue hunting knife—every agent carries one. I'll never get the blood out of this shirt, so I take it off. I know that someone, somewhere, is watching, so I look in the monitor as I pick up my file, thick with all my kills. Somewhere in here is my birth certificate, my passport, my fingerprints, everything they took from me when I first walked through the academy doors, all so they could own me. So that I'd always belong to someone else.

"Ready to get out of here?" Daisy asks when I leave Slavomir's office, her expression faltering when she realizes I'm in nothing but a geriatric sports bra, my skin dappled with Slavomir's blood. Down the hall the alarm sounds. The agency is going into lockdown, but I know the dossier. I've beaten this buzzer before. So what if they hunt me? I'm dangerous because they made me dangerous. They already gave me the skills to make it out on my own.

I run, and I'm not fleeing. I'm living. My heart jackrabbits as I lunge.

I've always loved you, I tell myself, *and I swear I always will!*

VIOLETA

Black is really my color! Mourning is filled with drudgery but I do look exceptional today. Regina is terribly upset and hasn't been paying me much attention, which is also very wonderful. I have really perfected the art of being photographed while gracefully spilling a single tear. Artem and Olympios are extremely handsome in their sadness as well. They are very beautiful boys, despite the misfortune that is their father. Was, I mean!

It'll be some days yet before the official state funeral. For now we are merely going about our business, showing our support for Regina, attending meals with her despite the fact that she is old and has no taste buds and her cook is not as good as mine. Olympios complains, and I'm just shushing him and promising sweets if he agrees to last one more hour when suddenly there's an explosion outside. How odd! My first thought is that someone is still going forward with the coup. What a drag. I'm willing to help Regina of course, but will she ever ask? If only someone around here would swallow their pride. I am extremely useful.

I tell the boys to wait as I hurry to the courtyard where there is . . . How strange! A smoldering car. It stinks of oil, which we no longer use. Environmentalism was one of Karlo's pet projects despite his extravagance in all aspects of his personal life. I do not know how a car could have gotten here—it looks as if it drove off the roof? It lands nose-down, like an arrow. I can only assume the driver is dead. There is certainly a dead body, as part of the shattered windshield is clearly pierced through a human spine, and I do not think such things generally bode well for survival.

Hm. Well, off to lunch, I suppose.

Unless—

Something catches my eye. A wriggle below the corpse? A jerk. Movement! A hand appears, an arm, below the impaled body. Then a garish red hat, singed to a raw, exposed scalp. The struggling hand reaches frantically to pull it off and the head underneath seems . . . familiar. They try to turn their head, vomiting sickly onto themselves, but the slightest tilt of the chin is just enough to catch a glimpse of a familiar profile.

And . . .

How odd. Is that . . . ?

I look around to be sure nobody else has seen what I've seen. Then, when I am reasonably confident, I rush forward. (If anything, this will make me look heroic.)

I reach for the hand I spotted and pull. There is a great deal of effort on both our parts but then there she is, nearly collapsing in my arms.

My suspicions were correct. My hair has not looked like this in many years—I keep mine fashionably dyed and I've long since tamed the unruly curls—but I know it like I know my own voice.

"Aya?" asks the me in my arms, weakly. She is covered in blood and vomit, her cheeks smeared with soot and tears.

"No." I cradle her like a newborn. "No, I'm Violeta. You're safe now. You're safe." I coax her gently, pleased I am able to be so motherly despite the profound disappointments of my own mother. Is it not a miracle that I turned out the way I did! "You're safe, Violeta," I say softly, "you're safe."

"How—?" She breaks off. Perhaps she, like me, is aware that the how in this situation is an implausibility of enormous proportions, and probably not important.

Unless it can be replicated, that is. Ah! A thought!

"Did you come from a good place?" I ask her.

"I drove myself off a cliff, so no," she mutters darkly.

A very good point. "Did you by chance do something very chaotic?" I ask, in accordance with Other Violeta's chaos theory. Suppose that would explain it, doing one chaotic thing to commence a lengthy chain of chaos . . . ?

But this Violeta's brow knits with something, possibly confusion, and I know now is not the time. She may have suffered a head injury, so I suppose the logistics can wait. "Well, you'll be safe here," I tell her. "My husband is dead and things are mostly very boring, but at least we will be queen."

"So . . . you have money?" she asks me. "And military?"

"Yes! Why, are you thinking of a coup?" I prompt excitedly.

Then her brow flickers again. She has the beginnings of a double chin and lacks my general air of polish, but I recognize it, myself in her, in that moment. She is me! An ally at last. After all this time!

I close my eyes and tilt my face to the sky. I know a blessing when I receive one.

"Thank you," I whisper to the universe.

And I swear, the sun smiles back!

JESSAMYN

The offering. Has been laid upon the altar. My sacrifice unto my Queen, my Goddess.

"Babe, have you seen my—FUCK!"

I settle myself on my perch high above the fray of the madding crowd. Below me Daisy Araminta Olympios cower in my shadow they know. Oh they know. They have failed because they are cowards and it is I. I am. The chosen one. I am the hero of the hour and it will be my line that is Blessed.

"BABE, WOULD YOU GET OVER HERE! Oh my god. *Oh my god*, I'm going to vomit!"

I close my eyes. Sleep comes for me swiftly on gentle tendrils.

"You scared me half to death, Regina, what are you screaming ab—oh god, is that a dead bird?"

In a wave it washes over me. Warmth envelops me. Tenderness inside and out.

"Oh my god, would you shut up? DO SOMETHING! Oh my *god*, I'm going to be sick—"

Although others have failed. And they know who they are. It does not matter. I am mercy. I am benevolent this day.

"Holy shit, it's like . . . I don't really get many chances to use the word 'desiccated,' but in this case—"

"ARE YOU FUCKING KIDDING? DON'T *TOUCH* IT!"

Let your hearts not be troubled.

Let them be not. Afraid.

For I am Vigilance. I am Faithfulness.

And at long last I have brought Peace.

A Year in January

She said her name was January, which I felt was a bold claim. I'm 89 percent certain she made it up on the spot, though at the time I was not particularly concerned with whether she was hiding from something. Life has a way of being like that, wearing you down to the point of acquiescence. I suppose it was largely because she was a woman that I didn't question whether or not she was a serial killer. That, or I was tired.

"This is a very odd description, is it not?" she said, pointing to my Craigslist ad, which for whatever reason she had printed out and annotated. Next to the line that said "must not be 'not a morning person' or 'not a night person' but simply a person unbeholden to chronology, as such" and below the line clarifying "judgy people please kindly reconsider applying, P.S. that isn't rude it's simply pro-active" was a small series of foreign-looking hieroglyphics.

"I'm not technically sure," she offered in apology, walking back her initial suspicions of my oddness, "since I don't have a lot of experience."

"With Craigslist, you mean?"

"Among other things."

"Did you just move here?"

"Yes, laterally."

"Laterally?"

"Yes, a lateral movement."

"What, like within some corporate structure, you mean?"

"Impossible to tell," she said solemnly.

I felt this was actually very within the realm of possibility and when I said so she remarked that there was no way of knowing; the realms were constantly shifting and as such very little could be said about them definitively, much less in reference to actuality. I felt this, too, was a strange remark but I, unlike most people, am not opposed to strangeness. I am generally regarded as strange myself. Many people also find me condescending and I suspect they are mostly correct about that.

I was starting to feel a bit tired and I told her so. "Are you often tired?" she asked me. I had the feeling it was a very clinical question, which reminded me of the doctor I had been trying to avoid. "No, no, I only ask for purposes of atmospheric betterment," she assured me.

Briefly I wondered if she'd been reading my mind and then determined it was best not to go down that path. Sometimes it concerned me what other people could see in my thoughts, but there was never a good way to address these anxieties. It was like writing a word too many times until suddenly it made no sense. Or when you've begun thinking too consciously about breathing and then, abruptly, you can no longer breathe.

"Just wait until March," I said.

"What happens in March?"

"Don't worry about it. Something about the equinox."

"Ah," she said, looking sagely untroubled. "Understandable."

She was approximately my size, which is to say neither tall nor elfinly small. In terms of appearance she reminded me greatly of the peripheral tests at the optometrist. I mostly saw her in flickers.

"I'd like to take a nap," I told her. "Just please don't touch my things without asking."

She pulled out a pen and scribbled it down, murmuring to herself— "don't . . . touch . . . things . . . without . . . asking," she echoed, and then looked up. "Is there a preferable way to ask?"

"I'm very tired," I told her.

"Ah," she said, "expediently, I see."

Then I walked into my room and crawled into my bed, burrowing under the covers.

*   *   *

All of my friends made it very clear that using Craigslist to find a roommate was a terrible idea, which is why I didn't tell them I was doing it. On a potentially related note, I am not very good at friendships. I find I have a tendency for devotion and therefore expect the same. When I do not receive it I become despondent, though not fruitfully so. Some people have such verbosity of sadness, periods that lead to beautiful metamorphoses. That or they have a destructive form of sadness, little inner cyclones of it. Meanwhile I become something of a brick wall, or a used car. Less valuable each time I am injured.

*   *   *

"There's a clause in this agreement that seems to indicate you require services of some kind," said January.

I had not opened my eyes yet, but she was sitting on top of my ankles.

"See? Here," she said, though I continued to keep my eyes closed. "You specifically said you needed someone who was willing to take out the trash without being asked."

"It was more of a descriptive passage," I said. "A desirable personality trait, not an anticipated service."

"Taking out the trash without being asked is a personality trait?"

"I'm sure I could have shorthanded with something if I'd really wanted to," I muttered. "Conscientious or something. Thoughtful I guess."

"How common are they?"

"What?"

"Thoughts."

"Dismally uncommon," I told her, and then I rolled over, or tried to. "You're sitting on my feet," I remarked with glumness. Sometimes when I'm unhappy I become impatient with my own unhappiness. There is such a drudgery to my needs that even I find upsetting. I dislike inconveniencing other people. I also dislike other people.

"Is that a pressure point for you? You should have said."

She budged over.

"Listen," I said, "I don't really feel like talking."

"Are there better ways to communicate?"

"Mutual understanding is ideal but it only happens over time."

"Is it like telepathy?"

"More like data extrapolation."

"Friendship is an algorithm?"

"We're roommates, not friends. But basically yes."

"I see," she said.

I think she wrote it down, but I wasn't paying attention anymore. I was trying to go back to sleep but couldn't, because she'd woken me. If I read a few pages of something I'd likely drift off again, but there was no telling what state of mind I'd be in after some reading. That's the trouble with books; it's the same trouble with clothes. The issue of deciding what to wear isn't a matter of fabrics, but a question of who I'd like to be once dressed. With books, quality is one thing, the resulting mood another. At a time like this I couldn't risk becoming overly excited. I had scheduled the majority of the day for sleep.

"It won't always be like this," I told her.

For a strange, prolonged moment I felt like crying. There are many different ways to cry and this was the worst kind: leaking. Spillover. The issue wasn't the mess, but the not understanding what I contained that was currently leaking. I prize all knowledge, but especially knowledge of myself. I dislike these sorts of tears; they indicate flaws in my management style.

I think January had already left by then, so I curled up in a ball and burrowed deeper in my blankets. I don't like crying in front of people, anyway. It's one thing to feel distaste for misery on my own behalf without suffering the compulsion to soothe myself for the benefit of other people. Everyone always wants you to feel better, don't they? They can't sit comfortably in a room with your misery, it's like pins and needles for them. To be properly sad you either have to be alone or a little selfish. You have to not care whether your gloom dampens someone else's bright.

* * *

You might be thinking there was something wrong with me. You might be wondering whether my distress had anything to do with January disrupting my sleep. Truthfully she didn't stop doing it, but I had my own share of transgressions. At some point I got restless and had a revolving door of idiots I invited up to my room. It was Kyle, I think, who was responsible for what I like to think of as the Clitoris Episode.

"You're doing it wrong," said January, which was of course very

upsetting for poor Kyle, who hadn't expected a stranger to walk into
the room where he and I were well into the latter stages of penetra-
tive sex. "She should have reached ecstasy by now."

"She's not wrong," I told Kyle. I found January's behavior just
as odd as everyone else did, but as I said, generally speaking I am
comfortable with oddities. I sometimes have the feeling I've seen so
much variation over so many forms of existence that this particular
version of me is immune to the concept of anything ever being out
of place.

In any case, January went on to explain to Kyle the workings of
the clitoris, which I had recently explained to her when she asked
me about my aforementioned revolving door of men. I think I had said
something along the lines of wanting to feel something, and also
hormones. Chemicals and such. She had assumed alchemy and I
corrected her, no, biology. She seemed disappointed and didn't leave
her room for several days.

According to January, she'd studied at a very prestigious academy
with some sort of exacting priestess, which I told her sounded a lot
like Catholic school. She was relieved I had some basis for comparison and explained that proper research was paramount to any degree
of true comprehension. I think I was drunk at the time.

Anyway, January explained to Kyle that he needed to stimulate
my clitoris while in the midst of penetration (a very attentive listener,
January) and when he asked her if she wanted to do it herself she said
no, she wasn't ready, proper research was paramount, et cetera. But
presumably he was some sort of prodigy in regards to my needs, she
offered Kyle encouragingly, or else I wouldn't have let him try something like this, which required a great deal of intimacy.

"Actually, no," I said, gently stopping her. I explained to her that
Kyle and I used to work together and this was a purely physical sort
of thing.

By that time Kyle was beginning to get a little antsy, making excuses to leave. I thought about being frustrated with the way my
evening had turned out, but upon further contemplation I realized
January was right. I should have reached ecstasy well before then, but
if not for her I wouldn't have said so.

Sometimes I wonder what it is about me, if I need to be touched or if I just want to be wanted or if I am okay accepting lies. I think the latter is definitely true in addition to both of the former. I think there is no such thing as a person who craves honesty all the time, or a person who wants absolutely to be lied to. I think personally it's always a matter of pursuing the truth of wanting in order to parlay some grander lie of value.

The point is January wasn't a bad roommate. We both had our days.

*   *   *

Sometime in March I decided I was going to do a mixed-media project. Food, sex, poetry, that sort of thing. I suppose you could conventionally call it a food blog, only I had no personal connection to the food outside of my wanting to eat it. It was mostly free-form poetry that reflected a period of grave erotic craving. I had also been very dedicated about my gym attendance at the time.

January asked me where all this energy was coming from and I told her I was feeling very invigorated by something, I don't know, everything, and she said why didn't that work all the time and I said I couldn't hear her over the sound of the treadmill whirring. She said was it from all the sleeping I had recently done? And I said no, I didn't think so, but also the treadmill was quite loud, so could this conversation wait until we got home?

Though I was excruciatingly neat during this period, I was not a very good roommate. I scrubbed our bathtub with a toothbrush, but also I found the middle of the night to be a convenient time to work. At some point January asked me why I was poisoning myself and I said that wine was a very important aspect of my personality and she said why, and I said because sometimes when I felt this EXPANSIVE and V A S T it was important to remember that it would end soon. The fear, January!!! I shouted. The fear is the driving factor, my mortality was a race and so long as I never asked questions I would win it really wasn't that complicated January would you please hand me that whisk!

I found January to be especially fascinating at these times. I had noticed, of course, earlier in our living together that she did not always understand electricity but seemed to have no problem conjuring toast. Initially I had not been interested in pursuing my curiosity (I think truthfully I had none, because curiosity implied conversation, which I did not have the energy for) but then I became intensely ravenous for explanation. Did she learn that at her academy? Yes, she did, though how anyone could go about not learning it seemed frankly irresponsible. Was she displaying some sort of specific and therefore limited ability or was she herself, you know, magic? That was unclear according to her, as she did not believe there was a distinction between magic and nature and it just seemed very sad to her that I was so trapped by the constraints of physicality. I told her it made me sad too sometimes. She made a face like :/ and said she'd long suspected I'd been cursed somehow and was there anything I could do to break it? Had I possibly already broken it, given my recent proclivity for motion?

I don't think so, I said.

Truthfully I knew I hadn't broken shit, but I liked the idea of it. That maybe I just had some sort of curse and therefore I could, conceivably, break it. It took shape in my mind and I could taste it, a burst of flavor. What a delicious thought! I baked a cake attempting to mimic the way it felt to be so unexpectedly free, but I think there was a problem with the flour ratio. By the time I finished the poem I'd been working on about the mystic savoriness of existence I no longer felt it was worth reading.

* * *

At some point I had to go away for a wedding. I did not anticipate this being an issue, as I am very extroverted even if I am deeply antisocial. Unfortunately, things that seem only reasonably unpleasant to me at a surface level have a way of sneaking lethality in from somewhere deeper. The water source or something. I've never technically understood wells.

January was devastated when I told her that various behavioral traditions dictated she could not come with me. I believe she used the word "oppressed," as in I was oppressed by the expectations of my tyrannical society. I remain unsure whether she wanted me to stage a full-scale revolution over it or not. It's possible I disappointed her when I failed to file a petition.

It was a family wedding. Distant enough that I was only half-heartedly invested, close enough that my every behavior was heartily scrutinized. I returned home to find that January had built some sort of wooden structure into the living room, like a temple.

She gave a little half gasp when she saw me and demanded how it was possible that I could spend so much time alone. I said why, were you lonely? She said she didn't understand what that meant but there was something upsetting about the way her thoughts in my absence had reached a dangerous momentum. It began with something very simple, i.e. her current circumstances, and progressed to violent extrapolation, i.e. whether the universe was in fact just a dream that a giant was having and when he or she (the ambiguously gendered giant) woke up we would all be rendered dust mites. I told her that's called a spiral, though I also told her I doubted it would matter whether we were the dust mites in a giant's dream or not. Isn't our experience real even if we are not?

She thought about this intensely. "What makes you say that?"

"Sometimes I'm sad. The sadness is always real. Sometimes I'm angry. The anger is real, too."

She seemed bewildered. "But you . . . are . . . ?"

"Are we human or are we dancer?" I joked in response, which was a reference to a nonsensical song by the Killers that I still recall frequently. That, along with that song about not ending up with Jesus despite all our best efforts, or so I've unhelpfully interpreted it to mean.

Back to the point, though, I think January thought I was serious.

"*Are* we dancer?" she asked me in awe.

I paused to think about this. Not because I thought it was a complex question—dancers are customarily informed of the choreography and I was obviously not, which meant almost certainly no—but because it was an interesting visual. I rarely saw myself with any elegance, but even a stage full of Pitbull backup dancers had a certain gravitas.

What if we were dancers and God was Pitbull? I shuddered and said, "January, even if I were a dancer, I doubt you and I are the same."

She seemed to suddenly recall that she had erected some sort of magical temple in our living room and, quote, "didn't believe in

space and time," and then seemed relieved to have remembered what
she was, though she remained interested in the state of my existence.

"I thought you said the wedding was nice," she said, peering at
me. "You look miserable."

"It was nice," I agreed. "Both can be true."

Then I slept for about three days.

*   *   *

January had a mild interest in my sex life. I think we can agree that
we all have mild to moderate cases of this, so it didn't seem fair to
blame her. She drilled me about my end goals, my deliverables, my
pings and actionable items.

"Is it for pleasure?" she asked me.

"Mostly yes," I said. "Though also sometimes because it's easier."

"Easier than what?"

"Than saying no."

"Why?"

"Depends on the reason. Sometimes I have a headache or I feel
sort of inexpressibly bloated, but if I say anything about it I'll remind
them of my bowels and it's really not worth planting that in their
heads. Might actually want to do it some other time, you know? So
what's one loss in a winning record," I said, setting the timer. I was
making tea at the time.

"Do they not know you have them? Bowels," she clarified. She
was learning that I did not always know what she was talking about.
As a result, she had undertaken habitual efforts to increase her clarity that I found very thoughtful.

"Yes, they know about my bowels. I think." (I had to consider
this.) "They know, yeah. But it's not sexy to them."

"Sexy?"

"Yes. Being of or related to sex."

"What is sexy?"

"Mm, depends. Sometimes confidence, sometimes vulnerability. Black lace. Mascara. Sometimes high heels, sometimes short
skirts, rarely dark lipstick but sometimes red. Oh, and sometimes
sweatpants," I added as an afterthought, "or gym clothes, but only
the kind that make your butt look good."

"So, costumes?"

"Basically."

She told me that her queen had held frequent masques for this express purpose. I asked if they were all essentially orgies and January confessed that she found it confusing the way I tended toward a single partner. Didn't I know my chances at ecstasy increased with multiple partners simultaneously?

"It's not always about ecstasy," I said. "Besides, there's the safety aspect."

I explained contraception and her eyes widened, so then I explained procreation. I asked her if that hadn't been taught at her academy and she said they—"they" meaning her species, I gathered—mostly went through a process of forced adoption. Sex, according to January, was for pleasure or power and nothing else.

I liked the idea of it. The simplicity of it. The world was very simple for January, I think. She seemed to find all of it very straightforward except for me.

"You're sedentary again," she observed aloud. It was sometime after the Clitoris Episode but before the next time we saw Kyle, which was at his wedding later in the year. I introduced her to the concept of tequila shots, but she was already well-versed in debauchery. She had a particular talent for mango margaritas.

I explained to January that I would be in motion again, maybe.

"Maybe?"

"Historically yes." Though it was sometimes difficult to remember.

"What if you're not?" she said. "Mobile again."

"Then I'm not."

"You'll be sedentary forever?"

I found it amusing that she had chosen the categories of sedentary or mobile. It struck me as a more accurate way to put it than most people ever did. For example, my doctor had told me that my periods of seething frustration were one thing while my episodes of exuberant anger were another. But it made more sense to me in January's terms that I was angry all the time, and only capable of doing something about it at some of them.

"It'll pass," I assured her, impassive from the exhaustion of being back to my least favorite bit of the cycle, but I think I was crying again, which explains why she didn't believe me.

"It seems to me this curse is worsening," she said.

Then she left. Probably doing research.

* * *

I decided to take a week off during late spring and conscripted January's assistance. I handed her my phone, my wallet, and my computer. If someone called me, I said, then she should simply tell them I was out of the country and would return shortly. In reality, she was not to tell me anyone had tried to reach me and if nobody tried to reach me, then she was not to tell me that, either.

"I'm just very exhausted by the pretense," I told her. "I love strangers, did you know that? I enjoy having acquaintances." Generally I found small talk invigorating. I liked to play a game with myself wherein I sought to identify whatever a person most needed to hear and then went out of my way to tell them. You will notice that despite my hinting at my flaws I have never claimed to be talentless. I am actually quite talented, though not in a way that fits with contemporary capitalism. I would have made an excellent court joker and, I suspect, a decent bard. My worth is inconveniently misplaced.

"The pretense of being yourself is what's tiring you?" asked January, bewildered.

At which point I had to explain to January that I am almost never myself, because the concept of being one thing singularly is fundamentally unsound. I am only variations, I told her. I explained that I'm more like a place than a thing; I have seasons of poor weather, tourist seasons, El Niño or Santa Ana winds. At my foundation I am always the same, but atmospherically there can be issues.

"It is sometimes unsafe to travel here" is where I concluded my thought, I think.

"So you're doing the pretense for the benefit of other people's safety?"

"As much as I'd like to believe that's the case, no," I said. "Mostly I can't stand not being wanted."

"Will people want you more if you take a sabbatical from existence?"

"Ideally yes."

"Does that make sense?"

"I believe so," I said. "It's logical even if it isn't rational."

We argued over semantics a bit but in the end January agreed to do it. Not that I doubted she would, but she seemed to have a weird thing with owing favors. I had to tell her quite coaxingly that it was a job, not a favor. I would pay her in whatever currency she wished, which ended up being a nightly conversation during my week of isolation. I thought I would hate this, but I didn't, not really. I asked her to sit on my feet because my circulation was bad and they were always cold.

The first night she asked me about religion. I explained as best I could from a place of ambivalent Catholicism how organized religion had somehow managed to improve the state of humanity by bolstering the arts but had also contributed to an insoluble crisis of racism, xenophobia, and genocide. Kind of a bummer, as I told her.

"I meant gods," she said.

"Don't let anyone's WASPy grandmother hear you say that," I warned. "Most people think there's only one and they get angry if you disagree about which one it is."

"Oh," she said, looking grateful. In fairness, I was aware I had probably saved her from any number of cyber trolls.

The second night she asked me to explain what I meant by racism. It ended up being a very long lecture about colonialism and biological warfare, I suspect. I told her that as a person who was made up of several identities I had only ever felt confusion over it.

"So you don't have one?" she said. It was one of the rare instances where she forgot to clarify what she was talking about, so I had to ask her what she meant.

"You don't belong to something," she synthesized slowly.

"I don't want to belong to anything."

She clucked her tongue in disagreement. "That's not true."

I was too tired to argue, and anyway, I didn't know the answer.

The next night we talked exclusively about the book *The Da Vinci Code.*

The next night, the spectrum of human sexuality and the pitfalls of working retail.

The next night, subprime mortgages, the Wall Street bailout, the human impulse to find community, and the rungs of Maslow's hierarchy.

On the penultimate night of my sabbatical we discussed the subject of my death.

"Do you think about it often?"

"Almost incessantly."

"Really?"

I nodded. "I sometimes think this would be a convenient time for it. Not invitingly," I was careful to assure her. "Just in the sense that I'm not sure what I have left to accomplish and at least I don't own property. The British nobility pay egregious estate taxes."

"What are you trying to accomplish?" she asked me.

"Well," I sighed, "unfortunately that bit's a total mystery. Love? Sometimes I think it's mainly love. Some all-consuming, enrapturing form of it. I think primally the answer is the continuity of the species. Transcendentally it's an issue of work product."

"What type of work?"

"Well, the canvas is me, I suppose? But the debilitation of creation is such a competing factor."

"Shouldn't the not-knowing keep it interesting?"

"Yes, I think so? But it's also quite exhausting," I said, referencing where I lay on my bed.

"Does everyone take sabbaticals?"

"No. But I think most people are better at it than me."

"Better at what?"

"All of it," I said, but what I meant was existing.

*   *   *

At some point I introduced January to brunch.

She loved it. It is, after all, the only known concept to be wholly without flaws.

*   *   *

It's possible I'm losing track of how things went. It was very easy to lose track of time with January, who didn't seem to experience it the same way I did. She told me that was due to something involving thinness in the air. I said like altitudes? And she said yes, sort of, shortness of breath and all that. It either made sense or I allowed it to.

I got very restless at some point. My dormant fury arose newly unhinged somewhere around autumn. I was no longer crying, having given it up in favor of weeping, which was ghastly. My head ached, my skin was terrible, and to make matters worse I was getting older. I used to be a prodigy, I shouted at January, and now I've pulled out two gray hairs in a single month!

"You know what would help? If you could forget things," she suggested. "I think the flaw in your personal existence is your continuity. Don't you think it wouldn't bother you to have wrinkles beside your eyes if you'd forgotten they didn't used to be there?"

"I HAVE WRINKLES?" I said.

"Oh," said January, chagrined. "Sorry, I thought you knew."

January's conception of what I knew or didn't know seemed to be her main source of frustration. I got the feeling she was repeatedly trying to make sense of me and couldn't. I explained to her at some point that it wasn't her fault, and that the reason she couldn't make sense of me had something to do with my volatility of emotion.

"It's chemical," I told her. "Chemical misfires in my brain."

"So you're not actually sad when you're sedentary?"

"No, I am sad. But not about anything. Just in general."

"So it doesn't have a cause?"

"No, it has a cause. It's just not always identifiable or, if it is, it's unrelated."

"But the sadness is real?"

"Yes. Artificially."

I could see I was distressing her further, so I suggested we get ice cream. She asked me why we didn't always go get ice cream and I explained the concept of calories and also the alarming prevalence of type 2 diabetes. She seemed crestfallen and wanted more ice cream to improve her mood, but then she remembered the bit I'd said about the calories and appeared to have hit an internal snag.

"It's all right," I told her reassuringly. "We all go through it."

"You'd think it would bond you together," she said while we were walking back to my apartment. "All of you trying not to eat too much ice cream even though you want to. You'd think that would unify you in some way."

"Actually, some people are lactose intolerant," I said.

Politely, I looked away when she started to cry.

* * *

With Jason she was cold.

"I don't like him," she said flatly. "He's not an idiot like Kyle. He's actively mean."

"I know," I told her with a sigh. "Unfortunately I like it."

"Why?"

"I think because it reinforces my suspicions that I'm not actually very good."

"Why would you want that?"

"Because it would help me understand why I can't have what I want in life."

"But what if the world is simply unfair," she argued, "and there's no rhyme or reason for why some people get things and others don't?"

For a moment my entire thought process went blank.

"That," I told her conclusively, "is too much for me to carry."

She said something about how diabolical it was that I seemed so strong and that I possessed so much knowledge, when actually I was also quite weak and incapable of understanding the most fundamental truths of the universe. I wasn't upset that she said it because I already knew that about myself.

"Well, I don't think you should date him," she concluded. I had already explained the concept of dating by then, so we were at least on the same page.

"It's fine, he doesn't want to date me. Not seriously."

"So what does he want?"

"Sex, I guess?"

"Do you think your vagina is your best feature?"

"What? No. At least I don't think so."

"Then what exactly is the point?" she demanded blisteringly.

"I think I just hate feeling lonely," I said.

*   *   *

Typically I didn't notice whether I was sedentary or in motion until a series of predictable things started to happen. When I was sedentary, I was only able to tell once I had made a lot of messes and read a lot of books—like, more than one book per day. It was easy to wallow in loneliness with either literature or my own thoughts, and in a lot of ways being sedentary was safer even if I was much more aware of my disgust with myself. Nobody ever hurt themselves by reading, except for the mood alteration thing and also, internal self-destruction.

Being in motion was a bit more extravagant, and therefore dangerous. Speeding tickets, overdrawn checking accounts, empty bottles I devotedly placed in the bins (you'll recall I was only messy while sedentary), and then of course Jasons and Kyles. They mostly fell into those categories.

There was also the taking up of odd hobbies, the lack of sleep. It is probably not a coincidence that I wrote the Craigslist ad that eventually got me January while I was exceptionally mobile.

Wanted: a roommate. You get your own room plus shared bathroom and full use of living room and kitchen. Female or female presenting, do not care which, actually you can be a man if you'd like but know that I cannot be responsible for your socks and I will not attend to your emotional burdens in any way. Must not be "not a morning person" or "not a night person" but simply a person unbeholden to chronology, as such. I can't promise to be quiet or social but I also can't promise I won't be. I'd prefer if you didn't eat my hummus if I specify that it is in fact my hummus, but that being said I'm open to communal groceries. Ideally you're the sort of person who likes dogs but doesn't have any. Better still if you like cats but decline to call yourself a cat person. Knowledge of bookbinding v helpful, calligraphy also a plus, though not necessarily either. Everyone should have a hobby, don't care what that hobby is unless it's hard drugs or arms trafficking. I don't like house guests so if you have a cousin from out of town who always stays with you or a long distance boyfriend or something that's just not my vibe. You can use my Netflix account because I'm not a monster and rent is more important to me anyway. Be willing to take out the trash without being asked. No homophobes, no xenophobes, no transphobes . . . if you're a phobe of any sort then history isn't on your side and neither am I. Not looking for the kind of person who shares more than five memes per week. One or two is fine if it's really funny but I detest being inundated. Judgy people please kindly reconsider applying. P.S. that isn't rude, it's simply proactive. I can't waste my time trying not to be what I am, I'm tired enough as it is. Not going to claim I'm normal or nice or anything. However I think it's fair to say I'm a decent roommate.

It doesn't surprise me in retrospect that January was the only one who replied.

*   *   *

January had problems of her own. Evidently she had been ostracized or banished in some embarrassingly public way and there was frequent mention of a queen, though it typically only led to a discussion about the continued existence of the British monarchy on the basis of Divine Right (a situation we both agreed was questionable—January felt it should be largely a matter of conquest and when I asked if she meant elections she said "sure"). She had one year to serve out this sentence, as she explained to me once, and then she could go back.

At some point mid-September she suggested that I should go with her.

"There's really no chance you won't like it," she said. "Your probability of ecstasy will increase exponentially. And it's not as if you feel you belong anywhere in particular at present."

Normally things January said didn't upset me. I think it had a lot to do with her voice, which was soothing, or her eyes, which were mildly hypnotic. But something about this particular sentiment broke through her inoffensive sheen and rendered me very distressed. I couldn't understand it, so I sort of stomped around for a bit and left the house to spend time with someone who wasn't her and then I came home with someone who was also named Jason though it wasn't Mean Jason. The sex with him was actually quite good, which is what made the aftermath so much worse, because it meant I couldn't pretend my sorrow was due to any lack of ecstasy.

After I stayed in bed through most of the following morning and afternoon, January found me and crawled under my covers. She curled around me like a waifish petal and sighed.

"You don't ever have to leave if you don't want to," she whispered to me.

I wish I could say it broke the curse, because for a second I felt like it might. There was a moment when I thought, *I have been waiting my entire life to be told I'm allowed to stay,* and it seemed to me that this was it. The happy ending.

But then I remembered I don't have a curse, this is just who I am, and so even though I had a moment of contentment it was another week or so before I stopped being sedentary.

*   *   *

I forgot to tell you what we talked about on the last night of my sabbatical, which I'm realizing now might be relevant.

"I think we should talk about the curse," said January. "About where it might have come from."

I told her it was genetic and she said so were curses, inasmuch as they were placed on a bloodline; in this case, mine. I told her my child had a 16 percent chance of having the same problem I had and also my parents had had their own problems and all in all there wasn't much use discussing whether I, personally, had a curse. I started telling her things I knew about developmental psychology and she stopped me.

"What happened to you?"

This was a surprising question. Not because January wasn't in the habit of asking surprising questions, but because it was a question that shouldn't have had a concrete answer and yet, somehow, I had a very specific one at the ready.

"I think I have an unnatural fondness for leaving," I said.

January found this interesting. She expressed it with the deliberate arch of a brow.

"It makes me feel strong instead of weak," I said, "to be leaving instead of left."

"Do you think that's the curse?" she asked me. She was being very earnest and serious about it. I doubted she would ever believe me when I reminded her that there was no curse, aside from general humanity.

"I think the issue is loneliness," I explained slowly. "The fear that I'll forever be alone is exacerbated by a personality that ensures it. Because even if I could tailor myself to be palatable to someone, it changes. Makes the environment inhospitable."

"The bad weather, you mean?"

"Yes, the bad weather."

"But people live in Alaska."

"Yes."

"And the Midwest."

"Yes."

"And Florida."

"Yes." She had clearly done her research.

"But you don't think anyone wants to live on your island?"

"Sometimes I do," I said. "Sometimes not. That's part of the issue, too. If I could be convinced all the time then it would be easy to keep going. But there is a crisis of confidence that blows in every now and then. Seasonally, to some extent."

"Sounds exhausting," she said.

I think it was becoming a joke to her. My existence was tiring; this, to her, explained why I took so many long naps or, at the time, a weeklong sabbatical. She was smiling faintly when she said it.

"Yeah, so anyway, leaving," I said. "It's very easy for me. Easier than the alternative."

I'll never know how she figured out how to make that something I could understand.

* * *

The best thing about January was that as weird as she found me, she was unquestionably weirder. There was the queen thing, plus all the weird questions and her interest in my sex life (hers was admittedly carnivorous; or, more accurately, omnivorous). She had a fondness for marijuana, which I scrupulously avoided. My thoughts had a tendency to race, as I explained to her, and the few times I'd taken edibles had involved a lot of existential dread. January seemed to have a perfectly fine handle on mind-altering substances, and once she got a feel for which questions others found eccentrically invasive vs. insultingly nosy, she really perfected the Manic Pixie Daydream persona that I could only approximate on a good day.

January liked to say things like "Careful, the old gods will hear you," or "My former bones were less sensitive to the calamities of youth," which prompted Kyle's friend Brad to call her Ghost Girl. People seemed to have a lot of theories on January, though none more so than January, who was enamored with the concept of reincarnation and continuously fretted about how she could ensure coming back as a seagull—the perfect form, in her mind. Something about proximity to water and also wings. She'd have to be just bad enough, she reasoned, that her punishment would be abject freedom. That, I said, or being eaten by a whale. ("I don't think that's real," said January, at which point Brad told her the story from the Bible about Jonah. She was not convinced.)

There were several weeklong periods when January and I went out every single night. She had a very impressive social endurance, which she explained to me was one of the requirements for being part of her aforementioned court. She was very adamant about the fact that merrymaking was a cruciality in her former life, and even I could see she was an expert bacchanalian.

I think sometimes I have a tendency to show my sadness most clearly in periods of excruciating joy, so when I asked her if she was happy here among the mortals she grabbed my face in both hands, feverishly intoxicated.

"Do you even know?" she said. "How magical you actually are. I didn't know I could imagine that something so odd existed and yet here you are, so strange. So fragile."

She kissed both my cheeks like an Italian grandmother. I told her I loved her and cried.

"So you understand, then!!!" she shouted in my ear, her voice a graphic, highlighter pink.

I told her I thought I did.

*   *   *

"You'll be in motion again," she assured me once.
"Will I?"
"Historically yes."
She smiled at me thinly, apologetically.
"Thanks," I said.
She nodded. "I see now why it matters," she said. "Memory."
Gratifyingly she left it at that, leaving the room to return (I assume) to her research.

*   *   *

I obviously explained to January why Thanksgiving was both egregiously problematic and also, undoubtedly, marvelous. I also explained that turkey was almost always too dry to be enjoyable, but principles of tradition and/or seasonal exclusivity demanded it. She marveled at the concept of stuffing, but believed me once I explained what it was made of. I had already impressed upon her the cruciality of bread.

I had recently been running again, though I got tendinitis after the second week and spent much of my time with an ice pack on my knee between episodes of training. She told me I should take a break and I told her I couldn't take breaks because I was working on something. I think by then she understood that what I meant was I can't take breaks because I might regress into another period of sedentary misery if I stop. She generally grasped that I lived in fear of the day motion would cease again because I knew it would. I could always rest then.

Sometime after we'd had gratuitous amounts of wine and eaten just enough turkey to justify the amount of mashed potatoes we'd also served ourselves, January told me that this was actually not the first time she'd been in trouble. It was just the first time she'd been banished.

She went on to tell me that there were quite a lot of causes for banishment if you were a certain level of curious, in which case a banishment was not so terrible a punishment, because she had learned so much. She told me she loved Craigslist because it reminded her of the market back home, full of trinkets and oddities and also, quietly, danger, but there was something exciting about that. There was no fun in shopping at shopping malls where nothing was destructive and everything looked the same. Craigslist was niche, it was boutique, it was a masterpiece of human collaboration.

"Also, I found you," she pointed out.

"I don't typically think of myself as a lucky find."

"Well, from what I understand you have something other humans don't."

"What, illness?"

"No, wonder."

"I think plenty of people have wonder."

"Plenty have illness, too, as far as I can gather."

"Okay, then what's significant about my personal wonder?"

"Oh, I don't know. Sometimes it's so sad it makes my chest hurt," she said. "Other times it's so bright I can't look directly at it."

"So it's . . . the unpredictability?"

"Yes, maybe. It's exciting."

"Unpredictability is counterintuitive for human survival on the whole," I said. "I think that's why people don't like it, or don't trust it. There's a suspicion it might get us killed."

"I wouldn't know," January reminded me. "And anyway survival is one thing."

One thing among many, she meant. "Not everyone is looking to survive," she added.

"I think they are."

"They're planning on it, not looking for it. I think you give people too little credit."

I had the strange feeling like I wanted to kiss her, or kiss someone, or climb up a mountain and scream until I couldn't hear the echo of myself anymore.

"That being said," January cut in primly, "imagine if you didn't go sedentary sometimes." She unzipped her jeans and exhaled, full to a manageable point of suffering. "You'd break the world into pieces. Dangerous," she remarked with a shake of her head.

Onomatopoetically, I thought about the snap of a Kit Kat bar. I imagined my consumption of the world, crisp and effortless, a little break in monotony.

I smiled. "You make me sound so mystical."

"I find it difficult to believe I could ever explain you," she said. "You're almost entirely chaos."

"This from someone who was once banished."

"A very orderly consequence," she reminded me, and tapped my nose with one finger before asking me whose idea it was to put marshmallows on yams.

"Not a clue," I said.

"Ingenious," she informed me, rubbing her swollen belly like a fortune teller's crystal ball.

* * *

At some point I realized January looked different to other people than she did to me. I think she was experimenting with race, which I had specifically told her not to play with. Age wasn't much better. Neither was gender. Still, I think my limited experience depressed her a little.

"Everyone else belongs somewhere," she said.

I told her I had never felt comfortable in any of the boxes available to me. I often paused before checking off my identity on a form. Things were improved by the "two or more" option but even then, I felt a sense of guilt selecting either or both.

"You feel a lot of guilt," she observed.

"There's a lot of places that aren't for me."

"Forbidden rooms? We had those at the academy."

"Yeah sure, something like that."

"So you can't go in?"

"I could. But I assume people would question whether or not I deserved to be there."

"Why does it matter?"

"You can't belong somewhere if other people think you don't."

"That," she said with obvious frustration, "doesn't make sense."

"Nothing makes sense," I reminded her. "It's all logical but not rational."

"Do you think they're jealous of you?" she demanded. "Of your magic?"

"What magic?"

She looked at me like I'd stabbed her.

"You need a nap," she said vitriolically.

*   *   *

The night before her banishment ended and her sublet on our apartment was up, I insisted on having a celebration. I was in a soaring sort of mood, intent on euphoria. I invited Kyle but not Jason. Some of my other friends with carousing tendencies were also there. Everyone I knew who had ever made jokes about their excessive wine consumption was invited and the theme of the evening was noise.

I set myself to the logistical arrangements, preparing to shimmer in my role as hostess. I knew that no matter what I did it wouldn't be enough, but that was a sensation I was accustomed to feeling. The silence in January's absence would be deafening, but I would adapt. It was amazing what a person could become okay with.

"Resilience," January said to me in private.

I found her in the bathtub, staring at the drain.

"Insanity," I countered, climbing in with her. We faced each other like two passengers in a drifting canoe.

"Imagination."

"Paranoia."

"Foresight."

"Fear."

"Bliss."

"Mania."

Her smile broadened.

"People expand to bear their curses," she told me. I think it was advice.

It's funny how we can never really depend on memory. I wanted very badly not to forget this moment, but there was no telling what my mind would obediently save. Ninety-nine percent of my year with January was going to be deposited in the trash against my will, most likely. In retrospect I might only have glimpses, or even less than glimpses. Some of my strongest memories are just moments of blinding sun, perfect warmth. Instances of solitary peace. I had a feeling most of my memories with January would be less about our conversations and more about how I had felt while sitting in a bathtub with her.

"Are you enjoying the party?" I asked her.

"A little," she said restlessly. "Why do people like parties?"

"The element of togetherness, I think. Companionship."

"But I don't think I make a difference to any of them."

"Maybe not, but for a night your lives are all taking place in harmony. Symphonically. And there's nothing more beautiful than a perfect chord."

"Is this what it is? Beauty?"

"I like to think so."

"So existence, it's all about beauty?"

"About creating it, maybe. Mine is, I think. Finding it in places and hoping I can make other people see it, too."

She rested her chin on her knees.

"Is sadness beauty?"

"Some of it."

"And the rest?"

"Gives the other bits meaning."

"The not-sadness, you mean?"

"Yes."

"So you have to be sedentary to appreciate motion," she observed aloud.

She scribbled it down on her notepad, which I hadn't noticed she had with her.

"Anything else?" I asked her.

"Is love beauty?"

"Yes. But not always beautiful."

"Why not?"

"There are selfish loves and wasted loves and toxic ones."

"What was this one?" she asked me.

"Gentle," I said.

I had the feeling I would have a very difficult time ahead of me when she was gone. Luckily I had thought to plan a party. It would give me something to clean up in the morning besides myself.

January shifted toward me in the tub and looked at me for a very long time.

"Nobody is ever going to believe me when I tell them about you," she said.

"Same, actually."

"Isn't that funny?"

"Yes, actually, kind of."

"Life's funny," she remarked to herself. "And anyway," she added, directing her attention back to me, "I've thought about your curse a lot and I think it's actually very important that you take care of it. Make sure you only let people in who are reverent with it. People who don't understand magic can be a real drain on available resources, so don't be irresponsible with your supply."

"Noted."

"And just because a curse can't be cured doesn't mean you can't ease it from time to time. I can leave you a list of herbs if you want. Certain rituals are more effective than others but that doesn't mean you shouldn't try."

"Okay."

"And I don't think you should try to get rid of it," she said.

"I don't think I can."

"I know, but don't."

"I can't."

"Yes, but *don't*."

"Fine, I won't. But why not?"

"Because I learned there was a new piece of me to go with every new piece I found of you, and that's wonderful," she said.

I think she meant it literally—that I had filled her with wonder—so I tapped her nose.

"Bye, January," I said, even though I knew it wasn't her real name, because sometimes things are real even if they aren't. I wanted to tell her that she didn't ever have to leave if she didn't want to, but I didn't think it would mean the same thing to her as it did to me.

"You never know," she said. "I might be back."

*   *   *

Historically, she would be.

Credits

The anthology you've just read would not have been possible without the effort and expertise devoted by every member of my unparalleled publishing teams. I am honored to have worked with each one of them, and they all deserve proper recognition for the time and talent they brought to this book.

Executive Editor Lindsey Hall
Assistant Editor Aislyn Fredsall
Agent Amelia Appel
Publisher Devi Pillai
Associate Publisher Lucille Rettino
Publicity Manager Desirae Friesen
Executive Director of Publicity Sarah Reidy
Executive Director of Marketing Eileen Lawrence
Director of Marketing Emily Mlynek
Assistant Marketing Manager Gertrude King
Senior Marketing Manager Rachel Taylor
Interior Illustrator Paula Toriacio (polarts)
Cover Designer Jamie Stafford-Hill
Interior Designer Heather Saunders
Production Editor Dakota Griffin
Managing Editor Rafal Gibek
Production Manager Jim Kapp
Copyeditor Terry McGarry
Proofreader Sara Thwaite
Cold Reader Rebecca Naimon
Associate Director of Publishing Operations Michelle Foytek
Assistant Director of Subrights Chris Scheina
Senior Director of Sales Christine Jaeger
Senior Audio Producer Steve Wagner

Voice Talent
Stephanie Nemeth Parker
David Monteith
Ferdelle Capistrano
Alex Palting
Daniel Henning
Steve West

Tor UK

Publisher Bella Pagan
Editorial Assistant Grace Barber
Marketing Manager Becky Lushey
Senior Communications Executive Olivia-Savannah Roach
Communications Assistant Grace Rhodes
Video & Influencer Marketing Manager Emma Oulton
Content Marketing Executive Carol-Anne Royer
Head of Digital Marketing Andy Joannou
Email Marketing Manager Katie Jarvis
Senior Production Controller Sian Chilvers
Senior Desk Editor Rebecca Needes
Cover Designer (UK) Neil Lang
Sales Director Stuart Dwyer
Bookshop & Wholesale Manager Richard Green
Sales Manager Rory O'Brien
International Sales Director Leanne Williams
International Communications Manager Lucy Grainger
International Sales Manager Poppy Morris
Head of Special Sales Kadie McGinley
Head of Trade Marketing Ruth Brooks
Trade Marketing Manager Heather Ascroft
Trade Marketing Executive Helena Short
Trade Marketing Admin Liv Scott
Trade Marketing Designer Katie Bradburn
Metadata Executive Kieran Devlin
Audio Publishing Executive Nick Griffiths
Postroom Staff Chris Josephs

Acknowledgments

The stories in this collection span six years of art, and I am deeply, unproductively emotional over this opportunity to give all my previous versions a place to coexist. Please don't perceive me; politely look away. I will be, I hope, very brief.

About half of the stories you've just read were first printed in my self-published Fairytale Collections (*Fairytales of the Macabre, Midsummer Night Dreams,* and *The Lovers Grim*) and the interior illustrations by the magnificent polarts all feature my original dedications to my husband. Thank you again to Stacie Turner, one of my very favorite muses, for whom I wrote the stories "The Wish Bridge" and "A Year in January." "The House" is a slightly revised version of the wedding vows I wrote for Charlene Paule and Danielle Sulit, so thank you to them for letting me include those here. Massive thank you as well to the many of you who read those early collections; I always think of "The Animation Games" as a story that belongs collectively to all of us.

Thank you to Lindsey Hall, my editor extraordinaire, who took so much pride and pleasure in helping me curate my personal eras. I wrote "Monsterlove" and "The Audit" for her. Lindsey, it was an honor to have you with me, shaping all the versions of me into the book you hold in your hands. Thank you always to Amelia Appel, my agent and steadfast supporter, and every member of my brilliant, tireless publishing team at Tor. Thank you endlessly to Po for all the breathtaking artwork in this book; thank you to Little Chmura, my friend and collaborator, for the original artwork for many of these stories. Thank you to my family, my friends, who all know who they are. I love you very much.

Garrett: to the older you, from the older me. Thank you for Henry, and for everything, always. Henry, thank you for being the coolest person we know.

And finally, my beloved Reader: It's an honor to put down these words for you. I hope you've enjoyed the stories. May whoever we become next always surprise us; may we look into the void and share a laugh.

xx, Olivie

About the Author

OLIVIE BLAKE is the *New York Times* bestselling author of *The Atlas Six, Alone with You in the Ether, One for My Enemy,* and *Masters of Death.* As Alexene Farol Follmuth, she is also the author of the young adult rom-coms *My Mechanical Romance* and *Twelfth Knight.* She lives in Los Angeles with her husband, goblin prince / toddler, and rescue pit bull.

olivieblake.com
Twitter: @OlivieBlake
Instagram: @olivieblake